D1329115

HOW LONG IS *Exile?*

HOW LONG IS *Exile?*

BOOK I

The Song and Dance Festival of Free Latvians

A novel by

Astrida Barbins-Stahnke

In Three Books

Library of Congress Control Number:		2015914269
ISBN:	Hardcover	978-1-5144-0326-6
	Softcover	978-1-5144-0325-9
	eBook	978-1-5144-0324-2

Print information available on the last page.

Rev. date: 03/22/2016

To order additional copies of this book, contact:
Xlibris
1-888-795-4274
www.Xlibris.com
Orders@Xlibris.com
715279

CONTENTS

Dedicated to my brothers, sisters, and cousins
on both sides of the Atlantic Ocean

FOREWORD

The idea for a novel came to me 1983, at the Latvian Song and Dance Festival in Milwaukee, Wisconsin, when my friend, the poet Sniedze Ruņģis, at an early morning poetry reading gave a speech *Cik gara ir trimda?* (How long is Exile?). That question or cry brought to my mind the many experiences of our people's real escapes, sojourns, and mindsets into focus. As I participated and observed, the festival became a metaphor or microcosm not only of Latvians but of greater humanity, and as such it turned into an inexhaustible source for the novel I had wanted to write in answer to the often-asked question, "Where you from?" And so, when the festivities were over, my mind started composing and imagining, and as soon as I was back home in Collinsville, Illinois, I started writing. It was going to be a short book, which I wrote quickly. But when I tried the draft on my friends and professors at the university, they asked questions that required extensive answers. Those, in the end, became the content of the *How Long is Exile?* trilogy.

Many Latvian writers and politicians have written and told much about their escapes from home and adjustments in foreign lands, but hardly anything in English. I hope that my novel may, at least partially, fill the gap. *How Long is Exile?* focuses on the life of one woman, a widow Milda Bērziņa /Arāja /Hawkins, born 1931, and follows her until 2001, the year Riga commemorated the signing of its charter in 1201. It was a glorious 800 year birthday celebration for Latvia, with fireworks and reunification of people whom World War II had scattered throughout the world. It was there I decided to bring my novel to the end, thus allowing my heroine to enjoy her golden years at home, at least for a decade.

Book I. ***The Song and Dance Festival of Free Latvians,*** with its flashbacks, introspections, nostalgic memories, and melancholy takes place at the festival, with the main character's coming to the song festival to find a newer and freer self after years of mourning for her deceased husband Kārlis Arājs. In flashbacks she recalls her childhood before and after World War II, her years as refugee in Germany, the nurturing of her husband and children Ilga and Gatis in a quickly changing and confusing United States during the 1960s and '70s. The gradual opening of her homeland and the possible reunification with her sister Zelda, who had survived five years in a Siberian gulag, cause her further confusion and feelings of guilt.

Book II: ***Out of the Ruins of Germany*** is set in Germany, as it was in Milda's lifetime (fall of 1944 – 1950). This was the time when her sense of exile, with its pain and alienation became a part of her personality. On my family's escape road we saw many orphaned, dislocated children who suffered more than others from the war and its shadows, as they were in the care of related and strange adults, who also were displaced and broken down. This was especially true of women—young, single and widows—who had to carry the damages of war as best they could and sacrifice themselves for their own and other people's welfare. Such was the lot of Milda's Aunt Alma. *After* the war, followed years of uncertainty and waiting in refugee camps, set up by allied forces throughout the three free zones. Alma and her niece Milda settle in Esslingen, the largest all-Latvian camp in the American Zone. There both discover a rich cultural life. Alma resumes her acting career, while Milda matures as a gymnasium student and becomes an independent-minded woman. For her America shines like a distant lighthouse that eventually guides her ship to a new life of peace, love, and prosperity.

Book III: ***The Long Road Home*** makes Milda's promise to her Aunt Alma and also her own wish to return home come true. After Latvia became free in August 1991, Milda—as in reality many others— were free to return to their homeland and reclaim their Communist confiscated properties and reconnect with their relatives. But Milda (as others), learned quickly that the road home is long and complicated physically and psychologically, for the sense of home and exile suddenly turns upside down. Milda soon realizes that America is really her home, while Latvia has been an unreal realm, steeped in inaccurate memories and nurtured by romantic fantasies and wishful longing for a place of ideal and perfect harmony. When she meets her sister and comes face to face with real life in the homeland, the divide is impossible to cross, and the feeling of being a foreigner comes over her with a vengeance. And so she, as many other former refugees, cannot escape from the sense of exile no matter where they live.

Yet she, as others, at least on the surface, live *normal, productive, and good* lives—whether in the homeland or abroad. One way of easing their transplanting is by carrying parts of the foreign lands home as, long ago, they carried parts of their homeland into exile. Thus Milda cherishes her Aunt Matilde's hand-woven blanket on her escape road, and, upon returning home, she renovates her parents' once-lost apartment in the style of modern American homes. *She* wears sneakers and denim jeans as she moves about in Riga, ignoring the questionable glances of local by-passers. In the end, she finds comfort and peace in her repossessed home, her close friends and family, in nature's healing power, and the satisfaction of having fulfilled her destiny. Although her road of life has been painfully difficult and far beyond her understanding, it has also been enriching in many ways. To accept her fate and not argue nor continually trouble heaven with futile questions is the lesson she has learned, and that gives her peace and joy to live, to love, to forgive, and accept. Still, the sense of exile never leaves her, for it has become a part of who she is.

ACKNOWLEDGMENT:

How Long is Exile? was started so long ago that many people who were with me in the beginning no longer walk the earth. I remember with gratitude and admiration my excellent American literature and creative writing professors at Southern Illinois University, Edwardsville and Carbondale, who encouraged me to translate, write poetry, and "something or other from your experiences."

Looking back, I appreciate those who read the first drafts of my fledgling novel, asked questions and gave advice, when uncertainty and fears tripped me at every turn. I also want to thank my fellow Latvians, whom I met in the early 1980s, when the Iron Curtain was still a mighty line that separated and divided our people. The academicians, artists, writers, ordinary working class people, and relatives welcomed me as if I were an open window or door to an unknown world, and they, in turn, became open doors and windows to me. We trusted each other and learned much. At the end of my allotted time in Latvia, several of my new acquaintances wanted their stories told "so that you over there know that we are here." They did not have adequate language skills nor freedom of expression to tell their stories, as everything written was censored and those who tried to break through the Iron Curtain risked paying a high price. So, hearing such imperatives as "you must" and "we need it" put an obligation on me. But I too was afraid, for contacts could be traced, and I did not want to add to my relatives and others more problems than they already had. And that is why only now I decided to have my novel published, using the materials I gathered over the years, as I visited Soviet-ruled Latvia and saw the slow dawning of freedom's light.

As I immersed myself deeper into the writing process, many stories would suddenly come to mind, requesting to be a part of the whole. Long forgotten images, casually uttered expressions, and episodes from the war, subconsciously stored in my memory, would suddenly present themselves in snippets or flashbacks, which I sifted out and ascribed to my fictional characters.

One such image became the prototype for Milda's Aunt Alma: our family was moving into a large house in Oeslau, Germany. Because my parents were proficient in the German and English languages, a group from the newly settled regiment of African American soldiers (The US army was then still segregated.) moved our family from a musty basement to a stately house, requesting our parents to be the official translators. Towards evening we saw soldiers going in and out of the neighboring house, moving its owner and things out and their items in. Soon the quiet of the curfew evenings and nights was disturbed by strange singing and piano playing. When in the light of day I looked up, I saw a beautiful woman leaning out the attic window, smoking a cigarette. She spoke to me in the Latvian. That image of her appeared to me when I started to create the character for Milda's aunt, whom I named Alma.

In 1979, at a conference in Stockholm, Sweden, a relative showed me a photograph of his cousin standing between two men, flanked by a number of children. He had recently returned from a rare visit to the Latvian countryside. He told me how hard life was and that his cousin lived with two men and had born them children. When I raised my eyebrows, he said, "What d'you think! How could she have managed all the farm work alone, after years in Siberia?"

Ten years later, I put her on the burned-out farm I had seen on my first trip back in 1977 and named her Zelda—Milda's sister. The War had separated them by chance or destiny (in Book I). One made it to safety, the other did not. Such was their destiny. Such was the destiny of our people whose families were split at least three ways: Latvia, Russia, and the free West.

And then there appear the older women—on both sides of the Iron Curtain. They are the widowed mothers whose husbands had been deported or gunned down inside deep, dark woods and buried in mass graves. The women hold on to their orphaned children's hands, always worried and working, their faces lined with grief. Like my mother, they did not shed many tears, nor did they laugh much but lived through their children, while clinging to their good and bad memories—and hopes.

I am also thankful for the men I incorporated in my novel: there is the preacher (based on my father), who seemed fearless and, therefore, was able to help many during the war and later with the emigration process to America. Opposite him is Pēteris Vanags, the veteran. Vanags means hawk. He is most corrupted and victimized by the War and the Holocaust. Milda fears him but is drawn to him with his magnetic, sexual force. Both know that only love and mercy can save them, but such love is forbidden; therefore, it never dies.

The prototype for Vanags's image also appeared to me without warning, reminding me of the invalids who showed up in our refugee settlement and whom we school children had to entertain on special holidays. We were afraid of them, yet could not stop staring and crying tears of sorrow as we tried to imagine their suffering.

My oldest brother Zigurds, also a soldier, was drafted by the Germans in 1943, captured in Berlin in '45, and deported to one of the worst gulags beyond the polar circle, where he spent eight years. He was free to go home after Stalin's death. After Latvia regained its freedom, he reclaimed and rebuilt our confiscated family home, where he now lives. I am most grateful to him for telling us, his siblings, his gruesome tales of a life from which the rest of our family had escaped.

I must also acknowledge the contrived, though generally true-to-life, leaders of what I call *The Kingdom of Exile.* They were steadfast like Milda's husband Kārlis Arājs, who was a true hardliner and emotionally repressed. He was especially demanding of his wife and his politically liberal children and their friends of the 1960s and onward. However, without men like him—on both sides—there would hardly be any conflict and resolution in my novel, let alone in real life. Without such strong and principled men perhaps there would not have been enough anger and will to accuse and fight for freedom.

And thank you, dear Sniedze Rungis, for giving me the key words: how long is exile? and walking with me through the mysterious and rich global *Kingdom of Exile* described in these books.

Very special thanks and love go to my late brother Torilds J. Barbins, who from my teen age years on encouraged me to write, even giving me various assignments and, in 1974, sending me information about the Baltic Drama Translation Project at Southern Illinois University, Carbondale. I joined the project and translated my first verse drama *Zelta Zirgs* (The Golden Steed, 1909 by Rainis) and then continued with the verse dramas of Aspazija (1865-1943). Through the translations and research I discovered the riches of Latvian literature, history, and culture. Without my brother's pushing me ever further and supporting me financially, I doubt if my dream to become a writer would have happened. I miss him very much.

Finally, I want to acknowledge my family: my husband Arthur A. Stahnke; our children: Lenore, Karl, Carma, and John; our grandchildren: Dimitri, Natalia, Aaron, Jason, Alex, and Gabriel. All I write is for them so that they would know where I came from and how and that in making a good and safe home for them I found my home and fulfillment. Thank you all!

Here I have named only a few persons, but there are countless more who inspired, provoked, discouraged, and helped me. Such listing would be impossible and as tedious as the chapters of biblical genealogies. Still, I am grateful to all and to "all that I have met." But:

If we shadows have offended,
Think but this, and all is mended,
That you have but slumber'd here
While these visions did appear. . . .
Gentles, do not reprehend,
If you pardon, we will mend. . . .
So, good night unto you all.
Give me your hands, if we be friends,
And Robin shall restore amends.

(Wm Shakespeare, *A Midsummer Night's Dream,* Act V.)

Sincerely,
Astrida

PRELUDE

Riga, the capital of Latvia, in the late 1930s. It is a sunny September *day. An elegant slim brunette, dressed in a rust-colored suit and a matching hat that blends well with the turning leaves, sits on a bench in the Opera Park, near the fountain. Reflecting on the ballet performance of Peer Gynt, just seen, she watches her two girls feeding the pigeons. She sees the ducks also waddling among the birds, snapping up what they can and then escaping into the canal to swallow their finds. The thin and taller girl, about seven, is an exceptionally attractive child, with yellow princess curls. She is afraid of the birds and holds her arms tightly against her body, throwing out hasty little crumbs. She stands on her toes as if she were dancing. Her large blue eyes stare at the hungry birds and blink at the sun. She never lets her mother out of her sidelong glances, frightened of being left alone in a mass of feathers and trampled mud. She tries to keep her patent leather shoes clean.*

The stouter other girl, with straight dark blonde hair, about two years younger, is rather plain. She feeds the ducks. She stands with both feet on the ground and is going after the drakes because she likes their green heads. She screeches and laughs in her full voice, as she crushes her slice of brown bread in one hand and with the other sticks small pieces into the open beaks, unafraid, unconcerned about being splattered with the dirty canal water and the mud. The mother shouts out once in a while, exasperated, telling her to stay out of the dirt, to look at her shoes, but the child does not mind.

"Yes, they are sisters," she snaps at an old man who shuffles past her, pausing to ask his question and watching the children and the birds. Disturbed, the lady rises and calls. Brushing their hands clean, the girls race for the bench and their mother's outstretched arms. The golden-haired child wins and smiles up at her mother, who holds her tightly, while the other frowns and slouches against the edge of the bench. Mother sets her good little girl in the middle of the bench and, with her white handkerchief, scolding all the time, cleans up the naughty one. Then placing herself between the girls, all three sit down. Mother gives each girl a piece of candy, muttering some soothing, admonishing words. While the sisters suck and chew, Mother puts her arms around both, leans back, and for a quiet moment bathes herself in the setting sunshine.

As if rising out of the ancient moat, an old woman takes over half the bench. She is bobbing her head at the lady in greeting, much like the ducks and pigeons. She pulls from a burlap sack a crumpled brown paper bag full of hard dark brown crumbs and settles down, her gray skirt spread over her legs and large feet. The birds swarm around her, but she turns to look at the mother and children next to her. She cackles pleasantly, eyes peering at the girls as if they were a set of transparent figurines. She watches the mother rise and put white sweaters over the neat, slightly splattered navy sailor dresses.

"Pretty, pretty," she says and displays a toothless grin.

Suddenly, she takes the blonde child's hand that sticks out of a sleeve. She stares at it and says, "Oh, girly, what a life line you have! You will travel far, very, very far. You will go to strange and beautiful places and across deep waters. You will break hearts like sticks and marry a handsome man."

Mother helps her child pull the hand out of the veined claws; the child cries and hides behind Mother. But the other girl stretches out her hand and says, "Me too."

The hag focuses her piercing eyes upon the rough little palm and says, "You, too, will travel far, but oh, oh, it will be a sad journey, you will . . ."

Mother grabs her children and pulls them away, but the Gypsy half rises, as though getting ready to follow them, and moans, "Oh, dear lady, I meant no harm, no harm, if you please. But I see, my eyes can see far into the future. You, too, are on a sad, sad road, if you please, with no one beside you. Be careful, dear lady, do be careful!"

A crowd gathers. People watch and listen. Some shout at the Gypsy: "Go away, you dirty witch! . . . Leave us alone! . . . Tell your fortune to the birds!" But she only grins, nods, and throws handfuls of crumbs at the glutinous fowl.

Meanwhile, Mother and children backtrack in order to cross the quaint iron-railed bridge. They take the path along the other side of the rather stagnant canal. The girls glance across at the woman, who now possesses the whole bench, a mixture of birds all around her.

The distraught mother hurries the girls. They pass the newly erected Freedom's Monument, whose copper Milda (so named by the people after a mythological Goddess of Love) set high above on a slim obelisk, with outstretched arms, balances three golden stars and with her shining, inlaid eyes watches Latvia and her people. She cannot turn around to see the scurrying woman and her children hasten up Brīvības iela, which is divided by a walkway lined with linden trees. They hurry through the gold-leafed tunnel, past the Esplenāde, the Orthodox Cathedral, across *Elizabetes iela, turn right at Lāčplēša iela, and rush through the iron gate into their courtyard. Glancing around, afraid of pursuing shadows, Mother bolts the gate with a bang, saying, "The awful witch!"*

As they climb the stairs to their apartment, she comforts, "Don't be afraid, my darlings, don't let her scare you. The Gypsies lie, they are bad, dirty creatures." Shivering she unlocks the heavy oak door, and they go inside. She turns the key twice and gathers her girls in her arms, kissing their hair and faces, stroking them gently, whispering, "Don't be afraid, don't worry, it'll be all right, yes . . ."

The girls wipe Mother's tear-streaked face. Shakily, Mother rises to prepare each a glass of sugar water for calming the nerves and implores them to lie down. She tucks a down comforter around them and stands by until their eyelids close.

In the evening they hear father opening and closing the doors. All rush to meet him, to tell what happened. He pats his daughters' heads and kisses his wife's face. They gather around a richly set table for their evening meal, served by their faithful maid.

Hours later, from their balcony, the family admires the rising crescent of an orange moon in a cornflower blue, star-studded sky. The girls compete in naming the first rising constellations and are rewarded by approving nods and smiles. The girls notice their father's arm resting on Mother's shoulder, her hand holding his, her lips brushing the protective hand, moist from her tears. For a moment, both watch the parents, then lean over the railing and look down on the nearly empty street, counting the silent forms moving below.

"It's such a lovely evening," sighs Mother. "I wish it would last forever and we, too, just like this, always."

"Yes . . . It is beautiful," says father.

"But beauty is never lasting," Mother sighs again sadly, deeply, clinging to her husband, reaching for their girls, just as Nanny opens the door saying, "If you please, it's the children's bed time." Reluctantly the girls oblige, leaving their parents on the balcony, in each other's arms.

A while later, to induce sweet dreams and to accompany the couple's caressing whispers, Nanny softly plays the Melancholic Waltz.

PART I

THE SONG AND DANCE FESTIVAL OF FREE LATVIANS

THE FIRST DAY

Registration

It was the last day in June 1983, when Milda Arajs traveled on the sweltering highways and interstates from Grand Rapids, Michigan, to Milwaukee, Wisconsin. She drove to participate in the Seventh General Latvian Song Festival. The celebration would go on in downtown Milwaukee from June 30 to July 5, with the Hyatt Regency Hotel serving as headquarters for approximately five thousand Latvians. Free Latvians. “Latvians of the Free World,” the posters said, displaying beautiful singing young men and women in ethnographically correct costumes. There were many such posters in downtown Milwaukee during that one week, and they served well as signs and clustering points. They helped to lead Mrs. Arājs to the Hyatt Regency underground parking lot.

With her suitcases on the lobby floor, she waited in the check-in line. To ease the waiting, she leaned against a wall opposite the main pillar full of announcements and an enlargement of the poster, but then stood up, again balancing herself straight as a school girl. With tired curiosity she searched for people she knew, but the lobby was full of strangers. Self-consciously, she rested her eyes on the pillar and scanned the announcements, checking only the times and places, not the words, for they were the same—as at other festivals—and returned her gaze to the looming enlargement that also served as a kind of backdrop for the constantly shifting crowd. She noticed every precise line and shade of the nonsurprising design. The soothing traditional rightness relaxed her. She looked down, closing her eyes, when suddenly she blinked hard, as was her habit. Her sense of symmetry and order jolted, for she saw that the lower left hand corner was not properly glued down. It curled up, revealing a dull, glue-smeared underside that had evidently been picked on. Such sloppiness grated on her nerves, and she, automatically, pressed down the upturned corner, but it would not stick to the post and defiantly dog-eared as soon as she withdrew her hand. She repeated the gesture, and again the corner curled its own way.

Suddenly, other hands were pressing down the stubborn corner, while high-pitched voices threw out comments and advice. Then out of the mumbling, murmuring confusion, one voice came through in a scolding, admonishing tone she recognized as pure Latvian: "It is the back side we ought to be looking at anyway!" This caused a confusion; people turned to see where the words had come from, but no one claimed them, and no one went on with the idea. Only Milda felt suddenly the chill of air-conditioning and noticed goose bumps on her naked arms. She blinked harder as a slight shiver shook her, leaving her full of tremors like a wind-brushed reed at the edge of a stormy pond.

The other side!

How ridiculous . . . Of course, the other side was a dull white brushed with instant glue! Yet she turned her head again as if to read the poster's invisible cryptic words. Naturally the words and meaning would be the exact opposite of the visible. The backside would read "Occupied Latvians" or "Latvians of the Non-Free World." She imagined the costumes torn, the voices crying, and fingernails scratching . . . To stop the inner trembling, she pulled her checkbook out of her purse and opened it to verify her drastically diminishing balance. She tore out the already made-out deposit slip that would cover the cost of her room and pushed her suitcase forward with her sandaled foot. Meanwhile, her hand holding the check shook as if she were stealing bread from starving golden-haired children.

"But this is your coming out of deep mourning," her dream side explained once again to her practical counterpart. "You have mourned for four years. A normal widow can get by with only one, but you—"

"C'mon, sister," her voice of cold reason mocked. "Your mourning hasn't been all that deep. There are certain advantages to your widowhood, aren't there? For instance, the fine life insurance premiums and free movement such as you could never have with him."

"But freedom is also loneliness," her soul's voice sighed.

"Respect then. You have respect because you are lucky enough to be the widow of a once-prominent patriot," Reason assured her. "Much better than being divorced, like so many women your age are. So take advantage of your status! That writing on the front of the poster—so black and bold—includes you too. Therefore, act free! It's not hard. You deserve to be here and spend your money like everyone else. It's all so simple. Like Americans going to the World Series." The last words had come out loudly. Milda had actually said them. She was saying them to a woman next to her in line, when the latter had commented about the expensiveness of such festivals.

"Maybe you are right," the woman said still looking at the check in her own hand as if she hated to part with it. "I remember the times when this would have paid for a whole month's rent and food."

"We are the living proof of the American dream come true," said a male voice, and then the line fell as silent as the eye of a storm. Meanwhile, on the periphery, the agitated sounds of excited, convening people gathered force with every revolution of the large transparent, swinging doors.

Milda was moving up in line and felt the check lighten a tiny bit. "You have come because of the child, remember?" Her dream voice whispered. "Because of Ilga you have made this national pilgrimage . . . All right. Let the father rest in peace in his tuxedo and wrapped in the flag. It's the child, your living poetic child—his child also—that you must pull again to yourself."

She felt tears slowly welling from deep inside, blessing her sincerity, for she was most sincere. More than anything in her life, she wanted to be friends with Ilga. She wanted to do something grand with her, something rare and intimate before it was too late. At the moment she had no idea what it might be; yet somehow, she was sure that when, whatever the IT was, presented itself, she would know what to do. She and Ilga would grasp it together, and IT would carry them out of their exiled souls' stagnation into electrifying experiences of deep awareness and the endless possibilities of freedom.

Meditating on the great concept concealed in that last word, she had moved so close to the counter that she could see another poster behind the busy checkers. Its corners, she observed keenly, were as they should be: carefully glued down and protected from restless fingers. From her safe distance, the black lettering of "Latvians of the Free World" stood out boldly for all the world to see, like the engraving on a closed vault. Again she felt an air-conditioned wave, only slightly warmed by the checker's smile. She slid her deposit across the marble inset and, taking the chained black pen, signed in on the dotted line.

As she retreated from the counter, wading sideways through the crowd, key in hand and watching the bellboy with her suitcase hopping around her, she bumped into Pēteris Vanags, her late husband Kārlis's closest friend, the zealous lover of her turbulent youth, but an overbearing imposter ever since his arrival in America. *I certainly did not come here to battle with him . . . What's gone is gone, and he's been long gone from my heart, and that is the end of us . . . But oh God, is it?* She caught a glimpse of his ice-blue hawkish eyes and saw his wide, tarnished smile. His overly strong hand tried to capture her, and as always, she resisted. Coldly and wordlessly she confronted his whole ruggedly drawn face and invalid form until he, giving her a pained scowl, stepped aside while she, temporarily victorious, trusting the steel of her spine, slithered through the crowd as quickly as an eel and vanished into an open elevator.

The Program

Locked safely inside her regal room of dust-blue furnishings, Milda Arajs kicked off her wedge-heeled sandals and with a luxurious bounce fell diagonally across the king-size bed. Making herself comfortable, she took up the $5 festival program booklet and consulted it hungrily as if it were a menu. The festival was going to be very rich, but of course, she could not take everything in. Assuming that to be the case, she had not ordered tickets ahead of time because she did not want to lock herself into an organized straightjacket. This had irritated the chairperson of the Festival Committee, who wanted to sell tickets, to have sums and numbers penned in her ledger. Repeatedly, up until the deadline, she had telephoned, insisting that Mrs. Arājs make up her mind, which caused the latter's usually pleasant voice to rise and implore: "Will you please leave me alone!" Then collecting herself, she added: "What I do will be up to my daughter Ilga."

And now it might also be up to him—Pēteris Vanags, the Hawk, as she thought of him, playing upon his name, scowling and smiling at the same time, imagining a large hawk with one wing, circling high above his innocent victim, then swooping down and taking the helpless rodent or chicken to its nest, pressing it down with his talons and the strong, sinewy wing—ravenously . . .

In the lobby she had spotted the chairperson swirling about, sparrowlike, greeting everybody, presenting a puffed-up image. She had acknowledged Milda with a slight bob of her teased head and then lavished her overly familiar solicitations upon Mr. Vanags, who, after being chilled by Milda's cold shoulder, had joined a group of other men and stood leaning against a wall, smoking and pretending not to see the gray-haired busybody.

"Oh, how I've tried to block you out over these many years," Milda said when her eyes met his in a line of photographs. "But it's no good. Like damming up a brook with pebbles!"

She had assumed that he was overseas somewhere in Australia or South America because, after a May 15 gathering, she had heard people talk about him and other Amnesty Internationalists, saying that new projects and demonstrations were being organized worldwide and that Mr. Vanags, so they heard, was in charge of something or other. When someone asked if he would be back for the festival, a man shrugged and said, "I doubt it." Relieved Milda then walked away, and soon she and Ilga were making plans, coordinating their times, and selecting what to wear for the formal days and partying evenings, glad that everything was going smoothly with her and Ilga acting like pals—talking, laughing, posing in mirrors.

Now Milda was angry that Vanags had not forewarned her, had not let her know that he would be here, coming between them, circling about. But as she stared at his much younger image, her anger gave way to recollections, poking at her rising, smoldering desire.

She slid off the bed and mindlessly unpacked her suitcase until her hand stopped against soft velvet. It was the diary Ilga had given her last Christmas. Milda had tucked it inside her clothes, thinking that there might be blank spaces of boredom, when writing would help. Languidly she picked up the neat little book and stroked its red soft cover, then turned the tiny golden key and unlocked its blank pages. She read Ilga's inscription: "*Māmiņ, izraksti savu sirdi!*" (Mommy, write your heart out.)

"Sure!"

She left off her unpacking and pulled the quaint, slim pen from its loop and made herself comfortable in the corner armchair. For a while, she gazed at the cumulous clouds and their changing shapes that floated over a very blue sky. She thought about him and her and their bodies changing over time, while their emotions tumbled about in restless, self-propelled confusion. She thought of herself in years to come, when her soul, severed from her body, would likewise be floating somewhere in space, and when, perhaps by chance, some offspring of Gatis or Ilga would find her fixed words behind the little golden key and be amazed. She wrote in careful English:

On that day he was my destiny, the fulfillment of my craving desire, and therefore, I sought him in the brightness of that hot noonday sun. I ran to him—uphill—all the way until I stood in the middle of the dusty courtyard of his encampment, but it was not there I stood. I stood alone in the courtyard of my own want and wishes . . . in the desert of my raging soul and parched body. I envisioned him as the symbol of all I had lost—my country, my parents, my childhood. Hence, I flew to him—to cradle and be lost in his one-arm embrace, to live and give him life, if only for a moment, for one stolen moment of satisfaction. Dazed I looked for him, but saw him not, and then I was ashamed. I was ashamed for running up the mountain, hoping to find him there—waiting for me. I was ashamed of my own perspiration that enveloped me like a tight veil, like a transparent layer of skin that clung to me with its own odor, releasing more vapors of forbidden desire. Yes, I was ashamed. I shivered in my shame as all the windows of the block houses in that Mountain Colony of Invalids glowed in the sun and glared back at me. And then I turned around and ran. I ran away from my soul's desert, my body's cravings, and my shame. I ran down the same path

I had ascended. I ran fast, quickly, as in a dance—the quickstep. [*Oh, how I loved to dance!*]

And it was then, on my way down, I heard his footsteps like the winds upon a grating shore, when they push and pull the waters of the sea. I was afraid of being overtaken, afraid of drowning in his lust, and that was why I turned off the road and took the hidden path, which ended at the castle wall and the rosebush. He followed me, allowing for no escape, and so I turned around and my soul flew to delight herself upon his lips like a suddenly released butterfly from her cocoon. Our souls and bodies blended to satisfy themselves, aware of their torment and inevitable separation.

Oh, it was so long ago! And yet thoughts make time collapse. But no! Never again! I am content to be alone, to be free. I've come here because of Ilga, our—Kārlis's and mine—wonder child . . . to guide her, to help her find the way home . . . to protect her . . . yes!

She put down her pen and rested. Transferred on paper, her emotions raged and then subsided. She read what she had written and turned the key. *Now, my words, stay where you belong, all right? I'll be good.*

She hid the book back inside her suitcase and put on her glasses so she could read the fine print of the program book. After leafing back and forth through the impressive volume and lingering over more photographs, she marked the events she would attend for sure and those she might want to attend if nothing better came along.

First, she found the *Young Writers' Morning,* where Ilga would preside, and boldly circled it, again reassuring herself of being right in coming this far and all alone. She was annoyed, though, that the event was scheduled for eight o'clock in the morning, instead of a more decent hour. *And on the fourth day too! Who would want to get up that early for poems?* Still, she underlined Ilga's name and was proud of her photograph, which took up a quarter of the page. She studied it with all the full pride of a mother who bloomed in her child's flowering. Ilga, she expected, would read her best poems and in doing so would also diffuse her (a mother's) influence like sweet perfume all over the gathered congregation.

She tried to identify the other participants but could not, nor did she care much about them. They all belonged to the younger generation, even younger than Ilga. They were the children born in the comforts of exile parents, not in Latvia; hence, they possessed only an acquired and not experienced knowledge of THE WAR. Ignorantly, flippantly they tended to simplify the flight from the homeland and the hardships of their parents' and grandparents' years in strange lands; they minimized the horrors of communists and Nazis. Yet they talked. Mouths full of surface American mass media words, they talked about *their* frustrations, *their* ideals, and world peace; they expressed *their* opinions about cooperation, love, and universal friendship in *their* art and poetry, freely mixing words and phrases. They bragged about wanting to help end the cold war and open borders, which was not a bad idea, only no one knew what the right method might be. They argued for trust and communication with people who came to speak from behind the Iron Curtain. They welcomed and heartily embraced any and all *Soviet Latvian* defectors and envoys—prominent, clever poets among them—certainly dispatched by the KGB to upset the Kingdom of Exile. It did not seem to bother the young that those same poets, in years past, had openly supported the Soviet regime and denounced *bourgeois* Latvia—their elders' free and independent Motherland—Milda's and her parents' generations' Golden Age.

Naturally, their *ignorant* and *naive* sentiments upset the leaders who depended on solidarity. Especially angry were the fathers and grandfathers, the old freedom fighters, like Pēteris Vanags, who carried visible and invisible wounds. Aware of all that and of Ilga's Joan-of-Arc heroism, Milda was afraid that there might be, on that poetry morning, a direct confrontation, an unpleasant scene. She could already feel the pull in the tug of war between the generations, where she would find herself in the middle being yanked this way and that. And she would have to make a decision; she would have to choose sides.

The organizers of the festival, some, mostly the parents of these provocateurs, also flipping like pancakes on a hot pan, finally agreed that the outspoken young could not be dismissed lightly. They had dealt with rebellions privately in their homes and were afraid of further domestic revolutions, and so they agreed that their offspring should be given a fair chance, saying that they were happy that their sons and daughters bothered about these issues at all and had fun dancing folk dances and singing in the choirs and were not completely drowning into the notorious American melting pot like countless other immigrants.

Hearing that, the proud parents of poets and writers pointed out to each other their children's superior national commitment, saying that singing and dancing didn't require impeccable language skills and special talents, whereas writing did.

"But," rebutted the committee chairman, "what they say might not be what we and the people would want to hear."

"So you don't believe in freedom of speech? Of free expression of ideas, of democracy?"

"How could anyone accuse me that?"

"Well then . . ."

And so the program committee, after a long debate, had nominated Ilga (because they respected her late father) and allowed her to be in charge of the two festival morning hours.

Nervously, because Milda was never sure what Ilga might say, she doodled stars and flowers around Ilga's portrait, waiting for the telephone to ring and the expected voice to say, "Mamma?" But the silence was nearly absolute on the high floor; only, groaning, the digital clock flicked its red minutes forward. She turned over and contemplated the public recognition of Ilga. It certainly was also a reward for her raising her children in the true Latvian spirit, the way Kārlis had wished and she accepted. They—she admitted—had not fully succeeded with Gatis, their son, but *you can't win them all*, she had learned while living in America. Anyway, Ilga definitely balanced out his loss to the nation with her live, imaginative spirit and insights she was able to put into words so well, so uniquely well—in her opinion.

Things do even out in life. They do come together, sometimes in the strangest and most unforeseen ways. Musing, she imagined herself also being applauded for her efforts. She imagined how she would accept the honor humbly, perhaps with the familiar proverb: *The apple does not fall far from the tree* . . . Then she would say, "The truth of this, I must admit, at times could be disputed, because, as we all know, raising our children in this day and age, away from our beloved homeland and our value system can be extremely taxing. Yet I have no regrets. And now that my daughter is grown up and can claim to her name a volume of poetry, there is no question about the tree nurturing the fruit, nor the kind of exotic fruit it has turned out." She would say the last sentence humorously because she really did not feel, did not want to feel, pompous. *Ah, well, let Ilga take up the whole stage and speak for herself! Let the people see and judge and the critics analyze all they want!*

Turning away from thoughts and people that upset her, Milda examined the whole program. She crossed off the plenary session and church services, but marked *Homo Novus*, a musical set in the Riga of the 1930s. It promised a Broadway style, and it would be staged in the Pabst Theater. *Again a bit of Latvian spirit in a German* Stein . . .

Eagerly, curiously, she put a check at the Esslingen reunion. She marked the folk dancing show and the choral grand finale. Hesitatingly she put a question mark by the grand ball, stabbing at the dot, angry that Kārlis had died. He had been a smooth, wonderful dancer; they had danced through many festivals, always making a handsome impression, always setting an example of what ballroom dancing ought to be. She had not danced since his death, and even the minute question mark she formed with very little pressure, seemed to pull his eyes, like blue light bulbs of the underground, over her shoulder. She could hear his cold voice sneering, *Now, Milda, why even the thought? How could you possibly let another man put his arms around you?—I am not dancing either. So please don't put yourself on a slippery parquet.*

She took off her glasses, rubbed her eyes, and closed the program book. As she gave up on any calls from Ilga, she feared—or wished—that Vanags might. With her arms wrapped around one of the pillows she waited, again gazing at the sky, thinking and remembering, wondering whom she will meet and how the days will go. Suddenly the flaming ball of the setting sun filled the window. She turned and closed her eyes, losing herself in the pattern of the synthetic satin bedspread.

First Encounters

When she awoke, the room was veiled in dusk. The skyscraper city lights glimmered through the haze. Her stomach growled. Answering her body's urgent demands, she rose quickly and prepared herself for an evening out. In the shower she sang, "I'm gon-na-a wash that man right out of my hair," in her accent-laden voice, and as the last of the shampoo flowed down the drain and her hair squeaked clean under her fingertips, she decided that this festival *must* be a pleasant, unforgettable experience.

Dressed in a dark blue silk pants suit, the top of which she left open to display a glittering chemise of multicolored butterflies, she went to a Chinese restaurant across the street from the hotel. Paradoxically, she already wanted to flee from the Latvian crowd and sit alone in the contrived illusion of the even more remote world of the Orient where, she imagined, dreams could float freely like opium fumes and where she would feel no need for excuses or apologies because she was in Milwaukee, nor would she have to offer explanations about where she was coming from or where she was going.

Tomorrow. She mused, leaning back, nesting her cup in both hands and sipping jasmine tea. *Tomorrow I shall be totally Latvian. Tomorrow I shall eat sauerkraut and sausage, but tonight . . . tonight . . .* She smiled sympathetically at the shy waitress, who spoke with a very strong accent, mixing up the l's and the r's, as she groped through the strange English language and the vastness of America—much as she had in the beginning—over thirty years ago. With the help of signs and smiles, the waitress took the order of assorted delicacies.

Oh, this is a dream! Milda reveled, blowing on the tea as she waited for the food. When the waitress put the dishes down, she inhaled the spicy vapors and admired the artistry on the platter. "You *undelstand*," the waitress said, smiling, retreating to serve others. Left alone, Milda savored the food, relaxing, enjoying her sense of freedom without being responsible for anyone else. She was just allowing herself to drift away in the nirvana of the senses, when, suddenly, out of the darkness, a man appeared and stood before her whispering, "*Ak, mana miļā, tālā,* (Oh, my far-away lovely), you are here!" He put great weight on the word *are* and then smiled from inside his full beard. "Good evening," he said observing Milda's confusion. Quickly he reached his hand down to cover hers, causing some food to spill and making her half rise as on a teeter-totter. He managed to pull her close to him for one breathless moment but long enough for her to exhale, "Egons . . . You shouldn't . . ."

As quickly as he had made her rise, he left her sliding back into her seat and wishing she could keep on sliding. Flushed and adulterous, she watched him enter a booth very far away, it seemed. She saw his wife's ash blonde head lift slightly toward him and then bow again as he looked over it directly at Milda. She saw the same waitress, the smiles, the waving of menus, the setups of tea and cocktails, and at last the full tray.

But Egons's eyes did not leave her alone. They held her own with a dark mysterious force, charged with secret wishes and regrets. She was angry with herself for sweating and feeling those pangs of guilt that automatically accused her of being responsible for all the sins of the world. Yet she had done nothing—except, like some foolish Persephone—wandered off alone to hunt for the enchanted fern that blooms only on midsummer night.

Still, she knew, she had provoked and yielded. Never mind that she was surprised, acted upon—as it often happened, causing her parched body to respond. *Not again, not when I want to be liberated, be my own person*! But stubbornly her body signaled quite unmistakably that she had not freed herself from him. Time and circumstances had merely pushed him far back in her consciousness. "Frailty, thy name is woman!" she quoted Hamlet, not caring where the dim airwaves carried her voice. She was irritated. *Men*, she scowled and promised herself that this time she would not suffer; she would not allow any man to hurt her. She was too old—or rather, too mature. A free woman. *Maybe he will help me block out Vanags. Oh, but I must guard myself and, if need be, beat the men at their own game, make them suffer and long and tremble in guilt—that is, if it ever comes to that.* Had not some man said to her somewhere long, long ago, "You must learn to take from life what it offers to you in its own time and place?" In other words, be as aggressive as I and the world of happiness will be yours. *Well! Ah—but perhaps the Hand of Fate is reaching out, and he is here to protect me from the old Hawk . . . yes, I'll think about him and forget the other. I will not be tethered!*

She crossed her legs and sank deeper into the booth. She could not finish the food, but ordered a Scotch on the rocks, the first in her life. She forced herself to concentrate on the drink, measuring with her straw the width and breadth of each ice cube and noticing how each sip floated straight up to her head, slowly detaching it from the rest of her and taking her back to that night of water and stars and him . . .

Seven years ago, this Dr. Egons Lācis (meaning *Bear*) had wrought near havoc in her life. It was at a Latvian resort on the shores of Longlake after a midsummer night's celebration. She was irritated that Kārlis had rushed off to his cot, saying he had had a hard day and was tired. Being always supportive and understanding, she told him to go ahead and sleep. She was not tired, not at all. She would not sit two days in the car so she could sleep now! She came to celebrate, to honor ancient traditions! Such an excuse would help her husband to an easier rest, she told herself, and soon joined a group that came up the path leading to the clubhouse. Arm in arm, men and women stumbled through the darkness, singing folk songs, laughing, saying that they must respect their ancestors, who believed that sleeping on this night would bring misfortune and sloth. It would be bad for the crops and their gardens, they laughed, not to mention the harvest! But when they reached the clubhouse, they could do nothing with it because it was locked. On impulse, one of the men found an open window. He climbed inside and unlocked the door. Everyone barged in, found the full refrigerator with bottles of wine, some six-packs of beer, and a bottle of Irish Cream. They ate and drank what was there and, finding no liqueur glasses, emptied the salt and pepper shakers and filled them to the brim.

"Time for a swim!" said the same man, who now stood next to Milda, refilling her saltshaker. She giggled and told him her name, and he said he was Egons and this was his first time in this beautiful place. He told her he was living far north, in Canada, and that it was a shame they had not met before. At that her heart went weak so that her hand sought support on his arm, which he gladly supplied. They bantered back and forth while the more virtuous women quickly cleaned up, covering their tracks as much as possible. An older woman locked the door. The others, in the best of spirits, found the path that lead to the lake. Stumbling along, they sang *so the tree tops swayed and the rocks echoed*, as a folk song said.

Milda pretended not to notice the subtle nudge of this Egons, who had climbed through the window, unlocked the door, and was now testing the premises of her being. Gentlemanly, he slowed her down, protecting her from stumbling over exposed roots. Politely, he let others go ahead. When the party had disappeared around a curve in the path, he kissed her Humphrey Bogart style and she swooned. The next instant his warm hand guided her off the path, behind a large bush. There he cupped her face in his hands, watching her confusion and smiling down, as the moon shone upon her, kissed her again harder and deeper. Of their own mind, her arms wound around him and her hands brushed the stars that seemed entangled in his hair. Slowly he released her and, turning his head to judge the distance and direction of the singing, led her on a narrow path to a secluded spot on the quiet, reedy side of the lake. The distant singing eased gradually, and all around them lay the deep silence broken by lapping waves and the calls of whippoorwills. Lopsided, the moon hung over the hump of a mountain, marking the boundary of their newly discovered world of pure enchantment.

He stripped first and dove into the lake, darting fishlike through the reeds to where the moonlight cast its shimmering silver bridge. She stood on the edge, her sandals in hand, watching him rise up from the water. As in a dream, she heard him calling her, at first softly teasing, then growing louder like the serpent in Aspazija's drama *The Serpent's Bride*: "Come to me . . . Come, swim with me, the water is warm, the night is lovely." He swam toward her through the reeds, flipped over, then floated out, teasing, seducing, still calling her quietly, sweetly.

Her sandals fell from her hand. Her fingers tugged at her white gauze blouse and slacks . . . Amazed, she looked down on the clothes at her feet, lying around in folds like the petals of a daisy, while she, bereft of all protection, stood erect in the moonlight, all the while hearing his call intensify. Taking a deep breath, she dove into the water, cutting it where he had and rising to the surface up against his body.

They swam without a splash for endless moments like fish, wordlessly synchronizing, until a strong wave washed them ashore. He lifted her up and carried her over the grating pebbles and set her down upon fine sand. There, next to the water's edge lay an upturned boat. He seated her on that and rubbed her feet and legs with sand, massaging her whole body. When she stiffened, he cooed, telling her to relax, telling her that he was a chiropractor and that the massage was good and necessary, that her back and nerves were much too tight. And she did relax, as did her nerves and blood streams—slowly and pleasurably. In breathless awe, she watched his hands move over her, hoping that they would not fly away like the birds of the night. When he finished the massage, he rubbed her gently with sand, and when she was completely covered, he picked her up and took her to the water, never letting go, but slowly lowered her into the waves. After such an immersion, she felt purged, her body throbbing, trembling. She put her face against his chest and closed her eyes. Again he set her on the boat and dried her with his white safari shirt and helped her dress, then slipped into his white trousers, throwing the damp shirt over his shoulders, which glistened like polished amber in the light of the setting moon. Taking her hand, he led her to an empty trailer. On the small deck, he groped for the porch swing, brushing off the fallen twigs and things, and laid her down.

"I knew I would someday meet someone like you," he whispered when it was over, when her fingers were gently combing his hair as he knelt, kissed her face, neck, ears, making her writhe and repeat what could never be repeated, but her mind suddenly took control and, as kindly as she was able, eased him away. Still he lingered, still reached out, telling her how this could be the moment of consuming delight, that there was nothing to be afraid of. "Yes, there is," she whispered and turned her face away.

He tasted the tears and with one finger swept them aside, kissing her parted lips so no more words would escape and tucked her under himself, while her arms wrapped around him . . . When the deed was done, they rested. Startled by a whippoorwill's cry, they rose. He led her off the porch.

"Let's walk a bit," she whispered leaning against him, their arms crossing around each other's backs. So entwined, they walked about the woods, aware of other lovers. They talked in whispers as the night faded, the stars dimmed, and the whippoorwills quit their exclamations. The dawn rose slowly along the dark mountain ridges. When, unwilling to part, they lingered suspended between the cries of the night and morning birds, the air chilled them as with a whip. Reluctantly, sleepily, they pressed each other's hands and separated, each going off in opposite directions to their sleeping spouses, making up strings of false words as they groped for their cots. In the morning, upon late awakening, she found at her pillow a saltshaker full of black wild raspberries. Smiling she ate them one by one, then lay back on the rumpled pillow and closed her eyes. *Me thought 't was only a little midsummer dreaming. . .* She hardly heard Kārlis stepping inside, telling her to get up or they would miss lunch.

That whole summer, Milda walked off balance, the whole time living in the magic of that midsummer night. She wondered how guilty she really was and reviewed what had actually happened but instead of self-condemnation she felt nothing but pure joy. She was glad that she had experienced a world of love so completely different from Vanags's wounded passion and Kārlis's secure assumptions. She kept comparing this night with those other summer nights long, long ago, right after the war, when she was no longer a child and not yet a woman. Then while Aunt Alma formed her own truce with the Negro soldiers, in the large confiscated Lutz house, she had experienced her first kisses with handsome Gert. It had been pure, innocent romanticism, when she felt strange excitement from only sitting close to each other by a brook and reading Goethe's poems. On sleepless nights she had tried to write her first love poem, but it hadn't turned out. Embarrassed, she had torn it up and tossed the bits of paper into the wind . . . That summer, frustrated, and trying to ease her thrashing emotions, she wrote letter after letter to her dead Aunt Alma, who would understand her need to dive into dangerously deep waters.

As the summer burned itself out and she became increasingly frigid, she contemplated asking Kārlis for a divorce, but she could not find the right time. She saw that he didn't see inside her, didn't notice the storms of her heart and, therefore, was completely unaffected by her secret night. And she cared nothing for his nights of committee meetings and drinking toasts to Latvia's freedom. Alone and locked in the impasse, she let things take their own course without pushing them to any kind of dead end. Besides, she reasoned in internal monologues that she did not have the kind of strength that could deal with lawyers and settlements and the splitting up of the family. Her strong rational side forbade her to indulge in any such foolishness. Anyway, where would she go and what would she do? Egons did not call for her. In fact, she did not hear a word from him the whole summer, when every day the silence of the telephone and the emptiness of the mail box reminded her that the enchanting midsummer night was just that—an enchantment, a spell, and nothing more. It hung alone like that lopsided moon without a beginning and an end, like a dream, that had its own life and should be kept out of broad daylight and inarticulate confessions.

Often during the nights of that summer she tried to measure the space between her and Egons. It was more than a thousand miles, she knew without looking at a map. Yet in the morning, when Kārlis was gone, she would take up the heavy *World Atlas*, open it, and stare at the red lines that marked the concrete freeways. Any chance meeting or deliberate rendezvous was utterly hopeless. Only perhaps other festivals, other national consciousness workshops . . . Yet she dismissed any kind of planning as wrong and sinful. By September ("But I'll remember you, my darling, when autumn leaves start to fall . . ."), the acuteness of her aching, longing pain had subsided. She noted this one day with a touch of sadness. Daily needs buried nearly everything: she had to get her children into their school routines and help Kārlis keep his social and working schedules straight, prepare the meals, be ready for all the holidays. "Oh, the usual household chores are endless and ever faithful," she told her walls. "The dust always settles and waits for me." By the first snowfall, that summer dream night had melted away like the large, fluffy snowflakes on the windowpane.

She remembered that the autumn had been especially burning that year. The sugar maples blazed all over Grand Rapids and along the Michigan highways. Every fall Kārlis insisted on taking the family to Minneapolis to visit his friends in that Latvian community. He would always take the North Shore Drive because of the brilliant leaves and because the birches and pines brought him back to his birth town, the beautiful Madona, nestled in the quiet of upper Vidzeme. Milda, too, enjoyed those trips and felt one with her husband, as did Ilga and Gatis, who mimicked their mother's exclamations, teasing her, making everyone laugh.

But that autumn she saw the leaves and the colors only as symbols of all that is short-lived and illusive. Silent, unnoticed tears seeped behind her sunglasses. Sadly she was aware that within hardly a week all the brilliance would fade, and turning brown, the leaves would drop to the ground. When Kārlis asked her why she was so quiet, she confessed that so much beauty made her sad. When the children plagued her with questions, she ordered them to be quiet and said that she only tried to find some peace in the ordered transitions of nature, her greatest teacher and solace. On the homeward stretch, when the children slept, she consoled herself and willfully turned her face toward Christmas.

Years passed, and she forgot to think about Egons and that night and focused on her family and their daily needs. Besides, there were new events and festivals that demanded full attention. At those Egons was absent, she knew not why. More years passed, and time gently healed the wounds and scratches—until that day, when all her universe shook and left her lying on a sandy shore like a stunned fish. When Kārlis died, she was sure that it was the end of the world. Crying and mourning, she accused herself that his unexpected, rapid departure was her fault, that she had not cared for him enough and, therefore, God punished her. To punish herself she fell into deep mourning, wearing black and gray dresses, like a celibate nun.

But now, in this Chinese restaurant, everything was churned up again, and all she could do was distastefully sip the Scotch and keep her heart from jumping out of her skin.

Oh God, she sighed. *I thought I was healed, but these things never end*. . . She gulped large mouthfuls of her drink, but it did not anesthetize her as it should. Instead, her mind sobered, bubbling with rage and cynicism. She confronted his coaxing eyes that seemed miles away and then turned her gaze on the blond, innocent head. She wondered what it would be like to be married to a philandering husband. Kārlis had always been faithful, always where he said he would be.

When Egons lowered his eyes, she stared at the two red dragons in the corners of the restaurant until the whole place blurred. Only when the waitress asked if she could help, did Milda realize she was crying. She coughed, embarrassed, as the shy girl placed the check on the table.

"Would you like to pay now or later?" asked the girl.

"Later," said Milda and produced her credit card. The waitress left, and Milda broke her fortune cookie. "You will encounter strange adventures," it said. When the waitress returned, Milda signed the bill and pushed the half empty glass away. She rose slowly, being aware of his gaze over his wife's head. She let her eyes meet his for one moment and then turned and walked out of the restaurant.

*

When dizzily she stepped through the oval red door guarded by open-mouthed, fire-eating dragons, the night was neon blue. She strolled across the street as if nothing had happened and soon found herself securely back in her Latvian world, which temporarily occupied the Hyatt Regency. She felt herself being thrown into the lobby as from a high wave that hit a marble shore. Absentmindedly she meandered through the crowd, bumping into people and apologizing; some, saying *glad to see you,* offered their hugs, irritating her, making her worry that her suit would be left wrinkled and dirtied by fingerprints. *How Americanized they've become*!

She went in swerving gyres until a cluster of old friends from her Philadelphia era pulled her in an uncertain intimate circle. Relieved not to need her own willpower, she sobered up as she let them guide her to the exhibits and shops, in the large rooms on the second floor, where they bought things, until she, too, pulled out her credit card and bought a *sun ring* from an old, notoriously expensive craftsman. As happy as a little girl on her birthday, she slipped the ring on her right hand ring finger, saying that once—oh, ages ago—her wedding band had drawn its tight golden ring around it, *but, you see, the impression is already faded . . . and I am free!*

In the open hallway, she recklessly extended her arm full length and orbited full circle for all her friends to see her hand and admire the value of the ring. "Look," she said, "I want you to notice that the eye is no melted chip but the most exquisite amber. Just look at this poor ant-like creature inside!" The women drew closer as if she were a lab instructor.

"Just think," she continued. "This creature has been perfectly preserved before our civilization even began, before numbers could pinpoint time." She liked everyone's attention and went on, away from Egons's scorching impression.

"See," she said, "how its minute legs extend, how its head holds up, still struggling with the avalanche of resin that is trapping it unawares . . . It had no idea that the sticky wave both killed and preserved it." She tapped with her polished fingernail on the hard, round, clear yellow dome, teasing the ant into action. "It's hard to imagine that some long-spent wave tossed this particular bit of amber upon the Baltic shore eons ago and that it shines now, tonight, here on my finger, such an immeasurable distance away from its deep source."

"The same as you," one of the women said.

"The same as we all," Milda echoed. With that the mood shifted slightly, and the women silently looked at one another and at the people down below in the lobby.

*

"Let's go get a drink," Aria Brown broke in. Cutting off Milda's lecture, they found a table that allowed them full view of the lobby below.

"Well, here we are," Milda said after they had received their drinks and she was sipping sweetly on a grasshopper.

"Yes," Aria confirmed. "Here we are, and Latvia is still not free."

"To freedom then!" stout Skaidrite proposed, with matching jollity. They raised their glasses, imitating the gestures of men who had drunk to Latvia's freedom for nearly forty years.

"There are still so many of us, though," Milda said musing, poking her short straw to the bottom of her glass. "Even the prodigals have come back." She sipped slowly watching the people and the revolving doors.

"Like me," Aria said slightly embarrassed. "I can understand. They, too, have had their fill of assimilation husks." She went on talking about her American husband who could not understand her Latvian and other needs and had pushed her to the edge so that divorce was the only honorable alternative. She said that she was here to check out Latvian men. "I have come to survey the field," she laughed as she gulped down her martini. "Give myself that second and last chance."

"How could any Latvian choose to live among foreign people?" Ausma Vēja, another widow, wondered. "I don't understand. How do you deal with all our holidays and folklore?"

"The best we can," Aria snapped. "We educate, enlighten, penetrate and fry the best pancakes, we can, which is a lot more than some of you do, so be a little humble and open-minded."

Milda's plastic straw hit bottom, and she called the waitress. They giggled and ordered another round, talking softly about their friends who had broken away from the ethnic community and fallen head on into the melting pot of America.

"It's what my husband Kārlis feared most of all—subtle assimilation," Milda said. "Anything but that. Better marry any kind of Latvian than an American. At least, he argued, there was a chance of preserving the language and traditions. He believed that people marry societies more than individual men or women."

"I think that's true, very true, indeed," Ausma kept nodding.

"He should've run a breeding agency," Aria snapped. "Look at me! I waited for that fair-haired, blue-eyed prince but he never came. Our refugee boys, when I needed them, were tied to their mother's apron sashes. Or maybe I wasn't pretty enough. Couldn't sing high enough, didn't give a damn about cooking our *frikadil* and *beet* soups, and so I disqualified myself. Jim made me laugh. He made me forget the war and all that goes with it, and for that I thank him and love him still—I guess. It was not his fault he couldn't understand all our messy, tangled roots." Her voice broke, causing her eyes to go blurry. She shifted positions. "Oh, well . . . Let's see what's down there. There they are! Oh, the picture never changes, only the people. The ladies still walk with their heads high as if they carried a stack of books, and the men parade as though they won the *Three Star Medal*!"

"Our people always have good manners."

"Oh yes! Very!"

"We know how to keep in step."

"We've walked in step for a long, long time, from one strange land to another, carrying our story and our song," Milda sighed.

"So," Aria cut in, "maybe it's time we update that story and song. It gets boring for the teller and the listener."

"Where's this conversation going?" Milda lifted her eyes from the last dregs of her drink.

"How would we know?" Aria asked. "We're all mixed up."

"Confused," Ausma added. "We have waited a long, long time."

"The men," Skaidrīte turned to Aria.

"What men?"

"Those who were lost and now try to return," Ausma offered her opinion. "They must have been confused in the beginning, didn't know where things were in this country. Most children had no fathers, no guidance, so maybe they were afraid of being poor and so they became entangled with rich American girls and tried to blend in, but it didn't work."

"Yea," Aria said. "So they couldn't get used to white mushy bread and canned mashed potatoes. Once in a while they must have hungered for our solid rye. Yes, so now they've come back, I hope single and looking, trying to fill in the blanks. Maybe I can help some lost ram find his way back to the fold."

"Yes, maybe," Ausma sighed.

"You might have a chance, both of you," Skaidrite said, shifting her pitying eye from Aria to Milda.

"Thanks for the encouragement," Milda snapped.

"Hey! See that guy?" Aria pointed. "I danced polka with him back in Germany, in elementary school. We got our hands all sweaty, so I pulled my hand away, but now I'm sorry. Should've held on to him. He turned out quite handsome and all right. Yes . . . He used to send me love letters behind Jim's back way back in the fifties, just before our wedding, but I didn't answer. Another mistake. He looks good. I'll have to check him out." She giggled and searched for her pack of cigarettes deep inside her large, stuffed purse. "Ah, to be young again!"

"We were once," Ausma sighed again. "I met my husband in Philadelphia, right by the liberty bell, in apple blossom time. And then came the Korean War . . . So here I am—a not so merry a widow!"

"War, war, war!" Aria exhaled. "We flee from it, but it catches up with us. Our men have always been plucked out from our midst with cruel hands, but our leaders shoot their mouths off about how we marry Americans. What was I supposed to do? Be an old maid? Ha! Not me! But now it's too late, who would want me, who'd I want? It's like trying to get an old shoe to fit. Oh God! Wonder what Uldis married." They fell silent and watched the milling crowd.

"There are so many gray heads. Like cirrus clouds," Skaidrite noted.

"There always have been."

"Only now they belong to us, our generation, and that makes all the difference." Skaidrite said, sipping. "Our blossoms are falling one by one."

"Yes. Take a look down there," Milda looked up, touching her hair. "All those heads dipped in the same pot of yellow Clairol."

They laughed.

"And the men too, poor creatures," Aria smirked. "Look at their bald spots! At least Jim has a full head of hair. I'll say that much for him . . . Maybe I made a mistake."

They giggled uncomfortably and ordered another round.

"I wonder what they think, really," Milda turned somber.

"Who?"

"Those who went away, who broke off and now are trying to return. I wonder where their children are."

"Same place where mine are," Aria answered. "Who knows? Whirling and rocking about in the melting pot like caraway seeds in Campbell's chicken noodle soup."

Milda shuddered, feeling more and more the impact of the grasshoppers and noticing just then two of the straying men approaching, grinning as if they were God's gift to the whole feminine gender. They came like school boys ready to tug girls' braids. They addressed them familiarly with *tu* and in a horrid mixture of Latvian and English. When the women said nothing to lead them on, they offered to buy them drinks for old and new times' sake. Still, the ladies politely and aloofly turned away. They gave no nods, no sidelong glances. Nothing. Only the clear message of disapproval. In unison their rebuffs punished the cavaliers, and as if slapped, they backed off.

"The bitches," one grunted.

"Damned freeloaders," Skaidrite said. "I bet none of them has given a cent to keep this organization alive."

"I really hate people like that," Milda said. "They put me on the wrong side as if I were an unbending conservative, when I claim to be of a free and liberal mind."

The encounter spoiled their mood and again forced serious issues to the forefront. Milda tried to push the oncoming dark thoughts away. When she opened her eyes, she saw Egons, with his arm around his wife's shoulder. They stood at the far end of the lobby. She jerked and spilled her drink. Bits of it splattered on her suit. "Oh, damn," she said and rose. "Excuse me. I'm very tired." She threw some coins in the middle of the table and walked off. The close, smoke-filled air was suffocating, she mumbled standing up, looking for an escape, and smiling stupidly, forced her legs to carry her out of the maze. She walked lightly, hardly feeling the carpeted ground.

"She takes things much too hard," Aria's words reached her from afar.

Milda blinked as she pushed the elevator button, all the while aware of the involuntary movement of her eyes that happened always in the face of frustrating situations. She knew it was an inherited habit from her poor mother Katerina, who had gawked the same way after the communists took over Riga and when life became too heavy to bear. Now she, her lost daughter, carried the irritating, inexplicable mannerism on her like a talisman. It was her way of shifting her mind into different gears, of leaping over many blanks, cluttered perceptions, and memories. It was her way of punctuating her life and thought. With another hard blink, Milda threw herself back in time.

Childhood Recalled

"Can you imagine," Katerina Bērziņa cooed on May 24, 1931, cuddling her baby girl at her overflowing breast, "our Mildiņa is born in our own free country. She won't have to slave for any Russian or German masters like our parents. Like you and I!"

"Yes, my darling," Aleksis Bērziņš said, looking down on his wife and daughter leaning on white pillows propped against a brass headboard in the best hospital in Riga. "No, she won't have to struggle and fight for a good life like all our people," he said, handing the large bouquet of pink roses to the nurse, who stepped up to the bed with a vase full of water. "Lovely," she said, having made the arrangement. She curtsied, then left the happy family alone.

"What should we name our precious?" Father asked, smiling. "She's so beautiful."

"Yes, so lovely . . . Let's name her Milda—*Mildiņa,* after the goddess of love."

"You're my goddess," Aleksis kissed his wife on the lips. "Milda. Yes, so be it."

And *Mildiņa* was a lovely baby who turned into a most beautiful little girl. She had fine blond hair, with ribbons plaited in thin braids on work days, but on Sundays her nanny's Lidia's curling iron made princess locks that draped down over her shoulders. Strangers, friends, relatives, unable to keep their fingers to themselves, said she looked like a doll, but *Mildiņa* didn't like people touching her, especially strange, old women who reminded her of witches who climbed up braids and pushed children into hot ovens. When she cried in fear, Lidia put her arms around her and said that nothing bad like that will happen to her and read on until *they lived happily ever after.*

Two years and three months after *Mildiņa's* birth—it was August 26, 1933—Mr. Bērziņš took his wife again to the hospital. Some days later, he and *Mildiņa* rode the streetcar to the hospital. They found *Māmiņa* in a white room, lying in a white bed reading a book. Mr. Bērziņš handed her a bouquet of pink roses. "So we have another girl," he said and kissed his wife.

"Zelda," she said, smiling and closed the book. "Let's name her Zelda."

"That's a strange name. I don't think it's in our calendar," Mr. Bērziņš remarked, but Katerina said, "I like it." And so it was. Minutes later *Mildiņa* watched the nurse bring in a crying baby and lay it at her mother's breast. She didn't like it.

At home, in time, *Mildiņa* got used to her sister but didn't like her when she cried and Mother couldn't calm her down. Then *Mildiņa* cried even louder, and Mother scolded, whereupon the baby opened her little mouth wider, expelling her screams in waves, making Mother be mean and nervous. *Mildiņa* didn't like to sit in a corner, with her eyes closed and her fingers in her ears. She didn't like to see *Māmiņa* weep.

Zelda was a big baby, too heavy for *Mildiņa* to hold, when Mother laid her on her lap and she kicked and pushed, leaning forward, as if ready to go her own way. Mother watched her anxiously, but Father was proud when, at two months, she stood up, holding on to his thumbs. Zelda skipped the crawling stage and walked at seven months. She seemed to be talking before she could say words, and when the words finally crossed her fat little lips, they came out in groups, in sentences. "Amazing!" friends and relatives flattered, adding, "Wonder what will become of her?"

Zelda had brown hair. Milda remembered her braids strong and thick as ropes and that she didn't want her hair curled on Sundays or any other day. She was scared of the hot curling iron and screamed when unwanted hands touched her. Nobody called her a doll. They said she was as strong and stubborn as a little ox. No one, except father, called her *Zeldiņa*, for it didn't fit her. She was simply Zelda.

"They are very different," Father said.

"I wonder what will become of her?" Mother fretted.

"Ah, don't worry! She'll know how to fight her way in life."

*

In those good *freedom* days of the thirties they had servants: a butler, a cook and a housekeeper. Their governess, Lidia, was in charge of the after-school lessons of French, German and piano and their daily outings. . . ..

HOW LONG IS EXILE?

Milda, alone in her room, could not fall asleep. She tossed and turned, thinking about Zelda, her parents. Everything. She remembered pretty, cheerful Lidia, who took them to matinees, parks, and the beach. She taught them—even Zelda—how to eat in a cafe, how to properly fold a napkin and hold a knife and a fork. "You must have good manners. Otherwise people won't like you," Lidia said—always kindly.

Milda could still see Miss Lidia, skating over frozen canals, her red coat blazing against the ice, one hand tucked inside a black muff, the other extended like a ballerina's. Or up on the dune hills of Mežparks, giving her and Zelda a push on the sleigh and then standing up tall against the transparent pines and the blue winter sky. And even now she could hear Lidia playing the piano, softly, beautifully, her long fingers dancing over the keys . . . She often wondered whatever happened to Lidia when the war was over . . . She simply was no more.

Milda, as far back as she could remember, always knew that their mother, Katerina Bērziņa, was very beautiful. She was tall, and *Mildiņa* and Zelda seemed to be always reaching up to her, reaching for her hand or her face, so it would turn to look down on them with love and approval. Katerina's hair was chestnut brown. She wore it piled high like the poetess Aspazija. When she went out, she wore hats—large and small, with brims and with feathers, flowers, and ribbons, her face veiled and open, as would be proper. *Mildiņa* and Zelda also wore hats that matched their dresses in summer and coats in winter. Mother always coordinated their colors as if she were creating a painting. She also remembered Mother's wardrobe full of the most beautiful dresses, which she liked to touch. Each dress had its own feel, and each dress magically and mysteriously changed Mother into a queen, an actress, a Madonna, a lady such as the girls saw on magazine covers. She remembered how the clicking of Mother's heels made the whole household excited, for then something wonderful would happen. There might be company, a night at the theater, or a train ride to visit their grandparents who lived in Alūksne, near a lake and castle ruins.

Milda's father, Aleksandris Bērziņš, was a tall, light-haired man, who wore dark suits. *Mildiņa* seemed to be always seeing his dark legs like some huge pillars. Often, when in a good mood, he would lift her up and spin her around. Then happy and dizzy, she would still reel as she stood on the floor of their splendid living room or in the sunshine of their garden. He did not lift Zelda and spin her around. He said she was too heavy. Then Zelda cried and would not talk to anyone for a long time.

The Bērziņš family lived in a plush second-story apartment on Lāčplēšu iela. Mr. Bērziņš had been a member of the Parliament. After Kārlis Ulmanis became president, he became Minister of Education. Milda remembered how her father used to walk in and out of their glass-door apartment with a tall hat in hand and shining shoes on his feet. Dressed in dark suits and carrying a black leather briefcase, he exuded an air of great importance, causing all who might be in his way to step aside, including Mamma and the girls. In the evenings he read newspapers in his library and smoked cigarettes. Other elegant gentlemen frequently visited him. They would bow to Katerina, as she closed the doors behind them. Then the men would go into the library, while Katerina and the girls had to be very quiet.

Mildiņa was intrigued by the closed doors. Important things always seemed to happen on the other side of so many doors that opened and shut throughout her childhood. She imagined that once the doors closed, the men would somehow, magically, sail away on a colorful carpet to far lands where they would visit kings and queens and learn from them how to govern the country. (Katerina explained that the men who worked with papa had to be left alone so that they could learn how other people ruled . . . "Your papa will help to make Latvia into the most beautiful and best little country in the world," she would explain, talking over their little heads.)

In those distant years *Mildiņa* and Zelda so revered their father that they felt honored when he asked either of them to fetch his boots or gloves. Even Katerina treated him as if he were some maharaja, as she brought in a silver tray full of delicious cakes and tea in glasses set in silver holders and was happy whenever he asked her to join the company. Then she would sit on the edge of their dark red velvet settee, smile, and, sipping tea, listen to his every word. *Mildiņa* sometimes saw through a keyhole her father kiss her upturned face and pull her up close to him. When a strange feeling came over her, she stopped spying.

Oh, Milda would never forget her mother of those lovely days and evenings, when she would preside over elaborate dinners served in the mirror-paneled, chandelier-lighted dining room! She would then catch only glimpses of her as she glided across the parquet, her evening gown trailing behind her, hair piled high in beautiful curls shining with tiny gems, arms outstretched to welcome guests. In those days Katerina always smiled elegantly, charmingly, like a portrait. No crass words crossed her lips, no tears marred her cheek. Gentlemen kissed her hands, and ladies curtsied and brought her flowers. Occasionally she would entertain them with pieces of Brahms or Schumann, playing exquisitely, and only when Mr. Bērziņš so requested.

At times even the girls, all dressed up in organdy and sashes, could come into the parlor and charm the guests with carefully rehearsed sonatinas or poems. Oh, those were glorious moments!

But Zelda did not care to be shown off. She did not like to play the piano and said so, at times even in front of guests. This caused Katerina great embarrassment, and it was then that she would remark that nothing could be done. Fate had ruled: one girl was like Matilde, the other like Alma. They were Katerina's sisters. Matilde, the oldest, lived on a farm down in Kurzeme, while Alma, the youngest, was an actress in Liepāja.

Savoring that inherited blessing of being like Alma, *Mildiņa,* when asked to play the piano, patterned her movements on Alma's.

Ah, lovely Alma . . . She smelled sweeter than carnations; her lips burned redder than poppies. Her hair was the color of maple leaves in September . . . But Zelda would stiffen and in her awareness of her place on the family tree, would take on to herself all the coarseness of Matilde and, pouting, would lean against the wall, unmindful of soiling the tapestry. With a mean eye she would watch her sister receive white-gloved applause and praise from many fluttering red lips.

*

But then it all ended. It ended brutally and suddenly. It ended on June 17, 1940, when the Russian army, under the dictatorship of Joseph Stalin, having extracted certain consenting signatures from certain governing agents of the Latvian Republic, marched across the eastern border and commenced the occupation of the Baltic States.

Milda remembered the summer day. She was nine, Zelda—almost seven. The family was in Daugavpils, Latgale, for the song festival. The war was far away, and did not stop the special, garlanded trains from carrying choirs from every part of Latvia to sing together in one huge choir. The railroad station and streets of Daugavpils, as well as the country roads, swarmed with people, lighthearted and happy, as on any exciting holiday. The meadows bloomed. The lakes mirrored the blue skies scattered with white clouds. *Mildiņa* and Zelda argued about the animals that romped up in the blue meadows of heaven until they became bored and started chasing each other, laughing and irritating their parents.

Upon arrival in Daugavpils, Mr. and Mrs. Bērziņš left their girls in Lidia's care and went to line up for the grand parade that would wind its way from the center of town to the festival site near the Basilica of

Aglone. Milda remembered the streaming parade of choirs that wound their way to the *estrade*, filling the huge stage. She remembered the sunshine and the dazzling colors of the costumes and, of course, the songs—the same she would be hearing in years to come—again and again, arrangements of familiar folk melodies and patriotic songs, praising the country's beauty and the people's virtue.

Sitting in the audience, with Lidia between them, the girls found Mother among the sopranos and Father among the tenors. Zelda stood up and waved, but Lidia pulled her down, reminding both to mind their manners and listen. And they did listen until—suddenly—the music stopped. Out of the air, came the voice of President Ulmanis, even the children recognized. Most seriously and alarmingly he announced: "Russian tanks have crossed our borders . . . Stay calm . . . I shall remain in my place and you must remain in yours."

But the people did not stay calm. How could they? The whole hemisphere trembled. Even the children sensed that. And then the choirs burst into singing. United, they sang the National Anthem—the national prayer:

God, bless Latvia,
Our precious fatherland;
Where Latvia's maidens sing,
Where Latvia's sons dance.
Let us happily dance, in our Latvia!

They sang it many times, like a dirge, like an unrelenting prayer, crying to high heaven. An eerie stillness followed. Milda remembered people wiping their eyes with white handkerchiefs. She remembered Lidia clutching her hand as if she were afraid to let go.

At last, slowly, silently, the people disbursed and went to board the trains that took them home. Milda remembered the long, silent, ride back to Riga. It was a ride through a twilight night, which allowed hardly an hour's rest for the sun. Swaying between sleeping and waking, the sisters had no idea that they were already as if on separate trains, riding into a chapter of history, so long and tragic that it would determine not only the courses of their lives but the whole population of Latvia—even of all Europe— and the whole world for years to come.

What happened after the festival and the months and years that followed, Milda recalled confusedly, in flashes of terrible brightness and deep darkness. She remembered screaming loudly at night, not knowing exactly why and at whom. She thought all air was foul and poisonous, and there was nowhere to go, nowhere to hide. And when, some months later, President Ulmanis was deported on a mysterious train to an unknown destination and a new president took his place, not only the children but the whole population became orphans.

Thereafter, Mr. Bērziņš lost his position, as did most other leaders and government officials who would not support the occupation. He stopped wearing shiny shoes and hats and stopped carrying his briefcase. A miserable Russian family was moved into two rooms of their apartment. The servants and beautiful Lidia vanished, and there were no more parties with happy music. The grand piano was covered with a gray canvas and wheeled away by strangers. In frightful haste Katerina managed to pack some of her gowns and other fine things into a large trunk and smuggle it to her sister Matilde's farm for safe keeping.

Katerina cried very much. She cried in the night and the day as she walked about her shrunken apartment, never speaking to the strangers who now lived in her once-beautiful bedrooms. She often screamed when she heard the Russians lamenting and talking in their language, grating to her ears. For hours on end she paced about the apartment like a declawed cat. She twisted her wet handkerchief and sponged her swollen, bloodshot eyes with cold water.

For the girls, there was hardly anything to do anymore, as all the familiar activities—the walks, the lessons, the upbringing—stopped. "Oh, my dear babies," Katerina would wail. "What will become of you?" And then she would pull her girls to her full bosom that heaved from unceasing anguish. Where exactly papa worked in those days, *Mildiņa* didn't know. He was absent most of the time, and when he was at home, he moved about the neglected rooms like a punished schoolboy. He never asked either girl to fetch his slippers and shoes but picked them up himself. There were times when he would suddenly shout words the girls had never heard before, and then he would become morose, closed. He sold his and Katerina's best clothes and what was left of the furniture and the silver. Nothing seemed safe; so Katerina hid things from him.

One dark day he took the revered portrait of President Ulmanis off the wall, put it in the fireplace, and set a match to it. *Mildiņa* watched the flames eat up the face—the face she had always seen as powerful as a king's. Katerina let out a shrill scream.

"Papa is mad," she whispered coarsely, her eyes glassy. The girls watched her tears stream, and then they, too, cried while their father stood in the middle of the flames, his hands raised like a priest's. When the leaping red flames died down, having devoured the sacrifice, Mr. Bērziņš turned and said, "I have performed my last patriotic act. I have laid our great leader's image on the pyre myself. No dirty communist hand will ever touch it." After that they had eaten supper: a thin soup and brown bread.

On June 14, 1941, Aleksandris Bērziņš vanished. "I am going out to see if there are any cigarettes at the kiosk," he announced and opened the door.

"Don't!" Katerina gasped, her face whitening, her hands clutching at him. But he pushed her aside and went to the door. She rushed after him, and he embraced her hastily. "It will be better," he whispered into her hair, which she now simply coiled in a bun at the nape of her neck.

"Perhaps Hitler will drive them from our land and Americans will come to defend us." He opened his arms to his daughters. *Mildiņa* flew into them, while Zelda held back. His favorite, pretty one, felt her father's intense, loving pressure. She did not know that it would be their last embrace.

He walked out and never came back.

It was a clear, warm evening, ideal for the month of June, when blue twilight with silver stars shrouds the earth.

As soon as Mr. Bērziņš left, Katerina started pacing nervously, twisting her handkerchief and gawking in a strange twitching motion that scared *Mildiņa* and made her turn her eyes away. She seemed to pace forever, but at last she took up her stand by the open window. She waited silently; only at times and sporadically, as if slapped hard, her body twitched. The girls, like guardian angels, went to stand at her sides. Together they kept the vigil until the air grew cold. Then Katerina moved slightly away from the window and reached over to pick up her white summer shawl. She pulled the girls close to her, inside the circle of her arms, and covered them as with lacy wings. Numbed they sat and waited, silently staring into the night's ghostly darkness.

All was quiet in the streets, except at regular intervals sharp sirens sliced the air as mother/wife and children kept watching, leaning out, peering down into the dawning light as far as their sights would stretch. By and by they saw the sun rise above the housetops—a fogged up, cold silver orb, like a lost moon. Chilled, they collapsed inside the shawl. When the clock struck six, Katerina rose and closed the window.

German Occupation (July 1941, to December 1944)

About a week later, after Midsummer Night and St. John's Day that few dared to celebrate, *Mildiņa* noticed that the uniforms in the streets had changed from one shade of camouflage green to another. Words also changed from Russian to German, but the tones remained the same. By then Katerina Bērziņa had draped herself in black veils and hardly ever went out of her shade-drawn apartment. When, by necessity, she did venture past the courtyard gates, one of her daughters was always obliged to go with her and hold her hand.

Down in the streets *Mildiņa* heard whispers and saw people—groups of strange, frightened people—with yellow stars on the fronts and backs of their drab smocks. Soldiers with guns and huge, ferocious dogs drove them along the gutters. To her horror some of those men spoke Latvian, waving their arms that seemed stiff like logs. She saw that the arms were wrapped with red armbands with black, crooked crosses. She also saw the knee-high black leather boots and the riding pants bulging out above them. She was terrified of the men and the dogs, afraid they would grab her, Zelda, and Mamma, too, and push them into the sewage gutters, but she was afraid to ask questions or say anything that might upset Mother, who repeatedly told her to be quiet because *there were ears everywhere.* She did not understand what that meant; she only held on to Mother's black-gloved hand with more fright than she had ever known and stretched her steps so they would never step on the cracks. She observed that Mamma's face, draped in black, was now always turned toward the inside of the sidewalk and not the gutter side, where the hounded people shuffled along.

One day they saw the city burn and screaming they ran home, but they did not talk about the fire either. Days later the ashes spoke . . . In school, too, neither the children nor the teachers mentioned the fire that had raged through and about the synagogue. Neither did anyone dare to talk about the people with the stars. If anyone asked questions, he or she would be sent immediately to the principal's office. By the time the Germans settled in as the new rulers, the children, who had already learned the meaning of terror from the communists, expected nothing good. They remembered how the Communists had changed the air, even in her school, when a Red Corner was set up where President Ulmanis's portrait had been. The boys had to bow and click their heels, and the girls had to curtsy before the new portrait of the horrible man with a bushy mustache whose name was *Jāzeps Staļiņš.* When a brave, angry girl, on a dare, had yanked at the red cloth, the teacher had dragged her away by her hair. No one saw her again. Such things happened time and again: those children who spoke too loudly and seemed rebellious were suspended and their terrified parents called up for a scolding.

Now, under the new occupation, more children disappeared. Those who remained whispered to one another saying that the missing ones were Jews and that the Nazis put them in ovens and ground them up. They trembled from their own words and visions and hovered like lambs in folds, silent and shaking. Once, when *Mildiņa* asked her bench mate where their classmate Jēkabs was, the teacher made her stand in the corner. She was released only after she had peed in her pants. After that she was too ashamed and scared to speak to anyone, but went about with her head hung low, her eyes always looking out for black boots.

At night, and only rarely, *Mildiņa* tried to talk to Zelda about the things they both saw, but she also told her to be quiet, to keep her mouth shut. Sometimes Zelda hit her when she was crying, and *Mildiņa* spit at her, sick with fright. After that she really did keep quiet. She bit her lips until they became chapped and hard, but she couldn't keep her eyes from staring at the awful sights she met. Desperately she turned for love to her dolls, but even the paper dolls scared her. She had nightmares about their lying in gutters and being chewed by huge dogs. She would wake up screaming, but Zelda, with whom she shared her bed, would kick her and tell her to lie still. It was then she feared and hated her sister as never before.

Zelda, though two years younger, was bigger than Milda. She was tough. Time and again she talked back to Mother, scratched her hair and stomach and many times fought with other children, always getting the better of them. She ruled their courtyard and watched over *Mildiņa* whenever they played outside, constantly bullying her and making her cry. And then again Katerina would remark that Zelda was like Matilde and her delicate *Mildiņa* like her sister Alma. Her tone said that one was bad, the other good; one was coarse, the other refined. One was to be learned from how not to be, the other—how to be.

Milda remembered both aunts visiting them during those frightful years. Matilde always came bringing a basket full of food—bacon, honey, jam, butter, and bread—herself carrying the combined smell of all the items, and hugging her, Zelda, and Mamma in bulges of fat and sweat. She wore men's shoes and smelled of the barn. One time—and Milda remembered this with real admiration—Matilde opened the door with a loud laugh and a bang. She was carrying what looked like a guitar case. "This time I really fooled the *scheister* inspectors!" She lifted from the case a huge smoked animal leg. Even Katerina laughed a bit and set the kettle boiling, while Zelda clung to her heroic aunt. Matilde stroked the child's hair and talked excitedly about how there were soldiers in the woods and how the war would soon be over.

"Americans will come to help us," she declared. "Those German boys want to go home too," she said. "They are all sick of killing." She did not go home until everyone had eaten her fill and Katerina's face had softened.

In contrast, when Alma dropped by on her brief visits to Riga, she still wore beautiful clothes. In winter an orange fox hung around her neck, its green eyes shining. Alma's perfume wrapped *Mildiņa* as in a mist, filling their apartment with the fragrance of lilacs, even in winter. When she spoke, her eyes bright and her mouth red, *Mildiņa* watched entranced. Nobody else she had ever heard could speak so beautifully, so melodiously. She loved to sit next to her adorable aunt, breathing her in like refreshing air. But Alma, after distributing lovely little presents to everyone, never stayed long, and she never pulled anyone to her bosom.

Now and then, throughout the terrible, fatherless years, both aunts invited the sad broken family for visits, but Katerina always refused to leave her apartment. "I must stay in my place, come what may," she said, resigned. "What is my life now that all is gone, now that they have deported my husband, my joy and protection?" And then the tears would start up again and flow for hours.

In Milda's memory, those years had no lights. She only remembered movements of people through dark streets and rooms in shadows. Even the night darkness seemed darker in those years when the stars forgot to shine or when she forgot to look for them. The night and winter cold was biting and gray, smelling of coal. There had been snow on one of those Easters, and an untimely frost, Matilde lamented, had killed the early sprouts.

It was always cold then, inside and out. Occasionally their old butler would knock on the door and bring them an armful of wood. He would bow and start a fire for his mistress and she, overcome with gratitude, would weep silently, offer him apple peal tea, and try to say a cheerful word. The good man, whose hair had turned white inside one year, sighed for a while with her, patted the girls' heads, and, nodding and bowing, backed out the door.

There were days and weeks when Katerina, her daughters, and those occupiers, who shared the apartment, would be sick with contagious diseases, but there was no doctor to call because they had been deported or, aware of what was happening to the Jews, had killed themselves. Katerina nursed the girls through red measles and chicken pox, but when she herself was struck down with *grippe*, Zelda took care of her. She knew how to make broth, and she kept the tea warm at Mother's bedside.

Mildiņa did not like cooking and sickness. She only sat shivering at Mother's feet, reading and coloring, hardly saying anything. Sometimes she wrinkled up her little forehead and tried to comprehend the meaning of new words. *Deportācija* was a word she learned first. *Terors* was another, and *Komūnists*—yet another.

In that last she packed all the evil that her child's mind could fathom. That word had messed up their nice apartment and destroyed her good life. It had snatched away her father; it was killing her mother. It banished laughter. Without mercy, it destroyed all that was beautiful and created unbearable gloom everywhere. And it drove her into exile.

*

Mrs. Arajs shut her eyes tightly, blocking out the lights of the bright hotel. "Poor, poor *Mammīte*!" She wondered whose hands, if any, finally closed her eyes.

The elevators rode past her, packed full like the notorious box cars of the deported, as etched on her mind in black and white. While she waited for the elevator that would eventually stop, she thought she was again on a strange platform waiting for trains to take her away, far, far away . . . When her eyes opened, pulling her out of the dark cave of crowded flashbacks and into the loud, electric lights, she saw double images of her family, grouped as they once had been, in front of the leaping blue, gold, and red flames . . . In disbelief she stared at all the jovial people: *Why are you laughing? You don't fool me! I know that behind your laughter, smiles, easy talk you're trying to ignore memories that no frolicking could ever erase.*

Impulsively, with a motion that might beat down a burning coal, she pushed through the small band of people and hit hard the red upward pointing arrow. At her touch, the bell rang, and the elevator opened.

"Oh, for heaven's sakes! If it isn't Milda Bērziņš!" a shrill voice greeted her as the packed car closed.

"Hi!" Milda answered as she was being pressed hard against this vaguely familiar acquaintance. She smiled placidly, aware, as in a dream, of leaning against one side of a gentleman who felt and looked somewhat like Egons. He turned and nodded, but she detached herself as soon as there was room and watched him get off on the fifth floor.

"So you are here!" The same woman spoke again for all to hear.

"Yes, I am."

"That's fantastic," the woman beamed. Milda still could not place her in any definite spot or time in her life.

"Why don't you come up to my room?"

"Oh, I'm so tired," she tried to excuse herself and watched the numbers of the floors turn on and off. She had forgotten to press #10, and before she could decide where to get off, she was being pulled out on the thirteenth floor.

"You can sleep for the next five years, but not now. I'm having a party and you must come! There's plenty of wine and cheese."

"Well, all right," Milda gave in. "For a while."

THE SECOND DAY

The Morning After

Milda Arajs found her room about three o'clock in the morning and went to bed, aware that she was acting completely out of character and that she would have to pay for her digressions in the morning. She set the alarm safely for ten o'clock and lay her head on the unnatural foam pillow. She slept restlessly. Dreams, phantoms, memories, and fears crowded her sleep in kaleidoscopic confusion; they appeared in black and white, like old silent films, and in dazzling colors like splashes from the brushes of German Expressionists. They spoke in many languages, and she tried to respond in kind, mixing Latvian, German, and English in inarticulate gasps and accents. She dreamed of running down corridors with all the doors closed, when, all at once, the hallway carpets became rivers that carried her like a weightless leaf until, without feeling the impact, she banged against a black board. She was slightly conscious of having screamed, but she had not heard herself make any noise at all. She had uttered her nightmare shriek because Ilga had fallen into the river and was struggling with the black board and calling, "Mamma, help me! Save me, *Mammīt*!"

So violently aroused, with the night still wrapped around her, she threw off her covers and her nightgown. She burned in hot flashes that whipped her with lightning switches. She vividly remembered that somewhere looming large on one bank of her black dream river Pēteris Vanags had stood holding out to her his empty sleeve. "Wow! Am I glad it's only a dream!" she muttered, rising, with the apparition of an angry Vanags—such as she had never seen in daylight—hovering over her. Unnerved, she closed her eyes, hoping he would show that face again for her to evaluate, but it did not return. Still, she felt uneasy. She believed that dreams sent messages and wished there would be some Joseph or Daniel, who could interpret the meaning, but there was no one. *Another secret I must hide in my heart . . . I hate being alone in this strange, luxurious room, but that's what it means to be widowed: you're forever alone in strange rooms.*

In the bathroom, she glanced in the mirror, said *ak vai* . . . and, after checking all the locks, went back to bed. Curling up, she pulled the sheet around her, but was unable to relax.

At last, toward dawn, she fell into a comatose sleep, void of all dreaming, until the siren of her alarm clock raised her up. For a lost moment she sat, not knowing where she was. "Ah, yes, I am on a great and expensive holiday," she told herself and stretched the full length and width of her five-foot, six-inch and 130-pound frame. Her head felt very heavy, full of the previous day's baggage. After summarizing the assorted impressions, she returned her head back on the pillow. For a while she lay still, absentmindedly criticizing the ceiling and passively wondering why her beloved faraway Americanized son Gatis (now Garry) had not even troubled to disturb her in the jumble of the night's subconscious darkness. Then quite on impulse, she picked up the phone and ordered breakfast to be brought up immediately. But as soon as she put the receiver down, she felt the ghostly presence of Kārlis, who would never approve such extravagance.

"Then why did you leave me?" she demanded. "Don't you know that I'm doing the best I can?"

She heard water running somewhere and allowed herself the sensation of pretending that Kārlis was in the bathroom endlessly taking a shower. She sank deeper and feigned irritation about having to put up with his steam. His showers had always been too long, and he had always left the toilet seat up and the floor littered and slippery, expecting everything to be neat and dry when he came home in the evening. The last time she cleaned up after him, he did not bother to come home. He fell from the arms of Vanags straight into space, beyond the sun and the stars, or God only knows where Latvian souls were stored . . . Now, acutely conscious of being alive, Milda determined to do as she pleased. She would have her breakfast in bed, would not care what he might think. "You're dead," she groaned. "You took off and died. Took the easy way out, didn't you?"

The dry words formed balls of spittle in her sour-tasting mouth. "You left us all just like papa. No, worse: you dared to die in Vanags's arms, knowing very well how mixed up I am about him, how I *feel*. No, you didn't because I don't either. So there! And now I am doing what pleases me, and—I can live without you very well!" But she knew she was lying. She missed his protective authority, especially at this time and place, when she felt extremely vulnerable, when Latvianness, so condensed in one hotel, seemed hot and claustrophobic.

She had her breakfast in bed. She ate slowly, luxuriously, listening to soft music on the radio and expecting Ilga to call. When the phone remained silent, she, to her surprise, felt relieved. She assured herself that Ilga had things to do—or perhaps that she wanted her to be free to explore the world that had passed her by during her years of solitary mourning. "All right, my child. We're going to put the shards of our relationship back in order later," she said, quickly rising. She showered and put on her wrinkle-resistant, orange-white flowery polyester dress.

She glanced in the mirror and saw that it showed off her rather youthful figure quite well; the deep V-neckline and empire waist accented her breast line—*almost as it was then . . . Wonder if it'll ring any bells for him* . . . Ready to go, she slipped her feet into comfortable sandals and left the room.

Confusing Circles

Down on the mezzanine she meandered through the crowd, only partially exposing herself to quick touches and greetings. She stalked around the edges of the clusters, fearful of being pulled into intimate triangles where she might again lose her thoughts and her day. If the day before she had dived into the crowd, then on this day she wished to wade as in shallow waters, no deeper than her knees. She would protect herself from stormy waves and was on the lookout for anyone who might push her over. She wanted nothing heavy, but simply to bask in the abstractions and hazes of her national awareness, storing up its energy.

She strolled about, like an outside observer in a Henry James novel, looking at people as on multiple screens. She could not connect the people who scurried around with herself and her past; the setting seemed all wrong. Surrealistic. Latvians should be connected with meadows and the sea and woodlands, not convention centers. She paused as she heard familiar music coming from afar, yet grating on her nerves. It was the old, sprightly folk song about a rooster who runs to the village to wake up lazy girls.

The song blasted out full of static and then toned down, adjusted by some invisible hand. Soon more songs floated from the ceilings and out of the walls. The pastoral notes and words filled the air, and she didn't know whether to be glad or sad. *Oh, if only this would be real! If only I could now be in a modern Riga with my people, free and going forward, not always looking back!* She paced on, her eyelids blinking,

blinking their warning: *Be careful! Harness those feelings, control those longings, stop yearning for what you can never have. This is a cruel mirage! But don't miss what you are really looking for!*

She paced on, listening, trying to think more soberly about how the poor songs were also out of place, lost, like peasant children in city streets; she wanted to gather them up and lead them home. Her folk songs should not be amplified electrically; they should echo naturally over free meadows and in clear air. They belonged in old Latvia by the Amber Sea . . . But still, she listened and, listening, breathed easier, while Reason tugged, challenging: *But if you are pleased by the ancient melodies, might not others be also? And if others, then why not Americans, why not the world?*

She stared in a kind of abstract shock at the poster in front of her that said **Latvians of the Free World.** The perfect paper faces, with mouths wide open, suddenly seemed aloud and singing, not at all embarrassed, not at all protective of their voices but throwing out their songs to the waves, even the waves of air-conditioning. Milda saw that all the corners of this poster were glued down properly and nodded approvingly. She straightened her shoulders like the blond girl of the poster—so much like herself in another time and place—and walked on.

Good! Reason spoke, *let the songs be! Let them find their own way. And don't worry: neither the words nor notes will drop down and die if they cross over into what you call foreign ears. Did it ever occur to you that others might actually enjoy your songs and make more of them than all the conserving patriots? Just think, what Tchaikovsky, Sibelius, Beethoven would be without New York, without Leonard Bernstein? Or if you want to turn it around, where would the knowledge of Latvia be, if Vītols, Mediņš, Dārziņš, and the rest of our fine composers had conquered Carnegie Hall? Exchange, for God's sake, share, give! And let go. Don't bind your beautiful songs so they can please only your nostalgic ears! Quit being a dowdy mother who smothers her children with shawls while the sun is shining!*

Her heart pounded, ready to break the skin.

And don't confuse modernization with Communism and old fashions and ways with patriotism like Kārlis did. Break away from his barred mind and open wide your own mind and senses to their natural limitlessness, their curiosity and honesty. Remember your namesake Mrs. Milda Gramzda and your proud aunt and the ship that carried you to freedom, cutting the waters sharply, precisely.

She walked faster, bumping into people, hardly seeing them. *Go on! You won't disintegrate! Do not be afraid to see what you look at and listen to what you hear. And don't be slow about it. Others might get ahead of you, and then where will you be? Don't you know that the seams and the borders of the world are already tearing? Don't you realize how rusted through and through the Iron Curtain really is? The touch of a strong hand will make it crumble, you'll see, Milda Bērziņa-Arājs, you'll see, and then where will you be?*

She stopped short and stood still, looking down into the open lobby, at the escalators carrying her people in streamers up and down, ceaselessly, dropping and setting them on stable floors where they tangled in patterns of curious disarray. She paced on, noticing that the music was affecting others also; people looked up and around, smiled, grinned, and chatted.

In the Art Gallery

Mindlessly, because it was there, she walked into the art gallery and started circling slowly, stopping at each painting long enough to pay her respects, until one arrested her attention, drawing her inside its coarse, brown frame, making her freeze. The artist had created a strangely abstract winter scene. Milda saw at first glance the tree trunks, the outlines of hills and valleys, the touches of orange and purple on silver icicles. Gazing, she felt the tone, the mood and read *Life Suspended.*

Without even one ethnographic design, the painting struck her as deeply Latvian; such she could see the Latvian soul in its distilled purity. She stood facing it with her head slightly tilted, looking at the canvas, yet not seeing it all. After a long while, she shifted her weight and stepped to one side, all the while keeping her eyes focused . . . She blinked hard, her eyelashes fluttering confusedly, lost in the canvas maze . . . And then she saw it! The hills and valleys below the trees outlined the body of a female nude. It lay there so obviously, now that she saw it. She blinked again. The woman was not dead, only dormant, sleeping her winter's sleep, not on any fabled glass mountain but pressed down, into the ground, an imbedded fossil, yet remarkably alive.

Milda penetrated the painting, delighting in its truth too magnificent for words. Time slid away, but still she did not move. Soon she saw only the cold, suspended, naked body, while everything else, the trees, sky, and ice fell into the background. She stood there as in front of an open freezer, feeling the chill but still looking into it, still gazing.

"You enjoy the painting?" Egons asked softly, looking over her shoulder.

"Yes," she answered, her hand bracing her heart.

"Do you know why?" She heard the controlled casualness of his smooth voice.

"I don't know," she said with matched calm. "I'm no art critic."

"What do art critics know that you don't?"

"I don't know. I only see, and maybe I see it all wrong."

"What is right and what is wrong in art?" he asked coaxing. "What do *you* see?"

"Siberia."

"Not Latvia? Not our Latvian winter?"

"No. Because the cold is too pure, the ice too frozen . . . I see Zelda. My sister."

"Oh . . . You did not tell me. Is she in Siberia?"

"She was. She lived through it . . . I have to go."

Not daring to look up at his face, she slid out the door and escaped into other, more safely crowded, halls and shops.

Buying Souvenirs

She did not want to buy anything specific, but just to pass the time until her heartbeat became normal; on second thought, why not buy some souvenirs for her grandchildren or something for Ilga, but certainly nothing for herself. Oh well, perhaps a book . . . She never felt guilty about buying books even though, since the death of Kārlis, she seldom read books by Latvian authors. The classics she knew practically by heart; the new writers, suddenly so many, could neither hold her interest, nor surprise her senses. Sometimes she merely collected new publications out of loyalty and for decoration; they did look nice and rich on her shelves. Also, it was a way of supporting the life of the endangered Latvian language.

She browsed through the stacks of books, but nothing caught her eye. She did notice, however, that there were several books in English. Translations. She spotted *The Golden Steed* and *Kitty's Water Mill,* translated by Helga Williams. She made a face, glanced at the covers and went on: *How dare she tamper with Rainis and Skalbe?* Flustered, she decided to buy nothing, not after already spending so much money on the ring. She looked at her hand pleasurably because the ring added a beautiful light, like an evening glow, to her working hand, making it feel not only glamorous but supportive of her struggling culture. She smiled at the thought; it would be the excuse she would give Kārlis for her spontaneous purchase. She would say it seriously, though, and he would forgive her in due time. Now she forgave herself as her ringed hand touched other arts and crafts, looking right, while it glided over linen, wool, ceramics until it stopped on a soft pigskin purse. It was not, however, the fine shoulder bag itself that made her hand pick it up, but the delicately burned-in and tinted pastoral scene on its flap. She looked at it as if it were a snapshot from her old family album that was, alas, long lost somewhere in the folds of the Iron Curtain.

"You like it?" The craftsman asked.

"Yes." She saw a fertile valley with a serious barefooted girl herding a flock of sheep that grazed peacefully. "How much is it?"

"Seventy dollars," the man said. Milda set the purse down, ready to walk away.

"Wait!" called the craftsman. "You are a lady who appreciates good work. I can tell by the way you touched it. I'll let you have it for sixty." He reached for the wrapping paper.

"Forty-five."

"Fifty."

"Sorry. Forty-five is all I can afford, and I do appreciate the craftsmanship as nobody else would." Milda stroked the leather expertly. "You would not want to have your beautiful work go to those who're not aware of your soul inside it, would you?"

"And what makes you think of my soul?"

"I just know. You are inside this shepherdess. You must have been a shepherd in your childhood."

"How did you know?"

"From the way you arranged the sheep. Only a true shepherd would be able to do that so perfectly."

"All right. Forty-five," he said, opening his hand.

Milda gave him the bills, plus the tax. "I was a shepherdess too," she mentioned casually.

"Really? When, where?"

"In southern Kurzeme during the German occupation, when I was about eight or nine. It was only for a month. Visiting relatives. I'm actually a city girl—from Riga."

"Ah, yes, those were hard times," the man said, pausing to light his pipe.

"Yes."

"But I herded my father's cattle when we were free, during the best of times." He exhaled a large cloud of bitter smoke and then spoke from one side of his mouth, the other clamping the pipe. "What a wonderful time that was! Paradise, that's where we lived and didn't know it. But they knew! Stalin knew as he pushed his way across our borders and started butchering us. He knew a bread basket when he saw one, the devil burn his soul! I saw the Russian swine dig up our fields," the man looked for a place to spit, but instead turned smiling toward another customer, and Milda, pressing her purchase to herself, left the shop.

Unwanted Encounter

In the ladies' room she emptied the contents of her old, battered purse into the new one and threw the old away. She studied herself in the mirror. The purse will be better framed against her white linen dress she will wear on the Writers' Morning. The flowery polyester dress she had on was wrong, and hoping that nobody would stop her, she decided to run up to her room and change. If she hurried, she could still make the two o'clock symphony concert. *Idyll.* That seemed inviting, restful. *Letters to Peer Gynt*. Lovely! And both works by Latvian composers, of course. It was just what she needed: an escape into some safe haven, where she would only listen and feel.

Hurrying, she turned a sharp corner into the elevator hall, ready to push the UP button, when her step tripped on the carpet. Her hand pulled back and awkwardly grasped at the stultifying air. Inside a circle of portly men stood Pēteris Vanags. Clearly he was trying to persuade those around him of something or other. His right hand with a burning cigarette between his fingers beat the air, but as soon as he saw her, the arm, with the cigarette at its end, turned in her direction like a weathervane touched by an unexpected wind. For a second she held her breath, in a glance taking in the whole scene. She saw the left, dead, black-handed arm inside the sleeve also moving slowly upward like the barrier of a railroad crossing, and she stepped back.

"Aha, Arāja *kundze*," Vanags said, suddenly looming over her, "I have been looking for you."

"Really?"

"We have something important to discuss," he said.

"No, we do not," she snapped. "I have no time."

With that, she turned and, without the slightest backward glance, fled down the corridors toward the concert hall. She slowed down only when she reached the door and heard the tuning of instruments. Since she had not been able to change clothes, she was awkwardly self-conscious about being badly dressed and, attempting to be as invisible as possible, slipped into an empty seat behind a post. She hoped the young woman on her right and the bald man on the left would not notice her bare feet inside her sandals and the clingy print of her dress that glaringly clashed with her purse. But mostly she hoped no one would feel the trembling of her nerves and the beating of her heart in frustrated rage: *Why now? Why does he have to be here to spoil my first big leap to freedom? Why, oh why? I do not understand . . .*

After Kārlis died, four years ago, she had expected Pēteris Vanags to show up at her front door at any moment and make good on his promise whispered in the shadow of the blooming rosebush growing into the castle wall: "One day you will be mine." Yet he had not come. He did not drop everything and fly to her side. His tone of voice on the telephone announcing the sudden death had been aloof and polite.

When he arrived at Grand Rapids for the funeral, he stayed at a motel for one night—not even bothering to telephone her. At the casket, just before the funeral, he had formally expressed his sympathy to Ilga, who was weeping, but still produced an angry scowl. Rebuffed, he then took Milda's hand and, eying her through her veil and tears, pressed it sincerely enough for her blood pressure to rise and then let go. He went to take his place in the front of the procession, while she, leaning on Ilga's arm, followed the casket. He gave a sterling eulogy to the packed house of mourners but, after the burial, left abruptly for the airport. He did not stay for the reception, so there had been no chance for any conversation. Naturally, this had upset her, hurt her pride. In time she allowed herself to heal and dismiss him from her thoughts.

But that was not easy. Both men—the deceased and the living—usurped her mind night and day so that during the first days and weeks of her solitude, she lived more in Esslingen entangled in their peculiar triangle that rotated in circles within circles. She replayed all the important scenes of their drama, analyzed the characters, and puzzled over the possibilities of multiple endings. When she replayed the whole scene of her husband's funeral, she became extremely annoyed and confused, for death was no ending. So what would it be? How would she bring their drama to a satisfactory conclusion? What did he have in mind? He, who now had something important to discuss? Was he also reliving the past or had he forgotten his promise? Or . . . was he afraid—as she was? Were there new obstacles, or had another invaded his heart?

In her sober moments she understood that he might be embarrassed. Kārlis's death had surprised and shocked him as much as her, and he, like she, needed time and space to rearrange things and shift all images from past dreams to reality. She knew that time and age had worn down such passion as they had shared to mere tremors of nerves and irregular pulse throbs. She knew that no one could ever recapture lost youth, and every one alive feared the specter of old age; still, during those hard, empty years, shouldn't he have called—as a friend? Didn't he care?

Finally, depending on Time's healing hand, she also stopped caring and expecting, and gave up, determined to avoid any contact with this incomplete, impenetrable man (as she insisted on viewing him). And so she withdrew in her Grand Rapids solitude and picked up the old bricks of her earlier fears, guilt, and her late Aunt Alma's violent objections. She glazed it all over with Ilga's repugnance of him and felt satisfied. Brick by brick she constructed a wall around her and imagined herself safely boarded—like a Solveg, singing her song, or a Penelope, weaving a shroud. Singing, weaving, and embroidering, she focused on her adult children, who did not need her much, but mostly she nurtured her old, inexplicable fear of him. *I don't really know him. Who is he and what was he during the war? Why did Ilga, as a little girl, instinctively hate him? And . . . was there a connection with the other man who looked spookily like him? So who was he and where is his home?*

This double had suddenly shown up in the Esslingen DP food line and then vanished like some shadow. She had wanted to ask Pēteris if he knew he had a double, but there had never been a right time. Their encounters had been brief and fraught by too much fear and excitement, and when leaning against the castle wall after their hasty intercourse, she tried to pose a question to Pēteris about his counterpart, he had kissed her lips shut and then lit a cigarette. After he finished smoking and freed his hand, she weakly put her head in his lap and welcomed his hand as it slid inside the cleavage of her dress . . . In the bright glare of their pleasure, the stranger's shadow floated away with the white cloud at which she gazed through the canopy of pink, wild roses. She took her small note pad from her purse and wrote:

How could I then or at any other time ask for any references? Young and on fire for him, I needed all my strength to fight against my mind, my anger with blind Kārlis, and overbearing Aunt Alma. Yes. They all and my mind had aligned against my body, and I fought them. My fall was my supreme leap against those who governed me, and giving in to our mutual craving was proof of my strength and courage. I did not care then who he was, nor what he had been. Back in those days we all lived in the present in a true carpe diem *spirit . . . And all I know is that then, on that hot afternoon, he satisfied the longing of my body and soul as no one could and no one has since—no matter what the laws and rules. And yes, it is that—that vampire-like possession, that never-healing scar that his presence enflames, the same one that even now makes me weak—or strong. I don't know which. So why am I afraid? Is it his all-consuming power over me? Is it still alive and smoldering in him also? Is he also afraid and, therefore, careful? What is it? Is that what he wants to discuss with me now? Or is there something else? Perhaps some Latvian thing that he wants to talk about politely with me, the grieving Mrs. Arāja? Does he need me for a symbol, a representative or—for myself? Oh, I don't know! I don't know anything. All I feel again is the strong, unbending Hand of Fate breaking down my wall, playing with me, having fun with me, a mere mortal.*

As the instruments screeched, she stopped writing and watched people milling about. She thought about his black fist, much more polished and visible in the vast Hyatt Regency landscape than in enchanting Esslingen, where other veterans were worse off. Concentrating, she told herself that the fist was a symbol of the war and all that she had tried to escape and again, with a shudder she recalled her recent nightmare and Ilga's scream and his mean grimace.

She grasped her stiff leather purse like a life preserver, wishing she could talk to someone about her feelings, but there was no one, not even a psychiatrist who would charge by the hour; anyway, it would take up too many hours of explaining, of setting all in perspective so he (or she) would understand the causes and effects of her particular syndrome. So Milda kept writing in her journal and did her own analyzing: she thought about his lost arm and the black fist. Any fist is also a palm, she pondered. The victim is also a victimizer; the fearful could become the terrorist . . . She tried to imagine in Vanags's fist concealed scenes and secrets, mysteriously carried out in solitude, perhaps in circles of fir trees on freezing moonless nights. She had read about things like that. More and more tales of horror and mystery appeared even in common media nowadays. *Oh, what is the truth about him? And what is it about me?*

As if in answer to her silent plea, she saw him enter the hall and sit down close to the door. She saw him glance around until he spotted her. Seemingly satisfied, he turned away, when another big man sat down next to him. The lights dimmed.

Is he stalking me? Did he see me in the gallery close to Egons and the painting? Is there any place where his eyes cannot follow? Oh, I must be very careful or I shall never be a free woman.

Inside the Concert Hall

As she waited for the conductor to take center stage and lift his arms, her fingers nervously slid over the burned-in girl on the soft light brown pigskin. Uninvited, a scene, burned in Milda's mind, flared up: she was very little and very scared, when she saw Mother leaning over an open newspaper. Katerina's tears fell on the page and soaked into the print.

"*Mammīt*, don't cry," she said in a tremulous voice. But Katerina only sobbed harder. *Mildiņa* put one arm around Mamma's shoulders and drew her to herself, as long before the war Mother had drawn her. "Shh," she said, and only then did she see at what *Mammīte* stared. It was a photograph that took up half the page, showing a battlefield. Bodies, some in mud, some sprawled over a pasture, lay about scattered like boys' toy soldiers. One of the dead had his arm straight up in the air.

"Can dead people hold their arms up for a long time?" she asked.

"Hush!" Katerina emitted and, freeing herself from her daughter's arm, walked to the window and looked out for a long time. *Mildiņa* waited a long time for the answer that never came.

*

She shut her eyes tightly, as she had then, wishing she had never asked the question because perhaps then this scene would not haunt her. Katerina burned the newspaper.

Now Milda was sure that Pēteris Vanags would know the answer. He had lost his arm; he had been on the inside of horror. He had been touched by it, and it had stuck to him, tailing him shadowlike and frightening. She knew nothing about the particulars of his dismemberment, only that she had been afraid, yet longing for his touch, that she, even in their passionate embraces, had closed her eyes so she would not see the false limb. Afraid to know the real truth, she dreaded to be touched. Lately, she feared the truth whenever she heard and saw on TV how foreign veterans who lost out in World War II and lived in the States were being investigated. America, she knew, had no patience or sympathy for losers; only Viktors could boast of the stars on their epaulets and above their breast pockets. But whenever she saw uniformed men in parades on Memorial and Veterans' days, she wondered how much blood and how many secrets each man carried inside.

*

A sudden burst of applause threw her into the present, and she, too, clapped hard. The conductor bowed, then turned, raised his wing-like arms, and up rose the first notes of *Idyll.* Beautiful, soothing notes they were, expressing what words could never say but brought to Milda's distraught mind soothing images that for a while chased all gloom from her, as the south wind would chase away icy clouds. As the notes helped her to relax, she called forth all the loves of her life. She saw flowers and woods in spring and summer, and somewhere in these woods there was a golden-haired little girl, whom her cousin Juris carried through the storm, her drenched head resting under his chin. And—many years later—there was Gert lifting her off the boulder and placing her gently on solid ground . . . And still later, Egons swimming next to her in the moonlight. And yes, of course, there was the insistent, brooding, gloomy, irresistible Pēteris Vanags and—always (she had assumed there always would be)—her reliable, stable husband, Kārlis Arājs.

She replayed her wedding night and her daily life with the latter. Their life had been good and predictable; Kārlis had a steady career with an insurance company and had quickly been promoted and had risen to the top. He had a tenth story office with a splendid view and an efficient secretary. He knew all about investments and taxes and what was deductible and what was not. He managed everything well, including herself, he believed. And she, in turn, kept the house in order. They were kind and faithful to each other—except when Egons caused her to step outside the marital ring that one midsummer night and when Vanags, as their guest, eyed her disturbingly.

On the poignant strings of violins, she floated back to that one night on the misty, enticing lake, but quickly the sudden thundering drums beat her like fists. Still, spitefully, peering over to where Vanags sat, she gathered all of Egons's words and caresses around her and, again closing her eyes, rested her head against the marble pillar. Nostalgically, she assured herself that in her war-damaged life, any surprising romance was good; it offered compensation and respite from pain and heartache. *Even a moment of truth and beauty—is a gift of God, though inescapably painful,* Milda had set down in her journal . . . *During such intercourses are conceived thousands of poems and paintings that fill all the galleries of the world, which people visit, often enduring long lines. All identify with love-tormented heroes and heroines, and so the secret, forbidden pleasures live on through countless ages . . . Ah, yes, when such love comes as it did to me—unsummoned, uninvited—it must be cherished, for it never repeats itself. Love's face is not round like a clock's. Love is light and shade, whispers and flames; it breaks and mends; it inspires and makes the spirit grow and life open up in all the colors of its surprising prism . . . No, I shall never regret any part of Love. I must not ever! I might regret many things about life, but not that—never.*

The violins soared, and Milda swam in the secret deliciousness of all her loves, silently recalling some beautiful, sad and tragic words that her favorite poet Aspazija had written:

Love for me was like a visitor
That passing by stopped at my door
And slowly went away.

Sad are these lines, Milda mused. *Yet what if there had been no sadness, no pain? Doesn't pain define pleasure? What if all love, except that of Kārlis, had passed me by? What if?*

*

Another wave of applause startled her. She clapped her hands, half rising and looking about for the love that could not be hers and that could never protect her from Vanags's black fist. And sure enough, she spotted Egons's bearded face and his wife's head close to another post, her hands clapping, her face all aglow. With one guilty glance she saw how innocent the face was. It was the face of one who had not been in the war. A face of a baby born in the free world, only grown up, older. And then she knew what had attracted them to each other, so surprisingly, so naturally. It was the other side! It was before-the-war Latvia in its many shapes and sounds.

She and Egons were born there, before the war. They were linked by all they escaped, remembered and forgot. They needed no introductions, nor explanations. Their walk in the night had been beyond the sensual, she rationalized. It was, therefore, a good and necessary passage—even sacred . . . To his young wife, however, he would have to reveal his past as to a child. And like a child, she would listen yet never know, never understand, only smile with accommodating lips and go on serving him the best she could until he would become bored and run. He had run until he ran into her, Mrs. Milda Arajs, who was also running.

*

The orchestra started playing *The Letters of Peer Gynt.* Milda leaned back and listened. She closed her eyes and thought about letters. So many letters, some black-edged, had been delivered at her doors, and each had affected her life profoundly. In fact, so much of her life had been lived in and through letters. There was the letter of invitation from Aunt Alma, with a parallel letter from Aunt Matilde. And in Germany came the rare, tragic notes from the devious servant Ella, coaxing, calling her home—to an empty, ransacked flat. And more recently, the big one like a novella from Zelda. It was with her now. That letter had suddenly dropped lost Latvia into her arms so that she felt its close breath. At home, when she was sad and lonely, her hand, of its own accord, would grasp the letter, making certain it stayed always within reach, not misplaced or stolen.

As the music drifted around her, she thought she could hear the scratching of Aunt Alma's pen in the night as she wrote letters to Viktors Vētra—her only true love. But the letters were never answered. Unanswered letters . . . They were the great determiners of perpetual unrest and misery. They were the knives that eventually or suddenly cut lives in halves and quarters, on to infinity, leaving behind trails of dry ink upon folded, timeworn pieces of paper, the mute evidence of love and struggle and pain: something had once been; someone had once walked on this earth and breathed its air. Countless Solvegs had forever waited for their Peer Gynts to return, but they received only letters, onion skins from windswept dunes.

*

The notes struck hard, *con brio.* Milda's fingers followed the pianist's intensity, scratching at the engraved shepherdess, and from inside the leather, the child arose and stood before her. It brought a letter and handed it to her. The letter was from Matilde. It was an invitation to her daughter Anna's twelfth birthday. No one guessed that the Hand of Fate had used the human hand that caused the broken family to break further. It had caused the sisters to play a game of checkers. That was all. But it made all the difference: one sister was here, the other there.

Milda clutched the purse to her heart. *I was such a scared little girl and would not have been able to save the smallest, meekest lamb from even a little bad wolf . . . I could not have saved my sister, nor Raela and Estere. No one.*

She closed her eyes and remembered. She called back her little self.

The Shepherdess

July 1941. On a sultry day, ten year old Pasha, the Russian girl who with her mother and grandmother had been moved into two rooms of the Bērziņš apartment, brought a smeared envelope to Mrs. Katerina Bērziņa and withdrew to her quarters. The letter was from Aunt Matilde. After Katerina read it, she started crying and said, "No, no, no! . . . For the last time, sister, I say NO! I will not let my little girls leave me! Never!" She wrote the words she had spoken on a piece of paper, stuffed it into an envelope, and told Zelda to go and mail it. Scared Mildiņa, meanwhile, cuddled next to her distraught mother and was very quiet until Katerina stopped crying and said, "Child, open the windows. I want to feel the summer. I do have a right to breathe, don't I?" Milda obeyed promptly and watched the curtains fly out the window, where she remained standing.

"Get away from the light!" Mother shouted at a high pitch. "And stay out of the draft! Can't you smell how the air stinks?" Tears came to the child's eyes, and she went to her dark corner and her picture books that were left over from better times, times when she still believed in the good spirits of the woods and gardens and the white, gentle *dieviņš*, who blessed them all.

Sometime later, in answer to the letter, Aunt Matilde arrived without any warning. As usual, she carried into the apartment the full odor of the barn and hugged the girls and Katerina with her overly affectionate strength. Then she opened her bags and brought out the sausages and cheese and a bottle of fresh milk with cream on top. Without much fuss, she prepared a meal, and they ate. The girls tore at the sautéed, crispy browned hen's leg like two ravenous pups, upsetting a glass and spilling the milk. When Katerina yelled at them, they screaming accused each other, hitting with fists and words until they collapsed in separate chairs on opposite sides of the room, crying in bitter shame. Katerina only stared vacantly as Matilde separated them. Like an ocean she placed herself between them and said, looking down on her sister, "This cannot go on." Then she told the girls to please go out to play so she could have a quiet talk with Mamma.

When, toward evening, Matilde left the apartment all clean and aired, she said to Katerina tenderly, "Please, think it over. It won't be the end of the world." They touched hands and parted.

Zelda followed her aunt to the station, but *Mildiņa* stayed behind. "Zelda loves Aunt Matilde," she said softly to her mother when they were alone. "Is she really like Aunt Matilde? Was aunty like Zelda, when you both were little?"

"Yes, maybe, I don't remember," Katerina snapped back.

"And am I like Aunt Alma?"

"Yes, I guess so, yes, you are."

Therefore, Milda never could figure out why it was that shortly after the visit—it was in the middle of July, when the apartment was very hot and after she and Zelda had gotten into another savage fight over a piece of dry sausage—that Katerina said wearily, "The time has come for Milda to go to the farm."

Hearing that, *Mildiņa* threw a temper tantrum. She could not understand why Mother would choose to have Zelda stay with her, when it was she who begged to go.

*

Now Milda Arajs, the mother of two, relaxing against a marble pillar in the packed concert hall, understood. But not then. Then her heart ached . . . She shut her eyes and made the soothing melodies carry her back to Kurzeme—far, far away, through time and space. Drifting, she gently stroked the outline of the engraved shepherdess, forgiving everything and assuring herself once again that it was all right. It was so fated. She and Zelda had been assigned their separate paths, and nothing could be done about that. She also understood all too clearly that Mother had needed Zelda because she was the stronger of the two and knew that mothers can be very frightened little girls while little girls can be very brave and fine mothers. Only time and circumstances assign the roles and then put them to the test. Now she realized that Zelda had in her a measure of sustaining earth, while she (pretty *Mildiņa*) was full of flowers, air, and dreams for which Mother would have no use. And so perhaps to free herself from looking at wilting flowers, Katerina, the very next day, had risen early to pack the girl's small wooden suitcase. That done, she woke up her soundly sleeping children and ordered them to get ready. "*Mildiņa* must not miss the train."

*

And so a weary mother and an angry sister had walked pouting Milda to the train station. They walked without saying much to each other. Katerina steered the girls through the crowded streets and the rushing mob at the station with fierce energy, while the sisters exchanged hostile glances: *Mildiņa* was frightened and did not want to go anywhere, while Zelda so longed to go to the country and be free! When the train arrived, Katerina took the traveler's hand and guided her to a very black door and said, "Remember to get off in Priekule. Don't fall asleep and let them take you God knows where! Understand?"

"Yes, Mamma."

On that hazy morning *Mildiņa* hated her mother, and once inside the train, she never turned to look back. She did not lift her hand to wave; instead she hunted for a place to sit down and as soon as she spied an empty spot next to a window, elbowed toward it, stepping over a pair of large feet that belonged to a woman who was wrapped in a gray shawl. The woman watched as the child made herself comfortable on the hard wooden bench and approvingly gave her a hand. Safely in her corner, she still did not look out of the window, nor at the woman across from her, who displayed a toothless grin. Repulsed, *Mildiņa* shut her eyes, which burned with sties. She opened them when the train started pulling out of the station. Then she did look down at her mother and sister waving to her as though they were brushing her away. Bravely, she lifted her hand and waved, but quickly used the same hand to wipe away her tears. Moments later, the train was out of the station, ready to roll. It rolled across the wide Daugava and out of Riga.

As she felt the full weight of Mother's injustice, pity for her sister softened her heart, making it ache, mostly because Zelda would not get any candy at all and, therefore, would hate her forever. She pressed her forehead against the grimy window pane and watched the dark waters sway and heave below, leaving Riga with its houses and spires far behind. "Mamma does not love me anymore," she said and bit her lips until they hurt.

She put her feet on her suitcase packed full of clothes and one beautiful box of chocolates. As hunger gnawed at her, she wondered where Mamma had bought the box and why she had to take it all to her cousins. She had not even allowed her to taste one little piece. Zelda did not get one either. Poor Zelda . . . She had looked so very sad because she had to stay home . . .

In Jelgava, a woman with two big boys came aboard. *Mildiņa* sat up straight. She pressed her feet harder on her suitcase and again gazed out the window. She knew she would be sitting in her corner for many long hours before the train would reach Priekule. To help the time pass, she took a coloring book and pencils from her handbag and tried to draw a castle on a hill. She recalled stories her teacher had told about Kurzeme, and how, ages ago, there was a fierce battle around the castle of Embute, which was not far from Priekule. She wished someone would take her there.

She tried to draw a castle with a battlefield, but could not imagine how soldiers could fight when they were dressed in iron clothes. She wondered how anyone could pierce another man with those long sharp swords and then cut off heads. She tried to draw a soldier but could not. She shuddered merely thinking about such things, and when the two boys sitting across from her made weird faces at her, she turned away and thought about something else. She tried drawing witches and devils who were supposed to have lived in the woods, caves, and bogs around Embute, and filled up pages with princes, princesses, stepmothers, and kings who ruled the castle. She imagined the excitement of being a witch and riding through storm clouds with the moon and the stars lighting the way, but she didn't know where a witch would go. Would she ride all alone through dark nights without ever sleeping or changing clothes? Or maybe the witches had to stay in the air so the devils would not catch them and pull them into their swamps where they would do nasty things?

As she thought of the poor witches sinking into murky cold mud, she scribbled black lines across the ugly figures she had drawn and decided it would be no fun at all being a witch. She closed the notebook and put everything away and looked out the window. The train was dashing through woods. The trees seemed to be uprooted, running along as in a race. She closed her eyes and imagined herself escaping out of some deep murk and riding up in the air, round and round as in a carousel until she fell and bounced as against the edge of the moon.

"Girlie, don't fall asleep!" From far away she heard a woman's voice. "Where are you going?" She half opened her eyes and saw the toothless woman leaning over the space between them.

"Priekule, if you please," *Mildiņa* answered.

"Well, then you can sleep all you want," the woman said kindly and sat back. *Mildiņa* saw the boys again making faces at her, and she squeezed herself deeper into the corner.

"Stupid creatures," she thought and imagined herself being a beautiful princess, like Rapunzel, hidden away in a castle tower with clever flowers climbing bravely up to the window to play with her. "But I would push the prince off my hair, because I don't like people pulling my hair . . . The prince might look like this big boy with the dirty shoes. Brr-rr."

"Wake up, girlie," the woman was shaking her. "You have to get off soon."

Mildiņa opened wide her sleep-glued eyes and stretched.

"Priekule! Priekule!" A uniformed man called as he walked past their compartment. She jumped up and saw the platform sliding to meet the train. Balancing herself, she walked to the door. Through the window, she spotted her broadly smiling aunt and, next to her, her cousin Anna, who appeared about the same size as Zelda. On Anna's shoulders perched the baby Lilia, whom she had never seen and wondered where she came from, for no one had ever explained to her how babies come into the world and how they grow big; she had not seen many babies, so that each was a separate mystery. Lilia was so pretty—like her name—sitting against the bright sky, pulling her big sister's hair, and laughing.

As the train stopped with a loud exhaust of steam, Aunt Matilde rushed forward through the boiling cloud, and before *Mildiņa* had put her feet on the platform, she hugged and kissed her and guided her out of the station into such complete stillness that she feared her footsteps might even disturb the chirping of crickets.

Down on solid ground, they walked toward a carriage, where a dark brown horse stood, his head deep inside a sack of oats. As he, ears pinned back, knew his mistress was approaching, he raised his head high and neighed a greeting. Aunt Matilde removed the bag and set *Mildiņa* between herself and Anna, who held the baby tightly and motherly. The baby grabbed for the stranger's nose and giggled, making *Mildiņa,* too, laugh. Matilde patted her baby and, pulling the reins, cut the air with a whip. They were off.

Zibenis (Lightning) trotted through winding roads that shone golden in the afternoon sun. Still not quite awake and fighting sleep, *Mildiņa* watched the horse's tail swinging back and forth as if beating time and lulling her back to sleep, but she did not give in. She sat up straight and breathed the freshness of the air, looking at the loveliness all around, feeling as if she were being taken for a ride through pages of picture books. Anna leaned against her lovingly, embarrassingly, the way Zelda never did, and *Mildiņa* smiled back shyly, hopefully. The baby soon fell asleep, her head lying limp against *Mildiņa's* side. The closeness made her so happy that she dared not stir for fear of disturbing something as beautiful and fragile as a baby's dream . . .

Zibenis pulled them through little burrows, along golden fields, past a graveyard, and in and out of dark and lacy woods, winging with birds and dancing with squirrels. As they rode, all the hard knots slowly untangled inside Milda's body. She felt as her canary must have, when, in their happy days, Mamma had opened its cage and let it fly all the way to the curtain rod. She started talking more and more bravely with quick city words that made Anna regard her with sidelong awe. She wished they would ride like that forever. But before long, Matilde half–stood up, pulling in the reins and slowing Zibenis down. They rounded a sharp curve. The girls held on and screamed.

"There is our home," Matilde said. *Mildiņa* saw the red roof of a big white house shining through mounds of trees.

"Now, isn't it pretty?" Matilde asked looking down on her little visitor. "Aren't you glad you came?"

Yes, she was glad. Very glad.

Suddenly Anna screamed louder and then laughed as a man leaped from behind a tree on to the wagon. He did not seem to notice Milda, but she looked him over from his head down to his bare, sunburned chest and thought he was like Apollo on her mother's cracked vase. Only when she heard Matilde shout out his name did she realize that he was her cousin Juris. She had seen him a very long time ago—before there were communists deporting people. Then he had had a runny nose, and he had hid from her and teased Anna, making her cry. In those years he was Matilde's little boy. Atis was the big one, but *Mildiņa* knew that she would not see him . . . He had been *called in* the summer before, right after the communists occupied Latvia.

Mildiņa was not sure what *called in* meant; only she sensed that it must be something very bad because her aunt had wiped her eyes and blown her nose a lot when she had told the news to Mamma. Katerina then had put her arms around her big sister, and they had cried together. After a while they made tea and drank it in gloomy silence. They had talked in whispers about the Red Army being in Latvia, and then they had told the girls to go and play. Once out on the boulevard, *Mildiņa* had looked, but had seen no red people anywhere, only uniformed men with red stars on their coats. But she dared not ask any questions, not even of Zelda. Seeing Juris now so tall and handsome, she tried to understand how things and people changed. She never saw one color or size become another, nor one face give way to the next and the next until it got old and died like a flower. She wished that people would stay the same so she could really depend on their always being in their places and looking as they were supposed to. But even she knew that this was a silly wish. No one stayed in the same place. Papa was gone from their home, and Atis had not jumped out to meet them. Juris had grown up, and she was embarrassed to look at him. Suddenly she was afraid that Mamma and Zelda would not be in their apartment, when she went back home. She was afraid that the communists would come back to deport them also.

She screamed a shrill scream and held fast on to her cousin. The baby, too, let out a scream. Everyone shouted at Juris to slow down, and he did pull back the reins as they turned into the road that led to the white house. They rode through a green tunnel of enormous linden trees. At the end of the road, Uncle Imants stood holding the gate wide open, smiling like a full moon. When Zibenis stopped, Imants walked up to the carriage and helped the girls get out. He held out his hand to *Miss Milda*, looked her over, and said, “So our little princess is visiting us after all!”

"Yes," she said. They went inside, and there she opened her suitcase. She took out the box of chocolates and said, "I brought you a present from Mamma. Zelda wanted to come, but couldn't."

*

Milda Arajs reached inside her purse and peeled a lifesaver off the roll and slipped it into her mouth while the people applauded. She closed her eyes, savoring the sweetness mixed with memories far sweeter than candy and more bitter than gall. As the next number, *Fantasies Concertante,* was being played by a young pianist, she let her mind delve deeper into the quiet pastoral pressed on her purse and her memories.

*

That summer, almost exactly forty years ago, she, the little shepherdess, had risen early, put on Anna's outgrown linen frock and, after breakfasting and family prayers, had gone out into the yard, where every morning Uncle Imants held the sheep in a tight flock, while Duksis, happily barking, made the rounds. Anna, meanwhile, drove the herd of cows out of the stable. When uncle held the gate open, the flock and herd merged. Together the girls guided the sheep and cows down a cart road, past ripening fields of grain, on to the pastures. Barefooted and holding on to a willow switch of which even the lambs were not afraid, timid *Mildiņa* tripped over the rough road, trying to keep up with Anna. Many a morning the grass froze her feet with its dew, and she lost the sheep inside cushions of fog the color of their wool. But she didn't dare to complain, not in front of Anna anyway, who controlled the business of grazing with the full confidence of a child who knows her turf and performs her acts with the kind of eagerness that is meant to impress rather than reveal joy in the task itself.

The pastures scalloped the dark and mysterious woods that had been the hunting ground of the German noblemen for many years. The last was Baron Keller. Anna explained, the best she could, the relationship her family had with these lords and ladies. She bragged how Ingrid, the princess who had lived in the manor, was her friend.

The girls had many conversations about life and things, and as they talked they grew closer, sharing many secrets and dreams. On hot days, they sat inside the hollow of a huge oak tree on chairs Juris had made with branches and moss. Sometimes he visited them and sat especially close to *Mildiņa* and talked to her about Riga and the ships in the harbor. Then she imagined that he was a prince who had come to rescue her from an enchanted forest, but she kept those fantasies from Anna, because when Juris talked grown-up talk with her, Anna's face looked too much like Zelda's, and then she had an achy stomach and thought she was bad.

At noon, usually, Aunt Matilde brought their lunch. She came straight over the fields, carrying the baby under one arm and the food basket hooked on the other. Her whole face shone with bright smiles and beads of sweat, as she hurried over the field, at times skipping like a girl. Sometimes, when she was not out of breath, they would play hide-and-seek until she was out of breath and the girls were hungry. Oh, how good tasted the rye bread heaped with sweetened cottage cheese! *Mildiņa* said she liked the brown bread better than the creamy cakes in the cafes of Riga. Baby Lilia sucked the crusts *Mildiņa* didn't want until she fell asleep on the moss. Then Matilde would let the girls take up the piece of white linen and colored threads and continue working on their aprons, cross-stitching flowers and whatever else they wanted, as long as the stitches were neat and even and they would be proud of what they could do. "Idle hands are the devil's tools," Aunt said, as she knitted a man's sock.

In the evenings, the girls followed the cattle home. As soon as they drove the cows and sheep through the gate, which Uncle Imants held open and beyond which Aunt Matilde and a maid waited with buckets in hand, they were free. When Anna ran off, *Mildiņa* lagged behind because she liked to watch the warm white streams of milk hit the sides of the pails that sounded like the strings of an orchestra.

At supper, every evening, Uncle asked the girls if they had done their work well and with love, and they always answered with nods and smiles. Matilde then would look pleased and tell *Mildiņa* that now she had rosy cheeks and was filling out nicely. She didn't know what that meant; she only knew that she was happy, the way she wasn't in Riga.

On warm evenings, Juris would challenge the girls to a race down the steep ravine, across the valley, up to the river's edge. Juris was the first to throw off his clothes and jump into the dark stillness of the water and with his splash shake the twilight.

Anna, too, stripped and jumped, holding her nose, but *Mildiņa* never took off all her clothes. Left in her underwear, she waded into the shallow water cautiously, her arms crossed tightly. She read the pebbles and watched for crabs under the rocks. When at last she slid under the ripples, she splashed, holding her hands firmly on the sandy bottom, teaching herself how to swim. She didn't dare turn her head toward her cousins and see their nakedness. Especially when she looked at Juris, a strange feeling came over her.

On Saturdays, after the midday meal, the preparations for Sunday began. Aunt Matilde always cooked a double meal—one for Saturday, the other for Sunday. She baked a large loaf of white bread, rolled out sheets of dough for open face fruit and cream cheese pastries, while *Mildiņa* made buns on which, with eager help from baby Lilia, she sprinkled poppy and caraway seeds. Meanwhile, Anna and the maid scrubbed and dusted the rooms. When all was clean and the baking done, the girls went out to pick flowers and put them in vases. The house then seemed to stand still and hold its breath, as if afraid to soil itself. Meanwhile, Uncle Imants put his tools away and, together with Juris, brushed the horses, polished the carriage, and, last of all, heated the sauna, which hunched at the edge of the pond. The first threads of smoke rising from the chimney signaled that the week's work was done and that it was time to get ready to go to the sauna and wash off the week's grime.

Bathing was carried out like a sacred ritual the grown-ups enjoyed. Even Anna liked it, but *Mildiņa* wasn't sure. She didn't like to be naked and sweat in the hot steam like in a witch's cauldron and would not jump into the cold, murky pond. But when the ordeal was over and she had put on Anna's outgrown cool linen smock, she felt wonderful. She and Anna would then run into the house, to the full table, where the men were already eating, drinking, and telling jokes.

After supper, the whole household studied their Bible lessons. Anna and *Mildiņa* read the stories out loud with much expression. Anna, because she had gone to church and Sunday school every Sunday, knew many stories by heart, but Milda, who had been taken to the Cathedral only on Christmas Eve and Easter mornings, learned them for the first time. She did not know how to believe all that she read and confused the stories in the large black leather-bound Bible with those of her story books, forming her own inner world, where she would let no one in. She memorized each Sunday's *golden verse,* which all children had to recite in front of the class. When all was done, the kitchen cleaned, the verses memorized, morrow's clothes laid out, shoes polished, it was time to crawl into bed and sleep.

The Ozols family kept the Sundays holy as the Bible commanded. On Sundays they dressed up, went to church, ate good meals, and expected visitors. Uncle didn't work in the fields, and aunt didn't cook. All the maids did was milk the cows.

Milda Arajs, far away from those times, still felt that special Sunday air; she remembered how the fields and animals, the house and people were different. Even the rooster seemed to crow in purer notes, stretching his neck toward heaven. And of course, she never forgot the delicious pastries on the breakfast table, covered with an embroidered linen cloth, nor the sweet, creamy coffee the children were allowed to drink on Sunday mornings. Imprinted in her memory were the rides to *Bētele,* the little Baptist house of worship, about four kilometers from the farm. The three Sunday mornings she had been there with the Ozols family merged as if in one wonderful holiday. The whole countryside seemed to glow in a celestial light, as Zibenis, dressed up in his brass-studded harness and pulling the black *droška,* trotted down the silent road of packed clay.

The *droška* was too small for the whole family, so to *Mildiņa's* great joy, Juris held her on his lap, and she, too happy for words, leaned her cheek against his chest and listened to the skylarks. Inside the church, the long sermons bored her, but she listened to the singing of the choir, because Juris, too, sang, and she liked to look at him. Uncle Imants was the director, and Aunt Matilde sang solos about heaven and angels.

At home, after a hearty meal, everyone was free to do what they wanted or nothing at all. Aunt Matilde liked to lie on a blanket under the linden tree, but uncle, wearing a white shirt, walked slowly and heavily around the borders of his domain and watched his ripening fields, while the cattle grazed in the fenced-in pasture of thick clover. Whenever *Mildiņa* walked beside him, she liked to look at his face, wondering if perhaps Abraham and Moses had faces like his—shining from the light of God. Yes, those Sundays were in her memory as lovely and still as a painting on a museum wall—high and untouchable.

But the most memorable was the Sunday at the very end of August, when the *Bētele* Sunday School children were taken on an outing to the castle and woods of Embute. That trip was *Mildiņa's* dream come true.

She and Anna could hardly fall asleep the night before, but when she awoke, all was dark, and a mean rain beat against the windows. *Mildiņa* sat up for one miserable moment and then fell back, pulling the covers over herself and sobbing into her pillow.

"Get up, lazy, get up!" Anna yanked at the blanket. "Don't you remember, we're going to Embute!"

"But look!" she screeched.

"Get up!" Anna ordered. "It's only a cloud, I can tell, but let's kneel and pray so that Jesus will make it move away." Not believing, she arose and knelt on the cold floor. Anna asked quickly and simply for Jesus to move the clouds away and said *amen* twice. Then she helped her cousin to dress, told her to go wash her face and run on outside, where Juris stood waiting, while Zibenis impatiently clawed the ground. Juris lifted her into the wagon. Aunt Matilde handed each a basket of food and covered them with a large rubber sheet.

"Have a beautiful day!

"It will be a good day," Uncle Imants promised, looking at the sky. He gave Zibenis a kindly slap and walked back into the house. Mildiņa made herself comfortable next to Juris, who put his arm around her. Once on the road, she closed her eyes and let her head slump against his sheltering side. Never had she felt such ripples of excitement, never had she expected so much from a single day!

The rain kept pouring as they backtracked to pick up other children because Uncle had told Juris something about a mission and service, but she had not understood any of it and did not care. She was exactly where she wanted to be and wished they would ride like that straight to Embute, all by themselves. But soon Juris stopped at a gray hut. A boy in patched clothes ran out. He carried no bread basket, but grinning jumped aboard. Along the way, they picked up other children, all poor, all raggedly. At last they had come around full circle, at the edge of their own woods. Juris stopped at the Blūm's Inn. Milda lifted her head and saw the people Anna had talked about in a hushed voice, saying: "They're Jews."

Raela and Estere run out of the large glassed veranda, while *Frau* Blūms, dressed in a dark red robe, stood inside, waiving and blowing kisses. Milda tucked herself closer against Juris, as the two girls, wearing red capes, climbed into the wagon. Each had a basket of food that smelled delicious. Their faces were very white, and their hair very dark and curly. *Mildiņa* looked for yellow stars but didn't see any. Glad about that, she smiled at them, as Juris cracked the whip. Again she cuddled up to him, closed her eyes, and listened to the rain falling on the canvas roof. Slowly, sleepily she lost faith in the sun.

"Wake up!" Anna nudged. "Look! Jesus heard us! I told you! The sun is shining!"

The carriage had just come out of the pine woods as out of a green tunnel. *Mildiņa* saw little patches of blue behind the low gray clouds. The rain was nearly gone. The wind blew hard. Anna threw the rubber sheet off, and Juris let Zibenis feel the tip of his whip. The horse ran as in a race, his mane flowing in long brown streamers. Excited, Juris stood up, and the children screamed pretending to be afraid, as gusts of wind hit their faces. And then suddenly, the curtain of dark clouds was as if pulled apart, and the sun shone in full splendor. The church bells rang, and the birds trilled. When the wagon reached the churchyard, where other children and the teachers waited, a double rainbow arched the sky.

"God is giving us a beautiful day," said the teacher.

A bit later, the children climbed a huge wagon, as large as a German army truck, decorated with oak branches and garlands. It steamed and dripped, but no one complained. As soon as the wagon started rolling, they began singing and sang until the sun shone above the tree tops, and then they were allowed to reach into their bread baskets. They shared their bread, cakes, and berries; they acted politely as if Jesus, the Friend of all children, were in the wagon with them. *Mildiņa*, sitting between

Anna and Raela, thought that Raela was the most beautiful of them all. Estere was very quiet, always looking up at her sister.

Suffer the little children to come to me and forbid them not, for theirs is the kingdom of heaven, was the golden verse for that Sunday. They all said it together, and then they sang *Jesus loves the little children, all the children in the world.*

And so the day went on—perfectly, unforgettably. They explored the old castle ruins and played games. They ate lunch on white sheets spread out in the grass and sang until it was time to leave. The wagon rolled into the church yard just as the sun went down.

"Now all my wishes have come true," *Mildiņa* said late that evening, when they were home again, hungrily eating pancakes with raspberry jam wrapped inside. But the worm of guilt gnawed at her conscience as she thought about her mother and sister in their dark apartment in Riga. She wished that Zelda could have been with them and seen the caves and the woods. She would have told Zelda how much she loved her after all and how beautiful the world was and that Jesus loved her too, because he let the sun shine that day. Also, she was happy that Estere and Raela were now her friends and that some other day, before she would have to go back to Riga, she and Anna would visit them.

*

And so the days had gone by, at first slowly, then all too quickly. Almost up to the end of August, the weather had been warm and mostly sunny, watered with mild rains and cloudbursts trimmed in rainbows. But then late one afternoon, about the middle of the week, dark blue clouds suddenly appeared on the horizon and turned the day into night. The storm sent *Mildiņa* and Duksis under the branches of a huge fir, while the sheep, bleating pitifully, ran their own way. That day, of all days, Anna herded the cows on a far field edging the Blūm's property, so that she was no comfort. Shivering from cold and shame for having abandoned her flock, she huddled close to the dog, which whined and trembled. After an eternity she heard someone slushing over the field, coming towards her. She peaked from under the fir branches and, to her great joy and relief, saw Juris, all drenched in rain. "There you are, hiding like a scared butterfly!" he called into the wind.

He took her hand and lifted her up, tucking her inside his rain cape. She wrapped her arms around his neck and pressed her cheek against his wet face. Comforting and calming her down, he carried her over the soaking meadow, while Duksis slinked behind them, his tail dragging the ground. Not looking up, they did not see the low black cloud rise before them until, suddenly, thunder, lightning, and sheets of rain whirled round about as heaven and earth became one. A loud thunderclap and bolts of lightning threw them to the ground. They heard wood splitting and branches snapping. They held on to each other and flattened themselves on the ground, hoping for the mean cloud to blow over as quickly as it had come. When a sun ray broke through, and they raised their heads, they saw, on the other side of the meadow, the old oak tree split in half, right through its ancient heart. It lay sprawled out on the muddy field, with its roots hanging against the dark sky like red dripping hair.

"This is a bad omen," Juris said, pressing her tightly against him and running to the house. Once inside, he set her down in the middle of the dark room, where the family sat waiting for the storm to pass. Aunt Matilde helped *Mildiņa* out of her wet clothes and dressed her in a soft, flannel gown. She gave her warm milk with honey, and Anna put her arms around her, saying over and over how sorry she was for leaving her alone. When the storm was past and the first stars appeared, they thanked God for keeping all of them safe and then went to bed.

Some days later, after the fields had soaked up the excess water and the wind had dried the crops, Uncle Imants harnessed his work horses and set out to harvest the fields. Neighbors came to help, as did the German soldiers. Together they worked hard all day. They joked and sang as they cut, raked, and tied the sheaves into bundles and stacked them to dry. At the end of the day, after the evening meal, the officer announced that his regiment would be leaving early in the morning. It would be going to Russia. Silence fell like a bomb, followed by loud, excited talking in whatever language came to mind. Matilde gathered what leftover food was handy and, handing a bundle over, wished them well. Thanking her and stroking the girls' heads, the soldiers departed on command. The family watched them go up the road, afraid of what the morrow would bring.

The next day Anna drove the cattle close to the woods where the soldiers had been for most of the summer, but now were gone, leaving empty clearings and deep trenches. The cattle now grazed freely, while Duksis raced around the empty fields chasing birds. *Mildiņa* and Anna went to the spot where the big oak tree had stood and looked at the protruding stump. There they stood, their bare feet stuck in the upturned soil. "The tree had a heart and it loved us and we'll miss it forever and ever," Anna spoke as at a gravesite and started singing a folk song about trees that watched over orphans, while the sun ran its course. They sang more sad songs and hung garlands on the drying, bleeding roots, and then they sat inside the circle of vanished shade and watched the sun set. When they heard Matilde's *oo-oo!* they gathered the herd and drove it into the yard, which also was churned up and seemed sad and strange.

Early next morning, they awoke to an upturned world. The earth quaked. On the highway, tanks, infantry, cavalry marched past them. Juris and the girls stood at the edge of the highway saluting, welcoming the Germans, who would protect them from communists. But the soldiers ignored the children who tried to give them flowers; one stuck out his tongue, while others shouted for all to stand back. Uncle and aunt watched the fearsome parade from behind their gate, looking through the linden alley as through a gigantic telescope.

At the end of the cavalcade came the dogs. About a dozen German shepherds, all neatly lined up, pulled wagons full of supplies. When they reached the edge of the pond, closest to the highway, a loud *Halt!* made them stop. They were unleashed and ordered to the go to the pond, where they lapped the water ravenously and, again, on command, trotted back to their wagons. After they were harnessed and ready to go, the commander saw Duksis, a part-shepherd mutt and much smaller than the enlisted. Without a word, he took a leash, fastened it around the dog's neck, and dragged him howling to where the other canines waited, ready to charge. The children watched the confiscation and then ran to the house, as, suddenly, above the trees, in and out of the clouds, airplanes tore through the sky, displaying black crosses with hooks on their bellies. When the invasion, like a storm, was over, an ominous silence fell on the earth.

"War," said Uncle Imants eying the sky and earth. "It's come to Kurzeme. It's all around us. . . . Son, take Zibenis and run for the woods. Get lost. We'll say we know nothing."

But Juris answered that he was no coward and would go fight the Bolsheviks if they ever crossed the borders again. *Mildiņa* held on to his hand.

*

Late in the afternoon a new regiment moved into the Keller manor. A new crop of soldiers came to the farm and demanded milk, bread, bacon. They did not bother to introduce themselves. They were haughty and wore stiff boots and white gloves that would not be dirtied. Their faces were serious and frightening. Zelda and *Mildiņa* did not dare say a word to them, let alone go near the guarded manor.

"I don't trust those Krauts any more than their dogs. Thieves and killers is what they are," Juris said, hitting the table with his fist.

"Ah, son, they are only boys," Matilde said. "They don't make the war."

"But they obey, Mamma, and that amounts to the same thing." He rose and mockingly sang a popular German marching song.

"Oh, stop it!" Matilde shouted. "They are all God's children, and we must love even our enemies like the good Lord taught us."

"But they are Nazis," Juris repeated in an angry man's voice.

"Still, they are people, and I want to do them good," Matilde answered sternly and looked out the window into the starry distance. "I hope somebody is being good to our Atis and not calling him Red."

"Forgive me, Mother." Juris touched her hand and left the room.

"Our country is again caught under the wheels," Imants said and closed the Bible he had taken up for protection. "Hard times are ahead for us all as in the days of old with the children of Israel." He stood up and went to put his arm around his wife's shoulders. Together they gazed out into the night. "Our Latvian boys will be forced again into service, and we must be careful. The news on the radio is not good. And," he turned to the girls, "stay out of the woods!"

"We will," Anna promised.

"All right," Uncle said, and then they went to bed, but *Mildiņa* tossed and turned. She heard the clock strike nine, ten, eleven, but no sleep came. She wanted to go home.

*

But the morning did dawn, golden and pink, and the children rose as usual, and as usual, *Mildiņa* and Anna ran behind the cattle, feeling the exhilaration of the open, harvested fields. Because the oak tree was gone, there was no shelter from the winds that, as if untied, blew all over and tore at their clothes. The lead cow, sensing that all borders were lifted, challenged the girls at every step, racing like mad for the one field that was still green—the hectare of sugar beets, Uncle Imants's pride and wealth. Crying, the girls chased the cows out of the field, but they charged back, stealing and gulping. Duksis was not there to nip at their heels. Seeing the disorder, Juris raced over from the far field and drove the cattle out and, telling Anna to be more attentive, went back to plough the earth. In the evening, he had no time for play but stood glued to Zibenis, who stampeded madly, smelling the air, his nostrils enlarged, his ears pinned forward.

As the week pushed on, *Mildiņa* dreaded herding more and more. In like mood, the weather turned cold and biting, and the stubble scratched her feet. She and Anna had nothing to say to each other; the openness of the barren fields could not hold their secrets, which now seemed stupid and embarrassing. At night, they made up awful ghost stories, creating nightmares for themselves and screaming in their sleep until comforting hands turned them over.

"The children sense something," they heard Uncle whisper to his wife. "I tell you, woman, the times are hard, and the Lord is testing us again."

The following morning, the cattle scavenged the fields close to the Blūm's Inn. The day was foggy, the outlines of objects blurred. But in the fog the girls saw a truck and a car drive away from the inn. Anna shooed the cows to the border, almost right up to the cart road that led inside the courtyard. The girls stood at the outer fence watching and then crept along the white pickets. They reached the gate, which was carefully bolted from the inside. The house was strangely still. No dog barked. No people talked. Only the hens scratched around in the sand.

Anna pointed to the open door of the veranda and quickly unbolted the gate.

"You wait here!" she ordered.

Terrified, *Mildiņa* waited. She saw Anna go into the house and told herself that any second Raela and Estere would run out to play with them or *Frau* Blūms would invite them in for warm milk and bagels . . . But the next instant it was Anna who stood in the open doorway all by herself. She stood still like a wooden doll and said nothing. At last she moved her arms and let out one fierce scream, and with that she jumped down the steps and ran out of the yard, out the gate. She ran past Milda, past the cows and the sheep. She ran like a siren over the sharp autumn fields.

Mildiņa watched for some paralyzed seconds, deathly afraid, and then she, too, took off, leaving the poisoned fields and animals. She ran without looking back, feeling only the sharpness of the stubble cutting her feet and knowing that they bled. She caught up with Anna just as she stormed into the kitchen, screaming, pulling Matilde away from the stove, upsetting things.

"They're killed! They're shot dead!" Anna screamed over and over.

"What? What's happened?" Matilde held her.

"The Krauts killed Estere and Raela! In bed . . . dead . . ."

She wailed and pounded the walls with her fists as if they were faces. Matilde caught her and held her tightly. *Mildiņa* crouched behind a chair and began screaming for her mother and Zelda, causing Lilia also to scream. Anna raged on until Matilde slapped her face.

"Stop it!" she shouted harshly, then quietly, tenderly she pleaded, stroking Anna's hair.

"What did you see, my child, what did you see?" She rocked the big girl back and forth.

Soon the whole house became quiet, rocking in the eye of something too dreadful for words. At last Anna lifted her head away from her mother's bosom and said in a trembling voice, her eyes glassy with tears, "Mamma, Estere and Raela are dead."

"Oh God, dear God," Matilde moaned, sinking down on the floor and pulling Anna down with her. "Oh, dear Lord Jesus, oh God in heaven, help us!"

"Blood, Mamma, I saw them lying in their bed full of blood," Anna let out each word with a gasp, looking deeply into her mother's wet eyes and gently stroking her hair back in place. But finding no help, no answers anywhere, she cried again.

"Sh-shh," Matilde rocked her, pressing her face against her daughter's. "Was not *Frau* Blūms there?"

"No."

"And himself? Did you see him?"

"No. We saw a truck drive away, didn't we?"

"Yes," *Mildiņa* answered clearly. "*Frau* and *Herr* Blūms got deported," she whispered, glancing out the window, as if expecting the truck to arrive any second.

"Oh God, it's come this close . . . Oh Lord, do not leave us! Hear your children in their time of trouble, hear them that trust in you, in the power of your name," Aunt Matilde moaned, argued, pleaded.

"I want to go home," Milda cried out as the truth hit her, as she understood only too well, and as she remembered the uniforms, the dogs, the people walking along gutters, yellow stars scorching their gray smocks, front and back.

"I want my Mamma!" she screamed. "I want Zelda!"

Aunt Matilde pulled herself together and slowly lifted herself up. "Please be quiet!" she begged. "All of you. I will tell Papa. If anyone comes into the yard, and if anyone asks you anything, you know nothing. Understand?" And she walked out the door, muttering, "Hard times, hard, hard . . ."

Anna reached across the room and pulled her cousin and her baby sister to herself, and they all huddled together. "After you, they were my best friends," Anna sobbed. "We had so much fun last Sunday, and now they are DEAD!" She cried uncontrollably, hysterically, but *Mildiņa* held her tighter and said, "Hard times have come all over the world."

*

That same evening, Uncle Imants brought home more bad news: Dr. Rosenblum's house was burned down, with their good doctor trapped inside. People said that he himself put the house on fire. But who will know what really happened? The sky was overcast, littering the landscape with blurred shadows. No one could stop the scythe of Death.

*

On Monday Juris was drafted. From the open kitchen window Milda saw two officers on horseback ride into the yard. Uncle Imants met them, while Matilde came running out of the granary, tripping over the hens and geese, her face red and streaked with dirt. "*Was ist den los*?" she called.

But immediately she froze, still as a pillar. Milda saw the men dismount and explain their purpose. She saw Aunt Matilde pleading, saw them pushing her aside. Uncle was ordered to call his son, and soon Juris came out of the barn, holding on to Zibenis. The men evaluated the horse. Imants raised his pitchfork, and one of the men shouted, "One move and I shoot." The soldier took Zibenis, handed the harness to the other, and told him to wait. Then he stomped into the house and ordered smoked bacon and bread. Matilde set the slabs and loaves before him and watched him eat standing up. She poured more milk in his mug. He gulped it down, not lifting his eyes, pushed the mug aside and shoved a paper at Juris and told him to sign it. Imants and Matilde also had to sign. Satisfied, the officer clicked his polished heels and walked out saying, "*Danke*!"

Uncle followed, leaning on his pitchfork. Aunt Matilde and the girls watched the officer and Imants argue. They saw Zibenis stampede and heard him neigh, his head high, calling heaven. Juris rushed to his side, but the Nazis pushed him away, mounted their horses and rode into the leafy tunnel, pulling the captive horse by a rope.

"Zibenis is being deported," Milda whispered. She watched Juris standing in the middle of the driveway, spade in hand, then charge into the house, "Why didn't they let me go with my horse?" he screamed

"The swine," Imants swore. "Just like the Reds," he said, gritting his teeth and looking like a mad bull ready to charge. "Volunteered! Ha! Exactly how Atis was dragged away."

"We have lost our sons," Matilde said, not daring to look at Juris.

"The devils, all of them!" Imants shouted, "Same tricks, same phrases, same moves, to hell with all of them!" He shook his fists at the air. "My boys are now set one against the other . . . Our house is divided, and it cannot stand. Our country cannot stand," he said.

Suddenly Juris turned and, like Thor splitting rocks, smashed his fist on the table, his face hot with fire. "We'll make Latvia stand! We'll drive them all out of our land just like you did long ago. Latvia must be free again!" And he started out the door.

"Where are you going?"

"To sharpen my ax, Mother!"

*

Two days later the parents drove their son to the train station. Anna cried in her bed, holding Lilia tightly against her, but Milda went out and tied her blue ribbon around Juris's wrist. Silently, like a woman, she spoke only with her sighs. Juris lifted her face and gently kissed her lips.

"When I come back, I will marry you," he said and pulled her close to him. "Will you wait for me?"

"Yes," she said and flung her arms around his neck.

After that, she had no peace. All joy had left the family. Anna became sick, and there was no doctor. Matilde made the girls drink teaspoons of bitter medicine to chase their fears away, but they would not leave. Milda began nursing Anna the way Zelda had nursed her mother. She gave her tea made of flower blossoms and read to her, but Anna remained glum. At night, *Mildiņa* was sure she heard Mother calling her. *What's happening? Is Zelda also sick? Have bad men taken them all away or has Papa come home?*

She did not know what angels were speaking to her, who was pulling her with such force. Besides, she missed Juris terribly. The whole country, as far as she could see, had become empty, strange and cold. She could not understand why it was that the men always left as if they were born to do so, as if they came into people's families only to go out of them quickly and suddenly. She did not believe that Juris would ever come back and marry her. She knew that he said his kind words only so she would not cry. Her father had said things to them also so they would not cry. He never came back, and other men, those good soldiers in the woods, who had left their homes in Germany, would never go back either. Perhaps they would die in muddy fields with their arms up in the air like the soldier in the black-and-white newspaper photograph . . .

"Men go away and never come back," Milda told Anna, "and women must wait for them. Women must take care of things . . . That's how it is during hard times." But Anna did not hear her.

*

Early the next morning, her belongings packed in her little suitcase, *Mildiņa* waited for the wagon to pull up at the gate. Matilde fussed a long time in the kitchen, making up a basket of food to take to *my poor sister.* A bit ceremoniously she then gave *Mildiņa* a pair of mittens, moss green with white stars. She had knitted them in secret. "It's a reward for being a big help and a good little shepherdess," she said, stroking her head. "We'll never forget this time together, and don't you forget us either!"

Mildiņa curtsied and kissed her aunt's hand. Matilde turned away, wiping her face with a corner of her apron and took it off and wrapped a gray shawl around her. "It's time for us to go," she said, watching Imants pull the wagon in front of the door and talk to the lonesome mare.

"Why won't Anna come and say good-bye to me?" Mildiņa asked in a broken voice.

"I don't know. Don't mind her. She's not right. Not right since she looked death in the face. But, God willing, she'll pull together. She said she had a bad dream last night. You were flying away on top of an airplane, and then she said it was bad luck to shake hands; that's why she won't come out. I don't know where she gets those ideas, but she's hurting, that's all I can say. She has such a kind heart."

"Yes."

Mildiņa climbed onto the seat next to her aunt. Uncle Imants shook hands with her and then, giving the mare a slap on the flank, went to hold the gate open.

Once they were a good distance from the house, Matilde said, "Ah, they are good children, those rascals of mine. God gave them to me and now He takes them away, blessed be His holy name."

All the way to the railroad station they hardly spoke. *Mildiņa* watched her aunt's large form sway against the aluminum sky. She saw large silent tears roll down her coarse, sunburned face and watched the wind blow them away.

*

Mrs. Arajs roused herself from her recollections. The piano was still playing its adagio notes, which seemed to come from a different room, a severed lost world. She wiped her eyes with her white handkerchief, very carefully, as if she were wiping Matilde's eyes—something she had not thought of doing then, so long, long ago. Suddenly she became impatient, nervous. She could not wait for the last chords that always tidied up each work no matter how disturbing the movements. She sat up straight. She was burning hot, her hands clammy. She squeezed the handkerchief hard as if her hands, too, were crying. To stop the pain, she stuffed the wet handkerchief deeply inside her purse, swearing: *I'm not going to cry anymore, not over the things that happened so long ago in another life, on the other side of the Atlantic Ocean. God knows there are enough reasons for tears now, today* . . . For one, she could fill dozens of neatly folded men's handkerchiefs with tears over impossible love, love which could never burst into bloom like her red rosebush in the middle of her garden but which, instead, she had to bury deep in some hard darkness—the way she had buried the body of her husband.

Oh, how she could cry over that and over what the world made of love, the most mysterious and lovely gift of creation, the last tender remains of Paradise, the last link between heaven and earth! She contemplated the loves she had known, and she had to admit that she was really stirred only by the impossible, forbidden ones. *Such love is as it ought to be—burning, alive, creative. But I never gave up hope in an eventual flame. Like a stupid Cinderella, I scratched in the lukewarm ashes until the very end, until the prince I had chosen crumbled, shattering the glass slipper forever, leaving things between us unfinished, incomplete* . . . She reached again for her handkerchief. She was perspiring. Her whole body was crying.

Intermission

When *Mildiņa* nervously returned to Riga, she saw that not much had changed. Mother acted as though she had just been in another room. Only Zelda seemed taller and thinner; her face was very pale, as if chilled by early frost. She looked at her suntanned sister with tired, sad eyes and asked politely about the country and about Aunt Matilde and her cousins. Mother also sat down, and Milda, glad to escape the awkward silence, told about the murders of the Jewish children and about Anna. "It wasn't that much fun, she mumbled," looking down, twisting her apron string around her fingers so she would not have to answer more questions and see Zelda's eyes burning in envy.

"So the hunt is on in the country also," Katerina said. "Be careful what you say and who you speak to."

As *Mildiņa* was getting used to being back in the city, she tried to be especially kind to Zelda. She helped her with the chores and let her have the larger half of whatever food they shared. But it was not long before they fought again over bread and sausage.

Katerina, when she was not lying down or crying, hid behind pages of newspapers. Daily, she checked the lists of the killed, wounded, and missing soldiers, at times crying out when she recognized a name. *Mildiņa* checked the lists also, looking for Juris's name over Mother's shoulder, and when she did not find it, she thanked God, lifting her eyes to heaven. Of course, she told nobody about her engagement, which she guarded as much as her fears and memories and her softly changing body.

*

After the Holocaust of '41 had made many cities and towns *Juden Frei,* the German occupation continued, making life ever more difficult. Meanwhile, the radio told about the Front moving closer, pushing against Latvia's eastern border and calling on Latvia's young and not so young men to enlist and fight the Bolsheviks. Many were sent deep into Russia, where most perished in its vastness. Among them was Matilde's and Imants's oldest son Atis. That happened in the summer of 1944, but no one could tell on what day or month his young heart stopped beating. Thankfully, Juris was in the reserves in Prussia, which was closer to home; he sent postcards, even to *Mildiņa,* and she wrote to him, drawing pictures along the edges, but by the end of summer the communication suddenly stopped, and things changed; the frontline was up against Latvia's borders. Nervously people listened to their radios and watched the gathering of ever thicker and darker clouds above the eastern horizon. In whispers or cries, they talked about the possibility of leaving the country. Having tasted the evils of communism, no one looked forward to a second helping.

By September the people of Kurzeme saw refugee wagons pass over the highways toward Lithuania and on to Germany, heading west, even though no paradise awaited them there. Alerted, some people buried their valuables in the ground and traveled lightly, assuming to return as soon as the war would be over. And country folk gathered in their harvests, prayed and waited. When the front stood still for a while, hope sprung up, and work continued.

*

During such calm, one day, in early October 1944, a letter arrived from Aunt Matilde: "We invite you to come for Anna's birthday. Remember, it is on the eighth, next Sunday. *Katiņ*, if you cannot come, please let the girls visit my poor child who needs some happiness. So please let them come. I will be responsible for everything." But the next day, Aunt Alma telephoned and invited Katerina and the girls to a special one-night performance of *Faust* at the Liepāja theater, on Saturday, October 7.

"I am Margareta." *Mildiņa* heard, as she put her ear to the telephone. Alma's excited voice said *wunderbar* and *sehr gut*. And "I will be responsible."

Katerina listened with the receiver away from her ear. When Alma paused, she said flatly, "You know that I don't go anywhere, so why trouble me?" Alma shouted at her, "Are you trying to drive your children crazy? It's time you pulled yourself together and lived again! He wouldn't want you to mope all the time." Scolded, Katerina wiped her eyes and said, "Well, we'll see."

After she hung up the telephone, she cried helplessly but in the evening she said, "Oh, I don't know what to do. I have two sisters and two daughters, and I need rest. Each of you can go to one of my sisters. Maybe it will be safe enough. The war is still far away."

The girls looked at each other, pretending not to be too excited, *Mildiņa* said, "I want to go to the farm," just when Zelda said it too, screaming, "Matilde is *my* aunt." They pouted, squabbled, and then Zelda said, "All right, I'll go to Liepāja this time." But meanwhile, *Mildiņa*, in her imagination and remembering her rightful place on the glamorous branch of the family tree, was snuggling up to lovely Alma and inhaling her perfume. "No," she exclaimed. "I must go to Liepāja and you must go to the farm."

In a mad rage, the girls fell upon each other, pushing, kicking, crying. Katerina withdrew and waited from the other side of the room for the fight to stop.

The Game of Checkers

Then she set forth: "Why don't you play it out?" She took the checker board out of the drawer and set up the game. "Whoever wins may go to the farm, but the loser may go to Liepāja."

The girls set up the pieces and, all tensed up, started to play. Katerina refereed the short game with as great an interest as if she were watching some wheel of fortune. Both girls noticed Mother's sudden return to life and became fiercely excited and competitive. They looked down on the board, on the black and red disks on black and red squares. They watched their hands push, jump, kill. *Mildiņa* was clearly winning. She grew tenser, wide-eyed, nail-biting, keenly aware what the game was all about and, without even glancing at her sister, studied the board like men do. The only sound in the room was the ticking of the clock. It ticked away the seconds and minutes of each one's life. Zelda drummed her nervous fingers on the edge of the table, waiting. When the clock struck, she saw her sister's hand become stiff and curved like a claw. The claw pushed a black disk, forcing the scared, tight hand holding a red one, make three continuous leaps. The same hand swept up the black disks and set them down carefully, one next to the other. The claw made another small move, forcing the red queen slide diagonally across the board, killing the black men in her path.

"You win," Milda said and stood up. She looked down on the checkerboard, her field of battle, and uttered a sound of victory. Zelda shoved the hard board aside, upsetting her black captives. The girls watched them roll off the table, while a row of red pieces stood in a neat row, guarding the empty squares. Zelda grinned and laughed. Katerina cheered, wiping her sweating face, and waited for her daughters' reaction.

"I lost," Milda said sadly. Bewildered, she watched Zelda and Mamma. "That means I go to Liepāja."

Zelda stopped laughing. She stared at her sister with clear, sad eyes, and said, "Yes." Milda looked down in mock sadness.

"Fate has ruled," Katerina pronounced.

*

Applause. Milda claps. She leans her head against the cold pillar. She hears again the tuning of the instruments and waits for the second part of the concert to begin. *Avanti* and *Simfonija.* The works mean nothing; not one of the notes strikes a familiar chord, but they do not upset her either. She merely listens, her eyes closed, her fingers stroking the impressions on her purse. Again she calls the shepherdess back to life. Again she wants to see her child self, to talk to her, to scold her for missing the moment in her life when she could have been kinder to everyone. *But how could I know? How could I know that the simple game of checkers would decide our fates?*

Oh, how she wants to roll time back and pull everyone to herself! How she wishes to be able to go back home and explain things, tell Zelda she did not mean to manipulate the game, did not mean to run for the train quite so eagerly, so impatiently, and that during her times on the farm she had learned to love Aunt Matilde with all her heart . . . and Juris, her handsome, gentle cousin.

Neither had she meant to side so completely with Aunt Alma—not so eternally. "We are a part of both our aunts and our mother," she would say to Zelda. "Our blood flows in the same streams. We are a part of the same tribe, so to speak. I love us all. I carry you always with me, just like, I'm sure, you carry me. The destruction of us happened long before our little game. Our nation and our whole generation were brutally sacrificed for the absurd ideas of evil minds." She tried to tell all that to her sister not so long ago in answer to her long letter, but it did not help, did not change things. Nothing can undo the damage, any more than the explanations of an earthquake could reconstruct a city. The truth of their country's genocide remains: there is no Aunt Matilde, no Uncle Imants, no Juris, Atis, Anna, no Lilia, no little baby Benjāmiņš . . . Their lives have all been aborted, their genes swept off the earth . . . Zelda had so written years before any *thaw*—long before that explicit letter, but not in clear words. She had written in codes and camouflages . . . *Communists. Communism.* Milda shudders and remembers . . . She and Alma had escaped. The others did not.

*

Intermeco. The pianist strikes hard. Milda feels as if he is slapping her down, telling her she should pay attention to the music and stop stewing. She puts her squashed handkerchief back . . . *Ah, it's no use, no use at all crying over impossibilities and the unfairness of life.* She sits straight, admiring the dexterity of the young man's fingers rushing up and down the keyboard and then, as if exhausted, slowing down and lulling her back to the land where birch trees grow and nightingales and skylarks sing. The pianist also seems to be drifting into a dreamland, his face contorted with strong emotions, as if wanting to talk to somebody, to empty his heart, but there is no one who would really listen and understand. Milda knows the feeling, for she also has no one to talk to. No one. Not deeply, not from deep inside the truth of her being. Could she possibly discuss the essence and meaning of sexual desire and love with Zelda, or would Zelda, too, laugh at her as she had when they were children? Doubly wed as Zelda is, she still might not understand; still might make Milda, her older sister, feel stupid and frail. And could she, the respected Mrs. Milda Arajs of the émigré high society, really accept Zelda's base polygamy? Could Zelda's views and actions fit in a modern Republican value system? No . . . She cannot see any honorable compromise, cannot see even sisters of two such opposing systems and worlds clasping each other in harmony; she cannot see anyone strike the perfect chord between them. And so they have to struggle in their dissonances, go on out of tune and out of step. The best they could do, perhaps, is gather information about each other and then try to penetrate its meaning, know the most honest and simple motives behind each act. But that would be difficult, if not impossible. No one ever truly opens him or herself to such scrutiny, not even in courts of law. All relationships, but especially familial ones, are difficult to solve. They go on and on, branching out on their own. She knows that every human being possesses his and her own alarm system with its peculiar electrical network, which triggers its unique emotional responses that may be at variance with all others. So even if Milda could accept her sister, would her sister accept her? Could the perfectly balanced truth about each other save them? Could she find forgiveness through understanding? Could they forgive each other that they live in two different worlds and that the ocean rolls between them? Could they forgive each other's life patterns inflicted by war and politics? Can anyone take up arms against Fate, like Hamlet tried, and by opposing end them?

Milda imagines the scenes described in that one letter from her sister; she sees such violence as would not be shown even in X-rated films. It seems all so outrageous, so otherworldly, embarrassing . . . No. Milda knows she could never discuss her ideas about love and life with Zelda. The words would not come out right, and she doubted if she could ever look into the eyes of her sister and not flinch—not judge or envy.

Lately she had felt Zelda's sad eyes on her. She felt them especially keenly since the general, cautious contacts with Latvia had started up and whenever she heard others tell about their brothers and sisters whom they had left behind when the war and the communists came over them. She often thought she heard Zelda calling her madly, exasperated because she could not make the connection as she dialed wrong numbers on disconnected telephones. Sometimes she could hear the ringing in her ears so loudly that she would have to press her hands against them and shut her eyes and block out all senses. Truthfully, she cannot stand a torn up Latvia that close; it scares her. And that is why she would shout at Zelda, telling her over and over again, "I did not do it. I did not mean to do it! It's not my fault that you are on one side of the Atlantic Ocean and I on the other. You on one side of the Iron Curtain, I on the other. Nothing can be done about it, dear sister. Nothing can be done about anything. I could do nothing then, and I can do nothing now! . . . It is all in the hands of God or Fate, or just mere chance. Who knows? Who could tell us? It's not my fault that you must live in Soviet Latvia and I in the United States of America."

But when other émigrés talked about sending packages, she again heard Zelda calling. She saw her sister waiting for parcels in a crowded post office in Riga and then turning and taking the slow bus or train home and opening her door and facing her two husbands and her band of children empty-handed. At such moments of vision, Milda would appeal to her sister's practical sense: "Sure, I might send one or two packages, but where will that get you? It would be like throwing things into a bottomless well. My dear sister, I could never fill all your needs. Besides, if you only knew, how I hate to shop for bargains! Or must I confess that I really cannot afford to help you? We live by our standards, pay our bills, and you live by yours. Also, how can I be sure that my sacrifice would not be traded in your black market and thus subsidize your awful system? . . . Oh, I'm so tired! . . . And alone. Please, try to understand. I have no husband, while you have two. It's not my fault, not mine at all. It's communism. Leninism and Stalinism and all the open and secret pacts that put us where we are. We were only children, poor, innocent victims of dreadful forces."

As if released by the final chord, she, like the whole audience, springs to her feet clapping hard, forcing the young pianist to bow several times as he receives flowers, smiling and bowing again and again.

Intermission.

The audience returns to Part III: *Avanti* and *Simfonija.* These opuses again cannot hold her attention beyond the first movements. Fighting sleep, she gives up and lets the fine, plaintive strings, carry her back to those troublesome German times—her last days in Latvia, when she and Aunt Alma escaped, leaving all else behind. Hopefully, in God's hands.

The Last Train Ride

On October 7, 1944, Katerina Bērziņa and her two daughters woke up early so they could catch the eight o'clock train to Liepāja. Everything had been packed the night before, so all the girls had to do was dress and eat their oatmeal. Katerina seemed unusually awake. She helped the girls dress and then braided their hair, first Zelda's, then *Mildiņa's.* She stroked each head with a tenderness neither had felt for a long time, to which they responded with shy, tender touches and smiling, hopeful eyes. "Oh, how I wish Papa could see you now!" Katerina sighed. "My darling *Mildiņa*, you are growing up too quickly, and soon you'll be a very pretty young lady." When Zelda stepped up also to be praised, Katerina looked down sadly and said, "Only time will tell what will become of you, I cannot." Taking a deep breath, she pulled both girls to her heart and sobbed. "You will take care of yourselves, won't you?" The girls stood still for a moment then wrenched themselves free from Mother's tight grip and her heaving bosom. "Promise me, oh promise me that!" she pleaded.

They nodded and went to put on their overcoats. *Mildiņa* tucked her green, white-starred mittens one in each pocket, even though Mother frowned, saying that it wasn't winter yet. "You might lose them, you might lose everything," Katerina said, twisting her hair into a tight knot and pressed her hat above it. As is customary, they sat down for a minute in a circle, held hands, and wished each other well. With a last look to make sure nothing was forgotten, they left the apartment.

They walked briskly to the train station. Katerina held both girls by their hands and led them through the rushing morning crowd. She stayed dried-eyed until she set them on the train and said her last instructive words. Down, on the platform, she waited until the girls found opposite window seats and were settled down. Then both girls turned their heads down for one last look at their mother, who teary-eyed looked up to them. When the train started moving, Katerina waived with her white, tear-drenched handkerchief. The girls waved back. Mother trotted some steps after the train, still hitting the air with her hand until a cloud of steam settled on the platform covering *Māmiņa* as with layers of gauze. Only the white handkerchief attached to a black-gloved hand fluttered inside the fake cloud like a lost moth, until it, too, dropped out of sight.

The sisters did not lament nor stretch their necks looking back; they sat quietly, glad about getting out of Riga and looking forward to their upcoming adventures, each believing that her destination was the best in the whole world and the envy of the other. Once they had wiggled into their opposite corners—Milda in the forward seat and Zelda trying to be content with the backward one—the train crossed the Daugava and rode on smoothly through the wooded and harvested October landscape, Zelda leaned back and eyed *Mildiņa*, who fidgeted self-consciously, remembering the checker game and trying to stop her guilt from tinting her face. She avoided Zelda's sporadic, wide-eyed gazes, not quite knowing how to be alone with her. Turning away, she focused on the clouds that seemed very close—right over the edge of the fields. She watched them silently clashing in the wind, the dark blue ones and the white, somersaulting in a forget-me-not sky. She marveled at the changing hues and shapes, as one moment they appeared threatening, full of thunder, while seconds later they danced, silver-edged, like teddy bears or poodles or lambs. "It's pretty," she said.

"Our country is the prettiest in the world," Zelda said. Milda leaned forward, ready for a quarrel. "How do you know?" she asked.

"I've seen pictures. I've seen pictures of Germany and Russia and everything."

"I've seen pictures of mountains so high that the clouds sit on top of them," Milda snapped back. "You know," she went on, "when I'm bigger, I'll climb those mountains and sit on a pretty cloud and float away. I'll fly like a stork over Latvia!"

"Stupid," Zelda spewed out.

"I can't tell you anything," Milda said and, pouting, looked at the gold-trimmed autumn earth and the white birch trunks shining against the meadows and mowed fields, where cattles grazed peacefully. "You're right . . . this is the prettiest country in the world, but I want to see others." She leaned a bit forward. "I'm sorry you cannot go to Liepāja—to the seashore, where Latvia ends and where the sky hangs down like a curtain." But the words did not come out as she wanted; they got caught in her conscience, and Zelda knew it.

"You made me win."

Milda, pinned in the corner, hunted for words. "No, I didn't. I just lost."

"Don't lie to me! You never wanted to go to the farm because you don't like Aunt Matilde, even when you say you do. Mamma doesn't like her either. You both think she stinks," Zelda went on.

"I don't anymore."

"You're lying. You like Alma. I think she stinks. Mamma used to stink like that too, a long time ago."

"*Mammīte* never stinks," Milda said too loudly. A woman across from her shook her head and glared.

"I love Aunt Matilde. She smells real," Zelda was getting louder.

"Yes, I love her too and Uncle Imants and Anna and little Lilia—and Juris," Milda said, looking out.

"I love the way Aunt Matilde rides horses and milks cows," Zelda went on. "And the way she talks to Uncle Imants. She doesn't talk to him the way Mamma talked to Papa. She talks real."

"I love Juris," Milda said to her heart that felt a woman's pain.

Just then the old woman sitting in the far corner laughed a toothless laugh that gave her the creeps.

"I like the way Uncle Imants brushes the horses and talks to the cows."

Milda wished Zelda would shut up. She was irritated at the people all around who laughed, looking from her to Zelda, egging her sister on as if in a race.

"Shh . . . I like everything too, but I guess not like you," *Mildiņa* whispered and slid back into her corner. She decided to sleep for the rest of the way, pretending not to hear Zelda's words: "When I grow up I'll be like my Aunt Matilde. And you can have your Alma!"

The Sisters Separate

Riga . . . *Jelgava* . . . *Dobele* . . . The train rambled on, making long and short stops. The girls awoke. At noon people got out in Dobele, where the train stopped for an hour. It was a nice day, so the girls walked around, ate their sandwiches, and, feeling better, smiled at each other and promised not to quarrel anymore. They still had a long ride ahead. Back in the train, Milda told Zelda about her trip to the Embute castle. "I wish," she said, "that all of us could go there, but I can't.. . . I know you'll like it there, and you and Anna will have lots of fun."

"Yes, but I want to see the Sea and find amber!"

"When we grow up we'll do everything!" Milda said and then took her book from her handbag and said she wanted to read. The train continued on its way through woods and over harvested fields, past herds of cattle and through small towns. It chugged and rattled back and forth, on and on. People slept, talked, read. The sun slid toward the west, and again sleep made *Mildiņa's* eyes close and the book slide down.

Auce . . . Vaiņode . . . Milda barely heard it. And then: "Priekule! Priekule!" The same uniformed man she remembered from three years ago called out. She shook Zelda awake. Yawning, she stood up and gathered her things and put on her coat. "Now don't forget," she said, "that we must meet here on Monday, that will be the day after the day after tomorrow."

"I know that," Milda said. "I hope you have fun," she said and tears came to her eyes, which she brushed off, embarrassed. Zelda turned her face to hide her tears, and then the train was in the station. They saw Aunt Matilde, Anna, and Lilia running up to where the door might stop. When it opened, the sisters shook hands like grown-ups, and Zelda stepped off.

This was a short stop, but Milda also jumped down on the platform long enough to hug and kiss everyone. There was little time for words that tumbled about in jumbled phrases until the whistle blew. Matilde pushed a package at *Mildiņa* and helped her back up the steep steps. "This is for my dear *Almiņa.* There's nothing to eat in Liepāja these days, I know, so when you come back, I'll take you home with me for a few days and fatten you up, all right? I already telephoned your Mamma, so we'll see you soon."

Milda smiled and said, "Yes, I'll be so happy!" And then the train door shut with its loud bang. She elbowed her way back to her window seat and pressed her face against the cold pane and waved. They waved back, Matilde shaking her handkerchief as if it were full of dust. Milda fixed her eyes on the fluttering cloth that beat against the gathering grayness of the day and then vanished.

She did not know that they would never see each another again.

*

Hardly past Priekule, the train slowed down and stopped. It was announced that the train was being delayed. How and why no one explained. After a long time it moved some, but soon stopped again. Halfway to Liepāja, it stopped and stood still inside a wooded area, while time was running away and turning into darkness, rolling on like the huge cumulus clouds of the heavily lidded earth. From the dirty window Milda saw nothing but tall dark walls of fir trees. Through their needle branches flapped crows like black rags. She sniveled against the grayness and sank deeper inside her corner. The toothless woman who had laughed so merrily before, leaned over and gave her a red apple and told her that everything would be all right. "Little girl, I have lived long enough to know that all trains move on sooner or later. Now eat up! You look starved, like all city children these days."

Milda thanked her and tried to smile, but tears slid down her cheeks. The woman nodded and took another apple from her sack. She wiped it on her heavy gray skirt and gummed into it. Cautiously, because the woman looked like a witch, Milda took one small bite and chewed politely, her mouth closed. The apple was delicious, and she ate it up—core and all—and put the stem into her pocket. She had no idea that it would be over half a century before she would eat apples again from Latvia's orchards . . . As the woman had foretold, eventually the train did jerk and begin its chugging and rattling. At last it rode smoothly until it stopped in the station of Liepāja. Milda got off safely.

The Performance of *Faust*

A large, red-faced girl met her on the platform. She took the bundle of food, sniffing its contents, and then pulled frightened *Mildiņa* through the crowd, shouting, "If you don't know, my name is Ella. My mistress sent me to meet you . . . C'mon, walk faster! Why are you so late? We've missed half the show!"

Milda ran along with fast, long strides, carrying her suitcase that became heavier by the minute. She could not switch hands because the maid's grip was merciless. Numbed, she felt herself being pulled into a packed streetcar, where at last she could catch her breath, protected as she was by so many legs and hips. Still Ella held her hand, hurting her fingers until Milda yanked herself free and demanded to know where her aunt was.

"At the theater, *dura,*" Ella answered, retaking Milda's hand and holding it tighter than before. "We are too late, too late," she scolded for the whole streetcar to hear. Mercifully, the ride wasn't very long. Minutes later, they got off and rushed toward a brightly lit building nestled inside huge, bare trees.

Not letting go of the small hand, Ella pulled Milda through a large door, past a nodding watchman. At the wardrobe they took off their coats. Ella gave Milda's suitcase to the pale, black-clad woman on the other side of the half wall, who scolded them for being late. Then she handed Ella a metal number tag and, muttering, seated herself back inside the hanging coats.

The auditorium door was closed. "Because of you I couldn't see the beginning," Ella complained in a Russian accent. Milda was too tired to react; besides, she needed to go to the toilet but was ashamed to speak up. She was conscious of her crumpled clothes and thought about her blue pleated skirt and white ruffled blouse and blue ribbons her mother had ironed and wrapped in tissues and carefully folded inside her suitcase, laying her white stockings and black patent shoes next to them. "That will be all you need for dress-up," Katerina had said, adding, "don't forget to curtsy and look people in the eyes when you shake hands."

On the train Milda had rehearsed how she would greet Aunt Alma, but now all that was of no use. She did not look in the eyes of this coarse servant, and she would not even think of curtsying. "I must go to the toilet," she said boldly, and immediately her hand was clamped and she was dragged down the corridor. Ella followed her into a stinking stall, making *Mildiņa* so embarrassed that she could hardly relieve herself, but Ella showed no shame as she went about her business. When they came out, they walked more comfortably and in stride. To pass the time, they strolled up and down the circular corridor. Milda admired the photographs of the actors and actresses displayed on the wall and stopped at her aunt's portrait. She gazed at it in proud admiration until the doors of the auditorium opened and elegantly dressed ladies and gentlemen came out. It was intermission. The audience formed into a row, two or three deep, and conversing quietly circled the corridor until the next act was about to begin and the warning lights dimmed.

Again Milda felt Ella's hard grip as she was pushed with the crowd inside the auditorium and set in a red velvet seat, where Ella left her. Milda was glad to be rid of her and sat as she pleased, dangling her feet and looking all around. At last the lights turned off, and the black curtain slowly opened. Milda sat up and looked for her aunt.

At long last, Alma appeared dressed in white and as lovely as an angel in a painting. She sat in front of a mirror slowly braiding her long golden hair and speaking words Milda did not quite understand, but the sound of her voice was so beautiful, so clear, that she listened entranced. Throughout the performance, she followed the action and the changing scenes with greatest attention. Every move Alma made seemed wonderful. She was especially beautiful when she walked in the garden with Faust, who gave her a box of shining jewels.

The prison scene frightened *Mildiņa*, but she was sure Margareta would escape, that she would fly away on Faust's magic mantle. But it did not happen. Instead she was being dragged away to be killed.

Confused, *Mildiņa* could not understand what Margareta had actually done, nor why she would not run away when she had the chance. She hated Mephistopheles, who had a goat's foot and who told lies. When she saw women around her wipe their eyes, she also pulled her crumpled hanky out of her pocket and wept silently, politely.

The curtain fell after the singing of the angel chorus. She was upset that the ending was not happy, but went on clapping until her hands ached. When Alma took her solo bow, Milda exclaimed, "That's my aunt!" The lady next to her smiled. Men shouted "Bravo!" Alma came out of the curtain a second time and curtsied several times, as she received more flowers. When she was handed a huge bouquet of red roses, she nearly sunk to the floor, smiling, and then left the stage. The spotlights went out, and the chandeliers lit up.

Ella pulled her out of the auditorium. They went to gather their belongings and then pushed their way out into the lamp-lit darkness. After waiting a long time, they got on a streetcar and silently rode through the dim city. Milda was dreadfully sad and sleepy, and again her bladder ached, but she held on. There was no place to go. Ella yawned and left her hand alone.

In the small cluttered apartment she felt like an intruder. In one glance she saw the glamour and the disorder, thinking that there should not be so many clothes lying all over and open, face down books. She had never seen things in such disarray, not in Riga nor at the farm. The stale air smelling of ashes and perfume, bothered her, but she did not dare to open the large, bolted window. No matter what, she wouldn't ask Ella for anything but watched her alertly as a mouse watches a sly cat. Her hands turned into fists when she saw Ella open Matilde's bundle and bite off a chunk from the link of smoked sausage.

"Go to bed!" Ella ordered, chewing hard and drinking from a dark brown bottle. Burning in anger, Milda glared at her. She too was hungry, but said nothing. After Ella wiped her hands and mouth, she shoved Milda into the bedroom where, on a large bed, one side of the covers was folded back. "Sleep there," Ella said and closed the door. Left in the dark, *Mildiņa* undressed and climbed into the cold bed that smelled of Alma and lay very still. To stop from crying, she said a prayer, which gave her no comfort, no closeness to Jesus and the angels. Instead, the room filled with ghostly shadows cast by a lone street lamp. She stared at the lamp and struggled to stay awake until Alma would come home, but soon her eyes closed.

The Escape

The next morning, Milda awoke to Alma's humming. She opened her eyes slowly and was glad to see sunshine streaking through the curtains, lacing the walls with shadows. Squinting, she turned toward the window and marveled at a gorgeous crystal vase on the wide sill, full of dark red roses. With its sharp crystal knives it cut the sunrays into rainbow snippets and threw them all over the room. Dazzled, the girl's dreamy gaze danced about the room until it stopped at her aunt's more dazzling reflection in a gold-framed mirror. Not daring to disturb the vision, she held her breath and half closed her eyes. Her whole being thrilled because the lovely woman, clad in a long pink robe and coloring her lips red, had actually slept next to her. Gently *Mildiņa* touched the impression in the pillow and let her hand slide across the silky quilt ridge created at her aunt's rising.

When Alma finished painting her face, only then did she dare to utter a shy "Good morning." Alma turned, smiled, and stood up and, stepping over yesterday's strewn garments, cushions, and quilts, came towards *Mildiņa*, who was reaching out, but suddenly a cloud covered the sun, and a dark shadow eclipsed the room.

Milda fell back on her pillow, and looking at Alma, tried to separate her from Margareta. But try as she did, she could not draw a clear line between life and stage and did not know what to say to the apparition that was moving toward her. But just then the cloud passed on, and with one quick hand, Alma pushed back the lace curtain, completely exposing the vase of roses. Milda exclaimed, "I'm glad you're out of prison! Were the chains very heavy?" she asked.

"Yes."

As if catching *Mildiņa's* mood, the vase again went wild with rainbows, throwing them all over Alma and turning her into the celestial Margareta, who sang with the angels, desperately trying to save Faust from hell.

"Did you sleep well, my dearest?" Alma asked sweetly as Milda rose to receive a miniature hug.

"Yes, oh yes!"

Alma sat down on the edge of the bed, sinking deeply into the down comforter, smiling with her bright red lips. *Mildiņa*, warmed by such a smile, relaxed. They chatted while the fragrance of coffee filtered through the open door. Soon Ella, smiling like last night's moon, poked her face through the door to announce that breakfast was ready.

"Now get dressed," Alma said, cupping Milda's face in her warm hand and leaning over her so that the white fullness of her breasts touched the girl's cheek.

Left to herself, Milda slid out of bed and dressed carefully, putting on her blue skirt and white blouse, the fine stockings and the patent leather shoes. Because it was Sunday, she did not braid her hair but let it fall down her back. In front of Alma's large mirror she gathered it inside the length of a blue ribbon and tied a perfect bow on top of her head, but then, not wanting to look like a little girl, she slid the bow down to one side and reduced the loops. She smiled at her reflection, took a deep breath, and, stepping over the perfumed litter, went into the next room. She sat down across from Alma at a small round table beautifully set on the very edge of the disorder with a white table cloth and a rose-patterned coffee service. Throughout the room were vases full of flowers of every kind and fragrance.

"Last night's performance was wonderful, so magical, don't you think?" Alma cooed.

"Yes."

Ella also agreed and was almost kind as she brought a platter of open face sandwiches of rye bread topped with smoked sausage rings and boiled eggs. On a silver plate were cream puffs and slices of apple strudel. In a crystal bowl glistened the pears and apples of Uncle Imants's orchard. As Ella brought in one dish and removed another, she made unsolicited remarks, saying how much the *child* looked like the *madama.*

"It's the blood, it's all in the blood." She said she wished she had a pretty mother or aunt. "But what's to be done? We don't choose our mothers. Fate is fate." And she disappeared into the kitchen, back in her place.

Ella's statement, so full of biting envy, spoiled the beauty of the morning, leaving them in awkward silence. When Ella was out of the room, Alma hunted for a cigarette and, playing with it, explained in a very low voice that her servant was from the Ukraine and that she had *red leanings.* She had come to Latvia right after the 1940 communist occupation, but since she was a hard worker, when she wasn't drunk, Alma had let her stay on even after the Germans took over.

"But I don't really trust her," Alma said.

Ella pushed the door open and came in with a pitcher of hot coffee. Pouring it into Alma's cup, she gloated about all she had done to find the beans. "But where there's a will, there's a way, I say, and I bribed the sales woman, saying that we must have good coffee and cognac so we can celebrate my mistress's success on stage, I said, and put down a silver piece, and sure enough, before I stretched my hand to take it back, she had a bag of beans and a bottle on the counter. Oh, I know there are plenty of things hidden from the people. The class struggle goes on all the time."

"Please, be quiet," Alma said. "Don't give me a headache."

"Sorry madam, but I just wanted to tell you that you are a fine vehicle of culture. Soon we'll all be free and equal."

"Don't wear that word out!" Alma scolded.

"Sorry, madam," Ella curtsied and slid away.

Agitated, Alma broke the cigarette and put one half into a black holder. She smoked with short quick puffs, sipping her hot, sweet coffee. Milda, imitating her, sipped her hot cacao and slowly, carefully ate a slice of the strudel. The smoke irritated her eyes, and she rubbed them, wishing the windows could be opened, but Alma was happy and at peace. "Last night was like a dream," she said from behind the fumes, her beautiful head resting on the roses of the wallpaper, her eyes half closed.

Suddenly the telephone rang. Alma sprung up and rushed into the bedroom to answer the call. She stayed there a long time. When she appeared in the doorway, she was dressed in a dark blue traveling suit. Her face was a pale mask; her red lips twitched.

"We must pack up and leave," she said. "There is hardly any time."

Milda stared, as she swallowed her mouthful.

"The Reds have stormed into Kurzeme and aren't far from Liepāja," Alma said and went back into the bedroom. "I will not live in a country ruled by communists! I will not live under Russians . . . Never, never, never!" She spoke in a loud staccato.

"I want to go home, I want my Mamma," Milda spoke with clear, loud words and stumbled back into the bedroom, the sun shining in her eyes, blinding her, making her trip over clothing and furniture. She found her suitcase under the bed. Quickly she changed back into her traveling clothes, packed away her Sunday things, and, without even looking at Alma, pushed for the outer door and held the brass handle, ready to break out and run. But Ella's grip clutched her hand. Milda heard her husky, accented voice close to her ear, "You can't go anywhere, you little bourgeois snob!"

At that, Alma shouted, "Leave the child alone!" The grip loosened. The two women faced each other over the innocent head.

"So," Alma charged, "what you wanted has happened. The Reds have come back to finish us off, and you're glad. Well, you can go to them! Go, go on! Leave my apartment at once!"

"It's not your place anymore," Ella snapped back. "It is mine too. Now everything belongs to the people."

"Go," Alma said wearily. "Please go. Get out of my sight." She pulled some money from her handbag and shoved it at Ella. "Don't go about blabbing that I didn't pay your wages."

"Your German money won't be any good now," Ella said but stuffed the notes into her pocket anyway. She paused in the open doorway, putting on her drab, tight overcoat. Suddenly indecisive, she fussed with her scarf.

"Madam," her voice carried tears. "Madam, you don't have to leave. I could hide you. No one will hurt you. Your own countrymen, who during the revolution once guarded Comrade Lenin, have come to save us from the fascists. Soon we'll all be free. Back in our places—you on the stage and I here, if you will forgive me."

"Go," Alma said through tight lips.

Ella licked her lips and brushed her eyes spitefully and left, but moments later reappeared. "You won't get far. You will be back, but I better pack you some food. Who knows, the trip could take longer than we think." With sure moves, she went into the kitchen and packed a string bag full of food and set it at the feet of her mistress. "There you are, and fortune go with you!" Ella looked triumphant, almost pretty, Milda thought, like a huntress pushing a sharp knife through an unsuspecting throat. Then she turned and went down the stairs. They heard the door slam.

Left alone, they eyed each other. To Milda, her aunt now appeared exactly like Margareta in prison. She seemed dazed, wanting to flee and stay in her rooms at the same time. She clutched her throat as if she were choking, but there were no tears in her large frightened eyes. Milda timidly reached out for her hand and led her back into the sunshine. Next to the window, Alma sat down so they would be even in height and spoke softly, "Soon my friend will arrive and help us get to the harbor. We will board a ship that will take us to Germany. It will be a dangerous voyage, I want you to understand."

"But I cannot go with you," Milda answered with equal calm. "I must go back. I have to meet Zelda at the station in Priekule. Aunt Matilde will be waiting. It's Anna's birthday. I promised I'd be there, and Anna does not feel well, so I must go."

"You cannot go back," Alma said. "You must stay with me."

"But Mamma? What about Mammīte?" Milda asked, her eyes now as large and frightened as Alma's.

"I don't know. Riga is cut off. The telephones don't work."

Alma watched her niece's face draw together in hard lines, her chest heaving. "Don't you dare cry, or I'll leave you here all alone, and then the Russians will send you to Siberia all by yourself." She spoke in a hard voice.

Milda screamed, "Ņooo!"

A slap razed her face. She did not hear the knock on the outer door, nor its opening and closing. The man who had played the devil the night before suddenly stood next to Alma, pulling her up. She saw him take her in his arms and kiss her mouth. Milda cried out again, and again a slap singed her face.

"Silence, you little gnat!" Alma shouted in a devilish voice. "Not another sound from you, or I will leave you!"

Terrified, the girl fell into the ordered silence. She watched Alma walk to the foyer, put on her brown coat and hook the golden fox around her neck. She folded the *villaine* that hung over a chair. Focusing her eyes on the afghan's bright geometric designs that ran in a wide band all around its edge, Milda was sure that it was a gift from Matilde, which she had woven. Bringing up Aunt Matilde's image, Milda saw her sitting for hours and days at her loom, humming as she wove, as the colored yarns slid through her fingers. *Aunt Matilde will be with us. She'll keep us warm.*

"Let's not forget this," Alma said and, laying the *villaine* next to the string bag, burst into tears. She went back into the bedroom. The man followed. The door closed. Left alone, Milda picked up the string bag and, after looking at its meager content, went into the kitchen to stuff more food into it—whatever she could gather—until the bag bulged like a ball. She put on her coat and slowly buttoned it up and then put on her hat and tied the ribbons. She made sure her mittens were stuffed deep inside her coat pockets and sat down to wait.

A muffled scream from behind the closed door startled her. She sprang to her feet and tiptoed to the bedroom door, listening. Soon Alma let out another moan of great pain, followed by struggling words: "Don't . . . the child . . . no, not now . . . please." And then she heard a loud crashing of glass. Cautiously, she turned the handle and opened the door a tiny crack. She saw the large crystal vase on the floor, broken in half and the roses lying in a puddle. Alma lay sprawled across the bed, the fox tangled around her neck, its blind emerald eyes blazing. She saw her aunt's legs, shining and naked, wrapped around the large, strong man who was pressing her down. Unaware of the innocent intrusion, both went on with their strange and awful struggle.

Trembling, Milda crept back to the foyer. The moans and sighs filtered through the opening, while she sat until all was quiet. . . . At last, the door opened, and they came out and stood in the living room, which already had taken on an abandoned look. Noticing the quiet girl, they moved awkwardly apart. Alma calmly buttoned her overcoat, throwing the fox over her shoulder. The man inserted a rose in her coat's buttonhole. They kissed. Then without a word, he picked up the suitcases, and they went out the big double door. Alma did not lock it.

The man helped Alma into his black car and set Milda deep in the back seat between the suitcases. That done, he opened his door, slid behind the wheel, and turned on the engine. Feeling like extra baggage, Milda watched the two backs in front of her. They seemed like puppets on a sleeve, maneuvered by invisible hands, frightened, therefore frightening. When she saw Alma lean on the man's shoulder, she closed her eyes and relived that wonderful Sunday long ago when she leaned her head against Juris's side, snug and happy. She bit her lips to keep from crying out, as she realized that she was being pulled away from him also. *How will he know where to send his postcards? How will Mamma know where to find me? How will we know where to find each other?*

The scenes where she and Juris had touched her, joked and teased whirled around her dazed head. The wonderful moments lingered, making her smile and sending vibrating thrills through her tense body. She leaned back, dreaming, recalling, when, suddenly, with a slam on the brakes, the visions vanished. She remembered the bad Germans in uniform taking away Juris and his horse. *Does he still have my blue ribbon,* she wondered and, taking her hat off, pulled the matching ribbon from her hair and braided it into her fine hair, double-tying the bow. She put her hat back on her head and wept, the tears running down her cheeks into the ribbon. In a blur she saw people sliding past them, some running, others walking, carrying bundles, pulling screaming children.

"We will come back, won't we?" she dared to whisper, but no one answered. Waiting, she imagined herself grown up and Juris in a room such as they had just abandoned. Only it would be a neat room, with roses blooming in the window, not in puddles of water and broken glass. And there would be her whole family reunited, and there would be no war and no communists.

The car stopped again to avoid a child who ran out in front of it. She screamed. Alma turned, telling her to be quiet, but Milda did not look at her; she sank deeper down in the seat and became very quiet, very small. Sick to her stomach, she felt the woman growing inside her, while the child died away. She agonized in silent pangs of dread, fear, and guilt as the images of her parents, Zelda, and everybody she was leaving. They floated past the car window, waiving their handkerchiefs and shouting, "Don't go! Don't leave us!" But then the pain ceased, giving way to rising excitement like a wave heaving her forward of its own volition. It seemed to her that all of Latvia, in fact, the whole world heaved in a movement of cosmic pangs.

She heard the church bells ringing from every steeple, as though ringing in Dooms Day, while she was in a race—escaping, driving away to strange lands, across deep seas, just like princesses in stories! Just like the Children of Israel running into the Red Sea before the pursuing fiends would catch them. She sat up, clutching on to the seat so she would not be thrown so hard from side to side. To make her fears and guilt go away, she imagined herself coming home again loaded with gifts for everyone. She would bring something especially nice for Zelda and Anna. She would make up for the birthday present Anna never received. She would tell exciting tales about where she had been and what she had seen.

The car slowed to a horse's trot. It bumped about on the cobblestones, throwing her this way and that. The streets became more jammed, the mobs hovering like gray clouds, blocking the sunshine. Some people carried chickens in cages, while others dragged stubborn cows that mooed their deep, monotone protests, more desperate than the cries of their masters. There were wagons with beds, lamps, chairs. Children screamed, and adults yelled. Everyone was running, scurrying toward the harbor, toward the sea. Her bladder ached. Embarrassed, she sat tighter, counting the people, the cows, the cars. And then to her relief, Alma said, "We better stop at those trees."

The car turned off the street on to a road leading through the park, toward the seashore. They headed for the tall willow bushes and wind-twisted pines. For a moment it seemed they had awakened from the nightmare and were on an outing. Alma giggled, talking silly, looking for a place to stoop. The man said "good idea," and recklessly maneuvered his car and stopped. Seeing a sheltered dip, they bailed out. Milda watched the adults take off, up the sandy slope. They ran toward the thicket as though playing hide-and-go-seek until they vanished in the dunes. Milda stepped behind a nearby bush to relieved herself and stood waiting. Minutes passed. Cautiously she started walking on a path leading up to the pine trees and the ridge of waving grass. From there, she saw the sea—a sparkling liquid blue wall beyond which, she knew, lay the wide shimmering world. She did not want to go there. She wanted to go home, and, turning back, she walked quickly, hiding among the trees and being careful not to trample the underbrush where heather and tardy wild flowers bloomed. Farther on, she noticed fat, healthy mushrooms tucked inside the lichen, the kind people picked early in the morning before the worms would burrow through them. Her fingers itched, eager to pick all she could, but like guards, the red, white-dotted, fly killers stood in the way. She drew back. "Don't even go near one!" Anna had warned her. "Even the spores can get you."

Fleeing from the poison all around, Milda started running. Branches cracked under her feet and hit her in the face. The birds screamed at her from every bush, telling her not to leave these pines, the dunes, and the heather. "Stay, stay, stay," she heard the wind whisper as she hugged the trunk of a white birch.

"I can find my way to the farm," she told herself. "Like Hansel and Gretel . . . If I go the way the wind blows, I'll soon be on the road . . . It is not far, it cannot be." She was crying, looking at the sky, looking for the wind to guide her.

"Oo-ooo, Mi-i-i-ldaa! Oo-ooo!"

Alma was leaping after her, pulling her back down, back to the car. She was scolding, yelling, telling her how she did not want any trouble from her, how she expected absolute obedience or else . . . She heard Alma cry. The fox, twisted under Aunt's chin, glared at her. Beyond, on the sand-swept boardwalk, stood the man—last night's devil—smoking a cigarette. Milda was trapped.

They drove toward the harbor of warships and large vessels, the open passage to the outside world. Alma buried her face in her handkerchief. Her shoulders heaved, but the man looked straight ahead. After a long, tedious starting and stopping, they were again in the thick of the fleeing mob. People cried, ran, fell to the ground . . . There were so many. "Is all Latvia running away?" she asked, without expecting an answer.

"This is as far as we can drive, my ladies," the man said gallantly and stopped the car. Alma's face, as it turned toward him, was wet and streaked with makeup. The man took the face in his hands and kissed it over and over. Alma wrapped her arms around his neck and begged, "Please, come with me, dear Viktor! Won't you please come with us? How'll I ever live without you?"

Milda heard the name. Viktors, not Mephistopheles. The name turned him into a mere man, and then she pitied him. She wished he would come with them, but he kept saying, "I cannot, my darling, my beloved, my woman. I cannot." He said the words in her hair.

"Why? Why not? Don't you love me that much?" Alma cried.

He did not answer. He only kissed her and stroked her hair and the fox fur. "You must go, you and the child."

"Why, oh why, must it be like this?"

"I don't know. No one knows," he said, and then Milda saw his tears. "It will only be a while before this crazy war is over, and then you'll come back. I'll wait for you," he said tenderly.

"Swear!" Alma cried.

"I swear. I swear by the sea and the sky," he said. "I will wait for you, but you, too, must swear that you will come back."

"I swear. I will come back to you even if I have to swim the sea."

"And we'll have a beautiful wedding," he said looking in her eyes. "Meanwhile, I'll keep acting, keep the stage lights on."

Then he took the wilting rose from Alma's buttonhole and with the thorn stuck his and her fingers. Milda saw the blood run down in two little streams, like red threads. She saw Alma's white face, the parted lips, silent and pale. She saw the two hands meet and the blood flow down together until the palms were red, like a pool.

"You are mine and I am yours. We have sworn. The child is our witness," he said, turning to look at Milda, and pressed Alma's finger to his lips, holding it there until the bleeding stopped. She did the same to him. The ritual finished, he stuck the rose back in the buttonhole and looked at it as if it had eyes.

"Whatever happens, there will always be a sure role for a good devil—onstage or off, my sweet Gretchen," he said as he wiped the hands clean with his large handkerchief. Alma smiled, a resigned prison smile.

They got out of the car and pushed their way through the crowd, toward a huge ship. The noise of the refugees was dreadful and desperate. Above it all, German soldiers shouted orders and tried to keep the lines straight and fair. Viktors signaled to one of the uniformed men who promptly appeared. He put two silver *Lats* in his hand and said, "Take care of them."

The soldier clicked his heels and picked up the suitcases. Viktors followed as far as possible—to the very edge of the land. He kissed his beloved again and stroked Milda's head and stepped back. There he remained, watching half of his life walk up the ramp on to the boat that rocked over dark waters.

The soldier guided aunt and niece to the higher deck, where they found a sheltered corner. There he put down the suitcases, saluted Hitler, quickly turned and was gone. Alma plunked down on her suitcase and pulled Milda beside her. Numbly, they waited with other frightened people for an uncertain, blank time, as drawn of color as the sky above them. Unmarked, the hours and minutes faded with the day. At dusk the siren blew and the ship started pulling away from the shore. They watched some men below roll the huge spools of ropes and lift the anchors, disconnecting them from their beloved, ravished homeland. The ship turned westward.

The dispossessed clung to the railings, weeping, moaning, waving to their torn-off halves and to the land they were leaving. By and by they saw Latvia shrink away, become little, until it disappeared in the hovering haze. Alma stood up, pushing Milda aside, like an unwanted burden, and plucked the wilted rose from her buttonhole. She kissed it and tossed it into the sea. The tiny dot fluttered about for a few uncertain seconds until the sea swallowed it. She leaned over the railing and wept silently, waving her gloved hand with her white handkerchief for as long as her arm could hold out against the force of the wind and the night. Everyone waved; the handkerchiefs fluttered like ripped off seagulls' wings. When the wind turned and the waves dashed harder, Alma pulled her *Mildiņa* back into their corner and wrapped the *villaine* tightly around them. Their faces whitened, and their lips felt the salty air and tasted the salt of their tears that would not stop raining. Through them Alma recited in weary resignation Margareta's lines from *Faust*:

Meine Ruh' ist hin, mein Herz ist schwer;

Ich finde sie nie und nimmermehr.

As in a trance, she said the lines over and over. Milda did not understand what the words meant. She understood nothing. She was cold and put on her mittens, again remembering her other aunt, her cousins, sister and the sheep that gave up their wool so people would be warm. When Alma slumped farther over the railing, as if on stage, Milda pulled her back with a strong hand. In their corner, they cuddled deeper into Matilde's hand-woven *villaine*—woven so tightly that no wind could break through it. "How good this is, how simple and pretty is the design," Alma said. *"Maras ceļš* (Mara's way). It will lead us home from wherever we may be. We must never lose it."

"Yes."

The night slowly wrapped up the day, leaving an orange ribbon along its edge. Hungry, they took some bread out of the string bag and, scrupulously rationing each portion, ate slowly. As the wind blew harder, the fog cleared, and a broken, shamefaced moon rose above the vaguely glowing horizon. Soon the stars lit up the darkness. Milda found the large and small dippers, the North Star, and the Seven Sisters, but Alma stared at Orion or at some distant, yet undiscovered, unnamed star on which she could pin her hopes.

As the stars and constellations brightened and the Milky Way paved the sky, somewhere on the deck below a deep baritone started singing the Latvian national anthem. Soon other voices joined in, forming a mighty chorus. The people sang the anthem over and over, filling the night with their pleading, persistent prayer: *God, bless Latvia, oh bless our fatherland* . . . The winds blew harder, and the waves rose higher. It was a precious cargo the ship had to carry over dangerous waters to Germany's more dangerous shores.

*

Why is everyone clapping? Mrs. Arajs opens her eyes and rises. She must have dozed off. She feels lightheaded. The crowd around her sways and heaves. *A full ship over stormy waters, always rocking, always tilting up to the stars, then falling back, white foam splattering, dissolving, seagulls crying. My people. I am in the midst of my people, as in the middle of a great unfinished drama with thousands of acts and scenes, each with its characters, stereotypes, caricatures, real protagonists and antagonists, heroes and heroines.*

She looks at the faces around her. *Round and oval orbs, little circles, globes of separate worlds, each with his and her peculiar topography. His and her escape story, which, if spun, would crisscross and wholly entangle the globe, and there would still be loose threads—a world of untold stories, like history.*

She looks for familiar faces and smiles vaguely, nodding to some, but not reaching out. She reminds herself that she does not want to deal with Pēteris Vanags and takes the nearest exit out. It is four thirty. A long evening stretches before her, and she wonders what she will do with it. *Ah, I'll eat some of it away, slowly, bite by bite—have a hamburger with tomatoes and* pickles, no *onions, though, for obvious reasons, and then I'll go and see* Ancient Wedding.

Evening Entertainment

The musical in the Pabst Auditorium was very nice, relaxing and easy. Nothing to getting married in those good old days of mysterious antiquity. Boy meets girl or girl meets boy, and they marry. The girl is shy, the boy aggressive. The girl is diligent, the boy wants to play around, but the girl—a good girl, that is—keeps him reined in and away from the bottle. She never complains, never speaks harshly, only works and sings, sings and works and sometimes, all alone and with no one to hear her, she cries. Weeps, looks out at the stars or the sunset and lets the tears slide down her face. Her heart is always full of longing and dreams, but nothing can be fulfilled; pleasure is only for the maiden, while the married woman is duty-bound. On the wedding day, the groom and his attendants arrive at the bride's house, wide awake and singing the appropriate songs. The bride, already dressed and adorned, receives her in-laws with smiles and invites them to tables overloaded with food and drink. After the feasting that goes on all day, the bride turns her full hopechest over to the groom and then her family bids her a sad farewell, knowing that she is in for a hard lot.

In the groom's house, the bride and the whole wedding party are welcomed with another set of songs. The virtuous bride opens her hope chest and gives everyone a gift: mittens, socks, shirts—all things she has made herself. The kinfolk evaluate, examine, and, of course, approve. They sing her praises and wish the couple good fortune.

Another feast, and the sparkling maiden crown is taken off the bride's head. The married women replace it with a drab linen cap. The newly initiated wife submits and allows her hair to be tucked inside it, while the women, in words and songs, lecture her on work and duty. But before they are finished, the *panāksnieki* (pursuers), young men from the bride's tribe, charge into the yard. With mock bravado they try to rescue the bride, their sister, their sunshine. But of course, they cannot and give up, as foaming glasses of ale are passed around. After another feast, the pursuers return to their homes, and the bride and groom go to their room in the attic of a granary. The bride makes the bed. She spreads it with white linen sheets and petals of roses, and then the groom lays her down . . . While the cast sings love songs and lullabies, the curtain falls.

*

"Nice, oh, how nice!" Milda says and applauds.

The people don't stop clapping until the last scene is repeated. When the lights come on, she sees women wiping their eyes, smiling through their tears at each other; some hold their husbands tightly. What do they remember? What do they feel, Milda wonders. What secrets and wishes do these people harbor? Oh God, perhaps she's not the only one with an inner and outer life? She vaguely recalls Ilga reading to her some passage from *Lady Chatterley's Lover* and tells her that D. H.Lawrence wondered why the human race has so many secrets, if all people, more or less, feel the same and do the same things.

"But he's wrong," Milda assures herself. "People are more unique than that. I'm certainly unique."

*

In the lobby, she sees the same cluster of women with whom she had been the night before. They are laughing, talking loudly with mouths and hands, having a wonderful time. She feels like an outsider who wants to belong, yet doesn't. Spitefully, she does not wish to be coaxed, governed, observed. She turns, pretending not to have seen anyone, but Aria spots her and calls out, "Oh, hallo! Come join us!"

She smiles and says, "I'm so glad to see you!"

"What a delightful performance!" Aria says. "How nice weddings used to be in the good old days!" she goes on sarcastically. "Everything so simple . . . No divorces, no court costs, only silent suffering. Men turn to drinking, but women have the good sense to slip into a river, face down, forever."

"Oh, stop it," Milda says and lets the crowd carry her away. Everyone is having a wonderful time; everyone is ready for excitement, nightcaps, surprises because on this night the city of Milwaukee belongs to *Free* Latvians.

THE THIRD DAY

Meditation

Mrs. Arajs was waking up slowly, confusedly. Again her head ached from the day and night before. "Too much talking, eating, drinking," she said, turning over, pushing her head deeply into the foam pillows. The whole festival was becoming too heavy, like a huge burden, a task—an ordeal without any real hope of getting done with it. She thought about her garden and wished she were there, weeding. With the house and garden, at least, she always felt that wonderful sense of accomplishment: dough turns into bread; flowers grow from seeds; weeds lie in a pile at the edge of a clean bed, ready to be raked up and thrown away, and grass—green and soft under her bare feet—a carpet she, Kārlis, and God had woven over the seasons and years, from the beginning, when there were the words: Love, Hope, Latvia, Home. It was a dream of a myth—a faultless blueprint. Why had it vanished so quickly? She tried to remember her husband as he had been in his best years—the thirties, when he was so full of energy and ideas that she could hardly keep up. They had traveled to many burgeoning Latvian centers together with their children in the back of their station wagon. He had been strict with them: no eating or drinking in the car and no loud, silly talking. Instead, he used the travel times to lecture and enforce Latvian values drawn from history. When in the mood, he would recite whole epics as if he were some Sir Gielgud onstage, impressing his captive audience. He answered many questions, and together they discussed important ideas and themes. This would go on for miles and miles. When he finished lecturing, they would all sing, mostly folk songs, Ilga and Gatis competing with words and melodies. The whole family was blessed with fine voices, and often they performed as an ensemble at summer camp bonfires, delighting everyone. On their long trips, every two hours, Kārlis would stop at some park or rest area so the children could run around, play ball or Frisbee, while Mother set out a picnic meal or some snacks. “Time and life must never be wasted!” he instructed. He practiced what he preached.

It seemed to Milda then that such time and life would go on forever. She could not conceive of a house without small children and her good and faithful husband, even though he often left her alone. But she didn’t mind; she was happy and fulfilled as a mother. And she loved her husband. She loved his body, the muscles, the broad chest, and especially his handsome face like a work of art. She loved to kiss his lips and run her hands through his thick, blond hair. In public she was ever so proud to be at his side, knowing that they struck the image of a perfect couple, and when the children—well dressed and well behaved, holding hands—walked between them, the picture was complete.

The troubles that plagued her now, then were far in the distance and unimaginable. Vanags, too, was far away, on the East Coast, and when he did visit, he was a flawless guest, always bringing her flowers and keeping his distance, though at times their eyes would meet and for a moment—but only a moment—she was back in Esslingen. She would then avoid his seeking, penetrating glances and serve her company with smiles and good food. She trusted her house and home to keep her safe and protected.

Lying on her pillows in the luxurious hotel alone, she wondered how that life could have ended so quickly. How could her darling children turn into rebellious teenagers, it seemed, overnight? She and Kārlis had been totally unprepared for the metamorphosis, and she was sure that the shock of losing control had caused such stress that his heart gave out. The tension, high-blood pressure, and nervousness appeared then, as they argued about how to handle the children, who threatened to follow the American trends of disobedience and unguarded, challenging, self-expression. When the scenes of the sixties, with ugly language, dress, music, and manners invaded their living room via TV, Kārlis lost control and more arguments ensued, becoming loud and serious. After sensing that he was losing the verbal battles, he would fall into prolonged silences and lock himself inside his familiar world of Latvian hard-line politics. He then called Pēteris Vanags on the telephone, leaving Milda out. Jealously, she felt her husband's trust erode and give way to friction, hurt feelings, critical, sarcastic comments, and gloomy silences. As more problems developed, the tensions multiplied and the nights grew colder until, suddenly, it was over.

Oh, how I wish we could live our lives over again, she sighed. She did not want to rise, to walk down the hall and into the crowd. She did not want to see cheating Egons, nor aggressive Vanags. *Who cares, let them be* . . . Oh, how she wanted to go home, to the home that was no more and to the life that was forever gone.

She found the aspirin and lay back, waiting for the headache to go away. But it hung on, droning, until it latched on to the whole idea of this and past festivals: too abstract, too intangible. Ah, perhaps too much of a man's concept, too much theory and ideology, symbolism, though women participated in all phases of the complex organization. Still, all big words, frustrating concepts that never mentioned simple head and foot aches. "Those are for women to worry about," Milda said to the ceiling. "Nevertheless, I know what a symbol can feel. I know its flaws and the dangers of misinterpretation. I've been—maybe still am—one."

She rose, dressed, and went out toward the synthetic mirage—down long, carpeted corridors, softly infiltrated with folk melodies, and toward elevators crowded and noisy, going up and down. And when a strange but friendly hand pulled her in, packing her tightly with others, all laughing and speaking in the Latvian language, she lightened up. "Let's see what today will bring," someone said and she nodded.

Listening and Hearing

On the mezzanine, Milda paused to reverently salute the Latvian flag cascading from the opposite side, almost touching the heads of people down in the lobby, burying or blessing them. Just below, she watched a young mother with two small children, a boy and a girl. The mother, in a light summer dress, pointed up at the banner and spoke words Milda could not hear but knew by heart. The children, outfitted like dolls in national costumes, turned their angelic faces up. The children waved, but their mother quickly gathered them up and rushed away. Folk dancing practice, no doubt, Milda thought and remembered. She turned and meandered on. Suddenly a group of young people, also ethnically costumed, rushed past her as they raced for an elevator. They missed it.

"I'm burning up in these things," a girl complained in English. "Can't wait to get them off of me."

"You were cool last night," a young man said, enjoying his own cleverness. "Man, you can really move!"

"Oh, get off me!"

"I'm not on you." They all laughed.

Milda walked on past the open, critical looks of other elders and paused to eavesdrop at a heated conversation: "No, we should not go there as long as communists are in power," said an old man. "We must work from here, mobilize. Demonstrate. Tell the world. That is our mission!" He poked another man's chest.

"That's right!" A woman pushed forward. "Our young people must be warned." The dispossessed matriarch stepped inside the men's circle. "I just got back from Latvia, and things were nice on the surface, but I know what goes on below. The people . . ."

She took a deep breath, but the old man interrupted: "We must educate them." he said.

"We must watch the gates. The communists are sly," another joined in.

"But maybe things have changed," a big young woman said loudly, in a heavy American accent. "I was there also. Got back last week, and nothing is the way you all been telling us! It's obvious that the world is changing, and . . ."

"Nothing changes in that system," the same man cut in, looking over the top of his glasses menacingly. Mumbling, the woman backed off.

"You see," the old one went on, "regretfully we have no power of controlling such as her. She will do and say what they want her to. She is doing it already." He took a deep, overly exhausted breath, and sadly added, "That is the tragedy of exile."

"Oh, give me a break! What exile! Tell me how you've suffered all these years! As if I didn't know, haven't listened to you all," the accused woman charged. "You all act like Latvia is dead. Keep mourning, keep having these here dirges, watch for KGB arrests like you couldn't wait for the next scrap of bad news, so you'd have something to write in your stupid newspapers!" She took another deep breath and, pumped up, emitted, "It makes me sick." She turned and went down the hall, her bulky body swaying as on furrowed ground.

Milda walked on. Behind another post, people talked about the same thing: "This leftist liberalism has to be stopped. Our young people are getting out of hand. Even some of our own intellectuals suggest that we should start some kind of exchange program . . ."

"So?" a young voice cut in. "Why not?"

Milda kept walking. Unaware, she had circled the whole open mezzanine and was back at the elevators. The hall was empty and quiet. Her headache had come back. She needed to eat, but first she went to check the bulletin board. Perhaps there might be a message.

"Greetings! Good morning, Mrs. Arāja," a portly man, smelling of Old Spice, bowed. His thinning hair was queerly parted in the middle and plastered down in the style of the fifties—or possibly the previous century. Gallantly he kissed her hand and smiled as if his lips had licked honey.

"Ah, Professor Kungs!" Milda remembered, of course. She knew he had taught history at the University of Latvia and, therefore, was considered an expert—an authority, whom even Kārlis would not second-guess. Ilga was not allowed to, and Gatis never voiced an opinion or question. Milda had seen Prof. Kungs gliding as he bowed from festival to festival, carrying his mysterious briefcase like a shield, perhaps guarding himself from any new historical interpretations or from the young historian who was quickly usurping twentieth-century Latvia, and messing around with the Jewish question. In fact, at the moment, the culprit was holding forth at another bulletin board.

Now, standing next to such exile-shaking authority, Milda felt awkward; the man kept bowing, licking his lips. She focused on the mole of his cheek and said, "I still remember your lecture on Latvian morality."

"Good, very good!" He kept smiling, bowing, while Milda recalled him standing at a podium asking, "What then is each Latvian's priority, his moral obligation? His *summum bonum*?" To that he had quickly answered: "It is (1) the preservation of national values, (2) the fighting for Latvia's freedom, (3) the preserving and increasing of cultural achievements."

"And have you obeyed my words, Mrs. Arāja?" She heard him ask as if from far away. "Have you done your duty? What are your children doing now?" Milda stood like a school girl, blushing, not knowing the right answers, not being able to elaborate. "My son, my son . . ." she stumbled.

"And your daughter?"

"I don't know," she stammered on, feeling the laser of his inquisitor's eyes. The mole seemed to rotate. "I cannot give you a quick summary, not under such pressure, nor our limited time." She liked her words; she realized that she was a head taller than he. "This is a festival, not a classroom, sir, and we—Ilga and I—are not yet finished. We still have to see things through. If you please, professor, we have to define our own *summum bonum,* spoke the Ice Princess. "Good day, Professor."

After he walked away, she noticed a pair of legs on the other side of the bulletin board.

Meeting Helga Williams

"And what, indeed, are your children doing, Mrs. Arāja?"

"Helga!"

They shook hands. Overcome by mutual surprise, they stood for a moment mutely eying each other until Helga said, "How good to see you!" and stepped forward, her arms open, but Milda stepped back. The Ice Princess would not allow herself to be ruffled too quickly. Still, they talked, catching up with bits of their biographies as they walked toward the exit, away from the milling crowd. Once outside, they talked louder, freer, pushing back the walls of time and space.

"Seeing you is such a wonderful surprise," Milda said, squinting at the bright daylight. "It's been ages, whole lifetimes," she went on. They turned a corner. "This will be a good day for me, after all," Milda said, her spirit rising.

They had a healthy breakfast in a small diner on a side street, where they exchanged mutual compliments, commenting on their hair, dress, weight, and began indulging in old memories. After cups of black coffee and looking at photographs, they paid and left. Milda's headache was gone; relaxed, she linked her hand in Helga's elbow and asked about her family. Gladly Helga filled her in on the major details of her life: she now lived in a small town in Illinois, where her husband was a professor at one of the newer state universities that had sprung up after Russians sent their first sputnik in space.

Helga told her that they were lucky because it had been easy for her husband to find a good job. They had a ranch house and four children. "I'm just a housewife. However, I do have a Master's Degree in English and am writing and translating, that is, when I have time, when the children are in school. So I have somewhat fulfilled my dreams, while I'm also doing something for Latvia, I hope. I am trying to spread our culture through America's heartland, answering, at least partly, the persistent question 'Where you from?' whenever I open my mouth—in stores, schools, even gas stations. Oh, our accents are forever! And so I think we might as well make the most of the whole thing about being the nameless *'and others.'*"

"I know what you're saying," Milda agreed. "After all these years that rude probing really still upsets me."

"Yes, me too, but through writing I turn our particular foreignness into an advantage. You should try it also."

"Who would care? But I do keep a sort of journal and have written down some notes. I tried to keep a diary, but couldn't. I embarrass myself whenever I read it."

"Write fiction. It's more honest than descriptions of so-called truths, and it will get things that bother you out of your system."

Helga told her that she and her husband had recently come back from Europe. "We even looked into Esslingen, which is changed an awful lot. I saw no footsteps of ourselves anywhere, except in the cemetery, where some of our old teachers and leaders are buried. The bridge over the Neckar that we crossed every day has become a mere overpass, while a four-lane highway, with unending traffic, streams below. It runs next to the Neckar, where the footpath was, and where we used to take our long walks. Remember the time we caught our teachers smooching in the grass, committing adultery?"

"Now that you mention it." They laughed.

"Ah, there is nothing in the world as romantic as the month of May on the Neckar shores, where acacias bloom!" Milda sighed dramatically. "You remember how it was, don't you?"

"Yes, of course. Even our super moral teachers could not resist and stepped off the path."

"And the beach? The tennis courts? Are they still there?" Milda asked.

"No. All gone. The highway ground them up—with all our wonderful memories, but the whole place, in spite of all the expansions in every direction, seemed much smaller than it was when we were there."

"And the castle? It is still there, yes?"

"Yes, of course. The castle ground is now a nice park, and in the castle's fat turret is an expensive restaurant we couldn't afford, but the old stairway's unchanged . . . I found yours and Kārlis's initials—shallow and faded. The Old Town Square is also cut up, with a highway weaving down below, skirting the vineyards, polluting, making noise. It was sad being there all alone with no one to share the memories."

"And the clock?" Milda wanted to know.

"Still ticking. I went inside the Rathaus. To the toilet. I saw that huge clock wheel turning, turning as it did then . . . I felt on that day like my young self, looking into the future I had lived through. It was all so strange, so hallucinating . . . I don't know if you know that I've been to Latvia several times," Helga said.

"Really! No, I didn't know. It wasn't in *Avīze.* How did you do it?"

Helga told her about the procedures and the help she received from the Connection's Agency. "I did not go back to any memories because, as you probably know, Kurzeme is off limits. I went to Riga and saw it for the first time. No, the second. Father took me there once. So my homecoming did not hurt the way it would hurt you. Still, I think you should go back. It will be easier for you."

"We better not discuss this," Milda said coldly, stopping in their walk, disengaging their arms. "Perhaps you don't know our policy of solidarity, which prohibits us to involve ourselves with communist Latvia."

"I do know it," said Helga, also now speaking with cool reserve. "But I don't agree with it. I make my own policies," she said. "After all, I am an American citizen."

"So am I," Milda said, "but in my heart and soul and my family I shall always be a Latvian!"

Helga thought Milda ought to be saying this from a podium. "Heart and soul, yes," Helga agreed. "But what about the mind? What about making one's own decisions? How can we explain ourselves to our children if we are afraid and still live in a past that is long gone?"

They walked on in silence until they came to an ice-cream parlor and stopped for a rest. Licking their cones, they continued their silent and separate evaluations of each other.

"Tell me about your children," Milda said, trying to bypass that very controversial, provocative issue about contacts with Latvia, which dominated many conversations and caused many rifts in and outside every Latvian center. Helga smiled with a sense of relief and began talking, telling Milda that she, in fact, had come to the festival to escape the emptiness of her house after her daughter's marriage to a fellow student. A handsome, exciting young man from Greece. "Right now they are on their way to Arizona."

"Oh," said Milda. "My son and family live in Phoenix." She confessed to her fears about Gatis rejecting all his upbringing and told how he had left the house and family in spite of all their efforts to raise him as a Latvian. "He broke his father's already ailing heart." Milda said and told more—also about the circumstances of Kārlis's death. "His last stand was for the ideals and rights of a free and independent Latvia."

Helga listened, full of sympathy, saying how she had liked and admired Kārlis in Esslingen, when he was leading the parades "with you at his side."

Milda smiled. "All that is gone forever, like our youth."

"Yes. So it is . . . We should take a trip together and visit our children, make new memories for ourselves and them," suggested Helga, gladly, easily. "It would be such fun."

But Milda sat up as though she were freezing. "I could not." In short sentences, she told about her one visit with her son's family, ending with, "I never felt as alone as I did then, there in that desert."

They eyed each other and understood that such a trip would be foolish and impossible. Playing with a napkin, Milda asked, "How can you accept it?"

"What?"

"Your daughter marrying a foreigner, your grandchildren automatically becoming Americans, not speaking our diminutive, loving words to you in your mother's tongue?"

Helga hesitated, shielding her sorrow and guilt, then answered in what reminded Milda of her (Helga's) mother's voice, "It's not easy. Different cultures create strange mixtures, but what choice do I have?"

Milda looked at her with critical eyes.

"If I reject," Helga said, "I would surely be rejected, and if I accept, I hope I'll be accepted, and then my life should be greatly enriched. Besides, I love them all and I want them to be happy. They are Americans, who are free to live and make their homes as they wish and choose." She paused, contemplating an unknown future that lay literally beyond the sunset where her precious firstborn was driving away with a stranger from another civilization, from Ancient Greece, driving away even from the world she had hardly learned to know and love. The distance hurt, she tried to explain. "And, therefore, I came here—to this synthetic illusion. I'll miss her very much," she said, "but there comes a time, without any real warning, when a mother has to realize that she belongs in the past tense. She is become a background to her children."

"Ah," Milda sighed.

"Only then there might be a future."

"Of unreal, quick little snatches."

"Yes. Whatever, however. Quality time, you know. So perhaps we could do it, the trip, I mean," Helga said cheerfully.

"Well, who knows? Things do get in the way, but perhaps someday." Milda kept twisting her napkin, not knowing how to get away, how not to be linked with Helga for the rest of the festival. "I haven't seen the Grand Canyon yet, nor the Petrified Forest, or the desert in bloom," she said, "but now we should go."

They rose and left the ice-cream parlor.

"Being in the West is like being on a different planet," Milda said.

"All right, so much the better!" Helga seemed ready to fly. "Since we don't have our own country, let's at least inherit as much of the earth as possible. We do live in the space age, don't we?"

"Yes. So we do," Milda agreed, then turned to face her old friend. "By the way, will you be doing anything else here besides having a bit of reimmersion into our national consciousness?"

"Well, yes. I didn't tell you. I do some freelance writing and am always on the lookout for a good subject—interesting personality, situations, that sort of thing."

"I see."

"Talking about personalities," Helga went on. "I saw who I believe is Mr. Vanags, you remember him, don't you?"

Milda remained calm: "Yes, of course. I saw him also—at a distance. He is aged quite well, isn't he?"

"Yes, remarkably well. All studs and jeans and boots."

"What?" Milda broke out in cold sweat.

"Do you still keep in touch or has your fiery love burned out?"

"What are you talking about?"

"Ah, don't pretend, please! We remember Esslingen, don't we? Even I could see that you were madly in love with the invalid. You tried to hide behind the mask of your engagement to wholesome Kārlis. Mother and Vizma also knew but would not let on. So now, what's going on? Has he come to claim you, all dressed up and ready to sweep you away, like some John Wayne in a Western?"

Milda's face flushed in angry flames. "I don't know what you're talking about!" She checked the time on her watch and said that she was tired, needed a nap before the afternoon performance of *Homo Novus.* Helga took the hint and dropped the subject, saying, "I could also use a little shut-eye. The musical will be long, as we might expect."

"So you're going?"

"Yes. Maybe I'll see you there."

Homo Novus

The new musical about the *New Man* was composed especially for this festival and was premiered at the plush Pabst Theater. The story was about a new, modern, Parisian kind of Latvian man, a dandy of the booming, jazzy thirties. Milda had been too little to appreciate the period in a truly free Latvia, but she knew that it was the happiest decade in her parents' generation's lives and was much romanticized, especially in exile literature and music.

Sitting in an expensive orchestra seat, Milda waited for the curtain to rise. She was glad to be alone and away from Helga's overly familiar questions and disturbing assertions. As the lights dimmed, she looked all around, but did not see her, nor Pēteris Vanags. But Helga, who sat high in the highest balcony, near the rafters, saw her and wondered why she seemed upset and nervous. Not being really a part of the community, she could not understand why the issue about contacts with Latvia was such a firecracker. It seemed to her that people would be happy that the walls were falling, that Latvia was not dead and buried. So what was the matter? She looked down at the people, her condensed nation, from which she felt separated, yet to which she was bound by invisible ties that could never be cut, not even after decades in America.

During the performance she forced herself to be a critical observer, because the composer had asked her to translate the libretto into English. After reading the script, she had refused, saying that some things were better left alone in their original languages and forms. She had made more excuses, saying that she was too busy, too bogged down, but thinking how, as with other requests for translations, there were no guarantees that her efforts, in spite of her and the creators' wishes, would be rewarded and the translations ever performed. She fanned herself with the program. It was hot, the seats small and tight. She was hardly able to cross her legs. *Too long*, she muttered as the play went on. The equally overheated people next to her nodded, wiping their brows.

When the performance was over, Helga caught up with Milda and walked along side, deep in her own thoughts and not saying much to the Ice Princess, who complained about being hot and thirsty. It was a hard walk back to the hotel, especially when you wore high heel shoes and nylon undergarments. "Next time things should be planned better . . ." Startling Helga, a man's hand fell on her shoulder.

"Ah, it's you!" she exclaimed, stopping for a hug. He was a young New York artist she had met in Riga on her last trip.

"So how did you like the show?"

"Too long. Three hours!" Helga said quietly, smiling familiarly at him. "How are you?"

"Great! Fine!"

"Oh, it's really good to see you!"

"I didn't think the show was too long," Milda joined in. "I liked the sets and music. It's how I imagine the Riga we lost. Yes, I loved it and could watch it all over again."

"Not if you had sat where I did, but seriously, Riga, especially the old town, is still like that," Helga said. "It still has that certain look you've seen in old books and postcards. It's such a charming, mysterious city—in spite of the system or because of our people—those who work and preserve, who live there."

"Right," said the artist, with his arm still around Helga's shoulders. "I fell in love with it at first sight, and I'm going back whenever I can. Exciting things are happening there—in life and art." He kissed Helga's cheek and remaining close to her, said, "Thanks for opening up things for me, for guiding me on my way home." She smiled, what seemed to Milda, an overly intimate smile. He winked, gave her hand a squeeze and was gone. On his shoulder hung a bulging bag full of metal buttons that said *Save Latvia's Children.* He was selling those buttons for $3. The money would go to Latvia's orphans.

"He is a saint," Helga remarked and tucked her hand in the crook of Milda's elbow.

"I wish I could see my Riga again," Milda said.

"You can—with a little bit of trouble. It's there, as he said, stirring and waiting, like the submerged princess in our legends."

"Oh, do we only have this one legend?" Milda brushed at the heat, forcing Helga's hand to drop down like an unwanted nuisance. "It seems that we're always waiting for some frog prince to pop up and hand us the golden ball, only to be dropped again into another deeper well."

"Yes, we are circle bound, aren't we?" Helga said, chilled by the tone of her friend's voice. She excused herself, saying that she had to hurry. Her brother and sister were here, and she wanted to find them. "See you at the Esslingen reunion!"

"Yes,"

Milda's feet, in spiked heel shoes, hurt, and her back ached. She was glad to see Helga, with her wealth of information and energy, hurry down the street away from the hotel. Meanwhile, the sun was sliding down, enflaming the city, blinding her vision.

*

Taped on Milda's hotel room's door, was a message from Ilga, requesting Zelda's letter. *What for*? Milda wondered upset. She recalled her daughter's excitement the day that letter had invaded their quiet house. She could still hear Ilga's dramatic breathing as she clamped the sheets of rough paper close to her heart, exhaling, "Intense . . . My roots."

Yes, those ever-protruding roots! Milda kicked off her shoes and pulled off her sweaty clothes and took a nice, cool shower. Refreshed and glad to be alone, she settled in the bed against propped up pillows and took up her sister's expansive letter she had brought with her, not exactly knowing why. She examined it, envying the neatly slanted handwriting with the right pressure on the down strokes, the perfect loops. She used to make similar strokes and loops when she was in elementary school, where penmanship was stressed, for a person's handwriting—so the teacher assured—revealed much about one's character. Zelda's writing had been stronger, bolder than hers, and Mother had scolded Zelda for using too much ink: "You are wasteful. Why can't you write nicely like your sister?" But *Mildiņa* had not written nicely to save ink but because she was afraid to press her pen down. She was afraid the paper would tear and the teacher would look down on her and scold her, humiliating her before her classmates. She was also afraid of ink splatters, of ink running down a clean white page.

She studied the calligraphy of the old school and compared it to her own scribbling. She saw how the war had ruined her handwriting as it had ruined most everything else. She thought about all the schools that had tried to educate her, all the various pens and pencils her hand had pushed, as it were, across, over, and through three countries, languages, cultures. She saw the incompatibilities, contradictions, and irregularities and how she had tried to keep things pure and right but couldn't. She examined her low-crossed t's, the dots thrown here and there, and how there was no distinction between the up and down strokes.

"Low self-image," Aria had remarked, as she watched Milda sign a check. "I used to write like that, but now I'm trying to change. I cross my t's high and strong. I'm raising my self-esteem."

"I see, and you're doing an overly good job," Ausma cut in teasingly.

"Well, as our proverb goes, if a dog does not raise his own tail, no one will do it for him."

They giggled.

"Yes, we have enough proverbs on which to rest all our cases," Aria said, and then they had parted, as friends do, with quick fluttering of fingers and *see you soon*!

Milda blamed the pencils and ballpoints for her crippled handwriting, but she would not even think of regressing to a dip pen. She would not want ink-stained fingers ever again. Zelda clearly wrote with a dip pen, perhaps the same she had ages ago . . . *Time has stopped in Zelda's handwriting, while in mine it travels on and on . . . Yes, clearly our characters are different. Fate rules . . .* She shuffled the tightly written pages, trying to picture the kitchen table and the lamp by which her sister had written—a whole night long—dipping into her heart with the sharp points of Truth and splattering the coarse paper with her tears. Milda made herself comfortable and read the letter once again:

Zelda's Letter

My dearest, dearest sister, I cannot believe I am actually writing to you, nor that we're not two little girls, but two old women, older than Mammīte was when we separated. I still see you, so pretty and small, and I confess I am jealous of you, as I was then. I was so bad, so very bad at times, but God has forgiven all, and life has washed us clean of all our childish sins. I'm a slow writer, such a slow writer, and this pen is old, older than my hand maybe, so forgive me if you have trouble reading, and forgive the splashes my tears make as I write. I send you my tears also, tears of joy because I can write to you. I cannot describe everything—it would take volumes, so I'll try to concentrate on the main episodes, the sharp corners around which my life turned. I must write quickly so I can finish this in time for Mara to hide it in her suitcase. (What a beautiful girl Mara is! So smart, so confident!) But I digress, always digress.

Now, let's go back to October 1944, when we parted. We tried to get to Priekule, as agreed. It was October 8. (Always remember the dates, Mamma used to say.) Couldn't get through. Riga also was taken, the German soldiers told us, shouting, saying the front was only beyond the bend in the road. We could hear the shooting, and then it was evening and strange lights flashed on and off in the western sky. The Germans told us that Liepāja was being bombed, and then we were afraid that you and Alma were dead. You were cut off. Everything was cut off, chopped up like a slaughtered pig, and I wished I hadn't won the checker game. I honestly wished I instead of you would be dead because you were such a pretty thing, like a crystal doll. I was a doll of clay, rough with smudges.

I cried and cried. It was like an electric storm—fire flashes on and off, on and off. My screams set Anna and Lilia crying. Aunt Matilde was a huge post at the gate; she was a stone-cast monument in the cruel night sky. Then Uncle Imants shouted, "Get to work! We must get out!"

So we started packing, throwing things in sacks. The next morning, we were on the road. Along the way some soldiers helped us get through, but they all looked like they had already lost the war and would be dead by evening. When we came out of the woods, there was fighting right in front of us. I saw men lined up on their stomachs with guns pointing into a muddy ridge, and I asked, "Is that how war looks?"

"Yes. Be quiet and keep your heads down," Imants shouted and drove on, onto the highway, which was full of soldiers, tanks, trucks and lines of people fleeing, trying to get out of what we later learned was the Boiling Pot of Kurzeme, the last battles of the Eastern Front. Uncle, sharp and quick-witted as he was, turned off the highway and drove down a cart road. The horses went mad, Bēris jumping and pulling the wrong way the whole time, Mira scolding him, biting his face. (Mothers are all the same, no?) Airplanes rode low, dropping bombs right on the highway which we had left minutes ago. Uncle steered the horses toward a line of scrubs, where a river or creek would be. We bailed out. The wagon wheel rode over Anna's arm, but it was muddy so it did not break. We flattened ourselves inside the muddy embankment until the bombardment stopped. All was suddenly deathly still. As we looked over the edge, we saw tanks burning on the highway and bodies lying all over. Our horses were gone.

"Come!" Uncle pulled me up. "The rest of you stay here. Understand?"

Uncle and I followed the creek backwards, towards home, and there, after some hours, we saw our horses grazing in a meadow.

"Ah, they smelled familiar ground. Over there, see, at the edge of that forest is the house where I was born; here is where I grew up. I

used to skate on this river. The river knows me." he said and taking off his hat, kneeled down, pulling me down with him. He praised the Lord in a loud voice. And then the horses came up, trembling and submissive, and we rode them to the wagon.

Along the way we came across old Millers, our neighbor. He walked like some cast-off saint with a big stick in his hand. His thin white hair blew in the wind and his coat flopped like useless wings. He, too, had tried to escape but everything had blown up. His cart full of apples (He had prize orchards, you remember or no?) exploded. Turned into applesauce, ha, ha! His wife, poor woman, was killed. Uncle lifted him on to Mira and me on Bēris with him. The horses were excited and scared. They galloped through the meadow like the horses of fire in the Book of Revelation until they stopped at our wagon.

Matilde had made a fire and cooked some food. We ate and were ready to move on, not knowing what to do with old Millers, who looked at us with weeping eyes, then turned around and walked away, back to his smashed wagon and dead wife and to his death, as I found out later.

But we traveled on, towards the Lithuanian border, which was not far away. But as we approached the Sventaja River, we saw that the bridge swarmed with refugees; there were German tanks on the other side, while a new fleet of Russian airplanes circled above us. And then there was a dreadful BANG *like the end of the world, and the bridge blew up; it rose straight in the air and then fell down into the water. The water turned red from the blood, fire, and sunset. The whole earth and sky burned.*

Later, out of that hell came men with red stars in their caps and on their lapels, some spoke Latvian. (Oh, yes, there were plenty turncoats who helped Stalin!) They made a wall through which no one could escape. One man unharnessed Bēris, others plundered our wagon. Mira stood on three legs, unbalanced, lopsided, with horse tears running down her horse cheeks, her ears pinned back. Anna screamed so loud that she had to be tied with a rope, while I sank down against what straw was left and held her screaming hands. Aunt Matilde pulled Lilia close to herself and waited. Her face was fire and ice, her scarf a fallen halo, the fringes blowing in the wind. She lifted her face to heaven and prayed to God, who probably did not hear her. How could He? There was a war on His earth.

Soon another flock of firebirds dropped their deadly eggs in the nestling valley. I saw men and horses falling like bugs with feet and hands flying through the air. Then quiet. A pause, an intermission. Then Uncle Imants, his face statue-still, turned Mira around. We breathed easier; we even talked, "Look . . . see . . . what's this . . . and that . . ." Mira trotted home, back through the woods and the valleys she knew by heart. She seemed happy because she smelled her barn. And we, too, stretched our necks, looking for home.

In the twilight of that doomsday, we saw the house still standing, guarded by the bright autumn trees. "God has ruled," Aunt Matilde said. Imants took off his hat and said amen. Then we rode through the linden alley, aware that now Russian, not German soldiers watched us, squatting along the ditches. "We are occupied," I whispered.

"Keep your mouth shut!" Uncle hissed.

The next morning they threw the bodies of the fallen in trenches and covered them with earth. Our fields were littered with corpses of uniformed men—Russians and Germans—and we were not allowed to go outside until they were taken away. Afterwards, the fields looked as if giant moles had dug them up. It was not until spring that Uncle dared to put the plough to them.

That is how it was on that day, and how it was later, you can read in history books. The occupiers shouted over the radio and pasted signs on buildings that they had liberated us from the Fascists, but everyone knew that we were also liberated from freedom and everything we held dear. In school, our teacher said that the Princess was locked up in a glass casket and set on top of a glass mountain, waiting for the Prince to kiss her. Ah, yes . . . That waiting! That kiss! What does it all mean?

Meanwhile, in Riga, our poor Mamma, confronted once again with the Red enemy, broke down completely. The Russian woman who lived in our apartment had her put in the insane asylum, and there she perished. I never found out exactly when and how. It was the end of October when Pasha brought us the news. Matilde paid her with a link of sausage and sent her back to Riga. I cried horribly against Aunt's heart, and she cried too, but Anna only stared and said, "All the sisters are broken in pieces."

I stayed on the farm. And so for the next five years, even though life was very hard and the war had destroyed the land, we lived peacefully, working like slaves to fill all the norms Moscow demanded. Everyone assumed that, even though Stalin's name was feared more than the devil's, the worst was over. The war was being pushed off our fields and out of our lives. On March 19, 1948, as you may or may not know, Aunt Matilde gave birth to a baby boy. They named him Benjamiņš, and he was beautiful, the joy of our lives. With that new life, new hope for peace and better times returned. Even Anna was normal again, taking care of the baby, being a real help to her mother. Lilia was a strong girl too, now 9. So everyone was hopeful, optimistic, as the slogans told us to be. We began to believe and trust, but we were deceived. *On Good Friday—it was March 23, 1949—the sun fell out of the sky, and again darkness covered our earth.*

All Latvia trembled. The whole district of Kurzeme was combed for partisans and any anyone who helped them. Those farms that had not been included in the kolkhoz years before now were forced to join. The farmers were again weeded out of their land, and (we found out later) 90,000—including women, children, old people were deported to the gulags in Siberia. The red sickle cut off one neighbor after another. The whole land screamed and burned. Red terror spread like flood waters, deep and wide, and there was no place to hide, nowhere to escape. An Iron Curtain was all around us. We heard that on the English radio station, which was always full of static.

On that day—yes, it was Good Friday—a truck drove into the yard, and we knew the end had come. They tied Uncle's hands behind his back and pushed him into the truck full of men, even our neighbors. Uncle cursed screaming, "You, devil's henchmen, destroy the land and you will destroy your parasite guts! One day you will starve, you men of evil! Thieves and deceivers! The time will come when you will fall into the traps you set for others! God shall not be mocked!" But they kicked him while the rest of us howled. After the truck was out of sight, the militia ordered us to be ready within an hour. "We will be back," a yellow-faced man shouted.

We became a sinking island. Quickly and with shaking hands, Aunt Matilde sewed slices of dried bread in the hems of our dresses and stuffed dry fruit into the linings of our coats. She made small bundles of extra clothes, and then she combed our hair and washed our faces, her hands sliding over our skins, her tears falling.

"They're coming!" Anna screamed. Sure enough. We saw them driving towards us as if they were invited. They drove through the alley. Still bare, the trees looked like gigantic, mute, bewitched guards that could not protect us from the onslaught of Evil. Aunt picked up her sleeping baby, changed his diapers, and wrapped him in warm blankets. Holding hands, we walked out of the house. The militia men shoved us with their whips and guns, but Matilde turned and said, "You don't have to do that. We know how to climb wagons."

They drove us to Priekule, a distance away from the train station, and loaded us in a box car that smelled of pigs. In Riga they separated us: women to the right, children to the left. They tried to wrench the baby from Matilde's arms but she bit the hand that touched her and held on, saying you can kill us both now, but you will not take him away. We clung to her, but they pushed us away, and so poor dear Aunt Matilde went one way, holding on to her screaming baby, crying so that I cannot describe it, and we, the three girls, the other way. We were herded into a large schoolroom where other girls already squalled. Women in uniform hit those who cried with long whips and threatened the rest of us, cracking the whips over our heads, popping them like dull gunshots.

I tried to keep Anna and Lilia from screaming, I don't know how. I played with Lilia, trying to distract her, but she was no longer a baby and knew what was happening. She cried silently in her pillow and prayed to Jesus. We were going to be in this crossover place for some days, so we made a little nest for ourselves, making a ridge with our bundles. In the daytime we had to do certain chores that I won't describe. In the evening I told stories, one after another, until all around me the girls quieted down, and the women with the whips moved to the other end of the room and smoked. Oh, that putrid smoke! To this day I hate smoking.

Anyway, I kept telling the girls that if they were good they would see their mothers soon. But that was a lie; I did not believe it, and I was right. The mothers were gone forever. Terrible things happened all around us. The days had no shape, or color; the sky was a slit in the high window, sometimes blue, sometimes gray, and dark at night. And then one warm day, we were put into cattle wagons with bare bunks and a bucket in one corner for our poop and shipped off to Siberia. The trip lasted longer than a month, with long stops in the middle of nowhere. We gnawed on the dry bread until it was gone, and then we starved. Many died, the very old and the very young at first, but later also the bigger girls. I feared for our deaths, but we pulled through. We reached Krasnoyarsk and then were put on a boat and sent up the Yenisei River to Igarka, beyond the Polar Circle. It was a long, cold terrible voyage. Many did not reach the end. They put us in a barrack that had holes in the walls, where the wind blew through.

That is how thousands of our people were tortured. The trains were very long, long hanging ropes, not only for us, but people from other nations the Red sickle and hammer scathed. Few lived through it, I among them. Sometimes I wondered if it was a blessing or a curse to live; now I know. I was blessed, blessed and chosen. Don't ask me why. Like you. You, too, were blessed and chosen.

What happened to Uncle Imants, Aunt Matilde and the baby, I don't know. I have tried to find out, but no one tells us anything. They all died, that I know. Their names are not on any lists living or dead.

Lilia died within the year. She died of diphtheria late in the night on Christmas Eve morning. Earlier we had a quiet celebration. Someone very brave brought a small fir into our barrack, and we put a candle on top. A kind Siberian woman had baked cookies and brought them to us at great risk. I kissed her hand, and she said God bless you . . . We sang songs, quietly and in the dark, because that night we were watched with Herod's eyes. I had made little animals out of scraps of paper for Lilia and the other children so there would be presents, and we all played some games. We were warm and happy for as long as the big star shone in our window. But suddenly Lilia became sick. She burned with fever and choked as she tried to breathe. I took her and wrapped her in a blanket and running carried her to the hospital, if it can be called that. She hadn't grown at all and had been sickly, getting thinner all the time, her stomach bulging, like so many children's.

As I ran, she became stiff and very heavy. It was such bitter, bitter cold—the stars were gold drops of ice—but I ran, sliding and falling. The nurse was kind; she put her under steam and I thought she was better. Her breathing seemed easier. She smiled at me and clutched her thin arms around my neck. But it was only a pause. The White Angel already held her hand, and I rocked her quietly singing a lullaby, and then she gasped, turned blue, and died.

On Christmas day we buried her in the snow under a pine tree. I made a casket out of pine branches so the snow would not hit her face. My tears froze on my cheeks as I scratched the snow over her, all the while telling myself that the White Angel has carried her soul like a precious jewel to heaven and laid it at God's feet for a Christmas present.

I returned to our empty corner and there I cried my soul dry. After that I felt calm. No one close to me would suffer and die anymore. I was at last free from fear because I was not afraid of the White Angel. I slept much better, and I was busy all day. The nurse liked me and asked the authorities to let me work with her. I don't remember much about the years I worked in the hospital. They were all white and smelled of ether. Many children died in my arms, but I did not get sick. I was immune. Frozen. With each death I turned into a larger icicle. I was almost glad for every death that brought suffering to an end. Still, I prayed every night. I even prayed for you . . . I prayed that I would see you again. As long as I had not heard of your death, I believed you lived. And how right I was! Am I not writing you a letter right now? Letters are sent to the living, not the dead.

They sent Anna to some other place far away. It was right at the beginning. She, poor thing, lost her mind. She was always hysterical, always trying to escape by chewing the wires. She was wild and dangerous, hitting and smashing things and everyone in her way, as the mood struck her. She died at the end of summer, like all flowers. When I found out, Lilia and I cried terribly, but then I left it all in God's hands. The poor girl was so unhappy long before then—well, since you were there, when the Blums' children were killed—that God took pity on her and pulled her to Himself.

After the world's worst tyrant Stalin's death in 1953, I and a few others were set free. But it was not until the end of March 1954, after I had saved enough money for my ticket (yes, I was paid a meager allowance for working in the hospital), that some of us boarded a train marked "Riga." What struck me was that there actually were trains going to Riga! That there still was a city named Riga, with streets and houses and people! And the other thing that surprised me was that we met trains full of people going to where we came from. The sight was dreadful, like looking death in the face. Our ride home was long, months long. All of us were sick, weak from years of torment, but we were riding back to life. That was the important thing. Our hearts actually beat inside us, and they beat with wings when we crossed Latvia's border.

Once in Riga, I asked them to put me on the kolkhoz in Mazgramzda. I still remembered the names of supervisors and told them that I had been a milkmaid. They approved my request, so I was glad. I did not want to live in Riga. I feared Mamma's ghost and the faces of occupiers. I did not want to hear Mamma crying in the night.

It was early April when I got off at the same familiar train station in Priekule. I was 21, and the earth called me, and so I went, not to any kolkhoz, but back to Uncle's farm. I knew that only the country air could heal me, and if it wouldn't, I thought, I'd rather die lying on the ground than in a rat cellar in Riga.

I'll never forget that drab spring day I walked home. I saw no living man. I had shoes with holes, but I trudged on carrying in my bundle all I owned. I saw the empty farms, the granaries gaped open, burned out. No animals in the fields. Nothing.

After the 7km walk, I came to our alley. The trees seemed monstrous, forming a tunnel of mesh. But at the end was our house. (Listen to how I say "our"! But it was mine! It was now my only home on earth!) I walked to the house. It was half-burned and behind it the winter branches of apple trees switched the gray sky. I's afraid that some stranger'd come out and I'd be homeless again, so I stood a while at the edge of the yard, trembling. I saw the broken rope of the swing still dangling from the old birch tree.

The sun was near setting, the air misty, but the trees swarmed full of starlings, and they chirped and sang me—I thought—a welcoming song. Then from somewhere under the barn came a gray striped cat with three kittens. I bent down and stroked her. She purred, and my heart melted. The stored-up tears flowed and flowed. I thought I was going to drown in them.

"We have to build it all up again," I said aloud, stroking the cat and the kittens so hard that I think I hurt them, because all at once they scampered away, except for one white one with a black nose. I picked him up and held him very close to my heart.

I took a deep breath and walked into the house. The door was not locked. Matilde hadn't bothered . . . I stepped into the kitchen. I saw that only the front half of the house was burned out; I could see that the bedroom side was all right. The fire had stopped at the threshold. The kitchen nook was all charred like the inside of a chimney, but the tea pot from which Matilde had poured tea five years ago, while we waited for them to come, was still on the stone stove. I didn't dare stir anything because all was black with soot and covered with layers of dirt. I just stood in the middle of the ashes, holding on to the kitten. Then I knocked on the bedroom door 'cause I heard some strange noises on the other side. I waited, my knees shaking with fear. But no one called out, no one opened the door, so I pulled it open and out flew a flock of pigeons. They flew past me, grazing me with their wings. But there was nothing else. No human or dog. Nothing.

I stepped inside. There was the brass bed frame with a dirty mattress and bedclothes lying on the side. There was the dresser and mirror, all covered with dust, and the chest of drawers.

Oh, dearest sister! The sight pierced my heart with daggers. Again that horrible bad Friday stood there before me. No one had shut the drawers. They hung open with rotten clothes spilled and trampled in the dirt. And there, in the dirt, was Benjamiņš's white, rabbit fur cap half-pressed into the floor. It must have slipped out of Matilde's hands. I pulled it out of the dirt and held it. Poor, poor baby! His little golden head must have been cold the whole time in Siberia. Oh, poor, poor child, I cried. Poor, poor everyone! The children cried and screamed inside my head. Dear little Lilia . . . She stopped smiling and laughing once we were put on the death train, while Anna cried the whole time. Whenever the train stopped, she tried to run away. The guards had to tie her down. It was so horrible, so awful. I was afraid of her, afraid she would hurt Lilia. We were all so hungry, so starved and thirsty . . . Why? Why did they do this to us? What had we done? What crime had we committed that we had to be so mercilessly punished?

I was shaking all over again, and I fell to the cold floor and cried, howled, like a mad bitch. The kitten fell from my lap and ran off meowing. Then I was left all alone. I fell on the bed crying until sleep took mercy on me. At times, in utter darkness, I woke up calling on the Blue Angel of hope to protect me. (While in Siberia, I had invented angels of different colors!) And he did, for I slept well, resting on the wings of hope until the bedbugs found me. They crawled all over, eating me alive. Still, I slept on. I merely scratched the pests away, murmuring, "I'll kill you in the morning." But my sleep was full of holes and strange dreams. The grating empty darkness of the house and land kicked and stirred inside me like an unborn child, and I called to God out of the dirt and ashes, like Job.

I woke up to a beautiful spring day. The skies were full of white lace clouds. The skylarks carried their tunes to heavens. I tried to remember the names of other birds. I had not seen them for so long. Our little country, I thought, is so rich and noisy, full of all kinds of life, not silent like the Garden of Ice.

I was hungry, like in Siberia, and again the tears came, but I got up and started cleaning, scraping, talking to myself and howling dry-throated until my guts turned raw. I went outside because a rattling noise startled me, and there, I'm sure, was our old stork repairing his broken-down nest, the wagon wheel Uncle had put on top of the barn so many years ago—in another age. Soon the stork flew past me rattling louder, on his way back he swooped down and walked up to me cautiously, curiously. He stood there for a minute looking at me with one eye and then the other.

I said, "Labrīt!" I laughed. He was so comical! He actually bowed, the gentleman, and then he, rattling in quite a different tone, flew away. Back to work. And I, too, turned and went to work. I had so much to repair.

I found some twigs and started a fire by rubbing two rocks. It was fascinating. There really was fire inside those stones, just sleeping there, waiting to be drawn out. I rubbed harder, feeling a strange power as the first sparks jumped up.

I rubbed furiously, laughing, and behold, there was the flame! God's spirit coming down to earth. I would live! I carried the flame inside and set it on top of the cold stove and fed it more twigs. Dry faggots lay against the stove. Carefully I added them to my flames and watched the sparks fly. Excited I built the fire so big that it would burn for a long time. I went out. *The sun shone in patches of melting snow and thawing mud. I looked down into the well. The dark water reflected pale light, and I hooked a rusty bucket on the iron hook and sank it down into the well. The water was high, and the bucket filled easily. Laughing crazily, I pulled it out and took it into the house and filled the kettle. In a dark corner on a peg I found dried herbs and made tea and drank it. With its warmth, strange joy flooded my being.*

The earth had given me the water of life and I drank it! Again I went out and explored the nooks of the root cellar. I found some potatoes with long, white sprouts, and I took them inside and cooked soup—stone soup, as in our fairy tales. I gulped it down at one sitting.

Oh, sister, thin and saltless as my brew was, it was still mine! I was not swallowing the slop from exile's kitchens. I almost felt rich: I had fire and water! Were not those the elements God used when he created the world? And I praised Him saying, "Thanks be to God, who restores all things and who has crowned me with loving kindness. Even though I walk through the valley of the shadow of death, I fear no evil, for Thou art with me, my God and my Savior. Amen."

Are you surprised that I prayed? You remember how I hated to go to church. I hated the cold gray walls of the Dome. I could never imagine that God would live in such a place, nor that He would ever visit it on Sunday mornings, or even at Christmas and Easter to listen to people who only went there on those days, all dressed up, like Mamma.

I think about that huge stained glass window. I did not like it then, and I hate it now: that window pictures our misfortunes, the trading of our people into slavery. Whoever cut the glass and formed the images made it look like it was a pretty thing, with the sun shining through it. But the sunlight also made the priest's robe blacker and the pain of the peasant cheated out of his land more glaring. I remember telling Mamma I did not like that picture, and she told me it was art and that I did not understand anything. I had no sense of culture, she said. You told her—remember?—that you liked it, and I was jealous because Mamma smiled at you.

But—I get off the track again. I started telling you about my faith or religion. I'll go on, if you allow me, because my heart tells me to.

So even when I was little, I could not imagine God anywhere but out-of-doors. Strangely, I could imagine Him in Siberia. Oh, how glad I was that I had learned to believe in God and the power of His salvation through Jesus Christ, our Lord! I was glad Uncle and Aunt had been brave enough to take us to their little church, the one you, too, said you liked. You remember! You know, of course, that it was against the law to go to church once the Communists took power, and Sunday school was out of the question, but the Baptists took turns holding meetings anyway. Like the early Christians, they gathered in catacombs—cellars, graveyards, barns. Oh, how scary those gatherings were! Sometimes in the middle of the night, sometimes at noon when the cows rested. Uncle Imants built a cave out of sheaves of straw, and we would sing songs inside the gold. There he read Bible stories. Always about hard times that worked together for good: the Apostle Paul in prison, Joseph in Egypt, Daniel in the lions' den. He preached, telling us how God tested those He loved best, how suffering brought endurance. "We are living in hard times," he would emphasize, "but they will pass." Then he'd pray, crying so he could not talk, and then everyone would cry and say amen.

In Siberia I remembered all that and what he said, and my faith kept me strong, so strong I gave it to others, without saying any Bible words. I suppose the light of my soul shined so that others could feel God's warmth and His love, though so many prayers went unanswered. Still, I had no trouble imagining God there with us in the snow and ice.

That land of ice and snow, I imagined, was His winter garden. I used to tell Lilia at night before we went off to sleep that we were the lost children of Cain, who went out into the world with a mark on his forehead because he was very bad. I told her that we were punished because Adam and Eve and their son Cain had been very bad, and I told her that we should, therefore, be very, very good so that our children would not be punished and sent to this icy garden. I told her that if we should die in God's winter garden, a white angel would take us to heaven and God would put us right next to a star and we would be very, very warm, and we would sing songs with the angels all the time. We would even play harps. And then we prayed and went to sleep. So it was every night. Except sometimes I would lie awake thinking about how unfair all was, how it was unfair that people should suffer for what they had not done and how others never suffered for what they did.

I would think about us all as I looked through the small glass of the prison window and see the clear cold stars up there shining in a dark blue sky. But I did not think black thoughts about God. My thoughts about God were warm and pure. Many condemned prayed. Some prayed for death, but I prayed for life. I imagined Aunt Matilde's sighs and prayers like white wings flying up to the throne of God, cutting through the ice and snow. I imagined God thawing our prayers with His breath and warming the souls of all those who died in His winter garden.

But back to the farm!

Days went by. I worked from sunrise to sunset. After days of severe hunger, I dared to walk to the kolkhoz for food. The key keeper didn't report me. She remembered our family and gave me what she could, and then I was sitting on a green branch. It looked like God always sent His angels my way. I don't know why I was His chosen handmaiden. But you'll see how all things did work out for the good of me and you. I could write a whole book about it, but the night is too short.

So I must hurry and tell you about my two men, my good husbands, how it all happened because I don't want you to judge me badly. I hear that in America people think differently, the way the old church people thought, back in the dark ages. But perhaps I'm wrong. Life shapes thought, and my life is not like yours. Perhaps if I were you I'd judge you, I don't know, I want you to understand, love and respect me. I'll set down everything as best I can. So, here it is:

One day, about a month after my return, in the middle of May, while I was in the fields looking for last year's roots, a car stopped on the road and two men got out. I was naturally startled, surprised in my muddy boots, because the whole time I had been back, no one had stopped at the house. Only rarely an auto drove past on the highway. I cannot remember hearing a cow moo, a rooster crow, or a tractor churn. So you can imagine how surprised I was to see not one but two human beings in front of me, as if they had stepped straight out of the sun. They looked, with the rising sun behind them, very large and very stern, such as I had imagined the sons of God who in the days of old came down from heaven to marry the maidens of earth.

I trembled because I thought they would put me in the car and take me away. Deport me again. Ship me away from these empty fields, the charred house. But one of them only asked me for my name and wanted to know where my parents were. I told them they were dead. The men looked at each other. I looked at them. I was afraid they would ask me for more details, but they didn't. What was there to ask? Everyone knew what had happened in our land and to our people. No one said the word Siberia either. It's like it used to be by us about not mentioning the name of the devil, remember? "Call the devil, the devil comes." So we never said Siberia. Never.

"You're twins," I said, staring at one and then the other. Strange reflections, a double blessing or curse?

"What's it to you?" one of them growled, while the other looked me over from head to foot as if I were crossing a border and had handed him my passport. At last he asked me why I was alone. I told him because I am alone.

"It is not my fault I am alone," I said, looking him straight in the eyes. His eyes were clear, while the others' were bloodshot, but I didn't flinch. I did not say the S-word either. I only said, "They died in the place whose name is that word."

"And you still live in the house?" the bloodshot one asked and wrote something in his book.

"Again," I corrected him. "I live again in the part that is not burned out."

"Take us there," he said. So, of course, I turned and we walked toward the house. I walked ahead of them. We had about a kilometer to go. The fear of being deported had gone out of me, and a new fear

took its place. As I walked, I felt my legs go weak. I heard the men talking, hissing to each other and laughing, cracking jokes. And then the bloodshot one shouted in a tense, angry voice, "Faster!"

I obeyed. I half ran, but I did not stumble. I would not fall, I said to myself. And I would not cry. I would not show them my fear. I felt their eyes on my back. I was aware of the way my back moved, their eyes stripping it naked. I knew what they wanted because I wanted it too. They tailed me, their shadows over and in front of me, stretching across the fields, covering my thin dark line. I imagined their faces on the shadows and kept on running. The shadows also ran. The shadows were nice, I thought, well-built, handsome. They were not dirty or brutal or repulsive, except for the bloodshot eyes. The other man's eyes were blue and soft. Both had dark blond hair, unevenly cut with dull scissors. Both were prematurely gaunt, nervous, as if waiting for something to blow up.

As I ran, I wondered if these brothers were orphans like I, with no place to go, no place to call home. I wondered if they had been fighting with the Reds or the Nazis or burrowing underground with the partisans. Or—perhaps, been on opposite sides, like Atis and Juris, aiming at each other. But one thing I did know: I knew they would be hungry. And so, running faster, I tried to think of something I could feed them. Their shadows stretched farther over mine until all three became one, and I felt cold and hot inside the eclipse.

"Faster!" the blood voice shouted. I slowed down. I could have tripped them, but they also slowed down. We had reached the courtyard and were entering the old orchard, our uncle's pride. At the instant I felt them take in the whole setting. The orchard became my pride also. I had hoed around each tree and trimmed out the dead wood. As if rinsed with spring water, my eyes saw the branches and twigs full of sprouting buds. Light green daggers pushed through every crust. Even the oldest, gnarled apple tree was getting ready. Pink buds everywhere!

The promise of loveliness and fruit filled me with such joy that tears rose to my eyes, but I wiped them away. I did not look at the men. I had not turned my face to them the whole time. I only saw their shadows, now over the apple tree, and I felt their breathing. They were out of breath! I was not.

A pair of redbreasts was building a nest in a crook up high. The mother cat nursed her kittens in a sunny spot next to the barn, their tiny paws kneading her stomach as she lay with her eyes closed—happy, so content! She did not even turn her head to look at us people, she had her duties and we had ours. We understood each other.

"Go in!" the blood-eyed ordered, and I went to the front door and opened it. We stepped over the threshold.

"Not bad," said blue eyes. I was very proud that my corner was neat and clean. I never would leave the house without making my bed, nor the table without a clean cloth and a vase of flowers. I had not become sloppy. They had not done that to me!

The morning sun shone brightly through the old lace curtains. We stood in ripples of gold. Perhaps you wonder where I got the lace and things. Well, you certainly remember Mamma's trunk that she sent to the farm to hide until good times would return. It was hidden in the attic, and I brought it down. I found our parlor curtains and hung them up. I resewed Mamma's dresses, so that many times I looked more like a baroness—or like Aunt Alma onstage—than a lone farm girl. I liked feeling good and looking pretty, it was a way of keeping despair away. And I was pretty then, God forgive my boasting. Oh, how I blessed poor Mamma every time I opened the wooden lid of the large trunk! I could not have folded a better dowry had I kept myself at the loom throughout my ice age.

So we are in the room, in a pool of sunshine, and I fix my eyes on the purple cushion of violets that bloom in the middle of the table, filling the room with sweetness. I excuse myself and go behind the wardrobe door and change clothes. I put on a blue dress and pull the hairpins out of my braid I had coiled around my head. I know what the men see when I step out from behind the door. It's a woman they see, and I see—men. No man had looked at a woman and no woman had looked at man like that, not since the destruction of our world, not since our ancestors looked at each other after the plague. But now we stand on the morning of a new world and we see each other. A triangle. Oh, dearest Mildiņa, I don't know how to say it all! Time has dusted that day with embarrassment.

But then I smiled invitingly at one, then the other and asked them if they would like something to eat. I heard that my voice was soft, low. They looked at me and at each other. I offered them water from the well, and they drank from the same cup. Their eyes danced and burned, the bloodshot eyes glowing like coals. They stared at me, and I thought they looked like the bullock when Aunt Matilde took our heifer to him.

The men searched the cupboard, and the one with the red eyes grabbed a chunk of my unleavened bread, squeezed it and devoured it. The other only drank water. I told them that there was rabbit meat in the bowl, but they did not hear me. Instead, they glared at each other as if caught in a duel, as if tossing dice, and then one of them, the red-eyed, who no doubt was the oldest, moved towards me. I backed away until I stood pressed against the bed. The other didn't flinch. He only let his eyes slide over me, behind his brother's humped back, just as I felt the aggressor's heavy breathing against my face. Well, you can imagine—or can't—what happened next. I don't have to describe it, don't have to shout it from the rooftops for the whole world to hear.

I covered my face and screamed, but the other put his hand over my mouth. "Don't cry, beautiful," he whispered. "You would not want to go there, meitiņ, would you?" But there was no threat in his voice, only sudden, hot desire.

I tried to hide inside the sheets, but we were lying on top of them, and then again I felt the thrusts and the penetrations all through my virgin frame, while hands slid over my aching and burning body, never before touched by any man. Tears flowed down my cheeks, and cries came out of my lips. The second man stroked my head and put it against his heart, his hands strong but gentle, his lips kissing my mouth, and my hungry mouth kissing him. My whole body was like my earth, drawing in the rain and the rays of the burning sun, and there was no escape, for my wildly flowing blood drove me forward until we became one body and soul.

I felt as though I had stepped on grenades. Split into many parts. I did not know whose hair my hands pulled and whose lips my lips kissed because my eyes were closed. Aunt Matilde appeared to me, smiling, as she was when we took the heifer to the bullock, when for the first time I had seen the dreadful, horrible excitement of life springing forth! Oh, it was all so mysterious, so holy in its wildness! (Shivers run through me even as I write, forgive me.) And I remembered how Matilde's face turned red because I had seen it all and how, sweating, not looking at me, we hurried home, leading the silent heifer by the leash. The animal did not guess—or maybe she did—that the calf had already begun inside her.

So it was with me, so it must have been planned. Our twin girls—Jana and Zane—were born on February 14, on St. Valentine's day, in the morning. Oh, the birth was long and hard, the punishment for my pleasure. I labored day and night. I heaved, screamed, laughed. The midwife grinned savagely, as if she enjoyed my pains and said, "You should have cried then, not now." I answered her with one loud scream, and coming to my defense, the girls came out of me—first Zane, then Jana—with their strong, loud cries. Each weighed 4 kilos.

Two years later, came the boys: Jānis and Juris (March 16, 1958). And then I said to the men, "Please give me rest. I have given you your sons." Then I locked my bedroom door.

But how long could we hold out? Nature is stronger than a woman's will. Nature is a woman and wants man, and I wanted my two men next to me when the nights grew cold. I did not conceive for six years, but just when I fretted that God had punished us and made me barren, I woke up one morning in August and had to rush out to vomit.

Anna was born (it was a light, quick birth) on May 1, 1965. Everyone loved the sunny child, and now I had all the help I needed from her brothers and sisters, so it was not as hard as before, when I had no rest day or night. With Anna, I felt very good and was very happy. And why not? Our country was also blooming in different colors—the muted and bright colors of spring. People whispered that there was a thaw, that freedom was rising out of the ground like our wild, blue (blue means hope and longing) anemones.

Dainis was born on April 9, 1968. And then the Lord closed my womb. We three—our holy trinity—had done enough. We had given back to our nation the children that were ripped out of the land we now tilled. We told our children that the land was sacred, made rich over centuries with the blood of our people. We taught them early that it was our duty to love the land and to work with glad hands. And today, I can tell you that they are fine citizens who will one day raise our banner high and sing our songs so the world can hear them. Oh, I am getting flustered! So much to say, so much to reveal in one or two sittings. (I'm writing in the night, while the whole household sleeps.)

Still, I want to go back again to that first day and night, to our marriage without a preacher or judge. Just us three and the setting sun behind the lace curtains like a veil. For a moment, lying there, I cried out, "I am an animal!" for I was not ashamed, not at all ashamed. A great power was driving me on and on. I was Leda with the swans. I was Eve in paradise. I was our earth goddess Mara. I was chosen to bring life back to our raped earth and people. I am holy, I whispered with my next breath, lying there, between the two men, who had fallen asleep.

I was their cradle, their pillow, their comfort, for they murmured and smiled in their sleep.

We must have slept many hours, for when I opened my eyes, I saw the last rays of the sun cutting through the lace. I rose, bleeding and hurting with an awful pain. I wobbled out to the well and drew cold water and washed myself and put on a clean dress. I let the men lie on the soiled sheets—the proof of my purity—and went to prepare our evening meal. I made rabbit stew. (You should see me trap rabbits!)

When at last they woke up, we ate, the brothers praising the food, saying that they had forgotten how a real meal tasted. They seemed a bit ashamed, one saying that he will never hurt me again, the other looking down, not knowing what to do next, where to go from here. Then I rose up and said that we were now married, one in the sight of God, and that my home was now their home and that we would all be together forever. I made tea, and we relaxed and talked. I told them everything, and they me. It had happened with them as I had guessed, as it had happened with so many of us: their parents, good farmers, deported the same day as I with our uncle's family on March 23, 1949.

The brothers had been out in the woods and were saved. Later they escaped into the underground and lived like rabbits for some time until things calmed down. Then they joined the system. It was easier that way, they kept explaining, justifying themselves. "We had to live, had to eat, you understand," they kept saying, looking at me with sad dog eyes. I nodded. I understood. Young men are not made for burrowing; young men, especially our Latvian men, were made to walk in the sun and to till the land. I kissed them in turn, and for a long time we sat silently, our hands clasped in a tight chain, a link in our people's tragic history.

They were land surveyors and were staking out the land for a new kolkhoz. That's how they had come upon my fields.

They talked on and on, but my eyes must have been flashing lights because they suddenly stopped talking. I noticed that the bloodshot eyes had cleared, the blue irises swam in a cloudy white sea, promising that no harm would come to me. The men promised to measure around my fields and post signs against trespassers, no one would know the difference. Such were the times.

"It will be years before anything can be built here." The rougher man said. "The whole system is like a three-wheel cart without a horse."

I laughed.

"Meanwhile," the other said, "we will all live in peace."

"What are your names?" I asked.

"Žanis Ozols," said the red-eyed one.

"Jānis Ozols," said the other. "And yours?"

"Zelda. Zelda Bērziņa," I answered. "Žanis and Jānis," I said slowly, feeling the words in my mouth, crossing my lips in repeated whispers. Two men, I marveled, where there had been nothing. I was afraid I'd be an old maid, since there had been a genocide and a war that killed our men. But now I was sitting between two men. Twins. "Žanis, Zelda, Jānis," I whispered overcome by tears, "all words with five letters. A coincidence or fate? Or some prehistoric prophecy?"

"Who knows?" said Jānis, the gentler one, stroking my hand. "Life is not a sack of grain you can put on a scale and weigh out, nor a measuring cup with marked lines. This much and no more—one man, one woman."

"So here we are—two men and one woman, and isn't it good?" Žanis said and kissed my lips, pulling me close to him, but Jānis took me back in his arms, saying, "Leave her alone, we've had enough."

"Never enough," Žanis grunted but gave in.

This was interesting. I sensed that each would watch and control the other, like the right hand controls the left. I would be protected. They would compete, outdo each other to please me, and I would be safe. We would work together, restore and rebuild. And so it was.

Years later, I married Jānis legally because of the children and the way we have to put things down on paper and put carnations at Lenin's statue. But I must confess that it wasn't all honey and roses: Žanis was upset and brooded for days, but I told him that I loved them both the same. And, yes, I tried to please and satisfy both, but my heart leaned more towards Jānis, who was and is more tenderhearted, true to his name. He works around the house and garden. He likes to fix things. He rebuilt the house on the inside. He knows where to find nails and boards (I never ask), and he loves flowers and teaches me how to graft new varieties. We grow enough to sell in the market. Especially beautiful are the tulips in spring and asters in the fall. He talks to the flowers as he works with them. He tells me that they know what we need and that their heads jingle with kopecks. The kopecks add up and turn into rubles. There are so many statues now, and all need flowers, he says, and there are many holidays and people give flowers to each other. And so it wasn't long before we became capitalists, and Jānis built a greenhouse. We had a regular spot in the market in Liepāja, and we sold more on the side.

Žanis works the fields and is good with animals. He is stronger than his brother, more inside himself, brooding, hardworking like an ox. The old farmer stock. He makes the rocks sprout, I say. He started with one cow and soon had a cattle, but they smelled it out. "Capitalists," they screamed at him one day and put him on the kolkhoz and added our land to it. New management had been sent upon us, and everyone suffered again, but not like before. No deportations. With that threat gone, the men started to fight for their rights, and we were allowed to keep our house. We went on working, meeting all norms, and soon Žanis became the overseer, and then it was easier for all of us.

Meanwhile, the children are growing up. I don't know who is whose father, but they look like their fathers, and are strong like our name—Ozols. They are all well-schooled. Our country school is good and strict. Now the four older ones work in Riga and come home when they can. They have their lives and friends. We don't meddle. Times have changed, they live in a modern world, and they forget the old and don't care to hear all our stories. The younger ones are still in school. Anna is very musical and has set her eyes on the conservatory in Riga. Dainis plays the flute and writes poems. He is the great joy of my life because he is still with me and reads his poems to me. Such is life.

Zane works for the Intourist Bureau. It was meant to be like that: how else would I have found you? How else could I write so openly? She found your daughter's friend Mara and brought us together. It is not a simple procedure. They have to be very careful. But she is clever, my Zane.

So, you see, God has blessed us, and we are happy, like the children of Israel and Jacob and Joseph of old, who faced many trials and tribulations, but came out strong, blessed by God.

But again I am off the track. There is so much to say, a lifetime to press onto a few little pages.

In the morning, the first day of our life together, they went away, and I was afraid that they might go and report on me and again I would be driven away in a cattle wagon. I was afraid, lost in my fears; we were all conditioned not to trust anyone, and so I trembled the whole day. But in the evening they came back bringing some clothes and a bottle of champagne. We clanked our glasses and drank. They had also found a link of sausage and black bread full of caraway seeds. They know a woman who had baked bread for 70 years—through all kinds of times and rulers. We feasted and danced to our own singing and whistling. Then we swore that we would be true to each other. They kept their word, and we never left one another again. After that I was not afraid, but love flowed out of me like sap from a birch tree.

Well, what do you think? How do you see me, my rich sister, the beautiful and fortunate? Am I bad? Are you better? Oh, Mildiņa, so pretty and pure as I remember you, can you understand me? Can you understand that the land needed all our strength? None of us could have done it alone, but together we had the power, like electricity that sparked light in the darkness you were blessed to escape.

Can you understand that for days after the first day and night I would wait for the nights and cry out with such joy I never thought possible? The men, too, were happy, not ashamed or jealous. All their life they had shared what they had, even their mother's womb. They, too, had been empty and scared, becoming brutal and mean without even realizing it, stealing and lying, prowling the woods like wolves. Suddenly they had a home and a woman to love, even if it had to be shared.

For as long as I could I kept the secret of the two heartbeats underneath my heart all to myself. When they found out, they practically worshipped me like I was the Holy Mother and outdid themselves in helping me.

Love, sister, we learned, can only be destroyed by hate, not more love. Yes, I was dizzy with happiness. From the Garden of Ice I had entered the Tropics. Love had come to me like a fiery angel, unannounced, unexpected. It had reached to me its healing hand at a time when I felt eaten up by sorrow. I was like a worm-infested apple—ugly, alone, pressed into the ground. But love found me. It picked me up and through its magic the worms and rot disappeared. The cured apple now glowed as on a tree, beautiful, shining in the sun. I never thought of myself as beautiful before, but after love touched me, I became lovely, singing all day. I have not stopped praising God for all His goodness. I remember Job, who was the Devil's game. But he held out and God blessed him.

Well, yes! I must tell you that I found Uncle's big Bible he had hidden away. Together, our family reads it every day. (All the fathers of old had more than one wife and many concubines who worked together so that the will of God would be done, so that the world would be peopled.)

The reading of the Bible still is our secret, for if we are found out, we would be publicly scolded and punished. So far no one has touched us. The little church is burned down, so there is nowhere to go. Trees grow inside the church, and sometimes on Sunday mornings, we all go there and sit with the trees and pray, pray for a time when young men will rise and rebuild and the Word of God will again be spoken from the pulpit. I see that day. I know it is coming!

Yes. Everything for me is different than I imagined. I did not blush at all with my husbands. I could not imagine something as stupid as a maiden blush—not after what I had seen or where I had been. Nothing was at all like I had read in the stories Mother kept on the shelf before it all happened. That age, with its shelves of gold-leafed books and shining crystals, for us was shattered. We had, without anyone asking our approval, inherited a hard clay age, and we had to live in it. Yet I felt, in those early days of our spring love, like my fields must have felt after a drought when water soaks through them and brings them to life and puts them to use again.

Life! Can you understand our celebration of life, when, the next Saturday evening, we heated the sauna they had repaired and went in it together, as our people had done for centuries, as Uncle Imants and Aunt Matilde had—God rest their souls—and come out cleansed in body and mind?

Afterwards, the men put on their shirts, new shirts I had made during the week from Mamma's blouses and slips. I put on Mamma's folk dress, the one she wore at the song festival, remember?

Yes, so it was . . . We sat around the table eating the bread I'd baked in the large clay oven Jānis rebuilt. The loaves were perfect—well-risen with hard crusts and firm texture. Oh, so delicious! And then we sang and talked and loved all night until the larks woke us with their trilling. Can you understand how beautiful it is for a woman to put her head on one man's heart and her foot on the other's? My little Mildiņa, have you ever slept with two men? Have you ever slept with one?

*

Milda let the letter slide out of her hand. She remembered its impact the day she received it. She had felt insulted with such probing questions put to her across miles and ages. What standards of morality, what rationalization! It was as if she had watched an X-rated film; sexually aroused, she had risen from the sinful trance mortified that Ilga would get a hold of the documentary and make it public.

"Communism! Communists did that to her," Milda said to the walls and went to the china cabinet in the dining room, tempted to open a bottle of vintage wine, but the vulgarity of a bottle emptied or even half-emptied in her desperate, frustrated solitude scared her. What if she developed a dependency? What then? She knew people who had gone that way, miserable creatures. So she had merely looked at the crystal glasses behind the beveled doors and remembered Kārlis and the days when those same glasses were full and ringing with toasts. Full of fears, ignorance, and tales of horror, the old refugees had vigorously drunk toasts to Latvia's freedom and independence, while Baptist believers prayed on their knees for the deliverance of their brothers and sisters, *who suffocated under the yoke of communism.* No one knew then when or if the Iron Curtain would be lifted or wear itself out. They knew nothing definitive about what was going on in Latvia; she certainly knew nothing about Zelda, who had not responded to her albeit feeble attempts to find out and resume some kind of communication.

After she had read the letter the first time, even the empty, dust-filmed wine glasses seemed to mock her. In her confusion, she had put on her walking shoes and gone for a long walk through the streets of her neighborhood.

Meanwhile, Ilga had found the letter bulging out under a Better Homes magazine and read it. "Wow! Intense," she had said excitedly, as soon as Milda came through the door. Eagerly Ilga had put on the kettle, and over cups of tea, they talked for hours, their eyes dancing and cheeks blushing. For the first time they talked like equal adult women, not like mother and daughter. Having read and discussed its content, Milda hid the letter and made Ilga swear that she would not talk about it, would not write or tell any of her friends and others that such a letter existed because, if it became public and Zelda were found out, she might be summoned for questioning and who knows what suffering and persecution would follow. All knew that the guards stood at every border crossing, and Big Brother was watching. Besides, the so-called thaw had come to an end, so it was rumored, and news of renewed oppression regularly reached the Kingdom of Exile.

Reaction

Lying on the quilt, Milda remembered her own wedding. It had been very properly conducted—with Mrs. Arāja as manager—in a DP revived old Latvian Lutheran church in Brooklyn. "Leave everything to me," Mrs. A. had insisted and, never admitting that Milda might have the least objections or suggestions, forged forth with the plans. Whenever Milda voiced the least objection to her betrothed, he reminded her that Mother knew the etiquette of Latvian upper circles and would do things right. Milda, an orphan, of course, did not know the procedure and would make mistakes and, therefore, cause embarrassment, Kārlis let her sense. And in the self-conscious, class-struggling community, embarrassment was a serious offense. Besides, Mrs. Arāja let her son know that they were not only transferring but establishing tradition. She knew her son's wedding would be remembered, copied, talked about, and she would not take chances with letting the least little thing slip out of her control. So even before Milda got off the boat with the Baptists, whom Mrs. Arāja with Kārlis at her side hardly acknowledged, she had the blueprint laid out in her mind. She measured Milda with her eyes—the bust, the waist, the hips.

She bought the satin and lace dress and the long white veil. She found the sponsoring couple who would lead them to the altar and the prettiest little girls who would carry the veil. She insisted on white lilies because she had carried lilies when she was a bride. She ordered and bought the tuxedo for her son. (*Rent? Why, what kind of a country is this, where men aren't married in their own cloths? Besides, every cultured man needs a formal suit.*) She made up the guest list, to which Milda injected that she wanted Miss Egle and her daughter Emilia, and the Gramzdas to be included. Mrs. Arāja nodded, looking pained. "The Baptists won't come," she said lighting a cigarette inserted in an ebony holder and coughing. And she was right. The distance from North Carolina to New York was too great and expensive. But Miss Egle came, fragile and silvery gray, she leaned on Emilia's arm. "This is a very happy day for me too," she said as she kissed the bride with a mother's kiss. She gave her her heirloom silver tea set, which Milda treasured more than any other gift.

Milda went hot and cold when she saw the name of Pēteris Vanags at the top of the list, but could say nothing. When she was informed that "regretfully" he would not be able to attend the wedding, a boulder fell off her heart and her steps became lighter. She liked to think that it was not the unnamed trip but his sensitivity that kept him away, and in appreciation she sent her silent thanks to him on the night waves.

The wedding was splendid, of course. The bride—most beautiful; the carefully selected guests—happy, dancing, and feasting long into the night. Over all, Mrs. Arāja, dressed in regal blue chiffons, reigned in confidence; only at times, after smoking her extended cigarettes, she absented herself. Milda saw her out on the balcony coughing and swallowing pills.

*

Mr. and Mrs. Kārlis Arājs honeymooned in the White Mountains in Maine. Kārlis drove a brand new Ford. He had rented a cozy cabin surrounded by birch trees. "This is just like Sigulda!" both kept exclaiming. "Just like Latvia!"

The memory of the wedding night did not thrill Milda, who never confessed to her husband that he was not the first. Counting on his innocence, she closed her eyes and watched, comparing and contrasting. The next day she was in a bad mood and the next night she said she was tired, but the third night, not to hurt and offend him, she whispered that she was happy, very happy and that her tears were tears of joy. With each day she became more willing to submit to his wishes and demands and at night, forsaking all others, she helped him to perfect their bliss. Still, in the brightness of sunlight, as she watched her white wedding bouquet wilt and dry up, her whole being seemed to wilt with the lilies. Toward the end of the honeymoon, Kārlis sulked and smoked excessively, reminding her that she was his. When she iced up, he told her with hard words that she was impossible to please. "You are selfish," he said, scaring her. She begged his patience and forgiveness. "Yes, I forgive you, but you must change your attitude," he said with rising confidence. She did change, and surprisingly, she felt cheerful. *It is good. It will be all right,* she assured herself.

The weather was fine, exhilarating. Full of energy, Kārlis talked about the future; they laughed and teased each other as they went boating and hiking and, in twilight hours, relaxed over glasses of wine. One day, hoping to be helpful, Kārlis bought her *The American Bride.* When he paid the bill, he winked at her suggestively, making the clerk smile. "Maybe this will help you," he said on their way out of the small shop. Milda could have slapped him, but slammed the door instead. Back at the cottage, to distract herself and please him, she read the article he had earmarked on adjustment to married life. She tested herself on "Ten Easy Steps to a Happy Honeymoon."

Confident that he had adjusted and she would soon learn from him and the article, he let the intimate things take their course and talked about his new job with the insurance company and how, after a period of training, he would be transferred to a new branch in Grand Rapids, Michigan. He said they were really lucky: Michigan was a beautiful state and Grand Rapids and Kalamazoo were becoming important Latvian centers. He ("we") would help the process; "we" would make it happen. Milda listened. "Where you go, I shall go . . .," she said, smiling with some conviction, trying to be deliberately happy.

Pleased, Kārlis said they would not have more than two children, unless they were girls, in which case "I'll give you another chance." They would raise them as Latvians but, of course, educate them as successful members of American society. "Their hands can belong to America, but their hearts must belong to Latvia, free Latvia, that is . . . This will cost us . . . We'll have to be strict."

Milda nodded, watching his excitement wax, as he envisioned an orderly future in an ordered Latvian society.

"You will do as I say, won't you?"

When she hesitated, he explained that in a proper household only one person should rule, otherwise there would be anarchy. She agreed. (Rule #1: *Make him feel that he is the boss.*)

"I have great plans for our life," Kārlis concluded, pleased with her submission. "And soon our serious life will begin." He was impatient to act, to make waves, and move on and up. He wrote notes for himself, smoked in chains and left her alone with the magazine or in the kitchenette. The smoking gave her headaches, but she suffered in silence and was glad that his company had allowed only one week off.

*

Milda's head hurt from all the reading and remembering. The room had no air, it seemed, and Ilga did not call, did not knock on the chained door. "I didn't come here to brood," she told herself and decided to purify her soul and go to the concert of religious music. She would be late, but so what? Religion was eternal and timeless; God had not created clocks.

The cathedral was packed, the heavy door closed. No more tickets. Locked out, she walked slowly down the steps, looking at her feet and the sparkling quartz in the concrete. She found a bench under a tree and sat down, squinting at the setting sun. She could hear the music coming softly through the open windows, its melodies bathing her soul and calming her mind.

"So you, too, are cast out of heaven!" Aria, Ausma, Skaidrīte, all on high heels, their dresses slightly transparent appeared before her. They covered the sun. Startled, Milda took off her sunglasses and looked at them. *Are they always tied together*? she wondered, but said nothing.

"Let's try Hell's Kitchen, since heaven isn't open to us," Aria proposed, making others laugh, covering their mouths.

"I wanted to go there in the first place," Skaidrīte said, "They're my kind of poets."

Milda hesitated, thinking that she really did not like the poems that came out of that kitchen, nor those arrogant New York poets, who certainly would not bother coming to Ilga's early morning performance. Yet she rose and joined the united front.

The hotel suite was crowded and loud. Cheap glasses clanged; the air was smoky, the lights dim. Aria & Co. pushed toward the gallons of wine as Milda backed out the door. She escaped into the empty corridor and took the elevator up to her room. Nothing seemed more inviting than her luxurious bed, the colored TV, and a late supper brought to order.

THE FOURTH DAY

Poetry Recital

The most important day of the festival dawned sunny and bright. For a while Milda Arajs lay in her bed dreamily lingering in the past, then shifting into the unknown future, wondering what it might or might not bring and reveal. She tried to divert her thoughts away from Zelda's ever new, ever puzzling letter, which alerted her sense of self awareness and examination. *Who am I really? What would I be if I were there and she here? What is now my responsibility? Oh, I don't know, I just do not know . . .* She threw off the covers and got out of bed. *Ah, there is never enough time for repose and clear thinking.* Zelda, Ilga, Vanags—all circled about in their own courses. Vanags noticeably kept his distance, perhaps giving her time to think and wonder, leaving her alone until after Ilga's big morning, though he had already darted down hawk-like, too close, invading her inadequate sleep and causing her to dream about Kārlis, who had appeared, only to quickly fade away. When she tried to run after him, she could not move her legs fast enough and woke up in a sweat. And there was Egons. She bumped into him and his wife often as they went from one event to the next. He always acknowledger her with cheerful, casual smiles, while she, nervously, hurried past him with a light wave of her fingertips.

Ilga . . . She worried about her daughter, whom she would meet in a formal setting in her debut as a new, upcoming poet. She was nervous about what Ilga would say, how she would impress, and how she would be dressed. She was sure that whatever she said or did would be original and unexpected and there would be a reaction, a disturbance that would ripple throughout the Kingdom of Exile sooner or later, for she would make people think, reevaluate themselves, be angry or pleased. She would urge them to go forward. But where was forward?

Milda wanted to go forward with the young, but was afraid of the old, the memory of her husband, and the hard lines of such as Mr. Vanags. Imagining a showdown, she sighed and hoped that her daughter would be careful when she attempted to hold up a lamp or a torch and lead her and others on and out of the present stagnation to new visions of truth and illumination . . . *Or am I expecting too much of her*?

She glanced at the clock and saw that it was time to get out and face the day. *Yes I'm nervous, and why shouldn't I be afraid of regressing again back into my role as the eternal mother of a willful, eternal child?*

She dressed carefully, putting on the off-white linen dress she had embroidered with meticulous care. Her amber brooch, pinned slightly above her heart shone out of the firmament of her being—pure, transparent, encased in silver. Her hand, with the matching ring, holding the tan purse with the evocative pastoral scene blended perfectly, while her Stride Rite tan pumps raised her as on a platform. She applied a light mask of makeup and styled her hair, pulling it back and away from her face and twisting it in a French roll, allowing some stray strands to fall where they would, softening her formal look, as would befit the early morning hours. Finished, the reflection pleased her, although it appeared somewhat strange and contrived—too folksy perhaps and a bit too motherly, too much of what she was actually trying to leave behind in her quest for a truer and freer self.

"Mirror, mirror on the wall. . ?" she started asking, but she stopped, knowing full well that the glass would say, "But your daughter . . ." *Oh, but I feel no pangs of jealousy! Only the usual melancholic sadness of universal Time passing over all of us . . .* She remembered Helga's somewhat forced assertions about mothers moving to the background and stepped back to see herself in the full-length mirror. *Not yet. My life did not end at forty, neither at fifty, and before I go downhill, I'll still climb—as long as I can.*

Background for Ilga and Gatis? Perhaps only for a part of me. The other part is mine and is just beginning to crawl out of the old skin. Besides, no matter what she says, Helga is and will remain a separatist, for whom even our midsummer nights are only shows and games, not the very depths of our culture . . . How could she be married to anyone who does not understand that? How could she give up our special traditions for a life in some small Midwest town with an oversized catsup bottle for a water tower? What is she and what does she want from me now? Another story? Am I her source material for some novel that will never sell? Or is she really a spy—going in and coming out of Communist Latvia so freely. Oh, well . . . we'll understand it all by and by . . .

*

Down on the mezzanine she stood erect, watching the slowly awakening crowd, as unwanted anxiety held on, churning her empty stomach, making her perspire and go cold. She swallowed a drink of water from a wall fountain and went into the ladies room. From her stall she heard a woman grating away: "I wonder what that Ilga Arāja will say this time. I don't like her tone, do you?"

"Na yaa-a," a voice neighed. "What's to be done with the young?"

"She's not that young. She looks gray, how do they say it? Burned out, if you ask me."

Milda held on to the wall. Far away she heard water running over muffled voices and soiled hands, over words, *smoke . . . drugs . . . mother . . . red . . . blacks . . .* until the faucets turned off and the doors closed.

Milda came out, washed her hands, dried them and looked in the mirror. She was all there. The words had not disturbed even her stray locks. Elegantly she walked out onto the carpeted hall and into the auditorium. Like a wounded deer, she sidestepped other feet and found her expensive seat. With the hard, habitual shutting of eyes, she forced all darkness aside and pulled from her purse a perfectly folded white cotton handkerchief and blotted her face. As she replaced it, she looked down into the mirror inside her purse. The faithful little glass betrayed nothing. The face that looked back at her from the darkness was actually calm and profound. Meanwhile, the hall was filling up nicely, surprisingly for such an early hour. Every seat in her row was being taken; a man sat on her left, a woman on her right, pressing against her on both sides. Irritated, she smiled politely and stiffened her spine.

Minutes later, the lights dimmed and Ilga was tapping the podium. The people quieted, and the large chandeliers that had made the hall morning bright turned off. "Let us change time and place," she said. "A poet has the power to do so," she continued. "Let us make evening out of morning, for it is evening—in Latvia."

A soft wind of whispers blew throughout the auditorium as it slowly fell into darkness. Then one by one, girls dressed in white, like some prehistoric vestals, lit the long white tapers that lined the stage and, their task finished, slowly receded.

Ilga tapped the microphone, paused, smiled and introduced the young poets, who took turns airing their amateurish verses that could not keep Milda's mind from wandering. She heard non-poetic, unintelligible arrangements of words. She also heard the Latvian language pronounced in heavy accents. The r's slurred, the t's ticked against their American palates, and the stresses fell on the wrong syllables. She caught grammatical errors that dated her and made her cross her legs the wrong, uncomfortable way. She blushed as she listened to one girl saying something about fertilizing herself and coiling into her own womb, giving birth to herself, delivering herself out of her own self, all wet and slippery, into a wet and slippery world. She heard murmurs in the audience and the EXIT door opening and closing. Loud, undeserving applause slapped her ears. She did not clap. She could not. She longed for real poetry—for the lyrics of Aspazija, Rainis, Skalbe—not a bombardment:

Bombs missiles grenades—
rat-ta-ta-tat rat-ta-ta-ta
hands hands our hands dropping the bombs
shooting the missiles
creating the wastelands the deserts of ashes
your hands and mine dropping the bomb
dropping the horror from heaven on earth
killing the children the white and the black
the yellow and red bringing back hiroshima
bringing in rigoshima
sending our brothers to hell
ringing the apocalyptic bell.

*

Milda leaned forward. She stared at a young man, long-haired and mustached, wearing thick glasses and faded jeans. She pressed her fingertips against her temples and, finding her opera glasses, drew him close to her eyes. She recognized in the aging hippie the kid who had disturbed the one class she ever taught at a summer camp. Now he stood before the audience like an apparition reading some free verse about another Hiroshima where ape-men scratched all over the globe; they scratched in the ashes, the dust of a burned-out world looking for new life. The poem grew tiresome, full of images about women swimming in newly created rivers of ashes like female otters looking for shores, for places of safety to give birth to their ape-fetuses, damaged by radiation.

Oh, dear God! Milda sighed audibly and recrossed her nice legs. Not wanting to look at him, she looked again deeply into the amber of her ring and the trapped ant. It seemed too large, and it seemed to be looking and crawling at her. She felt her perspiration. *These halls never have enough air!*

"I think he married the communist," the woman next to her remarked, doubtless encouraged by Milda's sigh.

"Ah," Milda sighed again.

"Married a Red spy—how else could she get here?"

"Shhh," the man on Milda's left emitted.

But she was too churned up to be so simply hushed. Her thoughts raced in reverse. She remembered the poet as a teenager, who, in the beautiful setting of a wooded camp, kept asking if Latvians also killed Jews. She had replied that as far as she knew, it was the Nazis who did that, not Latvians. He said he did not believe it. He said he had Jewish friends and then he asked why people here did not worry about the oppression of other nations and races—like in Africa and Central and South America.

"And did our president really send his army with drums and trumpets to greet the Russian troops in 1940 when everybody was busy and unsuspecting, enjoying the song festival?" Milda had vaguely remembered the president's voice coming over the loudspeakers at that song festival, but she hadn't heard that he actually welcomed the oppressors. Could that be true, she asked the kid and said that she never heard such a thing, hoping to shut him up just when he asked: "Mrs. Arājs, do you believe in the principles of democracy?"

She had not prepared herself for such questions and stood before her students feeling undressed. Nervously, her mind had groped and stopped at Estere and Raela bleeding in their beds. She blinked and saw yellow stars, and finally said she did not know the answers to questions she would not dare ask. When others became disorderly and asked loudly *Why? Why? Why did our soldiers defend and protect Lenin? Why did our soldiers join the Nazis*? she dismissed the class.

The next spring, to get away from it all, she pleaded with Kārlis, asking him to take her to the Tobago Islands. "It would be so good for both of us because it would help us understand Latvia's history, and besides, Dr. Andersons is so scholarly. It would be fascinating to go and actually see the places that this professor had found in the South Sea Islands and see Latvian names on nearly buried gravestones. "We might even hear the natives singing our folk songs, like he said, and we could actually walk through the ruins of King Jacob's castle! We would see the island of our own Robinson Crusoe! I just finished reading Green's *Tobago*. I'm so intrigued, so delighted! What a novel! Now that should be translated! I also read some of Rousseau's writings about the nobility of savages."

"Nobility of what?" Kārlis had asked and moved a little closer, and she had taken his hand, ever so lightly, and whispered *savages*, explaining how Rousseau had argued that savages were noble and that society corrupted them. They were sitting in their lovely arbor, she dizzy from the lilacs and he looking out into a star-studded space. Her spine coiled as his fingers strayed up and down her back and suddenly stopping with: "So it started with him then, actually."

"What?"

"Communism."

"But may I send in our reservations? . . . Then you could learn more about the roots of Communism—in their primitive, savage setting." She had stumped him, and the reservations were made.

*

They had a wonderful time in Tobago, listening to the professor's lectures, going about exploring overgrown cemeteries, sipping pineapple cocktails underneath huge palm trees. and swimming in cool, turquoise waters. It had indeed been paradise found. She returned to Michigan firmly convinced that Rousseau had been at least partially right, but Kārlis called her uncivilized and simplistic even before they deplaned. "My dear, are you ashamed for acting like Burt Lancaster in *From Here to Eternity*?" she had asked, but he just stared at the sky, waiting to land. Taking the hint, she never reminded him of the heat of the tropics when they lay between their cold sheets. Her back turned, she cried in her pillow as she hugged those memories, calming herself and excusing him, convinced that her husband, like many men of the North, did not or could not put his feelings into common words and actions.

Milda blotted her face with her crumpled handkerchief. She felt the man on her left. She saw his hands curl into fists, the veins sticking out and pulsating. She wondered what words, images or guilt had disturbed him.

"Connect!" said the next poet. "Build a bridge over the land and the water, touch your brother and sister! Go where the land calls you, go where your childhood sky bends over the earth, your earth!"

"That's better," whispered the woman on her right. "That's more like poetry."

But Milda did not respond. She was already transported back to the Kurzeme fields, back with Zelda. She recognized the words, slightly varied in arrangement, as those coming from Zelda's letter's post script, which had been missing from the letter. *So! Ilga had cut Zelda's confidential words only to pass them around and make art out of my sister's life!* Upset, she searched blindly inside her purse and found her sister's black-and-white family photo.

It is a recent one, not that of a young girl with muddy boots running through furrowed fields to her sensual bed; here a middle-aged, stocky woman smiles broadly and squints. Her arms are around two children—Anna and Dainis. Two young women, Jana and Zane, quite modern for the Soviets, sit at her feet in the grass; and two serious hefty young men, Jānis and Juris, stand behind Zelda, holding on to the low branches of an apple tree, all in black-and-white bloom. Framing the mother and children are two men, not the young men Milda imagined chasing her sister in their mad pursuits of animal lust, but middle-aged. Žanis is as heavy as a grizzly, grinning his bear grin. Jānis is taller, of slighter built; his face is turned toward Zelda with a kind of serious, intimate protectiveness. The men's clothes are rough. The women's dresses, in various prints and patterns, are rather too tight, too outmoded. Milda guesses that the material was pulled out of her mother's old trunk. She promises the picture that she will send—*as soon as I know how to do it*—more becoming yards of material and needles and thread.

"How can we connect?" the woman leans close and whispers, and Milda says, "I don't know."

The man grabs at the pack of cigarettes that stick out of his shirt pocket. Milda remembers what she wrote to her sister: "You live your life, and I shall have to live mine. Such is our fate."

With a guilty conscience, as, not so long ago, she licked the glue of the envelope's edge, she remembered being quietly glad that the Latvian Association had taken a hard line against relationships with Soviet citizens. She hated to shop and send. She did not have the resources. The hard line policy took the pressure off her and made her feel as though she were doing the right thing by not encouraging further contacts. It was enough that Zelda was alive and well. *May God bless her.*

The next poet took up the microphone. She was definitely not one of the young but an important and respected personality. She began, without looking at her open book:

Two Sisters

One was crystal, the other—red clay.
One danced in crystal-lit halls,
the other, upon her knees,
raked out potatoes, whole.
War parted them at once and
left underfoot for each,
completely different earth.
On her toes, light as prism-rays
from crystal chandeliers
one sister danced in the halls of state.
The other, heavy as clay,
remained at the boundaries of home,
always frightened by barred wagons
already set on the rails.
Crystal, with time, shattered and wasted away in dust.
Clay, long fired, survived long and hard years.[1]

*

With her whole heart in her hands, Milda applauded. The woman on her right blew her nose and wiped her eyes.

---

1 Aina Kraujiete, "Kristals un Māls" as translated by Inara Cedrins, *Contemporary Latvian Poetry*, ed. Inara Cedrins, University of Iowa Press, Iowa City, 1984.

"Now there's a good poem," she said. Milda nodded. Her eyes also blurred, and the image of Zelda appeared in the mock twilight like Hamlet's father's ghost. It looks at her again with sad eyes and talks softly through the flames of the candles: "What are you doing now, my little *Mildiņa*? Why don't we trade places for only this one hour? You know, it could have been different. I could be sitting in your chair with my legs crossed. Oh, don't look at my legs like that! If I had not walked in our clay fields and cow dung all these years and had not gotten so heavy from eating potatoes, maybe my legs would be as pretty as yours in silk or—what do women wear?—nylon stockings that are shamefully thin. And those beautiful shoes, so pointed as if you only had one toe on each foot. Oh, Milda, *Mildiņa*, how pretty you are! Still so young at your age! I could have been pretty too and you—I really wouldn't wish it on you—you could be as coarse and heavy as I'm now. I was not always heavy. You remember how skinny we were then, don't you? You do remember, no? But I got sickly and thin later, after they sent me there. I was starved and my stomach bloated, my guts gone bad, nothing working right. But that was then. Now I am such as I am."

Milda pinched herself, pressing her hands so tightly that the silver band hurt. Is she hallucinating? If not, who is that person looking at her from the flames, talking, judging and accusing—impersonating Zelda and all the other clay and potato sisters? *Had the postscript been that long*? She could not remember.

"I got heavy during the first ten years after the release. And then the men came upon me and I had two sets of twins, one after the other. We all were hungry and we kept eating potatoes with mushroom gravy. We dug potatoes out of the fields, the fields that were full of mines and hand grenades. There were many accidents all over the country. I saw a woman explode right in front of me and then a Gypsy, quick as an acrobat and funny went up in the air. When he came down hitting the ground he was all ripped up. I dragged what was left of him to the ditch and tried to put him together like some bloody puzzle. But he was dead. All the pieces of him were dead and charred. After that I was scared to go back to the fields. Still I went because we had to eat; the children and my men never had enough. So we kept digging like hogs. When we were lucky, we found other things—beets, carrots, rutabagas. Then it was good. I cooked soup, better than in the old days."

"That's no poetry," says the woman.

"Yes it is. A prose poem," another asserts.

Intermission.

Milda blinks and adjusts to the light, but remains seated. She sees many tear-filled eyes and hands wiping them and forgives Ilga for stealing the PS. It was more effective than any rhymed verse, she admits; besides, no one is looking at her but at his and her own other side—like that of the glue-smeared back of the poster down in the lobby. She cannot tell from the faces around her what the people are crying for. Is it for themselves or those on the other side of the world? She sits still. Her heart aches. She waits for her pendulum mind come to rest.

"Our children can talk about connecting, but we know better: a branch cut from a tree cannot be grafted on to an old trunk. A torn limb cannot be stitched or glued back," she hears someone say and stares at the empty stage.

*

As Milda considers whether or not to rise and stretch her legs, she sees Vanags enter the room and implant himself authoritatively among *the leftist elements.* Trying to make herself invisible, she slides down in her chair. Her heart throbs, while her mind wonders why he would be there. He doesn't care for the younger generation and their poetry. So, she reasons, it must be the politics. *Is he here to catch words for evidence and seek out those who had contacts with Soviet Latvia? Will there be the inevitable confrontation with Ilga?*

She presses her hands against the indignant, willful heart, when she sees Vanags stand up and look around. Seeing her, he walks back toward her, down the right aisle, moving slowly along the wall, giving everyone time to note him, no doubt gloating about still being recognized and greeted. Milda eyes him cynically, not looking at his face but his arm—the left arm that hangs dead at his side with the shining black leather glove, polished like a shoe, protruding from a starched white sleeve. The black, permanently dead fist seems to propel him, pulling him along the wall and making him stop at her row. He smiles and beckons for her to rise and move up front to sit with him, but luckily one of the organizers intercepts him and together they go out to smoke, no doubt.

What will happen next, she wonders. *Is Vanags being asked to address the assembly? To stop this morning-turned-evening? Will he stop Ilga from speaking?*

*

Milda twists her handkerchief, afraid that Ilga will challenge him publicly and turn on the lights—put him under some bright spotlight. She knows how much Ilga dislikes him and will say so if he spoils her show. She fears an uprising, a revolution of the young against the old. *Good thing this is only a festival . . .*

Ilga's dislike goes way back to a long gone November 18, somewhere, USA, when Kārlis spoke heroic phrases about Vanags and lauded his valor. "My friend lost his arm in the defense of freedom! Therefore, the wooden arm is a beautiful thing!"

Ilga adored her father but started crying when he shouted, holding up his own two living arms, saying that he never had to sacrifice as much as his best friend. "We owe eternal gratitude to men like him, and we must listen to what he says, for he knows the truth." Kārlis had pounded the podium and sworn that together they would fight communism to the end: "Until it falls from its own rut. For that *I would give up my right arm*!"

"Mamma, let's run away from that bad man," Ilga said out loud, "before he breaks papa's arm." Heads turned, and Milda put her hand over the child's mouth, while the embarrassed father shook a very pointed finger at them. The baby inside Milda had kicked furiously as Vanags spoke with even louder shouts, his raised false arm above all their heads. Ilga cried louder and Milda dragged her away. Everyone stared at them. Onstage, both men waited impatiently for the door to close. Little Ilga, of course, was later scolded and made to apologize to Mr. Vanags, but she was not sorry. Since then she hated the man with his black hand curled in a fist, and whenever Vanags visited them, she refused to shake his hand and stayed out of his way. It had been years since they last saw each other, but her hatred hadn't died; instead, gradually, as she grew up, he became a negative symbol, an object of general aversion and the cause for rebellion against the general *Establishment*. To oppose such as he had become Ilga's and her generation's noble cause.

So what's next?

Milda sits, feeling treasonous for keeping her secret connection with Mr. Vanags from her grown-up daughter. She could not admit to her that she pitied him and, in her way, had loved him most of her adult life. Ilga would be horrified and would certainly turn against her and perhaps abandon her—like her brother Gatis had. And then where would she be? What would her life be like in a dead and empty house in the middle of America's vastness? How could she explain to her daughter that she was actually glad that people still honored him and that the lost arm still guided him on to many stages all across this and other continents. His work of alerting the Kingdom of Exile to the ever-creative deceit of communism had kept him busy and far away from her house and home. *But now? What now?*

*

Milda sits up. The intermission is over. She tries to see who are filling in the front rows. She sees the editor of *The New Path* journal, which publishes liberal opinions as well as Soviet Latvian writers. Around him cluster the poets who have been to Latvia, those who, before their trips to the Soviet Union, had always read their works at similar song and dance festivals but after those odysseys, some hand had crossed them off the lists as favored participants. Milda sees them sit muted, no doubt wishing to be seen and heard, for they surely have much to say.

Scowling, she spots Helga Williams joining them and again wonders about her, pondering so many questions she had not dared ask her the day before: How exactly did she get into Latvia and why? Who paid her way? By what authority does she go in and out? How dare she also walk in and out of these halls of patriotic people, herself having chosen to assimilate and not even worry about the most central issues of national survival? And those translations? Are they any good, and who commissioned her? Milda is not sure about anything; in the dimmed darkness, she cannot tell the right hand from the left. She is only conscious and certain about one missing arm that is trying to reach her and from which she tries to flee. *Oh, it is so dark . . . I cannot see anything . . . Why, oh why, must I sit alone in this darkness? Why is no one I love beside me?*

*

"**How long is exile**?" Ilga asks. Milda sees her child leaning forward, her hair almost touching the flame of a candle. She speaks in a hushed voice, her large bright eyes like headlights.

"How long have we been in exile?" Ilga asks and then echoes her own words "How long?"

Her voice rings like a lament, like a cry from the very depth of her soul. She does not go on with the speech. She does not read any poems, nor does she recite—as she so brilliantly can. Instead, she drops into silence. She waits, waits for an answer, but there is absolute stillness in the night hall. The woman whose moist arm touches Milda's says, "That's not a poem." The man on her left leans forward, then back, grabbing on to his pocket with the cigarettes. Milda is hot and uneasy. She does not understand where Ilga is heading. She stands there like an evangelist, waiting for raised hands, confessing words. But there is only silence, for Latvian audiences (people of the cold, reserved North) are not like American mixes. Latvians listen, applaud, but say nothing. Still, Ilga stands, her arms open, fingers moving as though they were counting.

"How long is exile? . . . Tell me," she challenges. "How many years?" Milda makes a quick calculation: 1983 - 1944 = 39. It is an odd number.

"Thirty!"

"Thirty-five!"

"Forty!"

"Thirty-nine," Milda says not too loudly.

"Twenty-seven," says Ilga, looking straight at her mother.

Ilga is twenty-seven years old . . . Milda stares back at her alarmed—accused—as, one after the other, the numbers amplify. They are loud and sad like the crescendo of a requiem. They are like swaying ocean waves. Old and young voices, some with accents as grating as sand and others smooth like washed-up stones, tired, displaced stones crying on strange shores but still the only shores they know.

People like stones, Milda thinks. *Stone Age people. Stones having no recollection of the cliffs from which they were chipped, having no memory of the original fall or the coldness of the water when it first pulled them into its depth. Stones crying in the deep without a sound, crying in the darkness among dead ships that had lost their sails and their steering wheels, crying among the corals, crying to the strange fish that swim above them.*

Alma!

Milda calls up her deceased aunt—really her only mother and sister—crying, weeping at the edge of the Baltic Sea, as she writes that last note and swallows the pills. Milda sees the weary platinum-tinted head lying still on the rocky shore. She can hear the seagulls crying.

She also hears them crying on the other hidden, smeared side, around the old lighthouse deep in the Baltic Sea off the horn of Kolka, at the tip of Latvia, where the sea meets the gulf, where the sand bars shift back and forth every day and night and where the seagulls swarm in silver flocks, crying eternally.

"Oh God!" she prays. Then she hears, "Thirty, thirty-five, thirty-nine, forty, thirty-three, twenty-seven—"

She hears her nation crying, counting, chanting the years of its exile as if pushing black discs of an invisible abacus. They are pushing the single and the decimal rings with their sighs and moans from the left to the right. They have done it for such a long time that they have lost count of the years, but they will go on doing it because they need the sense of exile for their own relevance. They need it for their identity. Milda had never before heard the moans quite that way. She had never felt the one-wayness of it all.

"Enough!" orders Ilga. "I have had enough of exile," she says softly from deep within the candlelit darkness. "I want to feel at home . . . I want to go home."

With the last words the voice changes to that of a tired little girl, and Milda hears again her child whimpering in the back seat of their station wagon as she had done on many trips over many years, while they drove from one Latvian camp to another, from one festival to the next. But now, sitting in the dark and alone, Milda cannot reach over and stroke the golden head and say, "Hush, we'll be home soon."

"Can't we, your children, born in your exile, not ours, can't we call this land our home?" Ilga pleads. "Must we travel forever from one state to the next, from one city to the next, dragging with us forever our hot and heavy folk dresses of the distant medieval and dark ages? Must we forever carry the flag for which there is no mast? Must we be the ones who perch it on strange and high places where indifferent people, speaking American and every other kind of English and foreign language, wonder what is going on? Must we sweat under this flag, this maroon cloth with the white stripe down its middle?

"Yes, my friends, we know the glory of the flag! The symbols are accurate and have meaning: the body of a killed soldier was laid on a sheet. His blood flowing from him turned it red. The middle of the sheet where he lay stayed white. That was ages and ages ago. I know that ours is one of the oldest flags in the world, as old as boys, as old as blood and wars. They buried the soldier and made a flag out of the sheet. Ours is a blood-soaked, sad banner. Yes, we know that legend. Mothers and fathers, you have taught us that ever since we were babies. But must we carry it around us forever? Must we raise and lower it forever? Must we die under it?"

"Oh, Ilga, *Ilgiņa*, my little girl, don't cry!" Milda whispers, and the people around her stare. Do they, too, see the girl's father, the famous Kārlis Arājs on a hot, humid day in Washington DC, as he collapses and dies inside the flag? Can they hear Pēteris Vanags calling her, telling her how Kārlis, her faithful and gallant husband, died for freedom and the old glory and new hope of Latvia? What was it all about anyway, and what is Ilga really saying?

Milda is confused. Does Ilga blame her? Do the people blame her for Kārlis's hard and true line? For his and his like that have kept the borders tight? Who are all those in the armies of the cold war, anyway? Milda cannot figure things out as she looks at the left and the right and sees Zelda's picture, knowing *she* should go to her and have someone take a picture of them all together . . . Then there would be something to show, something to pass around.

Ilga does not look healthy. Is she really drinking too much—and smoking? Those dark shadows under her eyes are new. Milda studies her daughter with her opera glass and concludes that something does not look right. The Afro curls are not at all becoming to her fine Nordic features, so much like Alma's—or, really, like her own.

"Oh, dear God, help her," Milda sighs soundlessly so that the woman and the man sitting next to her will not hear. The man's breath is unbearable, and the woman keeps crowding her. Her bare arm wrinkles Milda's embroidered sleeve, and she pulls inside herself, wishing to crawl inside her purse. She looks at her watch and then at the suspended ant in the amber of her ring. It has been suspended for eons, and she wonders if it is easy to exist like that—eternally visible, yet forever unchanging.

Why must Ilga be so troubled anyway? Milda's mind races again through her family history and cannot understand why everyone takes things so hard, so seriously. Others don't seem to be suffering from the same intensity. Look at Egons's family and the ease with which he moves, even as he makes his smooth, tempting passes. She remembers how easily he lifted her at the edge of the lake and carried her to a safer ground, kissing her and whispering, "This is so good for us." And what about that beautiful young lady she had admired in the art gallery? Her golden hair was pulled to one side and coiled in a thick braid which cascaded over her full breast. Close to her ear an amber hairpin shone like a miniature sun, and her tailored blue silk dress was ever so subtly embroidered with *Mara's way* in gold. She had strolled around the gallery as though she were a live painting. People looked at her more than at the canvasses. She was Ilga's age, yet calm, poised—a proud Latvian. What had her mother done right that she had done wrong?

Had she and Kārlis indeed planted the privet hedge too thick and let it grow too high in order to keep their family world in and the other out? Were the hawthorn and quince bushes that enforced the borders too mean? Many times Ilga came in crying, her arms and legs all scratched up from crawling through the hedge over to the neighbor's yard where children played, making a lot of noise.

Gatis, too, had occasionally escaped through his secret hole, for which he was whipped by his father's firm, right hand . . . What kind of fences and hedges did other people build and plant? Or did they let the yards roll together in the open American style? In what kind of a setting was that beauty raised? Who was her father, who the mother?

"Where is my brother?" Ilga calls into the microphone for all the world to hear. She is leaning forward as though she were giddy, as though she were looking for him in the darkness, but she only meets her mother's frightened eyes. Milda, too, turns in all directions looking for her lost boy in the large crowd of displaced persons. Then blinking, she stares straight at Ilga, who need not shout because she knows where her brother is; she knows the address and the telephone number.

With the help of the opera glasses she can see Ilga's eyes grow moist. They are so remarkably like her father's, as they looked into their foggy bathroom mirror for the last time. Now his eyes are empty sockets; or if souls had eyes, they are perhaps far, far away from her—almost as far as they had been when she saw them for the last time—behind dark walls of time, behind clouds, planets, and stars . . .

"I am lonely," says Ilga into the microphone. "Where is my generation? Where are many of my Saturday School classmates? Where are they? Are they in or out of exile? Have they made new homes for themselves? Are they happy?"

She pauses. Her arms drop to her sides. Her eyes close. She looks like she is about to faint. She takes a drink of water.

"I am tired of exile," she says softly, barely whispering. "I want to go home," she insists, her voice suddenly putting on shoes. And then she reads one poem inspired by a letter from Latvia to a poet in New York. It is about a baby born on Christmas Eve in Vidzeme, in a barn: "For us each birth is a miracle, each child the son or daughter of God." Ilga had turned the letter into a poem as lovely as Silent Night. And suddenly Milda beams in unreserved pride.

"I dedicate this poem to my friend Mara, who went home," Ilga is saying. "Through her I am beginning to see an end to our long-drawn exile. I am beginning to see the change in attitudes, the dawning of a new era, as our old poets said a hundred years ago. A new relationship between the split halves of our people is taking shape, and again, as before, a woman will accomplish what so many men with cries of war could never do. Only last week I received the good news." Ilga pauses and takes another drink of water. Her face glows with her own kind of suspended excitement, the way it always does when she is about to disclose a special bit of knowledge: "I just learned that Mara has given birth to a baby boy."

She watches the audience turn into a dark, waving sea. "His name is Krišjānis. Named so after the saint who was present when Riga was built. He carried our ancestors across the Daugava River. So let us wish that this boy, too, will grow up and do great things for our people—the indigenous people of our land!"

Ilga motions the audience to rise. Milda watches the people get up slowly, cautiously, one by one—as for a standing ovation. Only Pēteris Vanags does not rise. He seems to have sunk deeply into the tossing sea of people. "Our anthem, please: *Dievs, svētī Latviju*!" Ilga's voice is loud and clear, commanding like that of her father.

A pianist, a young man with a ponytail, strikes the familiar holy chords, and the people begin to sing. Milda sings, tears streaming down her face. She—they all (even Vanags)—sing with their hearts, as on that boat at the beginning of exile, their faces turned toward the beloved land, to the East, where the sun is setting, only to rise again, when morning dawns.

The girls in white dresses blow out the candles.

Mother and Daughter

"Mamma," Ilga says softly, leaning above her mother. "Are you all right?" Milda feels the pressure of a firm hand on her shoulder. She smells the nicotine breath and stands up.

"What?" she asks, touching her temples.

The room, almost empty, feels like an overheated, unventilated cave.

"Oh. Yes, yes, I'm fine . . . How are you?"

"Famished."

"Then let's have lunch."

"All right, I was hoping you'd say that, thanks!" Ilga talks a stream and then says, "You look nice. What a beautiful dress! Did you do all that stitching?" Her fingers run along the embroidered sleeve, stopping and going on, her eyes full of admiration. "Amazing!"

"You may borrow it sometime," Milda says pleased.

They walk toward the door. Some people stop to talk to Ilga, paying only polite attention to Milda. They are those same *leftist elements* (as Kārlis would put it) who sat in the front row as though underlining the candlelit stage. *The support system,* Milda notes. The fat poet presses his stubby fingers into Ilga's thin shoulder; her eyes sparkle, but Milda frowns. This man had presented his poems in Riga, had them printed in *Dzimtenes Balss* (Homeland's voice). "The propaganda paper of lies," as outraged Kārlis shouted, after he read about it and identified the poet. "What a sellout in exchange for vital information about us who live in freedom!" Milda had not asked what that information might be; however, she had been equally alarmed and now was definitely suspicious of the seemingly rejected poet, who looked like he was enjoying the ostracism and Ilga's sympathy.

Milda breathes easier as soon as Ilga brushes him off and turns to embrace another dissenter from the rules of exile. *Liesma,* the Soviet approved press, had recently published a book of her poems, over which a wave of controversy ensued—not over the quality but the politics and price of a *Soviet* publication. ("Sentimental slop," Vanags had entitled his review in *Avīze*. Milda eyes the poet from the periphery. She remembers her from the first American Song Festival in Cleveland, in the early fifties, when the Latvian poets of *Hell's Kitchen* were young and their pens powerful. Then this poetess had stood tall, her thick black hair plaited and wrapped around her head; she had recited her sad patriotic verses beautifully, like an actress. Everyone admired and honored her for her beauty and her words. Over the years, she had, naturally, participated in all the following festivals—until she made her pilgrimage to her lost homeland behind the Iron Curtain and then written about her impressions, which were not acceptably negative. Since then she seemed to be standing alone, spiteful and still strong in the light of her golden years. No matter what the politics, Milda is sad to see her rejected and her hair short and gray. "The sands of time have also ground her down," she hears someone whisper and wonders what intimate words bring out the mutual tears, which Ilga gently wipes away.

"Ilga, *our* poet! *Our* voice! What a marvelous speech!" Helga brakes in, coming out from what seemed a locked door. "Right to the point! What an unforgettable, marvelous morning!"

"Oh, thank you!" Ilga beams, the tears still shining in her eyes. "You are another person here that I really want to embrace," she says, turning and pressing Helga to her heart. "Won't you have lunch with us?"

But Helga sees Milda's face and excuses herself, saying that she has another engagement, then tells Milda, "I'll see you tonight at our reunion."

As if whipped, Milda excuses herself and turns toward the nearest exit.

"What's the matter, Mother?"

"Nothing."

"OK! OK?"

"Excuse me," Milda says, and goes to the lady's room.

*

"What did you think of the speech?" a woman asks from a closed stall.

"What's there to think? I was surprised about the baby. Wonder how they deliver? Wrap'm up in red? Ha! Ha!"

From her cubicle, Milda hears more voices, their words half-drowned by flushing water. She hears her name, then the names and words: *Mr. Arājs . . . Vanags . . . Ilga should blush . . . What would her father think?*

"Yes, what would he think?" Milda echoes cynically but stays hidden.

"What will happen to us? Where are we going?" A third woman chants. Then a voice separates from others and asks, "Has this exile been all that long?"

Milda pushes the door open and steps out. She slowly washes and dries her hands. She touches up the stray strands of her streaked hair and applies lipstick on her dry lips. The ladies' room becomes quiet, eyes watching, hands washing, faces of imprecise time reflecting in the mirror, silent and flat.

"Mother, what's keeping you?" Ilga calls from an open door.

*

The high noon hours are hot and muggy. There are hardly any Americans in the streets. The Latvian language is spoken all around in various accents and degrees of perfection and imperfection. But no matter, Milda likes the sound. She imagines how it would be to actually live where one's own language were spoken all around and so taken for granted that even small children would speak it without thinking, automatically, without feeling different. So she and Ilga converse loudly, freely, as if the streets belonged to them. Milda is glad that Ilga answers her in calm, unwinding tones.

They walk toward the yellow arches of McDonald's because Ilga had turned that way, and Milda had long ago quit arguing against the mighty power of The Hamburger, as she had quit raging against the infinite packages of Lucky Strikes that cycle through Ilga's purse, hands, lips, lungs.

"I almost feel like I'm in Riga," she says. "It's so strange to walk in a city where our words run around in the streets. It's like a dream."

"Yes."

"It's how it'd be if we weren't foreigners."

"I know."

"It would be nice."

"Yes, but maybe not as interesting."

"Oh, my child! Are you still looking only for what's interesting?"

"No. I'm looking for some sense, some real truth about who we are and where we're going." Ilga stops, making her mother stop also. "You know what? We could go there. We could go where people speak Latvian in the streets."

"There is no such place. Riga is full of Russians."

"How do you know? You don't really believe all what *Avīze* says, do you?"

They walk on.

"Everyone who's been there, that I've talked to, speaks about that special feeling of being in a *Latvian* city," Ilga stresses the big, important adjective and takes a deep breath. As they wait for the green light her eyes, moist like her great Aunt Alma's, pierce Milda's shifting glances. "Would Mara have gone to Odessa or Vilnius or Tallinn? Of course not! She married a Latvian and had their baby in Riga . . . Our city, so why don't we go there too and back up our slogans with some positive action?"

"Or our credit cards."

They walk faster to beat the crowd of hungry people heading for the golden arches. *Life is a broad tempestuous sea,* Milda remembers the Baptist choir singing in Esslingen and wonders why it has come to her now, on this street, at this red light. *We—the foaming waves, rushing for the shore. For a moment we travel together. Next moment we break apart . . .*

"That's how it is with us," she says, more to herself.

"What?"

"Oh, nothing. Here we all are together for a day and the next moment we scatter like leaves in the wind, like waves in the sea. Such is the fate of our people."

"But Mamma, don't you see how by going there and adding ourselves we can change our course and keep Latvia from turning more Russian? What do you think?"

"I don't know what or how to think."

"Right . . . I see. That's our tragedy."

Vanags—the Hawk

McDonald's is packed with Latvians. The busy waitresses, asking people where they're from, are no wiser from the quick, smug answers. Milda does not bother to answer, but hands Ilga a ten dollar bill and starts toward an emptying booth. Just when her step becomes lighter and her thoughts freer, a man's familiar hand grips her shoulder.

"Mrs. Arājs," Vanags says. "What a coincidence! I have been looking for you."

"Really? I hadn't noticed," Milda feigns surprise and slides into a booth. She stares at the black leather glove and wonders why he doesn't get a white one for the summer. "What do you want?" she asks coldly, noticing how well the man has preserved himself and how he still stands out in the crowd.

"That is a complicated question . . . May I?" Without receiving permission, he slides into the seat opposite her, all the while eyeing her with his melting, ice-blue eyes. She trembles, her throat going dry and tight, her heart pounding, her eyes calling Ilga.

"I would like you to serve on the committee for our big international demonstration, coming up next year in Germany."

He speaks in a formal voice, and she, equally restrained, says that she has no desire to go anywhere and demonstrate anything, nor sing the same old songs in strange crowds and risk being arrested and dragged in front of TV cameras.

"We won't only sing and read poems. We will act." He lights a cigarette.

"What will you all do?" Milda asks.

"We will work out our hearts and souls for freedom and democracy . . . hopefully in Berlin, by the Wall. We'll charter a train and meet others from captive nations and go from there. Ever been back to Germany? And Esslingen?"

"No."

Vanags now leans over the table, moistening his lips, knowing that she remembers and by remembering desires him. He watches her eyelids drawing like blinds over her eyes and her hands clutching her purse. When her hands come up on the table, he touches her fingertips lightly, casually. He knows that he's awakening her dormant nerve endings, says, "Well, my dear, then it's about time for you to see the old world, and I would like to show it to you." Her eyes open and he looks at her intensely. His wooden arm swings slightly upward; the black glove comes to life. Still keeping up the formal tone, he says, "I would like you to be by my side when I carry our banner . . . in your beautiful costume . . . I remember . . . it would be quite in accordance with your husband's wishes. We talked about it the day he died. Do you still have his banner?"

"It's folded and put away."

"Well, then it is time for us to raise and unfurl it—as you yourself are rising out of the darkness of your grieving."

He leans farther over the table. His voice is quiet and close, making her go weak inside, coaxing her heart to reach out, but her mind holds her back, her fingers interlocked. She wonders what she should do, how to respond, for she knows that he is cautiously wooing her. *I feel the Hand of Fate upon me,* she says to herself and bows her head. He watches and waits, reading her thoughts, seeing that she is afraid, now that they are at last alone, albeit it in a crowded eatery. She breathes slowly, deeply, recalling, in quick flashbacks, many scenes of their youth on the other side of the world they once inhabited. How uncertain, yet exciting life was then! She smiles shyly, guessing that he also remembers—but what? What does he remember? What does he foresee?

So wondering, she tries to look into her own future and sees a dull, lonely year stretching before her, with nothing challenging or intimate except perhaps a letter, a card, a telephone call—maybe even from him—but more than likely from some other widows and charity volunteers, asking for help and money. Looking beyond 1984, she sees more years—if her health holds out—filled with concerns and worries for her son and daughter and the grandchildren, whom she does not know and doubts if she would recognize them outside their house in Arizona.

"Well, will you help and support us—our cause?" he asks.

"I don't know," she whispers, looking down.

"Please," he coaxes, "for his sake. Everyone thinks it would be very effective to have you there, up front, with us. We would remember our beloved leader and dedicate the event to his memory. There are a lot of people who still respect him and the work he did."

"Are there?"

"Yes, of course, and politically it would be a good time for effective demonstrations. At last we have Mister Reagan on our side. He knows how to talk to communists, and he needs us to help him attack the Evil Empire. Thank heaven, all the leftist liberals went down with Jimmy Carter. Jimmy! What a little boy's name for a president! . . . So the times are ideal. We can make a real case against Russian aggression and their idea of world communism and know that we would be taken seriously. It also helps our cause that communists are creating problems in Central America and that Poland is making world news. Yes, the times call upon us to act and you, my dear, could help save the world."

Milda looks up, befuddled. "What?" she asks as if waking from a trance. She sits up chuckling. Then trying to cover up her curiosity and interest in his grandiose proposal, she sighs saying, "Oh . . . oh, how long will all this go on—the festivals, these futile demonstrations, all that?"

"Always, my dear," he says, again looking intensely at her face, while his hand grips her locked fingers. One by one, her fingers open up and wrap around the lone hand and close down.

"Yes, there will always be a ball in some castle, and there will always be a poor Cinderella, only the prince will not notice her and the fairy godmother will be too tired to get her primped up and the clock will strike." She tries to sound casual and withdraws her hands.

"No, my dear, the time to prepare for the ball is now, and we shall dance the Tango as never before." At that his hand again finds its place in her warm, uncertain caress. "Yes, to be sure, there will be a ball and our people will dance again."

"Ah, these festivals only throw us off, push us into deeper unreality." She looks past him, glad that Ilga has not reached the counter and is chatting with people around her.

"Bigger and better," Milda keeps talking, "every time costing more and more." Her hands free themselves, leaving his alone, and hide in her lap. Vanags, his eyes questioning, drums the table as if signaling that their time may be running out. She hesitates, searching for words or help, then sees Ilga coming with a full tray. He sees her also and for a desperate moment his eyes plead with Milda.

"Hi!"

Ilga pops into the seat next to her mother. Spitefully ignoring Vanags, she spreads out the food and opens her mouth wide for the Big Mac. Milda picks a French fry out of the bag and dips it into catsup. Ilga looks from one to the other and knows that there have been exchanges and assumes that Mamma is threatened and vulnerable and needs protection.

"Why don't you leave us alone?" she asks irritably. When he does not get up, she raises her eyes to his. Like two stags they lock horns. "Don't you realize how irrelevant you really are?" she smirks. "Don't you realize that people see through you? You think we are so stupid that we don't know that you are scared and hiding?" Like an aggressive journalist she asks: "What did you do during the war? Weren't you also a part of the exterminators?"

"Young lady, you don't know what you're talking about."

"Yes, I do, you old hawk, and I wish you would leave Mamma alone."

"Ilga!" Milda scolds, but Vanags rises and leaves the booth. Moments later, they see the black-gloved arm swing past their window. He does not look back. Silently chewing, they watch him disappear around a corner—rejected, yet dignified, like the soldier he was.

"Perhaps you were a bit too harsh," Milda says. "You should not talk with your mouth full." She scowls at her daughter and watches her eat. Distraught, she puts her face in her hands and takes a deep breath. The scent her palms have absorbed overwhelms her. She keeps inhaling, allowing it to saturate her body and drive her away from where she is to where she once was—with him—in the town of climbing roses and vineyards. She wants to rise and catch up with him, apologize for Ilga, take his hand in hers and tell him, yes, that she will go, go with him—go to the Berlin Wall, anywhere, but that he must also promise that he will let her be free. Hot and perspiring, she wants to throw off everything that is contrived and false, even her dress, which is much too cumbersome and absurd in this place.

"It's enough," she says emphatically as Ilga empties her Styrofoam cup. "You're right, as always. We all have had enough of exile, at least the way it's been. It's time we follow our hearts' desires."

"Then you heard me, *Mammīt*?"

"Yes. Of course, I listened and heard—even what you did not say. Maybe the times really have changed and are changing, yet we see nothing because we may be looking in the wrong direction or are afraid to look." She talks rapidly, in guarded tones. "Perhaps we're all cowards, like poor Mr. Vanags, whom you push into the ground. Don't you see how he and many others are afraid of opening the doors? Maybe they don't want to open them, not really."

"But I do and you do, and so we'll go," Ilga says.

"Where?"

"Home. Back to the tribe. To Latvia. Will you take me there this winter?"

"So soon?"

"It's still far away. But I'd like to spend Christmas in Riga," Ilga says, excited, seeing a vision. "I want to make it a pilgrimage, a kind of Bethlehem. I'd like to bring gifts for little Krišjānis and Mara and Igors. That holy family, the one that is—at this point in time—uniting us, making the two halves one." Ilga glows in rapture, and Milda listens to her child, the poet, the future—and sees a way to her own liberation.

"Yes, all right. We must and will go," Milda says. "It might free us and really turn things around, break the walls and unite us." She wants to tell Ilga about the proposal Vanags had made but decides not to; she would have to explain and reveal too much, and for that the time hasn't come; besides, she does not want to spoil Ilga's vision of their doing something great, daring, and good together—just the two of them.

"Wouldn't it be neat if we could have one of these song festivals all together—you know, like one nation under God?" Ilga leans back and lights a cigarette.

"You're dreaming, my child."

"And what's wrong with that?" she asks but does not wait for an answer. "Let's go!" she says and rises. Milda obeys.

As they make their way to the door, out of the corner of her eye, Milda sees Helga in a booth on the far side of the restaurant talking to a man and a woman. On a peg she sees a fancy cowboy hat decorated with silver studs, and pretending not to see her, she pushes the swinging door.

Outside, with a small, casual wave of the hand, Ilga leaves her on a corner, facing a red light. The bright, sweltering street, streaming with people, becomes a vacant lot—empty, like her disturbed heart. She hurries to the hotel. She needs to wash her hands.

Intrusions

The telephone rings. Milda sits up, momentarily confused. The intended nap had turned into hours of deep sleep; shrill sirens sounded somewhere below or above, and the telephone rang insistently like a crying child.

"Hallo," Milda said uncertainly, propping her head because it was so heavy.

"Mamma?" Ilga's voice—so much like Alma's—came over the wires.

"Yes . . . Where are you?"

Ilga was staying with friends and would be back in the morning for the festival's Finale. "So don't worry and think about Christmas in Latvia! Dream a while, Mamma, and . . ." The operator cut in. The three minutes were up. Disconnected, Milda slid back onto the pillow. She turned on the radio and listened to some string quartet playing a Mozart number and mindlessly picked up her program book from which fell Zelda's letter. She reread the part about her and the two men running over the field to the burned-out house. Aroused, she wrapped her arms around herself, letting self-pitying tears fall on the loose pages. "Why don't you give me one of your men for a Christmas present? She who has two men, let her give one to her who has none," she said. "And I'll give you one of my coats. How'd that be for an even exchange?" She smirked at her own cleverness and thought about the red dress she planned to wear for the big Esslingen reunion, when another telephone ring startled her.

"Mrs. Arājs, my dear evasive Tosca, will you have supper with me?" Vanags's voice vibrated softly, invitingly, and Milda blinked her tears away. Zelda's letter fell on the floor. "There is a nice German restaurant down the street," he said. She heard his breathing, and he heard hers.

"Please," he added in a most intimate tone. She could hardly hear the word, but the desire inside it cried with a loud voice.

"No," she said and hung up. She watched the sweaty impression of her hand upon the receiver evaporate. *Can't he understand that I want to be left alone? That what's over is over? That Ilga and I have other plans?* Frustrated, she rose and went to take a shower.

Through the running water she heard a knocking. A soft, hurried knock it was. She pulled the large towel around herself and went to the door. Cautiously she opened it as much as the security chain allowed. She saw a slice of Egons with a large wrapped up parcel.

"Excuse me," he said. "I bought that painting you liked so much, and I'd like to give it to you now." He spoke in a businesslike tone. "May I?"

Quickly she lifted the chain, and he stepped inside. He closed and chained the door. He leaned the painting against the wall and turned toward her. She watched him take off his jacket, his tie, his shirt and so on. Then he pealed the towel off her, all the while his lips kissing her face and neck and whispering sweet words. "At last I found you . . . at last we're alone . . . it's been agony . . . you . . . so close, so far . . ."

Her conscience rose up and beat against her desires arguing, hitting her from within, throwing at her his wife's and children's blurred images. But his kisses blotted them out one by one, his lips telling her to relax and give in, saying that love was a surprise, a gift, to be taken when it came, that it could not be stored for some good and safe time. "Once it's gone, it's gone forever. missed . . . What we have is between us—we're not taking anything away from anyone because it's nothing they have."

His doctor hands knew all the crucial points of the flesh and worked until she thrilled at what he was holding out for her, and she received him with joy.

They indulged until the streetlights came on, and then he left her. She had missed the supper she was going to have with some old friends, and she would be late for the reunion. The telephone also had rung, and people had knocked on her door, but she picked up no receiver, opened no doors. She was drinking ambrosia in big, full gulps, consciously trying to saturate her whole being so that there would be something to draw on after she returned home to her loneliness and her empty house.

"Love of the moment . . . so delicious," she whispered, when they lay in each other's arms. "I never was very good with long-term, duty-bound love . . . marriage . . ."

"Shh," Egons kissed the palm of her hand. "Love like this has nothing to do with marriage."

But then he glanced at his watch and quickly left the bed. She watched him dress and open and close the door. Not a single word for tomorrow and tomorrow and tomorrow. Only a hasty, flat kiss on the cheek. *Must be his style.*

She also slid off the bed and went to finish her shower. She styled her hair and put on the red dress. In the mirror, a woman on fire confronted her, smiling, then laughing and crying. *Oh, who are you? What are you? What is a woman?* She turned off the light and, for a moment, stood in the twilight, calming her nerves and senses. Then she picked up her beaded handbag and rushed out of the room and down the hall, down to the ballroom where things had already started and would go on until morning. Such were these festivals, such were her people who neither started nor quit things on time. She trembled, charged with sparkling energy, ready to dance, to go where she had never been, glad that Egons had made no promises, put no restrictions on her that would be binding and messy. *Oh, what a psychologist he is! How well he understands and knows women! How he can heal and injure!*

The Reunion

Flushed and disoriented, Mrs. Arājs, once upon a time the most beautiful girl and outstanding student of the Esslingen DP class of 1950, paused outside the heavy closed door on which a sign said ***Eslingena***. Her heart beat with mixed excitement, making her dress shimmer like flowing lava. As she reached to press down the door handle, she felt herself regressing, going back, back to the time when she was a student, taking down dictation. Now she was late for class, a lost Cinderella, with bare feet, waiting for the clock to strike twelve.

Suddenly a familiar heavy hand falls on her weightless, trembling hand. It presses down, and the door opens. Milda blinks. Grace Kelly in *High Society* the morning after. She shields her eyes from the floodlights of other eyes. Red and black rings, single and clustered, float in her pool of vision, and she, too, floats: a little girl with yellow princess curls, she is running among sticky pine trunks, blowing bubbles. Lidia calls out, "Don't run too fast! Be careful!" But the child trips, slipping on pine cones and the large, protruding roots. The bubbles spill. Her knee bleeds, and gentle Lidia blows on it and covers the scrape with a plantain leaf. "Hush, hush, darling! It'll be all right." The little one cries against a white, starched blouse. Her knee hurts, but the bleeding under the cool leaf stops. Lidia strokes her head and scolds Zelda for sliding down the hill on her seat. Zelda laughs and swings on a dead limb, "Look at me!" she shouts. Upset, Lidia pulls her down; she drags the sisters out of the park, and they ride home on a streetcar. *Oh, how bright the lights*! A young woman in a beaded dress leans on the piano and sings the old German *Schlager* about a man not wanting to be alone on a moonlit night. It rings a familiar tune in Milda's ears; Alma used to sing it once upon a time. Milda still knows the words.

"Ah, Oh-h-h!" Milda hears. She hears applause, loud staccato clapping as the hand pulls her against his chest and holds her like a shield. Her fiery pleated dress drapes him. She knows it's Vanags but says nothing. She feels the deadness of his one arm and the intense life of the other. Her body recoils in his vise. She blinks again. Hard. And now her eyes see. They see them all but recognize only the few she has met regularly at these and other festivals. She sees handsome Jānis Gramzda with his accordion, wearing a plaid shirt; he starts up *Atmiņā lakatiņš zilais/Mati kā saulstaru riets* . . . (In memory a blue scarf/hair like sunset/you come toward me . . .)

Everyone sings the old 1940s pop tune. Some rise and waltz away. Vanags holds her tighter; she hears and smells his breath; she feels him like glue. Their sweat mixes, and she shuts her eyes.

Suddenly a woman's hand takes hers and pulls her out of his clutches. Helga, the rescuer, is taking her somewhere through throngs of people, pushing through to a round table at the far end of the ballroom. There sits her little sister Aija, with her smart American husband, and demure Biruta, Jānis's wife. The two women chat and giggle as they used to under the Esslingen chestnuts, when they took their dolls for walks. They smile at Milda and go on sipping their cocktails. *How free and worldly the Baptist young have become!* Milda notes sarcastically, in self-defense.

Helga is with them but not of them, Milda sees at a glance—as before, as back then. She sees Helga's hand holding a pen and a note pad. She knows that her friend is always and foremost a writer and, therefore, assumes that inevitably she will be manipulated like a ballpoint pen. *Oh, let her! Who cares? Yes, perhaps, I may become a page in some story, who knows?*

Still, she is suspicious of this once irrepressible child with owl eyes, who has been to Latvia and back and seems to enjoy going against the current, while the whole society, herself included, flows more or less on the prescribed course—as Kārlis & Co. had mapped out in the beginning. Milda sits uncomfortably, fearing the association, fearing what people would say and think. But Helga excuses herself with, "I must catch an interview," and follows a young, rather exotic woman across the room to the open bar.

Abandoned, Milda glances around, looking for Vanags and finds him sitting on a bar stool, leaning against a wall and drinking. But his absent hand no longer wears a black glove; instead, a golden hook glistens, reflecting the dim lights. His gray suit has turned into a jewel-studded windbreaker. He wears alligator boots and faded blue jeans. She stares at the apparition, and thinks that their eyes are meeting, but she does not know those eyes. She does not know the man; the one she does know is nowhere. He must have fallen backward the moment Helga charged at them. Milda's body vibrates where his heart beat against her spine, where the palpitations of their pulses fused. Her senses swoon at the recollection of the sudden release of his grasp. A chill had hit her as soon as he vanished and Helga had appeared. She had stared at Helga, who stood before her, looking rather stupid, asking her if she were all right.

"No, I'm not," Milda had snapped, looking past her. She had tried to shake off the Hawk, but could not—they were stuck together. His trademark scent had descended upon her and lay tangled in her hair; her knees are weak and lock her in place . . .

She rubs her eyes and stares at the door, not trusting any of her senses, but the door is closed and empty, a construction of varnished boards. Insanely, her eyes jump back to the other man, who now slides off the stool and goes for the door, but Helga crosses his path. They stop. Milda sees that he is trying to brush her off, as he pushes his way through the dancers, but Helga follows him, her strong notebook hand now touching him, blocking his path, her lips pleading, eyes appealing. At last he gives in, and together, they walk out of the ballroom. The band, made up of aging Esslingen musicians, keeps on playing. She hears the lovely *Melanholiskais Valsis,* and remembers her parents standing on their balcony, their arms wrapped around each other.

An Interview

"Are you, please, Alma Kaija's daughter?" a white-haired elegant lady asks.

"Niece."

"Really?"

"Yes, really," says Milda startled. The table feels like a spinning carousel, a lost satellite, orbiting in space.

"*Labvakar,*" says the lady and adjusts a golden pen and a leather-bound notebook. She explains that she is from Sidney, Australia, and is gathering biographical information for a book on the life of actors and the theater during the transition years in Germany. She explains that she would like to know what happened to the glamorous and extremely talented Miss Kaija.

As she talks, Milda recognizes the once reigning queen and mother of the theater. She stands up, bows, and, apologizing, shakes the extended hand, respectfully, as she would have ages ago. She is awed at the once noble form so shrunken, so nearly invisible. After they sit down, the old Queen Mary clicks the pen open and rests the tip on a blank page, ready. But Milda is not quite ready and stares at the hand that will at last write down Alma's story the way she will tell it, the way she has wanted to tell it for years.

Milda concentrates, focusing hard, blocking out all distracting sights and sounds so she can see again the Gotland seashore she visited during the 1979 Free World Latvian Song Festival. She remembers making the red and white clover wreath and hanging it on a willow branch that leaned over the water at the spot where Alma died . . . and starts talking. She talks to the blue-veined, transparent hand, firm like a bird's claw, encased in antique lace, a full-carat diamond anchoring her ring finger.

"My Aunt Alma died, I imagine, like the weary seagull she impersonated, whose stage name she adopted. She died as she had planned all along and according to her own script."

Milda tells her how Alma had chosen their separate ways and countries, how she had married Vilis Druva and how she had planned to divorce him after she had lived with him for a decent time.

"But he refused. She wrote me how he said he adored her—for life, forever. He possessed and idolized her and hardly ever let her out of sight. Alma could never stand that kind of closeness, you may well imagine, but she gave in, and for a time they traveled together, mostly along the shores of the Baltic. No doubt, she wanted to know the shoreline, she would want to measure the depth of the water and understand the tides, the fish, the scavengers—everything. She let him film her. When I visited him, he ran film reels of my aunt. At home and out, but mostly along the Baltic shore—in all hours and in all seasons. He had also taken her beyond the Polar Circle, to Lapland and beyond, into icy enchantments. There are reels of that too. In all those films Alma seems happy. She smiles, laughs, walks in the flowers and tall grasses, and you forget she is actually with someone. On the screen she is always alone in the desolately beautiful landscape."

Milda waits for the strong, aged hand to catch up with her words. Waiting, she closes her eyes and sees the old films. She remembers her visit with Vilis and how they had watched Alma all night, sitting on his bed, much too close in that dark, crunched room—his and Alma's bedroom—like a box. And then without further prompting, he confessed that she had demanded a divorce in a most tragic and surprising manner, which, "naturally, I denied."

He had been in the middle of the stack of colored reels, when he suddenly stood up on the bed and grabbed the gymnastics rings that hung from the ceiling. He pulled himself up, did some tricks, and then hung there inverted, looking down, circling over her head, like a dark pelican in the shade-covered white night. She had crouched in a corner. But he stopped the film with his foot and turned on the light. Trapped, Milda had to watch his performance. She saw his body, tight and sinewy, overhead doing acrobatics, asking her if she, too, would like to try, saying that Alma would not, except to hang herself. She saw his inverted grin at that moment turn hard and his hand grip the rings, while his feet walked on the ceiling. The next second he turned the light off with his foot and was beside her, his hand grabbing hers, as she yanked free, telling him to leave her alone, while Alma was running along a shore away from his camera far, far away—a small dot into a huge red suspended sun.

"It was during Khrushchev's rule when my aunt received a letter from Viktors Vētra, to whom she was engaged shortly before our escape," Milda continued and briefly filled her in on the background. "I swear that no woman ever loved a man more than she loved him. When, in early fifties, she wrote to me saying that she finally heard from him, it was like the sun emerging after years trapped in an eclipse. A miracle had happened: her man was actually calling her home! And she, in spite of her hatred for communists, was ready to go. Again she begged her stand-in husband for divorce, and again he refused. From then on—my aunt wrote—he watched her all the time, day and night, locking her in, hiring others to watch her when he could not. Still, she managed to mail her letters to me. They were full of rage, telling me how she tried to kill herself."

Milda pauses. She waits for the hand to write it all down, then continues, trying to keep her voice from choking:

"And then I heard nothing until the black-edged letter came from Vilis, saying that she was dead. And I was—it was strange—I was actually happy because I knew that she had won their cruel duel. I knew that she had succeeded in that supreme final act of defiance, true to her character, dying beautifully, like Hedda Gobler. She did it—as she would—on Midsummer Night's Eve. 1978.

"Somehow she had escaped to the ship that took her to Gotland. It must have been during the confusion of the wild Swedish celebrations, when Vilis, though an abstainer, would be drunk with his fraternity crowd—the old 1936 Olympic team."

Milda sees in what beautiful, even script the actress writes. She watches her put the periods and commas, the dashes and quotation marks. She sees the hand waiting.

"So Alma went to the east side of the island. How she got there, I don't know, nor does he. She had picked the spot that was closest to Latvia, where the sea was the narrowest, the same spot where some of our refugee fishing boats had landed in the autumn of 1944. And there she laid down like Ophelia, with clover blossoms in her hair, and took the poison. She left a note in a wild rosebush. It said, *My only beloved, my darling, you see, I tried to reach you. I went as far as I could . . . My* love *for you is as eternal as the sea. Ever faithful, Kaija.*'

"When I was in Stockholm, Uncle Vilis, as he insisted I call him, showed me a letter from Mr. Vētra, stating that if his Margareta did not answer him by May 1, 1978, he would understand that they are no longer bound by their blood-sealed oath. He wrote that he regretted causing her any heartaches, and that he wanted to get married before his hair turned gray. I knew from my aunt's alarming letter that Vilis, the perfectionist, had fixed the locks and increased his watch over her, but once the time was up, it did not matter. Alma would be his forever, for as he said, what would be the use to escape? Where would she go? What could she do? And in his way, he was right. She was lonesome and alone. She was bored with the struggling Latvian theater and the old, tired exile society. There was never enough sunshine in Sweden, she complained. Also, she had not bothered to learn Swedish, and so she was locked up in another prison from which she could not escape.

She was completely dependent on him, and he gloated about that. He knew nothing about her soul and spirit, but controlled her body, as she put it, with all the laws on his side. He treated her attempts to escape as proof of female madness, and people, of course, were only too happy to believe him, since they knew him and not her. She did have a way of upsetting people, I must admit . . . To me he confessed that he felt guilty because he did not put her away and so save her life." Milda choked up and, after a pause, sighed, "Oh, my poor, wonderful aunt! A tragic victim of our exile. Please be kind to her."

She watches the hand write down the last words and make a neat and round full stop. The grand lady confirms some dates and places and then, extending her hand, thanks Milda, saying she needs to talk to some more people. Left alone, Milda wonders if she revealed too much, but it's too late. She watches the old queen go away and sees Helga coming.

"How are you?" Helga asks, sitting down.

Why is she so solicitous . . . What does she see, what does she know about me? But Helga only smiles with her father's smile, stares at her with her mother's eyes. That smile transports them back to Esslingen. They are on the flat roof of *Lido.* The steps are clean, and they smell the baked bread . . . They chat for a while and watch people coming and going, recalling faded names, scenes, episodes.

"How did we ever get this far?" Helga marvels.

"Oh, we are the lucky few, the chosen remnant of our people."

"So it seems. They—at least those who are here—all seem successful, well off, if not exactly rich, like you and me. Still, they act special, rather superior, don't you think?"

"Perhaps."

"Ah, yes, we are the survivors of the noble Aryan race," Helga says with mock pride. "We wear America well."

"And remember Latvia beautifully," Milda ads, while the music keeps on playing and people keep on dancing.

"Let's go," Helga says, "I have a story for you."

A Revelation

Mrs. Williams, with nervous Mrs. Arājs beside her, drove her VW to the outskirts of town, where she stayed in a Motel 6.

"They are cousins," Helga said, once they were seated on opposite beds, "And he has come all the way from Argentina to settle his account, so to speak, or have his revenge. What a fantastic story!" She opened a bottle of Riesling. "This is the most fantastic event of the whole gathering! Counterparts in the true James Joyce style!" She rose and unfolded a small linen cloth and covered the night stand. She set out crackers, a wedge of Brie, and a cluster of green grapes. "This is wonderful," she said abstractly, deciding how to begin.

"Tell me," Milda leaned forward, reaching for a glass.

"What I must tell you will be painful," Helga hesitated, "because there are things and topics we rather not deal with. They spoil the fun."

"Tell me," repeated Milda, "for once I need to know. So I can go on."

"Very well. But it centers around the Jewish question, about things we rather not discuss."

Helga rose and stood looking out the window into the night. Behind her, slumped on the bed, in red silk, lay the Ice Princess—now aged, tired, melting away. Trying to keep things on an even keel, Helga struggled to balance words against emotions, which smoldered and sizzled at the surface of their seemingly casual discussion, afraid to rattle and splinter their relationship.

Tell her the truth, Helga hears her mother from beyond the brilliant sunset. *Don't you see how she is tormented by not knowing? Don't you see that she needs to find her way home?*

Her head tilted, as if she were listening, Helga stepped back and sat down on the edge of the opposite bed. "They are cousins, as I told you—as he told me. Let's call him #2. As eighteen year olds they were drafted into the German army and eventually put in the 'final solution' squads that did their job in Kurzeme's war zone. They were supposed to execute all Jews, while the Germans held them at gun point. Only with our cousins it was different. Vanags #1, according to #2, eagerly joined the Germans. It followed, of course, after the communist terror, after his father had been deported and mother tortured by the communists in some cellar in Liepaja. It was in the blooming month of June," Helga's tone took on an ironic, sarcastic twist, "while red poppies adorned our fields, when Stalin raged like a struck boar . . ."

"Cut the poetry and all your fancy figures of speech. Tell it straight, whatever the truth may be."

"Yes. Well . . . His uncle, #2's father, had been shot down in *Zilais Brīnums, s*o the boys went crazy, the one being scared and immobile, the other turning aggressive. For a while they stuck or were stuck together. Our own heroic Vanags was always behind his scared cousin, pointing the gun in his back making him do the shooting. This for him, he said, was the worst terror of his life. While he squirmed, he knew that the elder, stronger actually began to enjoy the bloodletting and went crazy with killing, raping, laughing. Others took pictures which, after the war, appeared in Western newspapers and magazines. He showed me one photo he's carried with him all his life like some hidden charm. In the corner of the photo, almost invisible, he pointed out his cousin—your Pēteris Vanags."

"Mine?" Milda shrieked. "Don't editorialize!"

"Sorry. The Argentina Vanags is convinced that the gun pointing at his back is his cousin's and the young woman—the nude target—was the woman he actually raped while her mother watched. Then both—mother and daughter—were eliminated." Helga picked at the grapes, while Milda stared in wide-eyed horror.

"But we did not do it," she whispered, setting down the glass, covering her eyes. "Kārlis said we didn't. The German squads did it, pushed the guns on our people, made them perform unimaginable acts. I know that now we're stuck with the statistics. All else is lies. History lies. You lie," she cried.

"I wish I did," Helga said, "but I've suspected all along that the reason we—our people—have helped to keep the borders sealed on this side and not allowed contact, is fear and guilt. Fear of people like me and others going behind the Iron Curtain and finding out what really happened in those woods and dunes where all was secretly covered up."

"You lie! We are not like that," Milda spoke. "Maybe some carried things too far, but look what they did to us! We all know that. We were victimized from all sides."

"Oh, my dearest friend, regretfully, we ourselves have had a miserable, dirty part to play in our own history. It was not only they—the Russians, Germans, Fascists, Nazis, Communists. We also helped—in some way or other. Old people there, without much provocation, told me stories that would make your heart stop. Yes, it hurts . . . Systems are made up of people, and people do the most awful things—even when they would have a reason, the noble reason of justice and self-defense."

"I won't believe you."

"Your choice, but let me go on with the story." Helga filled their wine glasses. "After the war, the cousins became POWs somewhere in Belgium. By then both had lost their left arms, except #1 lost it in a bombing and—"

"Not in battle?" Milda injected.

"Guess not. He had cut loose, so his cousin told me, before the end of the war."

"I see."

"The real Pēters had been shot in battle, in the hand. The bullet sat there until his whole arm became so badly infected that it had to be amputated. I don't remember exactly what happened in what order; here his story got murky and hard to follow. Anyway, the cousins ended up together in the same camp, about the time of the Nuremberg trials, and everyone was scared because all who fought on the German side, for whatever reason, were labeled as Fascists. Our brave warriors . . ."

"Oh, stop being sarcastic!"

"I'm not! Maybe you don't know—we didn't either until much later—that my own brother, at the same time, was on his way to Siberia, a Russian POW."

"Sorry. Yes, all right. Go on."

"The conditions in the camp in Belgium were horrible, as we all learned, and the real Pēteris had gotten some other infection and was supposed to be dying. And that was when Pauls, that is, the Pēteris we know, cleverly swapped papers. Little cousin's papers were clean, while all the atrocities of the other were on his record. But at that time there was no way of proving anything. They looked so alike that the first was able to somehow escape, and I guess by the time the victim recovered and realized what had happened, his cousin was perhaps on his way to the hills of our Esslingen. His crimes were counted as heroic deeds, and we all honored him. As you know, he did not lose any time applying for his visa to America. Very cleverly he manipulated his story in his favor. He played the part of the brave, victimized hero to the hilt, and because his English was rather exceptional, he was welcomed for services in the U.S. government."

"Oh," Milda moaned. "I'm so tired. The wine's gone to my head. I can't take it all in. It's awful. I'm sorry I blew up. I'm so upset, so under stress. It's been such a draining weekend, but I see, I begin to see how things and people fit together, what makes them tick. Ah, maybe it's not as bad as I thought it'd be. The war's like a millstone around all our necks. It turns decent people into criminals and then punishes them for life, when normally they wouldn't do those things. He was just a boy, really, whose parents had been taken from him and executed for nothing. What would you do in his place? What would I've done?" She stared at Helga, who again rose up. "No, he's not, couldn't be as bad as you and his mysterious cousin present him."

"Not bad?" Helga faced her. "How bad must a man be and still get away? The man's a rat, and you've known it all your life! The only places where people with a record like that could hope to escape was Australia, Central and South America—Venezuela, Argentina. So innocent Vanags ends up going there, being a scapegoat for war crimes he never committed."

"How do you know?" Milda stood up. "It's one story against the other." She slumped back down and finished her glass. "You . . . how'd you know? What proof's there? The pictures are old, maybe doctored up, they used to do that, paste things, rip up and glue, didn't you do that? The glue back then was awful, I could never pick it off my hands, I don't know, I don't know anything, but he's got this power over me, I try to run, but I cannot, and I fall and fall, and you all just stare at me and don't know what it's like to be a widow and all alone night and day and night, mostly night, and I'm lonesome, Ilga doesn't call, hardly anyone calls that I care about and people don't know how to write either, and some men, I won't mention any names, just get what they want from me—sometimes—and then they run back to their wives, and I'm all alone, feeling like a bad, bad woman, when I'm not that bad, only lonely, I wish I'd be in Latvia, I'll go, I'll go with Ilga, and I don't care what Kārlis thinks because he's dead. Do you know what it's like to live with a dead man? No, you don't, your husband isn't dead, is he?"

"Please, stop."

"Well, what's the matter? Can't you take the truth, you fallen away Baptist?"

"This is not about me now, or is it?"

"I don't know what anything's all about. I just don't want you to say such bad things about the only man who really loves and wants me," crying, she grabbed Helga's hand and held it until it hurt. "Now you just keep your sharp pen out of this tough hand. Don't be so pompous and sure. Like I say, haven't we enough of poking in other people's lives, haven't we all suffered enough and paid for what we've done and not done? I didn't start any war, and he didn't either, and neither did you. We did nothing but run away—escape, when so many couldn't, like my sister and mother and poor, fat Matilde with her brood of disturbed, children who were taken from her. Oh God, my God! Why? You tell me, you preacher's daughter, why did the Lord God forsake us?"

"I don't know."

"And then there is poor Zelda, my sister, who's had to suffer like no one else here. How do we know which men and women are the guilty ones, which the innocent? It's been half a century, for Christ's sake!"

"Yes, you're right," Helga yawned, "but the fact is that one cousin banished another to a deep dark continent. For the Americans and even us, who became American citizens, those people did not count. They did not exist. So the first Vanags killed the second twice—or more. He assassinated him daily."

"Who're you to judge? Just be careful and keep your mouth shut and your pen locked! Who would have ever guessed that we might all churn up together like this?" Milda went to the sink and soused her face with cold water. "Anyway, he's rich, isn't he? He's done all right. He has a golden arm with a golden hook that catches things, doesn't he? And he gleams. He sparkles and shines and can afford to come here and make trouble."

"Ah. You ought to be a lawyer."

"Sure, I ought, but it's too late. I missed out on a lot of things serving my husband and family and Latvia—all for nothing, no rewards—just talk, gossip. We don't matter in world politics very much, do we?"

"Now let's feel sorry for ourselves. Well, yes. I asked him about his job or profession. So materially, he admitted being well off." Helga rose and made coffee. "He said he worked in amethyst and emerald mines and became rich, but his life was hell. He had married a Polish Jewess, who, he confessed, accused him every day of his life for killing her people, even as she traded in house after house, getting richer by the day from his digs. Some years ago, she died. They have a daughter who is a lawyer. She is here to file his case."

"Oh God! What else?"

"You saw her, didn't you?"

"Yes. She looked like a bird of paradise."

"He said that she is determined to go after the facts and the truth. So who knows what'll happen to our hero, your not-so-secret admirer. Time will tell."

Milda cried out, "So he had a horrible marriage. That certainly wasn't his cousin's fault. I bet no one bothered him about his papers or anything else, so why did he pop out of his mines now? . . . Ha? I bet he's mean and is looking for revenge. I bet you he's here to start a scandal; maybe his daughter is involved in some class action suit that will bring her more opals and emeralds. Maybe he has enhanced the whole story. You even said how this wasn't clear and that was uncertain."

Helga filled their cups with strong coffee. "I'm just reporting to you what I heard. I don't know what will happen next, and I'm not getting involved. I meant only to warn you."

Milda took the coffee and sipping spoke, brushing the tears with the back of her hand, blowing her nose. Churned up, she stumbled about and plopped into the easy chair. For a while they sat quietly, drinking the coffee, regaining their composure. Then she spoke softly, her voice breaking and choking up. "I feel so sorry for him, I wish I could do something, help him, he's not bad in his soul. He has not done anything bad that I know since the war ended, except his politics seems to me all screwed up, but so are other people's. I do wish he would have two arms, two hands, like all of us."

Tears ran down her face. Helga tried to dry them by pouring more coffee in her half-full cup, saying, "Hush, hush. It will be all right in the morning."

She drank the coffee, and heaved in silent sobs. "I don't know anything, it just hurts."

"The truth is bitter sometimes," she heard Helga as though she were far away, at the end of an inverted telescope, shrinking in size, while the words got big, like a lecture: "But it's better than lies. You'll see, you'll see. This will clear the lies about all of us, about lots of things."

"Shut up!" Milda rose again to her feet. She, too, could deliver! "What are you gloating for? What are you saying about us, about our nation and people? You're desecrating everything I've believed. You've led even my children astray! I don't know if I can trust you, no I cannot, you have cmmunist friends, and you only come here to watch us suffer in this long, lonesome exile, like Ilga says, and you don't care, you want to drag us all in front of people with your pen, but I won't let you, I don't even know you."

Helga let her rave. She took the insults, the verbal blows, as she had taken other criticism about her translations and her opinions that went against the ethnic grain. She knew elegant Milda was out of character, drunk, while she was much too sober, trying to be articulate, saying things that had been stored up in her life. She spoke softly, more to herself, more as if she were speaking into a hidden tape:

"I, too, raged when I learned the truth about us and our people. How our famous *strelnieki* guarded Lenin and our own young Marxists helped to bring down the Tsar and were all for spreading communism all over the world. And I cried when I read how in the Golden Age of Ulmanis, some social democrats were locked up and how when the occupations came, brother turned against brother, how the betrayals and lists were made by our own people. I even learned that my father's name was put on the list for the next deportations by the very same neighbor who had hid us in '41. My God, his son and I herded cattle together and wove baskets out of the same reeds! Oh, the stories about us—our people—good and bad, go on. I have heard plenty from those who have dared to talk to me, as if I were a mother confessor. Oh, yes! There is that other side, dear friend, our nation's other side—sticky and soiled. But we have to deal with it, and until we do, we'll never be made whole. You may do what you will, but you must know that only the truth can make us free."

"It's easy for you to preach," Milda mumbled. "You're not really a part of us. You're out there, coming and going, doing what you like, spying on both sides."

"If observing and thinking makes one a spy, then I guess I am one," Helga went on, prompted by Milda's words, knowing that there were people who assumed she was carrying information or whatever because she had been to the Soviet Union several times and nothing happened to her. "I don't care what you or anyone else says without thinking, but that doesn't make it any easier for you to deal with the two Hawks—pardon the translation—and what's happening with our people. It's never easy to come off ideals and see things for what they are. Not ideals and dreams save and help anyone—but love."

"Stop preaching to me."

"Well, if that's what I'm doing, then please let me finish the sermon: As these facts, this information came to me, as I saw it here and there, I understood that we are a nation of regular people and not some kind of minor super race, and that I am also a part of our nation—with good and evil in all of us, but also with rights like free people, and that we are not at all ended and safely occupied but are still very much alive and in place, going through the present cycle of time, here and now. I had to learn to see people apart from their political labels of right and left, of communist, democrat, fascist, nationalist. I saw them as they were—like me—like all of us struggling in a mad world, going through time and space, understanding some things but missing most, and then you know what? I felt love growing inside me that I would call divine. This love doesn't ask for perfection, although it is nice to have things perfect. It doesn't demand super intelligence and beauty, although it's great to be smart and beautiful. And so when I was in Latvia, when I saw what the occupiers had done, I felt I could only undo some of the evil with bits of good will. So I gave my relatives and friends what I had, but mostly I talked to them and I listened to their stories and their complaints and somehow they trusted me, and it seemed at those moments, those times together, we were all free.

"The taste of freedom was sweet! And then I began dreaming that if more people did that, if more people would chip away at the hard crusts of fear, something wonderful might happen. We all might learn to forgive and trust ourselves to be free, and in time, who knows? The walls might break down. End of sermon. Let's take you back. You all right?"

"Of course I am," Milda said. "Perfect, after your sobering sermon. Will there be an invitation for me to come forward and be saved?"

Helga didn't pick up on that and found her car keys. Milda wrapped herself up in Helga's sweater, talking on, saying, "The world is crazy. Politics is crazy and I have no idea who's right and who's wrong. I'm just so very tired, and tomorrow—or today, later, we have to get up, shining and smiling and singing. Thanks for the coffee. Wine goes quickly to my head, but it clears up just as fast, so I'm fine, just fine, thank you."

They walked to the car. "I mean it," Milda said, putting an arm around Helga's shoulder. "Forgive me if I said something I shouldn't, but who else can I talk to? I get so lonely, I'm so alone, and it'll start again this afternoon. Oh, how I dread that ride back to my boring town and empty house! But thanks, thanks for being a real friend. I do trust you, really, and we'll keep in touch. I'm sorry if I offended you, but what are friends for? I do love you from so far back that we cannot even remember ourselves anymore."

"Yes. It's all right. I love you too."

*

The highways and streets were empty as the two women, hurt and exhausted, rode back toward the Hyatt Regency. Each isolated herself in her own thoughts, memories, and visions. Helga was spinning another short or long story, while Milda wanted to erase the months between now and Christmas and fly home, her children at her side. Her mind was tearing down the old concrete walls, cutting through the barbed wires. She was thinking of even making a stop in Sweden to dig up Alma's ashes and bring them home in a golden urn. She cried and laughed silently, inwardly, through the tears, softly saying how all seems like a dream, how all the long way—the lifelong, extended round-trip—seems but a dream or a vision, a tunnel they all have endured and how they should come out of it, how it was about time to do so. Then she thought about Vanags—the two of them—and felt all her repulsion and fear falling away and being replaced by pity. With surprising sympathy she saw the men's bitter struggles with their other selves; no doubt, it had become a long struggle with many-headed dragons that lurked about wherever the guilty men walked. She realized that she had no desire to see *her* Vanags tried and convicted for war crimes or crimes against her heart. She knew deep down that he really loved her and—perhaps—wanted to hide in her, to escape the final judgment in the warmth of her being.

"Oh, I am so tired!" she said shivering.

She rested her head on the back of the seat, thinking, seeing doubles of all the people she knew, of all who were sleeping in the houses and hotels and all over the world. She imagined the two Vanagses always side by side, as she was with her sister, as Helga was with her mother, as Kārlis, even in death, was with the tragic president whose name he bore. She saw people wearing masks, hiding behind them. And these masks formed a mosaic of the most marvelous colors and lines. She could never understand, never fathom, and therefore, she was done with judging anyone or anything, for she, too, wore a mask and was a part of the mosaic she called life and that right now, in the middle of this clear, cool night, she was finally at peace. She looked at the brilliant stars and the waning moon like a deflated ball rolling in the vast firmament, forever mysterious, forever challenging, even though men had walked and floated on it and brought back hard, plain rocks. They must have felt like gnats on the moon's face that keeps on grinning, keeps the tides going in and coming out . . . . Milda winked at the moon, smiling.

"Tomorrow I want to celebrate, really celebrate, but I don't quite know what," Milda said when Helga stopped at the hotel door.

"Perhaps the birthday of your new, free self."

"Ah, that's too corny, but perhaps," Milda said, holding the door open. "And on second thought, you better write it all down. Our story hasn't been told. So good night and good morning! See you soon."

"Yes. We'll have to sleep fast."

"Right. Thanks for the ride!" She closed the car door, and Helga shifted into first gear.

THE FIFTH DAY

The Finale

Mrs. Milda Arajs stands at a curb in line with her people. One hand shields her eyes from the hot noonday sun, while the other holds Ilga's in a tight grip. They don't want to lose each other in the crowd that thickens by the minute. As many other women, they are dressed in their native costumes—one more elaborate and beautiful than the next, shining with amber and silver jewelry. The women, young and old alike, are poster pretty. **Latvians of the Free World**—united, seeing each other and trying to catch the world's eye.

And there are TV cameras and simple and sophisticated private cameras and videos. All are snapping, rolling reams of film, making the passing moments immortal. Mother and daughter smile into close-up lens eyes as they exchange intimate glances. They have found IT. IT will happen at Christmas, but IT is already beginning; like a concealed seed, the feeling and idea of true personal freedom will be nurtured throughout the advent months until it will grow strong enough to hold the idea, the hope and reality of true national rebirth. Milda is not sure about the practical road to Latvia. She could never retrace the road by which she and Alma escaped. She would have to find a new fast way through skies and clouds, not lands and seas. She will have to follow the compass of the heart, and the heart will have to be strong, full of love.

They hear music. The bands are in place; the choirs have lined up according to country and city, all costumed in ethnic cloth and jewelry. Milda turns to face the parade. She sees the banners coming up the street toward her: the blue banner of the festival, the American Stars and Stripes, the maroon-white-maroon, and behind them the singers and dancers. The scene is beautiful; the day is a lovely blue with white fluffy clouds.

Milda's eyes brim with tears of joy. Everything blurs. Caught off guard, she suddenly feels a strong, familiar hand grasping hers. She feels herself being pulled, and she pulls Ilga along, but Ilga doesn't follow. She releases her warm hand and runs backward, to her rainbow friends whom she will show *her rich heritage.*

The banners are over and around the people. Milda is wrapped up in all of them, bundled but free. The music of a marching folk song soars through her, and she catches the tune and sings: *Div' dūjiņas gaisā skrēja* . . .([*two doves flew up in the air, cooing* . . *will you or won't you come with me* . . .) Everybody sings, their faces peeking in and out of the floating banners. Milda feels good, as she did long ago at the head of the countless other processions, when she was young and the New World she was about to enter seemed like a nebulous mirage. She feels the strength of her legs, the erectness of her back, her proud head and the people's eyes.

Excited, she looks to the left and sees *her* Pēteris Vanags at her side, the American flag secured under his left half arm, the black-gloved hand unmoving like a spoke. The hand she is holding is alive. She attempts to stiffen her hand but cannot and stops trying, stops struggling and lets it go soft in his. It feels a welcoming gentleness, a tired grasping as though it were crying in the night. She pities the lone old hand that has not clasped its mate since the time when both were young and strong. The hands and arms have been separated for over a quarter of a century—like her nation, her people . . . Milda thinks about the symbols and signs and gently squeeze his hand. She looks up. The eyes in the shadow of the stars and stripes are blue like the sky but flooded as they were then—beneath the blooming rosebush. He lifts her hand, and his warm lips kiss it, gratefully, passionately. Her heart dances, her heart sings.

Unmindful of the exquisite union, the people march on, all looking straight ahead. But they do not see the Milwaukee Arena they will soon enter, nor are they going there. They are marching across lands and waters, through iron curtains and barbed wires, across meadows and dusty streets toward a statue of liberty named Milda, who, though wounded many times and lined with neglect and age, still holds her arms outstretched to heaven and holds the three golden stars over the beloved, suffering City of Riga. Singing the people march where the stars shine, dreaming of the day when, united and free, they will walk hand in hand down the wide Freedom Boulevard to the very end and then onward, to the *Esplanade*, where the ancient pines, deeply rooted, have been twisting their evergreen branches through countless winds and storms. Those pines, like the people, have had to twist and bend as other forces have twisted and bent them. The winds have broken many, but there are still many more that stand tall with no intention to twist, bend or brake. Every morning they greet the sun as it rises out of the sea—a ball of fire and light.

*

After the three-hour program, excited and full of wonder Milda lay on her temporary bed, on top of the slippery, satiny dust blue quilt. The beloved folk and patriotic songs that had resounded from the arena over to the Baltic shores and back only a short while ago still reverberate throughout her being, but they could not overpower the intense, persistent pressure and whispers of the man who had grasped her hand and held it so tightly and so tenderly that it still trembled from the seduction, the fingers curling reluctantly, impatiently around those abandoned rough fingers, so strong and determined. She put the hand to her face and pushed out of her eyes the stray, hot hair, but the hand would not slide down and lie on the quilt. It covered her face, letting it inhale deeply the man-scent it had absorbed. In slow palpitations, Milda soaked up the cocktail of nicotine, cologne, sweat. She swallowed the scent, her lips pressed against her perspiring palm, her body writhing dreamily in pleasure and pain and then lay still, thinking, calming down, trying to be reasonable, trying to decide what course to take, what road to follow. She checked the time and knew that the day was running out and she had a long ride ahead of her. More than ever she dreaded the long ride home, knowing that, on the hot freeway, the euphoria of this festival will again be only a recollection.

She rose and impatiently tore off her cumbersome, perspiration-soaked wool costume and slipped into her traveling clothes—a light blue denim shirtdress.

She packed quickly, rolling her things up and stuffing them into her suitcase. "I have to get out of here and fast," she told herself, "before that stupid committee meeting is over, before his hand touches me again." She was panting, wiping her eyes and face with that same trapped, obsessed hand, not using a handkerchief or a tissue but washing it with sudden tears of impatient rage and longing, letting the hand run down her neck, inside her dress where her heart hammered against her breasts.

She hardly heard the knock—so distant, soft, and calm it seemed. She listened, hoping and fearing, knowing that if she opened the door this time, she would never be able to close it again. She stood still, afraid of what she might do and say, wondering where the words would come from. She did not trust the impatient hand that already held the door handle, ready to give it that one fatal turn.

The second knock was louder, followed by three taps like some secret code. She put her eye to the peephole and saw him, his eyes watching the inverted telescope—waiting. She shut her eyes and opened the door. The next instant he was inside the room. The door closed. His arm immediately wrapped her in its vice, tightly against his perspiring, heaving chest, where she rested her confused head, silent and submissive, hungrily drawing in the same scent the hand had held out to lure her senses. She clutched the hand that had caressed her ages ago without really leaving her. The years since their separation when she left Germany, with all her determined plans for living a new life and forgetting the old, had not erased that long-ago impression nor its scent that had marked its territory.

Time, sound, motion reeled away; his silent pressure intensified, his shirt turned wet, his breathing short and shallow. She was being tossed back into the same dream she had sweated through on the first night of this festival, when she seemed to be drowning. To save herself, she raised her arms and let them slowly snake around him—one up his back, the other up and over the shoulder, bypassing that repugnant artificial limb and reaching for his head, the graying temples and that deep-set wave, the envy of other much younger men. Then his living hand lifted her face to his, opening her tightly shut eyelids so her eyes would look fully into his deep, dancing ice-blue orbs. She drew down her lids cautiously as her lips parted, her mind registering that the struggle—the nearly forty-year chase—was over.

He kissed her, embracing her with his leg, pulling her against him, into himself, letting her feel and know that he may be an aging invalid but that there will be certain compensations, that nature never abandons one completely. He kissed her deeply—the lips, the eyes, the ears, the open, hungry mouth. Then as she was swooning away, she felt herself lifted up and set on the bed, the slippery quilt, while he slid down. She groped for him, sinking her hands in his hair, but he slid lower, now kissing her feet, his arm sliding up and down her legs, her thighs, but going no farther, no higher. She curved over him, slipping down, inviting his head to pause at her heart, his hand to be scorched by the impatient, stored up flames that erupted from deep within her being.

But suddenly he let go and dropped her back into a stark, embarrassing reality. He stood erect as on guard—the soldier on his watch—ready for a new battle or dignified surrender. He sighed and, looking very seriously into her eyes, said, "At last . . . When and if we meet again, you will be truly mine."

"If . . . When?" she murmured.

"I don't know," he said as though he were far, far away. She reached for him blindly but did not, dared not touch him. "What don't you know?" she asked, but he did not answer.

She stood before him silent and distraught, now with eyes wide open and full of questions, asking him why stop now, at this thrilling juncture, knowing that they must go their separate ways, aware that this moment of ecstasy will never, ever repeat itself, thinking how IT would not matter, for after all, she was now a free widow and he a lone bachelor. Besides, it wasn't as if they had not known each other already—as if the rosebush had been uprooted, its buds wilted.

So why hesitate to seize the day? Is he punishing me, she wondered, as her mind projected as on a white screen the face of the other, full-bearded man, who only twenty-four hours ago had occupied the same bed. How could she now explain the agitation and relief she felt as she watched him go through the same door this one had entered? Didn't the latter know that the former had danced out of her life as painlessly as he had waltzed in?

Unflinching, she turned her eyes on him, asking, "Why the sudden morality? Why such decorum?" To push herself back into her accursed hostility, she conjured up hateful questions about his past: *Who are you? What is your code of ethics, anyway? Have you not killed men and raped women ages ago, way back in those impenetrable war-zone woods at the edge of some sandy pit full of dead bodies? So why are you here, standing straight and looking at me, perhaps judging me? What have you forgotten and what do you remember*?

"Who are you really? Tell me," she said, her brow furrowed.

"Not until you tell me who you are—really." He spoke with his accustomed cynical formality.

"I want to go home," she said quickly. "I must get home before dark."

"Yes. I'm also flying away tonight," he said.

"So soon?" she asked dumbly, like a wife. He raised an eyebrow and looked down on her. "I'll call you at midnight, only to make sure you're home."

"Only that?" she asked challenging, eyes, angry at her weakness, at the chase suddenly, unexpectedly having turned around, literally with a vengeance. She turned away and busied herself with her things, while he stood watching, but when she was just about ready to swoop past him like Scarlet O'Hara in *Gone with the Wind,* he reached in his pocket and withdrew an audio cassette.

"You must listen to this before we go any further," he said. For the first time, she detected an almost boyish hesitancy or fear.

"Why, what is it?" She felt her blood chill as she saw KĀRLIS written in red letters. "Oh," she sighed as he slid the cassette into her purse with a thieving hand—she thought. "Has he been watching us?" she asked frightened of the ghost.

"Perhaps," he said. "And until you know the truth, he will hunt us."

"What? What truth?"

She let go of the suitcase and sat down on the chair, motioning for him to sit also. They faced each another. He lit a cigarette and smoked slowly until she became invisible inside the fumes.

"I hate smoking," she said and tried to rise, but he put out the cigarette and pressed her back in the chair. "The truth is," he said, "that he knew it was I you really loved . . . Please, no shallow protests now! We haven't time for that. And he also knew that you were, are, will be the only love of my life. He knew it but could never face that fact and the truth about himself."

"What's that? What do you mean?" She asked. "Our marriage was good. Of course, there were problems—also ones you caused—but what marriage doesn't have problems of one sort or another? Still, we managed to iron them out. It was a good marriage. Yes . . . I am sure it would have been perfect if your recurring shadow had not come between us and if our children had been better, but . . . Yes, we loved each other."

"Sure you did," he said. "Perhaps, when finally—at our last meeting—the truth sank into him, it killed him. I don't know. You decide."

"He had a bad heart," Milda said softly.

"Yes, very bad," he confirmed.

She looked at him hard, questioning, feeling her blood go hot and cold. She was afraid. She wished he would comfort her, lay her down on the quilt and do what both bodies had so craved before all the talk. What was there to say, anyway?

Reading her mind most clearly, he said, "Not until you hear the tape. Not until you confess the truth to him." He stood up and faced her. "I do *not* commit adultery," he said with his peculiar sense of superior, self-imposed morality. She knew now for sure that he was accusing her. And she knew that he knew, had known all about her, from the time he chased her and made her leap over the bonfire and from that time forth until this moment—he knew it all. Angry, she looked past him. He let her stew for a while and then raised her chin with one finger and said, "It's all right. That's life. A woman's destiny is to love and suffer."

She frowned. She had heard that male cliché countless times before as if it were the eleventh commandment, one she thought she had obeyed to the letter. He saw her struggle, the guilty shadows flickering, but he did not want to hear any confessions, any explanations and kissed her gently on the forehead. "The tape will hurt you, but you must listen," he said, and before her tears might start flowing, he walked out the door and was gone. She quickly gathered herself and her belongings and called the bellboy.

*

Down in the lobby people rushed about, grinding through the revolving doors that threw them out into the real world. She caught Vanags's gray-suited back as it rushed for the airport limousine. The back at that instant had its own life and momentum, separate from hers. She saw other people reeling by. Aria said they should keep in touch. Ausma shook her hand politely, and Skaidrīte remarked how nice it all was and how she could hardly wait for the next festival.

And then a hand brushed her shoulder. She turned and faced Egons for a quick second, while his wife fussed with their children. He, too, seemed far away, unimportant, even a nuisance. She smiled and said good-bye, noting how easy it was, and then went to check herself out.

As she was making her way through the lobby toward the revolving door, she saw a service man scrape the posters off the round pillar. She saw **Latvians of the Free World** ripped up, the crusty backside exposed and dumped into a refuse bin. Turning away, she hurried down to the parking lot. She found her car, slid behind the wheel, and put the gears in reverse.

PART II

DRIVING HOME

After Milda emerged from the parking lot into dazzling daylight, she saw other festival guests hurrying, going this way and that to their vehicles and then on home to their *normal* abodes all across the United States of America. The Fourth of July flags still lined the streets as did the festival banners. She drove slowly, looking around, looking for Latvians, but not stopping, not saying *Sveiks!*. Her people had simply dissolved into the crowd—into the melting pot. *But not completely,* she held the wheel firmly, apologetically. *Not forever because we are not your usual immigrants, illegal or otherwise. We did not come here because we had it bad; we came because of the war. We fled. We were threatened by forces beyond our control and when the time comes we'll go home, we'll go back and rebuild—if we live to see the day. We are a proud nation, and we don't want to be a burden to anybody.* She imagined returning to Latvia, holding Vanags's right hand, but then confusedly, she reviewed the promise to Ilga that they would *go home* at Christmas to see Mara's baby, to make a pilgrimage. *How will those two possibilities go together? Where do I belong?*

In the traffic through which she maneuvered—the one-way streets, mergers, construction areas, confusing signs—she tried to imagine how it all would work out. Thinking, recalling, pondering she almost missed the ramp on to I-94. She slammed on her brakes. Horns blasted, but she held on to the steering wheel and merged into the fast freeway traffic, going home.

She cruised at 65 mph, allowing her mind also to cruise and guide her. As far as Ilga was concerned, she understood that the spurts of enthusiasm that promised the hope for a real turning point, for real change that would narrow the passages from spirit to spirit, make conversation easy—a two-way process—did not happen. The hope, perhaps mutual, did not coincide in space and time, and so each was, even at this moment, going her own way. *Oh, where is my daughter? And with whom? Oh—*

Ilga!
Childhood

Ah, Ilga, Ilgiņa, Milda's soul called. *My own little girl, where are you? How did you vanish and turn into a woman, a stranger I hardly know, hardly know how to talk to? I know that in your heart of hearts you are still confused, though you act poised as if you knew the way, as if you could lead us all home. I know that you're still running around looking for missing links, looking for those lost and hidden roots none of us can find? Are you more steeped in Zelda than in me? Or is Alma's ghost haunting you, looking for another tragic, beautiful body to enter? Who are you really, my strange, precious child?*"

To Milda's mind came the image of her imp-like, wistful child, who was the first to find violets in their garden in spring and the first to catch snowflakes in autumn. Ilga was always full of surprises, skipping on dangerous ridges, saying outrageous things, asking unanswerable questions. Her teachers had told Milda at a PTA meeting, "Your daughter is certainly resourceful and original." They said she was artistic. She wrote good stories and could draw like no other child. She read books well above her level. "She is too grown-up for her age," her seventh grade teacher warned, suggesting she read ordinary books, like Nancy Drew mysteries or *Little House on the Prairie*, not *Tess of the D'urbervilles.*

But Milda and Kārlis were proud of that kind of criticism and encouraged their daughter to go on, to challenge and provoke the whole system, if need be. They also made her feel proud of being Latvian and of knowing two languages at once and equally well. They told her that as soon as possible she should study another—French, German, or maybe Finnish, since Kārlis claimed deep Liv-Fino-Ugrian roots. But meanwhile she was very busy and very good. She practiced the piano every day and sang in the Latvian children's chorus and danced in the folk dance ensemble. Every Saturday Milda drove her and Gatis to the

Saturday School, where the curriculum and teaching methods were like those in the good, prosperous times in Latvia—the independent time of the twenties and thirties. "This is your most important school," Kārlis constantly pounded into his children in his voice of thunder, whenever they complained about not having free time on Saturdays like other kids.

But Milda feared his stormy, red-face rumbling. She saw how Ilga's defiant eyes flashed back at him, how her little mind was gathering its own storm clouds and felt them gathering over her own head as well. And sure enough, one fine Saturday—naturally, when father was out of town—the clouds came down in torrents of tears. Ilga stomped her feet and shouted that she would not go to *that* school. She said she had other plans and pulled at her hair, undoing the golden braids Mother had taken great care to braid. In her mad rush, the rebel smeared lipstick all over her mouth and stepped into a pair of high-heeled shoes. Yelling that Saturday school was stupid, she waddled out the back door and crawled through a hole in the hedge, and escaped form Milda's blinking glare. Milda rushed off to the Latvian Center with her good little boy, who sat invisible in the back seat of the station wagon.

No sooner had she reentered her house when the telephone rang, sharply, insistently. Tight-mouthed Fanny Brown called, asking her what all this was about and did she have any idea what her daughter was doing. "We're all upset," she said and hung up. Frightened, Milda rushed to the scene, two blocks over. From a distance she heard the loud blasting of a cracked record: "*I wanna hold your ha-and . . .*" She saw Ilga, doing a kind of belly dance. She had tucked an old curtain all around her and was whirling away, eyes closed, her red lips parted . . . *A miniature Alma on Walpurgis Night* . . . Milda stared, but the children did not see her, nor did the other mothers gathering around them, their faces moral and hard. Fanny watched from her steps, leaning on a broom. "*Hey, hey we're the Monke-ee-s, we're only monkeying arou-ou-nd* . . .," the children sang with clear, rock voices.

Milda pulled Ilga down from the porch—the stage—and dragged her home, half-naked as she was. "What were you doing?" Milda asked, unable to decide whether to put tears or anger in her voice.

"Dancing," said the child with a woman's voice.

"You were showing off, being nasty. Why, look at you! Look at your belly button!"

Ilga stuck her finger into the little dent and licked it. "Sugar," she said laughing. "It was only for the show," she said, licking her lips, putting the colored, sweet finger in Mother's mouth. "I'm Salome," she said, "and I was dancing the veil dance."

"How did you know about Salome?"

"I listen to all the opera," Ilga said. "Just like you. I hear what you hear when the radio is on." The child spoke again with the voice of a woman. Milda blinked and stared. She saw a tiny Alma grinning, knowing already the secret pleasures of sin and willing to take the punishment.

"Go to your room," Milda said scared.

*

When at noon she opened the bedroom door, Ilga was sound asleep on her bed. Her hair lay in scattered disarray all over the floor. Hardly any hair was left on her head. The pillow was wet and smeared with lipstick. Milda stood numbed. Her little girl looked like a boy, like *Gatiņš*, with an overgrown crew cut. Her lips were pinched, her eyes shut too tightly. Milda touched the head lightly. Suddenly Ilga jumped up and laughed. It was a wild laugh, hysterical and too old for her age.

"Stop it, Ilga, stop!" Milda slapped her face, the way Aunt Matilde had slapped Anna. "Quit this!" Milda's hand was stiff and cold. Scared.

Ilga collapsed in Mother's arms, crying. Milda stroked the head that felt like a brush as the child cried harder. When at last she calmed down, she heaved, "Wh-h-y did you do-o it?"

"What?"

"Hu-hu-mi-li-li-ate me i-in front of my f-friends?"

"I did not."

"You did so! You were unfair! Cruel like a stepmother!"

"I had to punish you. You were bad. You did not mind us. You know you must go to school every Saturday, you know we don't want you to play with neighbor children. You must play with our children so you learn our language well. And we don't want you to sing those songs. Don't you sing in the choir? Haven't I taught you so many pretty folk songs?"

"I hate them!" Ilga said. "They're stupid."

"No, they are not. They are beautiful," Milda tried to be as gentle as possible. "They are the same songs my mother and aunt sang to me. My grandmother sang them to my Mamma, and so all the way back, far, far back, when our sea washed loads of amber out on the sand." She stroked again the bristly head.

"Who cares?" Ilga was pouting, keeping her head tense against Mother's hand.

"We care, my precious. Your father and I care, and all our friends care."

"But I don't," Ilga pulled away screaming. "I don't care? I love the Beatles and the Monkees!"

"But they don't sing pretty songs that are for children. You are too little for all that."

"All what, Mamma?"

"Shh," Milda pulled her close. "You sing our songs like a little nightingale."

"What's a nightingale like, Mamma? You've never showed me one." Ilga became docile, curious, her eyes searching, as if looking for the strange, mysterious night bird. "I think I sing like a mocking bird." She giggled.

"Which one is that?" asked Milda.

"The gray one. The one who sits on the telephone wire all by itself and sings. It doesn't have its own song but copies all the other birds."

"Oh. And that's what you think you do . . . I don't listen much to these birds." Milda began humming and whistling the bird songs she remembered. And Ilga listened. She was laughing, smiling, the sunshine playing on her streaked face.

"Why did you cut your hair?"

"Because I was sick of it," Ilga answered. "I hated it. I hate when you pull and braid it every morning. No one has pigtails. I hate being different."

"But it was so pretty," Milda cried and knelt on the floor in the middle of the gold. "I had hair like that. It was long and my mother used to braid it every morning," she sobbed.

"Well, you can have it." Ilga stood up and spoke from above. She held out a handful of hair and said, "Take it. You can have it!" She kicked the hair around. "You can make a wig out of it!" She laughed. "Your hair is getting old."

Milda rose and slapped her across the mouth. "You will have to deal with your father—tonight." She walked out of the room, shutting Ilga inside. "And clean up the mess," she called in frozen anger from down the stairs. She heard a loud kick on the other side of the door, but she felt the kick in her heart; she felt that Ilga was kicking away her childhood . . . As Milda drove to pick up Gatis, she mourned for the hair in which she would never again pin a flower or braid a ribbon. She remembered Alma burning her first gray hairs. She remembered the ring of fire.

Months passed and Ilga's hair grew back. When it was long enough, Milda took her to a beauty parlor and had it styled. The beautician said that Ilga was one of the most beautiful children she had ever seen. "And so grown-up too!" Milda nodded shyly and looked in the mirror, but she saw not only her little girl turning into a woman but the reflections of all the women of her scattered family receding, going backward, diminishing into little girls, into lost embryos. She was glad then that Ilga had taken the scissors herself and spared her the pain. Besides, long hair was now in style all over and was associated with the Beatles, hippies, drugs, and the Left. "You must keep Ilga on the right path," Kārlis implored.

He spoke to his daughter behind closed doors that night, and for a long time, Ilga was a model child at home and the best student at both schools. She even helped Gatis with his Latvian homework.

That Christmas, she gave her mother a box in which, braided and tied with blue ribbons, lay her hair like some stray, captured sunbeam. With the present came a card Ilga had made: an angel with golden braids and her own pretty face. The card was inscribed in most careful calligraphy with the folk song every Latvian child knew by heart: *"Es savai māmiņai, kā sirsniņa azote . . ."* (I'm to my mommy/As a heart in her bosom/As a heart in her bosom/As a rose in her garden.)

The Teenager

But once Ilga entered high school, she progressed in every degree of difficulty. She chose to take up Spanish instead of the languages—French, German, or Latin—her father insisted upon, *the languages of culture.* When he said that, she challenged him, demanding *credible evidence* for *his prejudiced statements.* Whereupon his face turned red. Watching the hue deepen and spread, she stretched herself to her full height and declared that she was big enough to make her own decisions.

Speechless, Kārlis clenched his fists in persecuted silence when he heard her say that she planed to go to Mexico to study anthropology or join the Peace Corps. "Maybe I'll go to Africa to fight apartheid." Kārlis did not know what that last word meant and what armor Ilga would need, so he walked out, casting a scornful glance at the bewildered Mother, who had done her best. She, pale and sad, said to Ilga, "Dear, your hair is getting too long." But the girl walked past her, up the stairs.

From the way her behind swings, I swear she could be Alma! Milda stood until the upstairs door closed and then withdrew to the kitchen. When, an hour later, Ilga came down for her ginseng tea, her head was sprouting tiny braids secured with wooden beads of all colors. All evening Kārlis sulked and glared at her and finally spewed out *Holzkopf* (wood head) and closed himself up in his study. Gatis wanted to know what the big deal was, but Milda had no good answer. She could not put the symbolism into words a child would understand. Ilga winked at her little brother and said *right on.* Bewildered, Milda cleaned up the kitchen, and Ilga, in high spirits, stayed and helped.

"Things aren't as bad as they seem to you," at night Milda comforted her husband, holding the bedclothes open to receive him, but he said he was tired and turned his back on her.

*

Somehow they survived Ilga's high school years. She graduated with honors, elevating Kārlis and Milda among other, very proud parents. Beautiful in her *Zemgale* costume, her hair braided in one thick plait that snaked down her back, she also graduated with honors from the Latvian High School . . . Gatis adored her, while her parents, clasping their hands in nervous relief, congratulated themselves. The title of the main speech was: "*Latvijai ir nākotne*" (Latvia has a future)." And indeed so it had. The outdoor church of Longlake was packed on that sunny day. In the front rows sat the graduates, all in national garb, about one hundred proud young men and women. The whole atmosphere was charged with special excitement, as one by one the graduates walked up to the stage to receive their diplomas—with the national emblem and banner—like in free and independent Latvia. There was hardly a dry eye, when, at the end, the people sang

God, bless Latvia.

*

Ilga did not go to Mexico, nor to Africa. She did not join the Peace Corps. She stayed in Grand Rapids and from there, through the filter of the exile community, she began looking—probing deeply—at Latvia. She joined the invisible, inaudible Young Americans for Latvia League, which seemed like a swarm of gadflies that bit the old folks—the parents and the leaders. They stung where it hurt the most: at the idea of communism. They pulled the propaganda newspapers out of the waste baskets and read them. Some started to write to their peers behind the Iron Curtain and receive responses in normal human handwriting, expressing normal human interests, wanting normal things. Others went **home** and returned, insisting, "It's not the way our old folk say it is."

Simultaneously, their reports seemed enforced by the general belief, backed up with news reports, that there was a *Thaw.* The cold war, like all wars, had exhausted itself and was coming to an inevitable end, the smarter ones argued. At such news, Milda listened and remembered the preacher saying that things typically change with the third generation, which has neither the power nor fear of their grandparents and thus become catalysts for change. *Is Ilga in that category?* she wondered but did not dare reveal her thoughts to anyone, especially Kārlis, who became proportionately more hard-line and spent many hours in the night talking to his friend Pēteris Vanags, *who understands me the best.*

Meanwhile, as debates became more confrontational, certain brave youths decided to go to Riga and study the Latvian language there, even when their parents pointed out that the ancient language was no longer pure but full of acquired Russian words and idioms. Also, about this time a number of Soviet Latvian defectors showed up in The Kingdom of Exile. They dismissed the impressions of the young as naive with *their* true stories of horror. *It's why we wanted to get out.* They gave speeches about the ways of the KGB and how no one should be trusted, how there was no Latvia—not *de jure,* not really—but that it belonged to greedy, brutal Russia. They warned against contacts and listed the *native* people who, even without their knowing it, were *Communist tools.*

Still, the teens of the displaced smirked. They were critical of American past and present policies and also tried to set their elders straight: "You can't have fear and freedom at the same time; they're mutually exclusive." They knew about McCarthyism and the execution of the Rosenbergs and how mass hysteria could be created and manipulated and how political extremism pays off, especially during presidential elections. They knew about American military bases around the world and about the Pentagon and tax distribution. They had the statistics at their fingertips. And they knew themselves. They knew that they were not communists, but liberal, intelligent Americans. "We're not helping communism, but we are breaking through it, tearing into it, while you all tremble and go back to '41. It's become a joke, a hoax . . . Why don't you wake up and join the real world?" And so they dared to step inside the barred Soviet Union and breathe the polluted air themselves, testing all limits. "If I am perceived as red," a young man spoke up at some basement meeting, "and I know that I'm no communist but am treated like one, then it must be so with others. And the question I have is whether there are any communists at all anymore or are we dealing only with our fears and false images?"

"Or," posed another, "are these defectors actually agents who have come to remind our elders of old terrors? Are they, in fact, sent here to play upon the worst fears and prejudices of our parents so that Latvia *will be* kept forever closed? Could these be the rats that are sent here to check on how much power and control the leaders of the old ship still have?"

"Yeah!"

So the gadflies swarmed. Ilga constantly buzzed around the heads of her parents with questions and contradictions, but Kārlis merely shooed her off. Meanwhile, the young rebels welcomed every artist, poet, and musician who, came from Latvia and helped each one to find a place to exhibit or perform—away from the sacred exile halls. After the well-orchestrated performances, the free thinkers ate and drank with the guests, also cautious and secretly suspicious. However, with the help of assorted bottles, the beleaguered counterparts talked their short and limited nights away. They whispered inside secrets to each other and even indulged in very free and spontaneous lovemaking. But the faithful patriots also kept their vigils. They made lists. They knew who met whom. *Guilt by association . . . Suspect until further discussion*, etc., the young scoffed.

Pēteris Vanags telephoned more frequently, and Kārlis Arājs talked to him, behind his closed office door. After such talks, his eyes glowed feverishly. He was ready to charge, to organize, and write declarations. But Ilga charged back, with a swarm of gadflies at her command.

A major confrontation happened on a pleasant April evening. Gatis was not at home. Kārlis and Milda sat on the porch, swinging. Their peaceful garden, after a shower, glistened like a polished emerald slab. Suddenly brakes screeched, car doors banged, and through the gate came the young, with Ilga leading the way as if she were climbing a barricade. In her outstretched hand waved a white sheet of paper. She pushed it at her swinging parents, shouting, "Explain this, my father!"

She pushed the paper harder, right into Kārlis's face. He cringed and looked at it without uttering a sound, his ears flushed. Then he raised his eyes to meet Ilga's. For a moment their accusing, defensive glances locked, while Milda reached for her tea cup and held it suspended between the saucer and her lips.

"What about it?" Kārlis asked.

"Yes, what about it?" Ilga echoed coldly, cynically. "That's what I want to know. That's what *we* want to know." She moved aside, letting her friends have more of the porch, but they said nothing, used as they were to honor Mr. and Mrs. Arājs.

"Father, those are the names of our friends, people we know. People we live with," Ilga said quietly, looking down on her father, who leaned against the back of the swing, his chest barreling out. "Blacklisted," Ilga said, articulating every letter.

"Now don't you jump to extremes," Kārlis said defensively. Milda noticed the sweat rings of his armpits growing larger. "Those are only the names of people we are not sure of. They . . ."

"Yes," Ilga cut in. "They have been to Latvia, is that it? Is that their crime?"

"Yes. I mean, no . . ." Kārlis shifted around, swinging like a child, and looked at Milda for help. But she only blinked.

"All right. What about these? What have they done?" Ilga pointed at the names. "Zane, for example, why is her name listed? Is it because she taught us those haunting folk song arrangements of Dambis, Pauls, Kalniņš or because you cannot stand anything imaginative and modern?"

"Well, well." The swing creaked. "You are being disrespectful."

"And Viktors," Ilga went on. "What did he do? Showed slides of Riga, didn't he? Slides you never bothered to see. And Tamara. She read poems she brought out of Latvia, and did a fantastic job, by the way. Mamma, you would've liked them."

"Quiet!" Kārlis shouted.

"You would have, *Mammīt*, I know." Milda looked at Kārlis with scared little girl's eyes. Ilga said, "Pathetic."

Kārlis stood up. "Well . . ."

"Well, what, Mr. McCarthy?" Ilga spread out her arms, blocking his escape. "Where is this leading to?"

"I don't have to answer you. I rule this house."

"Yes, and the fuckin' bigoted minds too," Ilga's voice rose. "Oh, I knew something was brewing. All those quiet night phone calls from that Nazi Vanags and other hawks. But why am I surprised? We heard about the listing of people, only they were far away, in other cities. Just names, and maybe there was evidence. Some talk sounded convincing, as if there might be something real to this communist infiltration, but this is sick!"

"I did not make up that list," Kārlis said quietly.

"Oh, don't give me that! Without your blessing nothing is done in this whole Exile State."

Ilga lit an unfiltered cigarette. Milda gasped, knocking over the tea cup and spilling the dregs of linden blossoms. "Alma!" she said and rushed into the house and stayed there until the scene was over. She heard the continued confrontation from the other side of the wall. She heard words, phrases: *The Bill of Right . . . evidence . . . logic . . . love and human understanding.* She heard tears in Ilga's voice. She heard coughing and a long silence and then: "I am ashamed of you, father. For the first time in my life I am really ashamed." She coughed again. "If you personally did not write down these names on this paper, find out who did. Have that person send out an apology."

"Put that cigarette out," said Kārlis. "I didn't quit smoking so you could take it up. We'll talk about it later."

"You haven't given up anything. Now, erase these names! Burn the whole damn list!" Ilga screamed.

"I have no power to do that."

Ilga laughed. "Power? . . Power?" There was a long pause. "You mean courage, father." Ilga shifted into English. "Guts. Guts to be democratic in this great big super democracy that has fed and protected you—all of us—and guts to tell Vanags and the likes of him to fuck off."

"Watch your language, young lady."

"Sure, hide behind that. Throw me out of the house, have Mamma wash my mouth out with soap."

Another long pause. Smoke crept through her closed door, making Milda step back deeper into the kitchen.

"Put that obnoxious cigarette out!"

"Not until you answer some questions," said Ilga calmly. "First of all, where will this stop? And, second, who will stop it? And, third, who will be there to defend you or Mamma or me and Gatis when our names will show up on some future black list?"

"Why," Milda heard Kārlis squeak in a falsetto. "Outrageous! It will never happen. We live exemplary lives, that is, unless you . . ."

"Sure. Me. Blame me!" A fresh cloud of smoke hit the air. "Father, I am ashamed of you.— Why do you teach us to love Latvia? What has all my schooling in Latvian studies been all about? I simply don't understand. Why can't we touch this, our holy land and its people? Why?"

"I don't have time to answer your eternal questions," Kārlis said in a cutting voice. Milda recognized the tone. Her husband always spoke in that tone whenever he was faced with specifics that upset him. He always hid behind his lack of time.

"Exemplary lives," Ilga mocked. "Father, cowardice and injustice are not the examples I want to follow." Her voice broke. "I haven't time either."

Moments later, Milda heard the gate and the car doors slam and rubber tires peel away on the wet asphalt.

*

After the showdown on the porch, Ilga and her father fought their cold war battles with more diplomacy and avoided hard issues. Their eyes would look past each other, and their conversations turn shallow. They forced safe words like darts across their schism, words that barely revealed the surface of each one's totality. No important arguments tore up the harmonious Arājs's home; there were no confrontations. Therefore, to the busy, successful father all seemed well and settled. He congratulated himself again for having prevailed with his unbending discipline and principles. Only Milda, her maternal instincts alerted like an insect's antennae, picked up her daughter's restless tremors and silently monitored the degrees of difficulty of her maturing. She smelled not only nicotine, but much stronger scent whenever Ilga breathed near her. She saw wild, transcending ecstasies that set her daughter aahing and oohing over each flower in their garden, even the dandelions. Ilga's grades soared and plummeted. She stayed out late at night and overnight, especially when Kārlis was out of town busy fighting communism. When he was at home, Ilga stayed in all evening and went to bed at a normal hour but then left her bed, bat-like, after the house was silent. Milda, in her insomniac tossing next to her snoring husband's side, heard the exits and entries but said nothing. During the day she read *Dear Abby* and other columns that did not help. There was nothing that dealt with her particular *alien* predicament, and so she sank helplessly in her silent fears. She and Ilga hung on the edges of the great unknown, while people shouted ever louder on all the TV channels. It sounded as if the next byline would announce the end of the world, for which she was not ready. Wide-eyed, all senses alerted, she watched her babes turn into strange adults.

When, one spring night, the telephone rang close to her ear, she knew that what she feared had happened. She picked up the receiver on the first half ring, then said, "Right away," and, automatically dressing, tiptoed out of the house and drove herself to the police station. She identified herself in her accented dream voice and said, "Yes, that is my daughter." She saw the evidence, the dried weed, and posted the bond. She signed the forms for rehabilitating lectures and a work program. That done, the two cars—linked by mutual remorse, shame, and anxiety—drove through the empty night streets, which, rinsed by an earlier shower, shone like black patent. In the driveway, Ilga fell on her mother's neck, wept, and promised to quit all her bad habits and friends if only, if only she wouldn't tell Papa. "I swear, Mamma, I swear!" She sobbed. Milda believed her and told no one. But she remembered Alma. It was Alma reincarnated whom she dragged home, not her own dear child.

Once a week, for a month, mother and daughter spent an hour with a counselor, who rudely asked about the family background, and when Milda offered humiliated explanations, saying words about the war and family displacement, the woman was no wiser than before. She had, of course, no idea where such a place as Latvia was. "Honey, you're an American now, and you better go along with our rules and reg'lations."

"Stay to the point," Ilga said, tightly holding her mother's cold hand.

*

After the grueling sessions, throughout Ilga's junior and senior years, there were no serious confrontations, but then with the flight of migrating blackbirds, the problems returned. Milda observed signs of the same old patterns. She became more frightened than before and buzzed about like a bee whose honeycomb was being attacked. Still she said nothing. She could not sleep and would not dare to share her suspicions with Kārlis. She joined the Charismatic Movement and fell to praying. When that didn't help, she took up Yoga and tried to use the powers of her mind. She focused on Ilga. She concentrated. Her mind pushed at the invisible clouds of fear and darkness, and she succeeded, she believed. Ilga suddenly turned good again. She smelled of nothing but perfume and soap and Noxzema. She stayed in her room. Milda saw her from the garden sitting in her window nook writing poems, she assumed.

In time Ilga won small prizes, and everyone was nervously proud. Milda did not dare criticize. Yet she was not sure if what Ilga wrote could really be defined as poetry. There was something too weird, left-wing or left-handed, extreme. But her motherly heart raged and slowly turned to jelly, flooding her being for she saw and heard in each line of the free verse, with its staggered, off-center lines, the cries of her child's soul. It cried out against personal and global injustices. It cried for home.

At about the same time, during the late sixties and early seventies, the world not only opened up but seemed more frenzied, disrespectful of established traditions, which, among others, dislocated and confused the roles and manners of men and women. To those people who prided themselves and taught their children established manners and etiquette, the change was extremely upsetting. The world seemed to become ever more crazy, mad, shamelessly open about everything. The biblical forewarning that at the "end of times" the things that were whispered in secret and in darkness would be shouted from rooftops and in broad daylight was happening, and people, in their confusion, looked for causes and scapegoats which abounded in great numbers and various sizes, ranging from "the pill" to "the moon." Kārlis and his fraternity fellows were convinced that such monumental changes were a part of the communist plot of world domination. He felt that only George Wallace understood the dilemmas and hoped he would win the presidency. With those of like mind, he discussed politics over long distance telephone calls. He wanted to organize anti-communist demonstrations in front of the major state capitals and then expand to many parts of the Free World. *Communism must be stopped around the globe!* Yes, he would even be glad to send Gatis to Vietnam to help the cause, but on his TV screen long-haired men were burning their draft cards and shaking their fists.

To counter his fears, hope also emerged. Obscure, obliterated countries—like Latvia, Lithuania, Estonia—also popped up on the TV screen once in a while. They wanted freedom; they wanted recognition. In the USA, as African Americans demonstrated in the streets, other people followed suit and dug for their roots. They traced their genealogies—perhaps so they would not feel lost, so they would have a sense of belonging when the world would end, Milda thought, and was proud that, surprisingly, without warning, national sentiments and accents and customs became stylish—nothing embarrassing anymore. She was happy to see increasing numbers of Latvian young people show up for the local gatherings. Already half drowning in the melting pot, they tried to pull out; suddenly they wanted to study the old language and learn the ancient crafts.

Ilga embraced the trend. She asked questions about her ancestors, Latvian history, politics, and ideals, and Mother gladly steered her daughter deeper into her vanishing culture. Lost and exhausted from the pressures of American teenage life, Ilga for a while submitted to Mother's tight reins. Her friends likewise clustered around their elders' wisdom, once regarded as foolishness. From North to South and from East to West, especially in the stronger Latvian communities, a certain kind of hippie movement flourished alongside the general one that had steered all America and, in fact, the whole world on its mad, rebellious whirl.

The Latvian spin-off, however, separated and went its own way, all dressed in national costumes and wild flowers pinned in long, loose or braided hair. Hot dogs with sauerkraut in sweet-sour home-baked buns sold well at all gatherings. Young women sought out the older women to teach them how to bake rye and sweet-sour bread. Ilga was also eager to learn.

"It's beautiful the way we pass the starter from hand to hand," she rejoiced and never let Mother skip a week of bread baking. Sometimes Ilga helped to knead the hard, sticky mass. "Our bread connects us all," she said, her hands buried in the gray dough. Milda then likewise rejoiced, feeling very connected and happy.

"I know," Milda mused, her eyes looking out into space, remembering her good Aunt Matilde, who with her bread had tried to save her communist-torn family from starvation—until those cattle wagons rattled throughout the land and demolished everything. Still, she hoped, that the starters survived and lived in the shattered households and that even as she watched her loaves rise, women in occupied Latvia were baking the same bread as she and other free women. *Ever united, we are kneading and passing the leaven on*, she mused, *and the yeast ferments and makes the dough rise.* "This is a metaphor for freedom . . . rye bread and the hope of freedom keep our people alive," she said, turning her gaze to Ilga's buried hands, instructing her to souse the palms with butter so the kneading would be easier, telling her to knead until her hands became clean and the dough elastic. She hoped that Ilga would pick up the feel, the rightness of texture and never again lose it. She also instructed her how to preserve the starter in the refrigerator and how to pass it on and on.

"Intense," said Ilga. "Beautiful," she whispered, when done, kissing the smooth dough and marking it with a cross, according to ancient custom.

Likewise the Latvian language acted as an adhesive and gradually became elevated to an elite status, for only the sincere and the wealthy could afford the books, the schools, and the trips where the solidifying happened. In Kalamazoo a Studies Center was built. Eventually, though in very small numbers, students came from all over the free world. Simultaneously, at various universities, where energetic Latvian, Lithuanian, and Estonian professors taught courses in foreign languages, world drama, and literature, their syllabi included—in translation—their respective national classics. The greatest value lay in linguistics; therefore, the knowledge of the Baltic languages, especially Old Lithuanian, soon counted for credit and served as tools for research.

Certain scholars and laymen of Baltic origins decided to form a joint academic organization and named it *The American Association of Baltic Studies* (AABS). It published a quarterly, where academic, well-researched articles on serious topic could be published in the English language. The JBS would be an alternative to popular exile newspapers. Its contributors would generally be academicians, and their writing would have to comply to academic standards. Moreover, those immigrants and their educated offspring found in the AABS an organization which they gladly supported and where they could proudly participate and advance academically. Thus, like the fabulous yeast, consciousness grew, swelled, adding to knowledge more knowledge that went far beyond ethnic confines. AABS attracted the brightest and the best offspring of the old refugees and held conventions in interesting places, ending them with elegant academic balls. To these conferences also came scholars in carefully selected pairs from the universities and academies of the Soviet-guarded Baltic States. They also read papers (usually in the German) and mingled with their refugee counterparts, debating the interpretation of history and discussing the meaning of democracy. They compared methods of teaching and research and guardedly discussed the necessity of freedom and honesty in research and writing. Especially exciting were the first provocative, albeit cautious meeting and mutual exchanges of ideas which began during the so-called Soviet Thaw and continued on until the Soviet Union collapsed. Thus, by degrees, the hitherto closed doors and windows opened, never to be tightly shut again. Yes, Baltic Studies was interesting and fun, said one young and handsome, very bright, keynote speaker. The audience applauded enthusiastically. History was moving forward, as anyone could see and hear.

By the end of the seventies, those who had emigrated as teenagers from the DP camps of Germany controlled the AABS and made it attractive for future generations of *real Americans,* who were not only proud of their ethnic origins but welcomed integration and diversity. So this transition generation was able to go forward—beyond their parents' stories of persecutions and escapes and resettlements in the New World, where many had slaved in the cotton fields of Mississippi, sweated in the steel mills of the large cities in the North, and taken on whatever menial job would secure their emigration to the Land of Promise and Freedom. Though sympathetic, the ambitious young did not stay indentured in the locales of their sponsors but moved on. They did not care to listen forever about their mothers and grandmothers humbling themselves as maids and cleaning houses for their rich American sponsors and feeling guilty for being the heirs of their elders' continued sacrifice. They earned university degrees, understood finances, talked about investments and held top jobs as engineers, architects, teachers, brokers, professors. They and their children soon could afford things; they could afford to attend ethnic summer schools and even studies in Europe. Gradually this generation became the elite, the influential, the awesome movers and shapers of new attitudes and policies that truly changed the world.

In such enlightened atmosphere, the proficiency of native languages became the *in thing.* For the elders, it was a matter of showing off, like the displaying of rich plumes. Pushed into the background, the aging parents would judge each other's patriotism by their children's language skills and, therefore, would invest ever-increasing amounts in all kinds of activities and education as long as they were done in the right spirit—that is, the strong, unbending intolerance of communism and the unquestioning acceptance of traditions peculiar to the Baltic peoples. Each country displayed its treasures and beauty year after year, in festival after festival.

But those young people who could actually write—and write well—were practically revered; they were set up as examples and had sure access to many podiums and decision-making committees. Thus, in the shadow of the American Civil Rights movement and political debates, ethnicity flourished. Magazines and newspapers could hardly accommodate the influx of avant-garde poetry that revealed everything, even the cross section of a tear.

To Latvian newspapers and journals Ilga sent out batches of poems, which generally were accepted and printed. The large shadow of her father could not overpower her, and she became famous in her own right. The critic who wrote for *Avize* reviewed her first book harshly because her metaphors and analogies were *foreign* and, therefore, confusing and strange. Ilga and her contemporaries laughed at such criticism and went on writing their *modern* and *postmodern* verses. Other young would-be poets loved her for her daring and relevance; they admired her beauty and free style and clustered around her whenever she showed up. Thus exulted, she walked with her head lost in clouds, smoking unfiltered cigarettes, a notebook in her carpet bag. A friend gave her his own designed and printed T-shirts saying *Happiness is being Latvian* and *Hug me, I am Latvian*. Her banged-up VW bumper sported a maroon sticker with white letters saying *Sveiks!*

Still, all this did not erase Milda's maternal worries: Ilga was not turning out the way she had imagined and Kārlis had insisted. But what could she do? In modern America, mothers seemed irrelevant, even obsolete. Frightened, they seemed to stare out from behind screened-in windows and porches. Milda often stared out of her windows, watching the weather patterns and hoping for kind winds to clear away doubtful clouds.

Rather unexpectedly *Avize* started printing air travel advertisements, enticing the large reading population with super savers and packaged deals, which promoted travel to Eastern Block countries. Milda read those with great incredulity and amazement. She imagined herself flying to meet her sister and kiss the sacred Latvian soil. She envisioned the globe turning into a small ball wrapped in jet streams. Cautiously, she pointed out the ads to Kārlis, telling him that things were getting really exciting, that they, too, might be flying home soon, but he frowned, saying, "Would you expect me to beg entrance into my own country and pay my money to them who stole my house and murdered my father? I will never buy a ticket to a communist Latvia and neither will you!"

"Oh dear," Milda sighed, "I understand. communists made both of us orphans and homeless travelers and burdens to others, but my sister did not do it, and she lives and has to decide how to survive."

"And what good will it do to upset her life?"

"I don't know . . . Let's at least hope that these trends will steer our children in the right direction and that they will find a way to pay for the sins of the oppressors and the oppressed. I do hope that somehow together we—they—will boost national awareness in a changing world and that new times and attitudes will heal our wounds and broken heart." She stopped exhausted and waited.

"Hope what you will," Kārlis brushed her off and continued reading his own article.

Mr. Arājs's attitude, however, was not universal; others who had fled from their countries back in 1944, slowly, cautiously, one by one did buy tickets to Tallinn, Vilnius, Riga—via Moscow or Leningrad. They applied for passports and requested visas. Laden with goods and most anxious and tender feelings, they traveled back to where they had so painfully come from and returned sublimely changed, strangely complete but disturbed and very confused. Thus the clogged windows and bolted doors slowly opened ever wider, disturbing the Kingdom of Exile with uncertain winds and signals. The stories of the travelers varied: the negatives were easy to understand, but the positives seemed suspect of deliberate brainwashing; therefore, those who talked in positive or at least understanding terms about life in the Soviet Union were prime suspects, especially if they had gone back and forth with the help of the Connections Agency. *No one would give you something for nothing! Don't blow your stories into my ears!* So went the comments.

To warn and discourage people from believing that any real changes in the Soviet Union might be possible, *Avize* ran a series of horror stories about border crossings and reminded its readers that the Connections Agency was acting under the orders of Moscow and how it was an arm of the KGB. Still, that did not stop things; it seemed that, in fact, the Agency worked harder, welcoming the nations' lost sons and daughters without scolding them and in the style of old time hospitality. It called them, respectfully, *the emigrants.*

Pēteris Vanags and other hard-liners countered the propaganda with renewed vigor. He called Kārlis frequently and urgently, not bothering to excite Milda's ear with his seductive voice and phrases coined especially for her. *He is too desperate*, thought Milda. *Why*? But she never asked, knowing that the answers would be in the forthcoming article. When *Avize* arrived, she quickly found his article and read it. She did not discuss it with Kārlis but with herself in long angry monologues. While no journalist, she knew enough to spot bias, vague generalizations, and propaganda. She saw that Vanags had gathered every minute horror story and blown it up and dismissed everything that was positive as lies. He affirmed the warnings of other defectors who urged the exiles to break contacts, saying how hopelessly the land was polluted and the country taken over by Russians. "You don't want to go there. You don't want to have anything to do with those people. Don't trust anybody."

She saw how he confused his readers, how he and her own husband and others of like minds made the whole refugee community sick and how the sickness spread. Some became recluses, others depressed, and there were even cases of suicide. The disease was particularly contagious at large gatherings, such as the beautiful song and dance festivals, where people could not tell the sick from the well, the doubtful from the convinced. When word got out that certain places were infiltrated, nervousness increased. Yet no one bore any visible mark; no red star shone on anyone's forehead. And so it happened that often people would sit around tables, listen to each other's words, and wonder—could it be he? Or she? Or do they think it is I? Finding no proofs or evidence, they would joke and drink, and some would get very drunk and very loud and end the party with jolly old songs and more stories about war and terror. Afterward, they would drive back to their normal bread-earning activities or accredited studies, and they would say, "Who cares? We are so little, we don't matter anyway." But the behavior watchers remained vigilant.

And so people—the aliens—lived in the twilight zone between imagination and reality—between the Latvian and American worlds. Regularly they escaped from one into the other like the witches of old, who walked around in human form during the day but rode on broomsticks in the night. And they were haunted. Ilga and her friends felt haunted and fled from their mothers and fathers, but at other times they ran to them for protection. Sometimes Ilga would not show up at festivals even if they happened within a day's journey, while at other times she would travel all across America only to throw herself into the festivities like the princess in *A Midsummer Night's Dream*, when she, too, would fall in love with any ass and eat fern leaves until the dawn broke. Then she would vanish into satellite worlds, where her soul burrowed and where no one could find her, only to resurface when she felt like it, when she heard her blood speaking.

Only Milda, who suffered from a mother's incurable worries, saw how tired she was, how much she resembled Alma.

The College Student

In the fall of 1973, Ilga entered a college in upstate Michigan. She seemed a good regular student, with possible majors or minors in art, drama, English, history, sociology, or—just maybe—political science. She returned home on every holiday, bringing her books and telling stories about her creative friends and her exciting studies. Her parents were cautiously pleased because she finally appeared undisturbed in the old way. She had embarked on a new road and seemed to like the pavement. Father paid her way, and Mother slipped her extra money for a woman's special needs. All was well, they told those who inquired.

During her first summer at home, however, Ilga was elusive and brooding, her brow ever so slightly scraped with lines between her eyes. "I need this time to find myself," she told her parents, who thought she ought to be working at some job.

"Nevertheless, child, you should assume at least part of the responsibility of your education," Kārlis said and reminded her how hard he had worked to get where he was. "And your mother also labored as a humble domestic, and I would venture to say that she had no time—nor did it ever occur to her—that she should roam around in search of something that was right inside her. Of course, we were engaged." Kārlis glanced at Milda, who smiled back shyly, remembering how it was. How she worked for a year in a department store back room, wrapping parcels for deliveries and cleaned Mrs. Fern's house before going to work on Saturdays.

Every two weeks she visited her betrothed, herself paying for the round-trip train tickets from Philadelphia to New York City. Still feeling a bit guilty, she remembered, as their eyes met, how she had in her own mind insisted on reinventing her long-lost virginity and how the senior Mrs. Arājs, herself wishfully convinced, guarded that refurbished treasure with her constant presence during those visits. The matriarch had bought the white satin and lace long before Milda stepped off the ship, when the embarrassed and innocent Kārlis welcomed her at the shore. He had promised himself and his mother that they would keep their relationship pure so that there would be no accidents nor guilty stains on their consciences. True to his resolve, Kārlis, until their wedding, embraced his fiancé seldom. He kissed her with closed lips and open eyes.

"You remember, woman, don't you?" he asked over Ilga's head.

"Yes," Milda stuttered, "I wait—I mean I waited and paid for what I . . . my own way." She turned her sad eyes on Ilga, adding: "I worked my way into the rich life that you, dear child, now take so much for granted." She realized how poor she was at laying down the law—any law.

*

Ilga chose not to hear the troubled undertones of her parents. All summer she spent her days and nights around Longlake—her miniature Latvia, looking somewhat like a refinished period piece of the 1930s. She tried to reincarnate herself in her great Aunt Alma, whose 1947 photograph, taken in a dark DP studio in fabled Esslingen, she had pulled out of Mother's album, enlarged, put in an antique frame, and hung on her wall. She had found a flowered dress, similar to that in the photo, in a Goodwill store. She plucked her eyebrows, bobbed her hair, and applied lipstick with a fine brush so the lines were sharp and the lips, when she talked, looked like fluttering scarlet butterflies. She balanced herself glamorously on narrow-heeled pumps as she crossed and re-crossed the packed-down dirt paths of the reproduction of Latvia's fabled highlands. As she walked about, getting the hoped-for attention, she hummed old tunes, popular in romantic, lost Latvia. *Atmiņā lakatiņš zilais . . .*"

The magnet of the vanished decades of the thirties drew her back. She pointed out that it was the only complete decade her mother had actually lived in Latvia. This decade, with its gilded glamour and crushed parliamentary system, its decadence, its extremes of wealth and poverty, its yielding to President Ulmanis's charms and ruthlessness, and finally its sad dirges and war marches was, she realized with the sense of having discovered an eruption on a distant planet, actually the whole foundation of her parents' being.

"Hence," she deduced, "the thirties is also my foundation. I am also born out of that time. It is where I, too, come from." Having established that premise, she wanted to unearth its mysteries. But the more she looked down into the Iron Curtained folds, the more she became confused, seeing not the truth through the usual historical fathoms, but the reflections of the exiled consciousness which glimmered on ripples of good and bad memories as on a mirage. No one satisfied her curiosity. No one told her the whole truth and nothing but the truth.

Alone in her hypothesis, she struggled to form a clear topic sentence, but could not find the precise word, the subject—the nominative. Frustrated, she seemed forever forcing the strange pieces of her history together as in a gigantic puzzle, sometimes pushing so hard that the edges broke off, leaving the picture full of ugly holes and empty spaces. She argued for mysterious links and eternal cycles of her people's progression throughout the ages. She vehemently rejected the pat nationalistic segmentation of good vs. bad, Latvian vs. Russian, black vs. white, Communist vs. Free. At the same time, though, she argued with great passion for Latvia's freedom. She argued for human rights and sang loudly, *We shall overcome some day-a-a-ay.*

But the people in Longlake did not like the Negro songs, nor could they be excited about the rights the black people screamed about on TV and all over the country. "We also had to slave for what we now have," the legal naturalized citizens would state. "No one helped us when we came here with only a suitcase and our working hands."

Milda and Kārlis did not like the association with black slavery either and spoke to Ilga about it, but she snapped back, saying that actually the Latvians and African Americans had a lot in common. When Kārlis presented old arguments in favor of inherent differences of all races, Ilga screamed, "Oh my God! You don't get the point!"

The point, the focus of Ilga's concern, was not the Civil Rights Movement as such; for her it only served as a metaphor and a guide in search of her own roots. Her love focused on Latvia, the land she had never seen, but from which, as from an underground spring, all her life flowed out; indeed, all her sense of being. The deeper she stepped into her pre-history, the more she yearned to touch the land itself, to gather it in a bundle and carry it off, singing—barefooted and bare-breasted like her Jacobin sisters of the French Revolution, on which she had completed a course. She went to art museums and studied paintings of revolutionaries. She saw herself as the personification of Freedom. She imagined herself walking into the future, kicking up the dust with her spiked heels. That summer she also read the plays of the Latvian poet Aspazija and saw how all the great poetic/revolutionary minds were alike and how all the revolutions fed upon each other. "The ropes of countless revolutions push history forward," she declared to Kārlis, asking him if this would make a good topic sentence for an essay.

"Ropes don't push," he said. "Ropes, my dear, pull," he smirked, proud of his comeback. She crumpled up her paper and threw it at him.

"Calm down!" he scolded. "You should know that we don't justify revolutions, because they breed anarchy and communism. Misguided, usually very young idealists propose easy answers to complex issues, and so on, and . . ."

"You miss the point," Ilga broke in. She snatched the cigarette from his raised hand and finished it. Milda saw it all through the crack in the door. "Latvia is only a small part of the whole, which none of you see," Ilga said. "You just don't follow my thinking, both of you!" Insulted, her father departed, leaving Milda alone to smooth things out.

"We Latvians have not yet discovered our own history, so I must look for it myself," Ilga declared and, taking up her books and papers, went to her room.

She searched for *The Truth* all summer. Her curiosity was abnormal, her parents and teachers agreed. But she could not be stopped. Like a stone pulled loose, she went forward and down. She was satisfied with nothing less than the absolute truth, which she put on the oversensitive scale of her feelings. It was the needle of her soul that pointed out to her the truth, the only truth she learned to trust and to live by. And with that she picked up the truths and lies of others. Somehow she knew those people she could trust and those she could not; when she sensed bigotry or hypocrisy, she would drive her questions into her captives as if she were on a crusade until her opponents, her father included, lay exhausted and vanquished. Then she would triumphantly walk away, a cigarette in hand. But at the next turn, she would melt at simple sincerity and affection. She would extend her field of energy and in return sponge up the energy of those who responded to her need and enlightened her.

"Ilga is like cognac," Milda heard a young bushy-haired poet say. "She can only be taken in small sips. You could get drunk on her and she would leave you quicker than a hangover."

When Milda asked her daughter the meaning of such a comment, she said, "So?" And shrugging her shoulders, said, "I am a poet, and I live my poetry. I am an actress, and I test my lines on the big stage of this life, but . . ." Her eyes narrowed, her voice swam in tears. "But I am a damn good honest scholar, poet, and actress, and I choose my script and my own parts. My director is not some two-legged conceited asshole but Jesus, the King of kings and Lord of lords, whom nobody that I have met follows, not really." Milda watched her cry. *Like you, so much like you,* she said to Alma's photo on the wall. *I beg you, please leave my child alone.*

Ilga blew her nose into a Kleenex. "Mamma," she sniffed, "I am a good, honest woman. I know when I do things right. All the rest is bullshit." She sobbed. "Damn it, this is my life. Mine! It's my only turn in space and I want to orbit in my own destined way."

She orbited all summer, while the sun shone out from the heart of the galaxy with flaming indifference. All summer Ilga kept driving herself as she tried to penetrate the reservoirs of many lost, exiled, confused souls. She rolled out her soul like a carpet for those who wished to walk on it and enter the great parlor of her being. But, except for a few temporary adventurers of uncertain origins, most people did not even meet her at the threshold; they stopped like visitors or traveling salesmen and passed on. "She's crazy," some remarked. "Nuts."

Yet a quixotic aura did radiate from her, encasing her as in a separate orb. Gradually people became used to her caprices. They readily cleared the stages, as throughout the years, they were accustomed of doing for celebrities, including some poets. Thus elevated, Ilga seemed tall, larger than life, and people had to tilt their heads up in order to see and hear.

And Ilga? Ever so slightly she looked down from her spot of light into the dim, blurry darkness of her people. Sometimes she read her poems, but other times she merely spoke to the audience. She spoke then in a voice that reminded the old people of Aspazija and Biruta Skujeniece and Lilija Štengele. In that way she seemed to enlarge the small stages and rooms and surprise the audiences, for her poems arrowed through common clichés with laser-like precision and power. After such performances, she was exhausted, her spirit spent. She would then disappear.

She would disappear in search of the mysterious. She would look for it in the thickets and along the off-beaten paths. She loved Longlake—this closed national garden, where she proclaimed herself as a lost daughter of Eve. She assured herself that she had the right to eat every kind of fruit she wished from the thick-branched tree of human and divine knowledge. There would be no deadly danger in tasting anything, for Eve had already taken care of that; therefore, there would be no sin in her curiosity. She was too late in beguiling any Adam or serpent and therefore dared to go on and evoke the evasive, creative spirits through clouds of smoke and in the light of a full moon.

Snakes

Toward the end of summer, in a kind of folkloric jest, she passed the word around that she belonged to the cult of ancient pre-tribal, pre-medieval witches that were hunted down throughout German bishop-infested Livonia. To make people believe this, she said she had seen a vision. She said she had seen the outline of a snake inside the well-worn floor of the Longlake cafeteria. "It wore a crown and pointed northeasterly. She described how in a flash she saw that with the help of the snake she would somehow restore the balance between her Latvian and American halves. She said she saw the heads and the tails connected in a circle—the mythological cycle of life and immortality. She said it meant that Latvia would rise out of captivity and be free again. She prophesied a massive awakening that would shake up all Europe and spread all over the globe, but first someone had to lift this downtrodden spirit of Latvia (as symbolized in the image of the snake) out of the floor (the symbol of the Soviet Union). "And we, the people who live in freedom must do it! We must, with our own sense of freedom and truth and democracy, lift up our brothers and sisters so they can rise fearless, drop the old skins, and live in a new cycle of life."

The idea charged her to the max. She felt she was touching immortality. And so one morning, as in a trance, she left the cafeteria and went away into the woods. She gathered branches, careful to choose the right kind of hardwood, and that same afternoon she carved her first snake. After that, until the end of summer she carved and polished. She polished the snakes until they glistened as if alive. She sold them to her friends, but not the first one. That she carried with her like an icon. "I wish that all Latvians could have one of my snakes. They would unite us."

Soon a group of young, inquisitive third-generation aliens flocked around her, snakes in hand. She drew them to herself so close that they felt her breath and saw her heart beat through her thin dress. She told them that it was their duty to free Latvia, not with bombs, but with ancient wisdom and truth—like crusaders, only without the spears and daggers. In the remote cabin, where she stayed, at the very edge of the campsite, close to the forest, she gathered the young and curious. She retold the folktales and myths with a new, live voice. She told them about submerged castles where bewitched princesses waited to be rescued and where the golden key of freedom lay waiting for brave hands to turn it. Then she said that her snakes would provide only a visible symbol of things invisible, "Since freedom is invisible long before people recognize it . . . before action becomes belief. The trouble is that our people, especially here in exile, do not believe in freedom. They have given up. But you, you must listen to me. You must go home to our ancient land by the Amber Sea and take the hands of your brothers and sisters—actually your second and third cousins. You must carry freedom across the skies and the seas, but first you yourself must be free. Communism is not what enslaves people, really. Communism is old and tattered at the edges. You'll see how it will tear itself to pieces. Oh, it pretends to live on the economic level and is still guarded by the swollen leeches that infest the Kremlin, but wait until one brave hand pulls the gates open, and you will see the greatest miracle of modern times!" She spoke like Judith and like Deborah of the Old Testament, and her enthusiasm caught. Discussions flowed in secret, away from the eyes and ears of the elders, who came to Longlake on their vacations to bathe in their memories as in healing sulfur pools.

Among those who listened to Ilga's clear, enchanting voice sat a girl named Mara. She was from Philadelphia, dressed in tight jeans and a white T-shirt with the picture of the Latvian flag. As Mara's chest heaved in response to Ilga's call, the dark red lines wavered. When Ilga was finished, Mara rose and came forward, as at a revival meeting. She embraced Ilga and said, "I'll go to Latvia when I'm ready."

"Bless you," said Ilga. She noticed how young Mara was, how clear her complexion.

"I would like to buy a snake.".

"Bless you."

*

Still, Ilga's spirit ebbed and flowed, rose and crashed. She had no idea how to get from here to there, how to connect. She didn't know how to transfer her snakes to the other side and lay awake pondering, dreaming, imagining. During daylight, she walked about as if looking for some new sign, some specific signal. She roamed the wild areas of Longlake because only there, she believed, would she meet those spirits—also alien and in exile—who would care about Latvian needs and aspirations. She knew they were there, in the winding paths and thickets, flying over the water-lily lake on dragonfly wings. Why else would she have this certain feeling? Why else would her heart pound so? Why did she feel a kind of strange pull that tightened her nerves and tuned her senses?

And then it happened.

She was sitting in one of those long drawn-out meeting, where Professor Kungs droned on and on about "every Latvian's duty, his and her *summum bonum*." Quietly and half listening, she polished a snake with the finest sand paper that also sanded down the irrational-edged voice. She caught the words *summum bonum* and lifted her eyes. *The highest good . . . Yes!* That's what she was doing—seeking the highest good. Those words, the idea they conveyed, seemed to snake around her soul as she felt a strange pull from within. She sat up, listening, her eyes closed. And then as from a deep void, she heard her name, softly, coaxingly, as on ripples of the north wind, she imagined, and rose and walked out of the crowded, hot hall. She walked off into the woods, taking an overgrown, barely visible path. She pushed the branches and brambles aside with her hazelnut snake until she came to a small dell, where a circle of pines guarded the silence and wild rosebushes screened the view. She sat down on a stump, closed her eyes and meditated. Soon she heard the same call, as if softly blowing through the air. She rose and walked on, past thickets and old, burned-out campfire places. She came into another clearing and paused to breathe in the soothing menthol fragrance of the woods. When, relaxed and in tune with the universe, she opened her eyes, she saw right in the middle of the sunny quietness a baby snake. It was too little to be afraid, and Ilga, laying her wooden snake down close beside it, studied the green baby. She talked to it, and the thing rose up swinging its body in a twisted slow dance.

In a flash Ilga understood what she must do: she would carve baby snakes and transport them to Latvia through her friends, through those who believed her. She remembered Mara and knew she would help. And there were others, like her mother's friend Helga Williams and the poet Miss Roma, and, yes, other people, still strangers, but out there waiting for their calling, who would be glad to make a link in the chain that would bring the two sides of her nation together. Oh, what excitement, what marvelous mission was hers! She saw her role so clearly, and it seemed really so simple, so right. On each snake she would engrave a message of freedom. Her little green snakes would connect those who were not afraid and strong enough to want to be free. Her snakes would be the antidotes to the maliciousness of the mammoth mythical black snake of Latvian antiquity that, at the bottom of some mythical sea, was forever grinding flour for the poisonous bread of evildoers. Ilga would import into occupied Latvia a new breed of snakes! Not vengeful serpents, not poisonous black reptiles, but benevolent house and garden snakes that devour pests and disease.

As she pondered how she could make a change, a plan at last came to her mind: first she would send them to the poets and mystics, those who understood the old signs and symbols. Next, her friends would take them to the students and architects of the underground, those who also burrowed deeply into the roots and refused to obey the regime. In such manner, she would pull the spiritual resources of her people together until all evil walls would break down. The spirit of fearless freedom would then release the submerged princess, decapitate the black snake, retrieve the golden key, and unlock the doors and gates to the open world! Yes, she would make it happen! She saw it all in brilliant colors underneath the canopy of trembling leaves, where the forest seemed primeval.

She sat still, only slightly trembling, letting the impression sink into her whole being. She sat like a yogi, breathing deeply, holding her breath, then letting it out slowly. When she was done, she felt dizzy but happy. At last, she rose from the ground. She was certain that the invisible, exiled spirits had touched her . . . She stood in total harmony with the whole universe, hushed and bathed in pure sunlight. Awed, she performed the sun worship ritual and left the snake her hand had so lovingly carved in the dell as a sacrifice. Then gathering fresh branches, she walked toward her cabin.

When she stepped out from the woods and stood on the edge of civilization, she was aware that her dress transparently clung to her damp perspiring body. She glanced around, unbuttoning the top buttons, letting the wind cool her down.

Suddenly, the twigs crackled. A small voice said, "Boo!" and out from behind a bush popped up the white head of a small boy, about age six, all dressed in white linen. The shirt, embroidered along the collar and cuffs with serpent and earth designs Ilga could read at a glance, was neatly tied at the neck with a *prievite*. The shorts also were edged with matching handiwork. Only his feet stood in tube socks and sneakers.

"You should be napping," Ilga said, startled, enticed, as if the green snake had turned into a boy—the way it happened in folk tales.

For a moment they looked at each other. Ilga saw a bunch of wild flowers in the boy's hand. His hair stuck to his forehead. So he, too, was wet from perspiration. He, too, had taken strange, forbidden paths, and now their paths crossed. There must be purpose in that . . . Ilga smiled brilliantly and spoke to him gently. She beckoned, and he moved toward her cautiously, his little arm with the flowers extended. She set her twigs down and opened her arms wide, but the little creature held back, eyeing her, the eyes glimmering like those of greeting-card elves.

"Are you the goddess Mara?" he asked his voice more breath than sound. "Are you real?"

Ilga smiled wistfully, as one can only smile at innocent children of enormous faith. "Why, no," she said, but then not wanting to disappoint him, she added in a whisper, her hands now holding his face close to hers, "but I know her. I am her daughter."

"Really?"

"Really." She held him closer. "I just now talked to my mother." She rose, saying, "Wait, stay here!"

She ran to her cabin and returned with a pocketknife. With the boy, sitting close at her elbow, his flowers tucked in the décolleté of her dress, she carved the first miniature snake and gave it to him.

"Take, it," she said. "It's yours. You finish it. You polish it. One day it will take you to the land of Mara, to our dear little Latvia."

"Really?"

The little hand reached for it, but Ilga drew the snake back, teasing. "First give me a kiss," she said and bent down laughing, giggling. Quickly, the boy took her head in his hands and, pushing her down at an awkward angle, kissed her on the mouth. It was a man's kiss. She lost balance and fell backward, her hair catching in the brambles.

"What're you doing?" she scolded dizzily, but he kissed her again and then stood up, brushing off his shorts.

"Where did you learn all that, you little shit?"

"TV, of course. You're stupid. There is no Mara." The boy's face was red, his hair mussed, the neat shirt out of the elastic of his shorts. He backed off and then charged again, flattening himself against her body so that the flowers crushed. She pushed him off.

"Here," she gave him the baby snake. "Now run along, little boy," she said, envisioning a man evolving out of the boy in slow, circular motions, like a snake crawling out of his skin. She drew back in fear, while the offended boy stood before her, tears blinding him. Spitefully he grabbed the snake, but with his free hand delivered a heavy blow to Ilga's ear. Then he laughed a man's conquering laugh.

"You're bad," he said and, turning away, holding his snake high over his head like a jet plane, ran away. Ilga lay back. Bewildered, she stared at the sky, the trees, and the grass as if they had betrayed her. She was a weed yanked out of a sacred garden and left lying with her dirty roots exposed. Bereft of all beauty and truth, she pulled herself up and went to her cabin. Crying, she packed her things and drove out of the camp.

"The little bastard," she cursed as she speeded down the highway. "The boy is certainly the father of the man," she said aloud. Then she lit a cigarette and laughed a bitter, anguished laugh.

She could not hear with her battered, purple ear for a long time. All summer fell silent.

*

Still, she remained faithful to her vision and carved dozens of benevolent snakes and stained them green. In each, she engraved a message—a clear Latvian sign or symbol. "Those who know will understand, and those who do not, must not know," she told her creatures as she breathed on them.

Once her ear stopped hurting, she forced herself to forget the boy. "I have no time for hate," she said, watching a praying mantis gnaw on a sweat bee. "Life will teach him plenty." She convinced herself to be happy again because she was doing her part—all she could, all her voices commanded. And her friends who traveled to Latvia gladly did take her snakes along and returned with exciting stories and short messages for her. And so before the year was up, a brother/ sisterhood indeed affirmed itself. Ilga was ecstatic. She had made the connection! She had bypassed her father and Vanags and the rest of the old guard who watched the old rusting gates with hawk eyes. But those eyes also were old, blinded by cataracts, turned backward and inside themselves,. The eyes of the young looked forward. They were farsighted and clear.

Meanwhile, indeed, things were happening in Latvia: the sacred springs were cleared from communist debris, old castle ruins were being reconstructed, certain once-persecuted poets were presently reading their works not only in secret but in open crowded rooms and lighted concert halls. A national brigade, led by a poet, protected the ancient Kurzeme oaks from mindless saws. Sadly, some people were arrested and deported, while others mysteriously vanished, but their martyr blood watered the land for freedom. Ilga and her friends understood the full meaning of the reports and short notes that said, "The waters are flowing" and "it will be a good spring."

After such notes and secret discussions with friends around burning candles in smoke-filled rooms, Ilga worked harder. She carved deeper. The carving and polishing calmed her nerves and always restored her soul's delicate balance. All loneliness and isolation then would vanish like fog swept up by sunlight. Milda noticed that Ilga was becoming extraordinarily beautiful. Truly exotic.

None of the newspapers in exile or at home reported these small, symbolic events. *Those that have eyes let them see*, said the preacher, *and those that have ears let them hear. Let the wicked rage for yet a short while . . . The Lord God neither slumbers nor sleeps. The Lord God watches over Israel and also over Latvia.*

Passage

In mid-September, shortly before leaving for college, Ilga quit carving and decided it was safe to visit Longlake—now empty of its coast-to-coast summer crowd.

"Others can take up where I left off," she said into the cooling air. "My hands hurt."

She sat meditating in the same spot in the dell where she had come face to face with the little green snake, the affirmative messenger of the correct passage of her mission. Though it had happened hardly over a month ago, it seemed like a timeless span—like impressions, recollections, and dreams. She waited for more than an hour for a second, stronger vision, but it did not come. Only yellow and orange leaves slowly fell over and around her. She remembered with renewed annoyance the little boy and his big kisses. His image came to her distorted and grotesque in the form of a middle-age Lilliput, Milda had described to her when she was little, telling her about the circus that had come to Esslingen and brought with it the enchanting town of Lilliputs—miniature people from some land of mystery—and how they had done acrobatic tricks and dances. Ilga wondered whatever happened to them and the elves, dwarfs and other creatures of fairy tales Did they all disappear? Are their spirits still alive searching for those who believed in them and then clutching on with all their might, never letting them go? Feeling invisible presences in the quietness and not really wanting to be found by anyone or anything, she rose and with quick steps left the woods.

Out of breath and hot in the September afternoon's dazzle, she strolled about in the absolute silence of Longlake, basking in pleasant, strange, exciting recollections of all the summers that formed her past. Sadly she felt herself aging, growing away from those years, growing away from the dreams and frivolities, from the love sicknesses and bewitching idealism. Yet she loved Longlake passionately and patriotically. There was no other place like this on the face of the earth. It was built by so many memories and hopes of her grandparents' and parents' generations that were slowly passing off the earth and entering the gates of afterlife, even as she had entered the hand-carved gates of this mini world dedicated to God and Latvia.

As she followed the winding paths, her hands stroked the leaves along the edges. Her mind conjured images of friends with such force that she expected to run into them at every turn. She felt their aerial embraces and walked with them, her feet hardly touching the graveled ground. But she met no one, except the little woodland creatures, which, left alone, scurried about carrying supplies to their winter storehouses. She felt such great solidarity with them that she wanted to catch them all and, like Snow White in the Disney movie, hold them against her cheeks. "I have also come to fill my storehouse," she said to a squirrel. "I need to store up my energies for the winter." But the squirrel did not care. He ran up the trunk of an oak, his mouth acorn-gagged. Ilga watched him vanish and then walked to the parking lot, to her lone car, full of boards, wooden snakes, and other extensions of her creative self.

She did not get in but found her notebook and pen, because suddenly she felt a poem stirring inside her. She went looking for a place where she could sit quietly and write down the rising words. She was excited, like a woman in labor, even as she felt light, as if her muse were carrying her on dragonfly wings. She glided down into the valley and along the shallow bend of the lake crowded with water lily leaves that cupped themselves around scarce, lingering blossoms as fragile as hidden dreams and desires.

"You are so lovely," she told them and, walking up as close as she could to the swampy lines between land and water, she tried to catch one of the floating blossoms but could not. To her horror, she saw a black beetle land on it and trample all over its white delicate face; it invaded the yellow stamens with all its coarse natural rights. "That's how it always is," she sighed and went on until she came to the edge of the deeper and more active part of the lake. From there, it opened wide, glimmering as blue under the sky as the ever-open eye of God. She threw off her shoes and walked up the boardwalk, where she and her friends had sunbathed, touching hands, hearts, and the cosmos. She sat down, letting her feet dangle in the still warm water, her dress pulled high above her knees. She stretched her arms far overhead and watched her fingers stroke the sky, and then she relaxed, brought her hands down, and took a deep breath. She clicked her pen and wrote, **"Passage."**

If it came to dying this day
I would choose it I would swing open like cages
Clanging bursting seedpods
—my eyes like startled empty doorways—
and let these last hours of sky and shimmering
air cross the doorstep to burn me
clear of dust memory planet.
This acid season blinds me through and all my body
I'd corrode to white-ash all eternity
Would remain for me this cobalt sky birds flown
And climbing hurriedly away trees mute

And waiting rooted nothing
Moves but silent winter in its secret passage-way
Riding riding its shuddering
Horse of ice.[2]

Suddenly, the sand behind her creaked, and a very tall, very naked young black man stood close to the last bush near the rim of the land. He grinned, on first glance, a shy grin, as if she surprised him, as if she had no business being where she was. But then he stepped out in full view, in all his naked savagery as if he had come to reclaim the land and the water. He stood like man primeval, evolved out of the dark continent where Homo sapiens claimed their beginning. But as he moved another step closer, his grin changed to an ambivalent frown. For a tense, immeasurable time span he and the white woman sized each other up. Two frightened animals, lost at the water's and land's edges.

She moved first. Quickly she pulled up her legs, pulled down her skirt, and positioned herself ready to run just when he was nearing the boardwalk, and with his next step was already standing on it, blocking her way, panting in lustful, sooty certainty. For a moment he wavered, then, testing the boardwalk, began gliding toward her like an apparition, his dark nakedness propelling him, his arms already reaching for her. She chilled. One hand held on to her notebook, while the other clasped her pen, pointing it like a knife. Another breath and he was only inches away. She froze. But he simply brushed by, his shadow sliding over her and over the rippling, shimmering water. Entranced, she watched him swim away and then backtracked on the warm boards. As soon as her toes touched sand, she ran. Vaguely, she heard his swimming, rhythmic splashes. Her shoes in one hand and her poem in the other, she ran like a

---

2 *Ķekars*, poems by Sniedze Ruņģe in Latvian and English, Grand Rapids, MI: AKA Publishers International, 1985, p. 129.

gazelle, her whole body aflame with instincts of self-preserving fright. She tore open her car door, slid inside, turned on the motor, and peeled out of Longlake.

She drove right into her mother's kitchen, it seemed, where Milda was peacefully arranging buns on a cookie sheet. Hysterically, Ilga told her everything and then waited, but Milda only blinked, her fingers stupidly strewing caraway seeds on the buns. At last she said, "Maybe it's your fault. How many times have I told you not to go off by yourself like that?" Her voice turned to scolding. "And I've also told you not to wear those old dresses. They provoke. I don't like your skirt. Where did you get it? You should at least iron it, I'm . . ."

"Ashamed," Ilga finished. "I can't believe it, Mamma!" Her eyes like blue marbles shifted back and forth.

"What?" Milda seemed a confused, lost little girl.

"What?" Ilga mocked. "I was almost raped, and all you can say is *I don't like your skirt*!" She laughed bitterly, wiping her tears and staring incredulously at her mother, who muttered something about there being a songfest somewhere and helplessly seemed to recede. She was shrinking, going off into far distances, fathoms of deep time, through which Ilga could not reach her. Desperate, she wanted to hold her back, pull her down to herself, but she couldn't step out of her wounded prided. At last she said, "I cannot go back to Longlake, not for a long time. It's been invaded and spoiled. There's no safe place for my dreams to live."

*

The next summer she did not go to Longlake at all. She did not tell her friends what had happened. Her rational mind told her that the man had been only an incident, perhaps a lost inmate from the nearby asylum, but her emotions forbade her to enter the fake, polluted Latvia. Milda tried to reason with her. "Why must you always blow things up?"

"Blow them up? Mamma, don't you still understand that I could have been raped?"

"I know. All I'm saying is, please be more careful and don't provoke people with your dress and manner. Don't draw attention to yourself."

"Sorry! Sorry, sorry, sorry," Ilga snapped. "I can't afford anything you like, and I don't like so much of what you have. Why don't you pitch those ugly polyesters? They are so unbecoming, so un-Latvian." Ilga paused, realizing she had safely changed the subject to her mother's more comfortable state. "I got to go now, bye," she said walking to the door. Milda followed.

"But what do I say to people?"

"Oh, tell them that I don't like the food. Which, by the way, would not be a lie. The food is terrible. Awful. It's not even bad American." Ilga smiled provocatively. "Tell them—who ever asks—that I get sick to my stomach." She kissed her mother's cheek and left.

"I wish father were here," Milda said to the closed door. But Kārlis was far away—in Australia. He had been elected chairman of the worldwide anticommunist committee and was crossing the globe organizing *effective* demonstrations.

"You can deal better with the world than with your children," she said bitterly. "I cannot handle Ilga." She wept. "I simply cannot."

To free herself from worrying about Ilga, she decided to go to Longlake by herself for the volleyball tournament the next weekend. Her good son Gatis had left earlier for warm-up practice and might have some time to spare for his mother, who now pinned her hopes on him. She was so very proud of him because he had finished the Latvian language program with honors. All other reports were excellent and his volleyball points high. People said he was handsome, looking a lot like her. Such sons were lucky, they said.

When she found him at the lake playing volleyball in the sand, she was quite stunned: tall, suntanned, he sunk the ball down with ease, flying over it like an eagle over his prey. She stood still until the game ended and both teams raced for the lake. Like dolphins, the young dove in and surfaced up through the water and then raced for the raft. Like an island in the sun, the raft sank deeply inside the waves. She saw girls fluttering around the young men. Gatis pulled a yellow polka dot bikini-clad beauty up next to him and turned her over so that she would be above him like some delicious fruit. Milda turned around, fighting off images of herself beneath the blooming rosebush. She turned away and walked rapidly up the path toward the cafeteria, where her generation sat wearily on benches that had no backrests. She was hot and flustered, shocked and excited. *It's time I talked to my son about the facts of life.* She knew that Kārlis would not, could not do it. *I must spend more time with him, not be so tied up with Ilga.*

*

Therefore, Milda was greatly relieved when, in late September, Ilga eagerly left for college. Even before the old Volkswagen drove out of sight, Milda looked forward to hearing from her, thinking how they communicated much better by long distance telephone than directly in their own hallways and square rooms.

In due time Milda did muster enough courage to have several mother-son conversations. She tried to explain things to Gatis, who listened patiently, asking mock questions, and trying to keep a serious face until he burst out laughing. "*Don't worry about me, Mamma,*" he said and left the house with his volleyball in hand.

With her worries so easily snatched away, she seemed lost. She looked around—at her things and house and decided she needed new colors on and around her. And so throughout October, she changed the wallpaper in her living room from beige stripes to golden scrolls and painted the dark hallway a bright yellow. That done and pleased, she emptied her closet of all her polyester garments. The next day she drove to the nearest shopping center, deposited the box at the Goodwill truck, and drove to an expensive boutique. An hour later she came out wearing a brown tweed pants suit with the *necessary* accessories, shoes and a purse. She carried a box in which, folded in white tissue paper, lay a size 10 red silk dress. Kārlis would not like it, she knew; it would be like a red flag to a frustrated bull, but she didn't care. She would not even show it to him but stick it under their bed, where he never looked. And she would say nothing yet about planning to buy at least one pair of designer jeans and some comfortable sweaters.

On her way home, in high spirits, she prepared a careful statement in defense of her *extravagant impulsive buying.* She would tell him that expensive clothes paid off in the long run and that she wanted him to be pleased with her during this new fall season. *We'll just have to see how it goes. He may not even notice me or the house.* But she blessed Ilga and could not wait to call her.

*

Ilga changed her image once again during the summer between her junior and senior years. She pitched her dresses and skirts into the Goodwill bin and found inside the store other people's discarded faded jeans, full length and cutoffs. She rummaged for tailored shirts and man's jackets. She was quiet, thoughtful, depressed, as though a plug had been pulled out of her spirit. She did not carve a single snake but tried to sell her surplus in the off–Main Street art shops of Grand Rapids and the renovated alleys of downtown Kalamazoo. She was always in need of small cash, not caring much for large sums. Whenever she made a sale, she smiled a child's smile and again disappeared into the shadows.

Mostly, she lived at home and kept a steady schedule of rising in the morning before nine and going to bed before midnight. She was polite to Milda and nice to her brother and her friends. She showed the required, noncontroversial degree of respect to her father, who that summer worked very hard for global freedom. He was assigned to go on several long trips—even to Venezuela and Brazil. These trips lifted his spirits to seventh heaven whenever he traveled in the company of suave Pēteris Vanags, who hammered the hard line with much greater force than Kārlis ever could. Vanags, insisting that nothing was changed, kept pounding his convictions into the conservative and uncertain war-damaged minds of the old emigrants whose reference point was always June 14, 1941. To support his arguments, he presented evidence from the horror stories of recent defectors, who were flown from one community to another to speak about how things *really* were in the Soviet Union.

Milda, too, as she listened, swung safely to the right and rejected all leftist arguments and impulses. She was ashamed that she had actually laughed the day she had cleaned her closet. Her red dress, still new, mocked her and she was afraid that, lying wrapped up under her bed, it would become tight around her hips. To measure herself, once in a while she pulled the dress out of hiding and, holding it up to herself, posed in the mirror. *There will come a time,* she murmured as she thought how Kārlis would never see it and how Vanags would be enflamed with desire, setting her also on fire. She was determined to watch her diet and count her calories.

Normally, when her husband was away, she stayed close to home, lost in her garden and thoughts. She updated the family album, and she sewed and then started embroidering a fine linen dress she might wear at some song and dance festival. She also stitched a new Latvian flag to replace the faded one that Kārlis was carrying all over the world. She made it out of very expensive wool, guaranteed not to fade. She planned to unfurl it as a surprise, when he returned.

The days still dragged, and she missed him, wanting to tell him, to bring him back to her eager and yearning, and, as she watched her needle dance and weave, she decided to give a garden party in Kārlis's honor and invite as many important guests, as the garden could hold. Also Pēteris? At that thought the needle pricked her finger and her face swelled from an unexpected surge of blood. *But I must—for his sake, for my husband's sake . . .* She resolved to be strong. Planning and anticipating, she looked out at their garden and was pleased that she had tended it well; the flowers rewarded her with their generous array of colors and fragrances. She was happy. Excited.

*

Kārlis returned home at the end of that summer suntanned and in high spirits. Milda received him with open arms and hungry kisses. "I missed you so much and love you beyond reason," she whispered leaning against his heart, knowing that he was pleased and glad to be home, even though his arms seemed heavy around her.

The garden party on Labor Day was a great success. Vanags, dressed in a white linen suit, came with pink roses for the hostess. He kissed her hand and then removed himself calmly to join the men, who, as usual, talked about wars, politics, and sports. They ate, drank, and smoked heartily, leaving the women to themselves. Ilga, dressed in baggy cotton pants and an elastic red top, was also present, as was Gatis. Both were subdued and stayed out of any discussions about politics or any other hot issues. Ilga was particularly irritated by Vanags's presence and his eyeing her mother, who was clearly agitated. *What's going on?* she glared at them and then at her father, whose eyes were blinded behind his dark sunglasses.

"It all went quite well," Milda said to her husband after the last guest—Mr. Vanags—left. To erase the kiss he managed to press on her lips when he caught her alone in the hallway, she held Kārlis's hand tightly as she watched the culprit slide into a taxi. "I love you," she whispered to her faithful husband, but Ilga told her dad to take off his sunglasses.

After Kārlis adjusted to being home, he seemed perplexed about Ilga's behavior. "What is she doing now?" he asked Milda, who caught his accusing tone and did not know how to answer him. She, of course, knew that Ilga's outward transformation was calculated. Ilga had confessed that she was giving up on romanticism with its witches and ideas about souls and spirits and had embraced the ideas of higher humanism and rationalism. She was enlightened, she said, and grown up; she was free and self-contained! To prove that, she showed Milda her A's in logic, political theory, and systems of government. During the summer, trying to get a head start for her 500-level classes, she had read Machiavelli's *Prince* and Plato's *Republic*, Voltaire's *Candide*, and Thomas Paine's *Rights of Man*. Guided by the great, enlightened minds, she giggled at romanticism with uncomfortable, cynical staccatos and criticized her parents and their friends as being *misguided national romantics*.

But she mainly left them alone, as one in a hurry to win a race would leave a slow competitor behind. She had only two weeks left before classes would start, and she needed at least an outline of her term paper ready for her Soviet Politics course, for which she had pleaded an incomplete. And so one day, she slowed down and asked her father for help. "I have decided to write my paper on Latvia's political changes between 1934 and 1940." She explained that she would focus on the rule of the last president Kārlis Ulmanis. "What I want to know is: did Mr. Ulmanis, with his *coup d'etat*, actually pave the way for the communist takeover of 1940?"

Hearing this, Kārlis raged, shouting, "It's a lie!"

Scared, Ilga backed off, still challenging him with her steady clear blue eyes, and asked in a calm, reasonable voice: "But what is the truth, father! I want to know. I really want to know the truth. I am supposed to write an objective analysis," she said.

"The Truth is," he said, bringing his voice down, "that ours was the best among other small democracies of Europe and . . ."

"How was it a democracy if it was ruled by a dictator?" Ilga cut in. "What about the *coup*?"

"No blood was shed. Only some social democrats and communists were jailed for a short time."

"Jailed?"

"My child, times were dangerous, and the parliament was split and not acting in the best national interests . . . But why do you have to get involved with things you know nothing about?"

"Precisely because I know so little," she said evenly. "Because Latvia interests me, and because my professor asked me the same question I am asking you for which I had no clear answer. Father, I must know and understand that period so that I can understand the present and myself as well as the changes, which are happening right now . . . et cetera."

"What's your purpose? What is behind all this?"

"Pure and simple, father. Intellectual curiosity, if you know what I mean." Her voice grew louder, clearer. She went on: "My theory is that Latvia was not a mere innocent victim of her history, as we have been led to believe, but that it actually is responsible—at least partially—for creating its own chain of events. We are the last link of that chain, but by no means the end one. It will go on." She talked calmly, herself surprised at that calm, aware that the knowledge and insights she had gained through her studies buoyed her above her flustered parent. "So how much did our president contribute to our destruction?"

"Don't you dare badmouth him! When we elected our leaders, we honored and believed in them . . ."

"And obeyed."

"Yes! Not like in this great country, where as soon as a president is elected, every Dick or Jo thinks he has a right to pounce on him. Even his bathroom and bedroom aren't safe."

"But isn't that how democracy works?"

"I refuse to discuss this any further with you," Kārlis said, his face turning red.

"But why?" Ilga persisted.

"Because the name of Latvia is sacred in this house," he declared. "Our history has been written. We carry it in our hearts."

"I agree," Ilga said. "But I want to be intelligent about it."

"You're insulting me," Kārlis shouted. "You are no historian, and I don't approve of these so-called term papers, where any fool girl can say and write what she wants, even before she can carry her own weight.

"I am not a fool," Ilga said and dramatically lit a cigarette. "I need to go to the library. See you."

With that she was out the door, leaving the air stirred up. Left defeated and fuming, Kārlis found Milda, who was outside tending her daisies. He charged her with bad mothering, with letting things get out of hand, with not keeping the promises of her wedding vows, and succeeded in reducing her to the level of the daisies, her whole being soaking in tears. For a bitter moment; he looked down on her, and then he turned about and left her and the house. *He carries the world on his shoulders*, Milda excused him.

Days later, he took off for Brazil, with Mr. Vanags joining him in Florida. Meanwhile, at home, the air seemed to clear. The daisies lifted their heads and bloomed, and Milda went about her daily chores. But Ilga, frustrated and feeling rejected, turned to her: "What's Papa's problem anyway? Why does he get so worked up about a president?"

"Ah, dear, you don't understand. He literally worshipped the ground he walked on," Milda said and retold the story she had heard in the bathhouse in Esslingen. "Mr. Ulmanis actually put his hand on your father's head and blessed him, so he feels he is commissioned to carry on the unfortunate president's ideals and lead our people until our country is free once again."

"Oh my God!"

"Yes, with God's help . . . someday."

"But how? What will be the steps? And who are *the people* anymore?" Crying, Ilga cross-examined her mother like a prosecutor, making Milda also break down in tears and beg to be left alone, saying that she was only human. Exhausted, Ilga apologized and threatened to give up her project. For a day she moped around the house, thinking how little time she had, but during the night a violent storm broke a pine tree at the edge of the yard, barely missing the house. "We could have lost everything in a moment," she said, looking out the window. "I mustn't give up!" she said and before the sun was up, her mind was cleared and her energy and purpose resurged. Feeling the opening of classes only a week away and her incomplete grade turning into failure, she started digging deeply into the forbidden holy decade of her parents' youth. She dug up old magazines and newspapers in various basements; she wrote to different people and interviewed those who would talk to her. Finally she closed herself in her upstairs room and wrote, carefully blowing her smoke out the window.

When her first draft was finished, she tested its arguments on poor Milda, who could not match her daughter's sophistication and her sharp intellectual brass, for she had never had—could not have had—a graduate or even an undergraduate course in Latvian history, not to mention political science or critical analysis equal to her daughter's. The war had blotted out her chances for a normal education, and, feeling deprived, she reminded Ilga that she was ignorant about many things.

"Nevertheless, I did finish the gymnasium with top honors. But there had been no opportunity for me to go on to college after I came to this country. I had to work and could hardly find time to learn the words of everyday *American* English . . . My dear child, you must understand that I come from a simpler, but a very rough, very tragic age . . . Further education for me—and him—was out of the question. We—your father and I—were engaged, saving pennies. I cleaned Mrs. Fern's house, I . . ."

"Oh please!" Ilga cut in and left the kitchen.

After the door slammed, Milda sat confused and silent, a gray mouse, looking out at the world with blinking, wet eyes. She remembered . . . She recited the hard lessons life had taught her. She told herself that she knew life before it became history. Her teachers were women: her mother and aunts—Matilde and Alma. And the children: Zelda, baby Lilia, Juris . . . Anna's cry and her bleeding feet made up a most heavy volume of history that would not fit on any library shelf. Yes, and Alma, who wrote history in letters; she punctuated it with pebbles on the edge of the Baltic Sea and threw the content upon the cold, dark waves . . . What could her child—who, thank God, had been protected from it all—know? How could the unaware American professor who perhaps had seen no other but American shores, evaluate anything? *Ak vai* . . . She went out and talked to her flowers.

However, when Ilga eased up and was kind, Milda's curiosity unleashed itself. Some little questions started popping up. She cautiously asked Ilga about her assessments of the *dictatorial rule*. Yet she would not go into details, for Ilga would only use the first question as a springboard to another and another, leading to the inevitable arguments that would leave Milda feeling guilty for breaking parental and political solidarity. But when left alone, Milda reflected on what her daughter had learned and ponder these things in her heart. When, just days before her departure, Ilga again asked questions, she sighed, saying, "It hurts me to talk about those times and our president, who was deported and died in Siberia, no one knows where." With tears filming her eyes, she told Ilga how *her* father had burned the president's portrait and how the whole country felt orphaned without him.

"Our president loved his country," Milda said, wiping her eyes. "And all I know is that the years he ruled were the only golden years we had. Why must you tarnish them with cruel, cold, impersonal statements and questions? Does it give you pleasure to upset me and your father?" Ilga, taken aback, paused and faced her mother, but she resisted her impulse to take poor Mamma in her arms and comfort the refugee child hiding inside the woman. Gathering her books and notes, she excused herself and left the house. She drove to the library. She had to finish the draft.

Her work was a chaotic jumble. *Organization, class, is most important . . . Yes, but how?* Ilga pondered, as she drove through the rush-hour traffic. *Introduction, body, conclusion* . . . Statements needed to be backed up by evidence and illuminating, illustrative examples. She had to arrange causes and effects in logical sequence. Words, sentences, paragraphs had to be coherent, relevant, and reasonable. Footnotes were always a pain, and the professor was old-fashioned—a real stickler for what everyone knew were minute details . . . Once she found her corner in the library, she carefully reexamined the guidelines and spent hours making an outline. The last days and night Milda hardly saw her. She was writing, typing, revising. Finally, she checked the transitions and spelling, then shouted with joy. She saw an **A** like a distant light in a foggy sky. She raced for that light.

*

About the first week in October, Ilga sent home a copy of the title page: *Latvia under the Dictatorship of Kārlis Ulmanis, 1934–1940: The Golden Years?* They saw the A+ and the comment: "Excellent! Best work I've received from either graduate or undergraduate in all my teaching. You might consider working this up for publication. If you have any questions, come see me." Ilga wrote a separate note to her elders: "You may frame it." No other news.

"I forbid you to react to this," Kārlis commanded his wife. Dutifully she obeyed, and all communication between daughter and parents broke off. Ilga did not come home for the Christmas holidays. She sent no card, no presents. Early in January Milda called her dormitory, but there was no answer. Weeks later, Mr. And Mrs. Arājs received a letter from the dean stating that their daughter had been missing and asked them if she had dropped out. Kārlis was furious, while Milda prepared for a nervous breakdown. Fortunately, Gatis needed her, and her husband would not put up with careless meals and a sloppy house. "She'll call when she needs money," Kārlis said, with no pain in his voice.

*

Sure enough, in the spring, Ilga telephoned, reversing the charges. Still, she did not tell her weak-voiced Mother where she was or what she was doing. All Milda gathered was that she lived somewhere on the upper edge of Michigan. Slowly Mother's nerves recovered and she waited . . . At last, on a balmy spring day, her lost daughter suddenly showed up and fell in Mother's wide open arms. She looked gaunt. She was dressed in a crumpled pair of brown slacks and a wrinkled shirt half open, revealing nothing underneath. Milda bit her tongue and allowed herself the release of a tearful reunion. Ilga explained nothing, and in a few days, she was gone again. Throughout that spring, she kept dropping in and out of the house, picking up her mail and scraps of food. She asked Mother for loaves of bread and came home only when Kārlis would be away. When Milda needed his help and advice, he scolded: "You pay too much attention to her . . . That's what she wants you to do."

"So?" Milda looked in his cold eyes. "I am her mother."

"Yes, I see . . . I haven't time."

*

By spring, the worn-out family accepted Ilga's comings and goings. The parents agreed that they would not get all emotional whenever Ilga showed up at the house but would treat her with studied indifference. Ilga understood the game but was upset: *My parents don't care, they don't ask me anything, they don't know what I've been through* . . . She took a deep breath and said: "Incidentally, I did submit my paper to several journals, but all I got were rejections, saying that there was no general interest in the subject."

"Oh," said Kārlis.

"So, Father, don't worry," she said, savoring his vague, curt reaction. "Superpowers don't give a damn for midgets. After all my work and our arguments, I realize that we are interesting only to ourselves."

"Well," Kārlis elaborated: "I am certainly doing all I can to alert the world, and in time it will hear us. The morality of superpowers is always tested by the treatment of little countries—like a tree is tested by its fruit."

"Sure," said Ilga, and with the whole subject settled, the family reached an equilibrium of sorts—until after Gatis graduated.

Gatis Arājs

He graduated from the American and Latvian high schools in the spring of 1978. Milda photographed him with both diplomas and framed the photos. Within a week they were ready to be hung on the *biography* wall above the miniature Latvian and United States of America flags respectively. A made-in-Germany alarm clock, shaped like a globe, ticked in the middle of the bookshelf immediately below. Kārlis pounded the new nails with proud force, hammering close to the second- and third-place ribbons for swimming, math, and reading contests and slightly below an earlier photograph of the Latvian volleyball team of which his son served as captain, while Kārlis coached—when time and duties allowed.

"Nothing but absolute discipline," he told the team in the locker room. "Complete concentration . . . mind above emotions . . ."

And the team had won game after game. "These games teach you, my boy, how to live. The same rules apply . . . Discipline, mind over matter, concentration is what makes men out of boys."

Dis-ci-pline. Mind. Con-cen-tra-tion . . . The hammer pounded the wall. The pounding echoed throughout the house.

"Done!" He put the hammer down. The parents looked at each other deeply, respectfully. Something huge was indeed finished, and—behold!—it was good. They deserved full credit. Hadn't they also worked for all the ribbons, trophies, and diplomas? Why shouldn't they beam at the wall in front of them?

"This wall cannot hold any more nails," Kārlis said and put his arm around Milda. "Well done, Mother," he praised and kissed Milda's forehead. "Our son will now go toward a bright, good future. Many roads are open to him."

"Yes," she said, eyes brimming full of joy. "You are right, father. You know so many things." She squeezed his hand and leaned against his heart. Both felt the fluttering heartbeats of their married oneness; both felt complete, perhaps thinking that they deserved a vacation.

But Ilga saw the wall and the parents from another angle. She saw them as one body with two heads—male and female—framed in a blue window, like a canvas. She clasped her hands over her mouth, held her breath as though before an altar, and exhaled only when she felt Gatis creeping up the stairs and looking in from the hallway. The parents turned and reached out to their children.

"Because of your diligence, I shall reward you," Kārlis told his son. "You need not work this summer, but you may spend it at Longlake. You need extra time to improve your language skills—secure them, so to speak—so that when you go out into the world, you will not forget the important lessons of your youth." Gatis appeared pleased, but his eyes looked past his parents, out the window, where the birch tree, planted at his birth, waved its lithe branches in the warm June breeze. He went to the window and opened it wide.

"In the fall you will be going on to Lansing, to Michigan State. School of Engineering," Kārlis said. "I have already talked to the dean, and he assured me that there will be no problem in getting you admitted. You may take this as another graduation gift." Kārlis paused. "If it surprises you, I am pleased. I meant to surprise you."

The father talked on, laying out his son's future. Everything was figured out in fine detail, down to eventual marriage and the inheriting of this, their house. As he talked, his spirits improved. Enthusiastically he looked into the future and not at his son, who had slid across the room and slouched against the frame of the open door. Nor did the father look into his son's eyes that studied the frayed carpet. At last he stopped talking. Mother and sister sat on the edge of his bed. They listened carefully. When Kārlis was finished, all was quiet.

Gatis straightened up and, looking slightly down—Milda noticed with alarm that the son was taller than the father—said, "*Nē*." No.

Taken aback, father glared. Ilga grinned, and Milda was surprised that this little word was actually a part of her boy's vocabulary. And then to prove that he really did know the full meaning of that crucial word, Gatis prefixed every other very active verb that Kārlis had stated in the positive with *ne*, thus negating everything—his father's dream, the future, and himself. The conflict ended with Kārlis swearing, Milda crying, and Ilga drawing in extra oxygen and holding her breath with slightly shut, expectantly moist eyes. Gatis left the squared triangle as one would leave sculptures in a museum. The sculptures turned to life only after the door slammed.

"What's the matter with him?" Kārlis shouted.

"Oh, he is scared of the future," Milda said softly. "It's another stage."

"I think it's a new drama," added Ilga, "and our baby is going to write his own script this time." And she, too, went out. Milda and Kārlis did not know where their children were that night. But they came back tired and hungry the next day, and no one dared to say anything.

But right after the Fourth of July, even before the star spangled banner had been put away, Gatis shocked them further: He brought home a girl. "This is my friend," he told his parents in English. "This is Angela Viviano." *An Italian and Catholic, of course* went through the parents' minds, as mutely new warning signals collided across the room.

Finally Milda said, "How do you do?" just as Ilga came bouncing down the stairs, full of exaggerated cheer, whistling some Latvian marriage folk tune. She stopped short and looked down on the scene in the living room as if it were a TV show, where the sound wires were broken.

At last Gatis spoke, adjusting the volume uncertainly: "Mother and father . . ." The English words had a cold sound in the house of the displaced Latvian patriots. "Mother and father," Gatis stammered and went on. "Angela is really my fiancée. We are engaged to be married." He swallowed and blushed, yet his words had been clear and brave. Milda immediately noticed the tiny diamond shining on Angela's finger and did not know what to say or do. She stood holding on to a shelf full of books, waiting for Kārlis to make a move.

However, it was Angela who quickly stepped forward, hugging and kissing both parents on both cheeks and then stepping up to Ilga and hugging her too, saying, "You're now my sister."

But Ilga remained aloof, watching, her eyes sliding over the collected faces. "Yes," she said. "Is this an end or a beginning?" she wondered.

Milda appreciated Angela's beauty but thought that she was too friendly, too improper, and certainly not suited for her *Gatiņš.* On what should have been a formal occasion, Angela had come into their house wearing a T-shirt that was very tight across her full breasts. The shirt displayed an array of hearts and flowers and L O V E in hot pink. Ilga knew that the shirt was a gift from Gatis and that it carried a load of symbolic meaning, which would further upset the parents. She recalled that some days ago Gatis had wrapped something pink in a white tissue and, startled by her, had covered everything with his body. Sensitively, Ilga had pretended not to notice, but she had. She had seen the prelude to the drama, which was being performed at this very moment.

Gracefully she slid down the banister, but remained holding on to the railing.

"You look pretty," Ilga told Angela, fixing her eyes on the bright red shorts that matched the tiny hearts across a silently heaving chest. She wondered how Gatis had mustered enough nerve to go out and buy red shorts, knowing full well that those shorts would walk into his father's house where nothing had the tint of red. Ilga watched and waited for an awkward moment, as if posing for a camera. Nothing clicked.

The next second she took the last step down, into the living room. She walked inside the awkward circle as a tribal queen and, taking hold of Gatis's and Angela's hands, faced their elders and said, "Well, so my little brother is engaged! This calls for a celebration. Of course, Mamma and Papa, they will stay for dinner! I'll put a bottle of champagne in the freezer.

Sweating, Kārlis turned to Milda and mumbled, "Yes, of course."

Angela's face lit up, her white teeth flashing in a glorious smile, her dark eyes casting velvety glances into Kārlis's blue icy stare. Instantly she moved toward Kārlis, freeing herself from Gatis's hold, and embraced him. Milda watched her husband's awkward arms hang for a second in a sort of paralysis but then tighten around the girl's T-shirted shoulders. She watched Angela's breasts flatten against his chest and her full lips giggling and brushing against his cheeks. Milda coughed and excused herself. "I must go to prepare the meal," she said. Her accented English stabbed her own ears.

Later in the evening, sitting in the formal dining room and dressed in his light suit, Kārlis seemed unusually lively. Milda suspected that he misunderstood her intention of teaching the casual and intruding Angela good manners by serving the meal in the dining room instead of on the porch, where they usually ate in the summer. She suspected that no one understood. In fact, she could not quite understand herself as she pulled out the china, the silver, and the white damask. Did she put on her dress only to make a sharp contrast between herself and Angela or did she dress as if in armor because she needed protection against an invasion? She did not know. Did not know what to expect next.

Ilga also stepped into a pair of tight-fitting shorts, and Gatis looked as if he were on his way to a tennis court. But Milda was most surprised at Kārlis, who generally, as a matter of principle and etiquette, would not allow anyone to sit at their dinner table with exposed elbows and knees, now said nothing but presided at the head of the table spreading out his white, starched napkin. *Has he actually capitulated*? Milda wondered. *Or has he stopped caring? Is he, as they say, burned out?* Her puzzled mind tried to fit things together, as she set her gold-rimmed Bavarian platter of chicken breasts in front of her husband.

Angela had seated herself at Kārlis's right arm, with Gatis on the left. Ilga sat across from them, eating and watching and being especially attentive. She kept filling the goblets and glasses, as she carried the conversation in charming, affected phrases. The whole thing was a game, a charade, Milda sensed, and could not wait for it to be over. Meanwhile, Angela talked to both father and son. She babbled and fluttered nonstop, asking questions and making frivolous statements about emigrants and foreigners generally. She compared the Arājs with her grandparents who had also come from "the old country." Her grandpa had worked on the railroad and grandma had made spaghetti and pizza, which the neighbors bought because it was so good.

"You mean you're from right here, from The Hill?" Ilga asked.

"Naturally. They started out on The Hill! What self-respecting Italian wouldn't?" Angela went on. "And naturally, they opened a restaurant. I still remember Granny stuffing me like an olive," she talked on, "always stuffing me, but I'd not eat more 'n one helping, because I'd not want to get fat like her 'n Mamma, you know . . . I really admire you—can I call you Karl and Milly?—for teaching your kids the old language and everything. I can only say a few words in Italian, but not enough to speak it or anything." She looked up at Gatis and said, "I'm so proud of Gaty 'cause he knows this language, I think it's really neat."

"And you will not let him forget it, yes?" asked Kārlis.

"No way!" Angela said and put her hand on Kārlis's hand that held a silver knife. "I'll make him teach it to our kids, if I can help it. We'll have a dozen little hybrids." Angela laughed but suddenly a poke in her side from Gatis shut her up. She frowned and turned to serious eating.

Milda held her fork and knife tighter and looked at Kārlis, whom she could not figure out. He seemed entirely too mild. She darted accusing glances across the table, but he remained untouched. Shouldn't he be clarifying to this Roman intruder that with them the learning of the Latvian language was much more than knowing a few phrases? Shouldn't Angela be made to understand that with them—and naturally with Gatis—Latvian culture and language were sacred? And didn't she see, Milda wanted to ask Angela, that they had raised Gatis and Ilga to be Latvians in all they were and did? Frustrated, she carved the chicken breast, taking its tenderness for granted and not even tasting her own creation—roasted chicken soused with delicate dill-and-chive-flavored mushroom cream sauce.

Why didn't Kārlis take the trouble to explain to their future daughter-in-law that, for their family, underneath everything lies the hope that Latvia would one day be free and perhaps their children and even grandchildren would go there as builders of a free, democratic country? Why was Kārlis only eating and drinking, when unborn generations of their seed were at stake? What was happening to him who had always held the flagpole so firmly? She now observed how weakly he held his silver knife and how his little finger, it seemed to her, coaxingly brushed against Angela's hand.

Milda was losing her sense of reality; her thoughts, dreams, visions were mocking her. All the years she had spent teaching her children the Latvian ways now seemed to have been a foolish waste of time. Everything seemed futile, irrelevant. Angela, clad in her T-shirt and red shorts, shook things up—even Kārlis—she was certain, as she watched him eat the dessert.

Suddenly, with a surge of something like rage or jealousy or inexpressible confusion, the scenes of those long-gone tropical nights in Tobago came to her in all their high tide. She saw Kārlis as he was on those nights; she remembered his face, his strong legs as they braced the waves and pulled her toward him, into him until it was over and they lay on the beach, digging their feet into the sand and repeating the act again and again. Across from her, Kārlis's face was like it had been then, on those hot nights. His eyes, turned on Angela's shirt, roamed as they did when the lopsided tropical moon shone upon them. Now she saw those same hungry looks falling on Angela. *Oh, the champagne has gone to his head*! *Still, must he eat the strawberry desert as though he tasted kisses?* She had never seen her husband enjoying strawberries and whipped cream so much. From her end of the table, the strawberries on the crystal plate and the hearts and flowers on Angela's shirt hung ripe for picking. She wished she had baked some kind of pie instead.

Angela praised the strawberries. She said, "Oh, Milly, they're delicious! You'll have to give me the recipe!" Shockingly, with her fingers, she picked up a large berry and put it between her teeth, the attached whipping cream smearing her mouth. A bit embarrassed, she giggled, swallowing, then took another berry, put it between her teeth and offered half the fruit to Gatis. When he didn't know what to do, she took his blushing face in hers and brought it down, over her, and inserted the tip of the berry into his closed mouth. After a while they swallowed.

Ilga said, "How beautiful, how poetic! Now let Papa have that kind of a taste too."

Milda said, "Ilga!"

But Angela, laughing, picked up another strawberry and, leaning toward Kārlis, offered her full mouth. Kārlis bent down and received as much as he could. Milda saw his lips touch Angela's and his hand press over hers. She saw him swallow everything and ask for more. Ilga gloated and filled up his glass, but Milda rushed into the kitchen to brew a strong pot of tea.

When she returned, the company had risen and were going out into the garden. Ilga was lighting the candles in the Japanese lanterns, while Kārlis took off his white jacket and loosened his tie. Gatis, an aerosol can in hand, shot poisonous arrows at invisible insects. He told Milda to stay back, get out of the way. *My little Gatiņš,* Milda recalled, *slaying monsters in the night, playing Sprīdītis . . . How quickly he's grown up! How manly sounds his voice!* She stepped aside, out of his way, into the soft light of the paper lanterns.

Everyone found a place to settle for tea. Milda did not know why Ilga was trying to turn the night into some oriental dream, why she insisted on jasmine tea instead of Milda's English Breakfast and why she brought out china cups without handles. *Hiroshima, Mon Amore.*

Milda, not knowing the reason why that particular film came to her mind at this particular time, remembered how moved she had been, how she had cried over the destruction of a small country like her own and a tragic love affair—also like her own. But she tried to smile and brush all images away, aware of the silence that fell on all, as they sipped the tea and watched the moon—a silver disk in a starry sky.

"Say something in Latvian," Angela spoke up. "I'd like to hear what it sounds like." No one came up with the desired something. Ilga complied:

Še skūpsti manu muti!—Manu muti
Ir skūpsītijušas Izraeļa meitas.
Šais lūpās vācu skūpstus, dotus tev,
Daudz-daudzu saldību no visiem ziediem.

Ilga bowed and Angela applauded, saying "that's pretty, what's it mean?" And Ilga translated, saying:

Here, kiss my lips! My lips
Have kissed the daughters of Israel.
In these lips I have gathered kisses for you—
With much sweetness from all the blossoms.

She explained that the words came from the drama *Joseph and His Brothers* by Rainis and that she was reading it. Angela listened and said again that it was beautiful, like an opera. She said she didn't realize that there was love poetry and opera in Latvia. Gaty had told her nothing. Ilga recited more, and Milda was surprised. She had no idea that Ilga had memorized so much. She picked a rose and gave it to Ilga, while Kārlis pulled Angela down on his lap. Milda saw his hand, and a foolish, wandering, lost hand it was, groping in the dark for what could never be grasped. *What fools may mortals be*, Milda thought and wanted to laugh out loud, but, of course, she didn't. Instead she thought about Alma in the role of Dina as she stood onstage in paper moonlight: Dina had come to find her Joseph and offer to him her kisses and her life. Oh, it was so long, long ago! Milda opened her eyes that began, stupidly, jealously filling with tears. Mercifully, she saw Gatis disengage Angela from his father.

"It's time to take you home," Gatis said, taking Angela by the hand and dragging her along.

*

When Gatis returned a couple of hours later, the ripped up family was in the TV room watching *The Tonight Show* but not seeing anything, only hiding in front of the television set so they wouldn't have to talk. As soon as the light-blinded young man came into the room, Kārlis hit the "off" button and rose. He rose as if he had awakened from some dream that others also had seen, a dream that had not been curtained by shut eyelids and the darkness of the night. It was his turn to blink, to flinch and attack:

"What are you planning to do with this Italian?" he demanded.

"That Italian's name is Angela," Gatis answered, "and I plan to marry her."

"We cannot allow it," Kārlis said and looked at Milda.

"Then," Gatis, grinning down on the man who had begotten him, said, "I will have to go against your will."

"In that case, I shall have to disown you because I cannot have you marry a foreigner—no matter how charming." He coughed, trying to clear the static from his voice.

"In that case," mocked Gatis, "I shall have to make my choices."

"Papa," interrupted Ilga.

"Quiet!" Kārlis thundered, matching the rumbling thunder outside. Milda rushed to close the windows. She saw the tall trees flapping and waving, twigs snapping. She was frightened as she saw ominous symbolism in the violent acts on nature's stage.

"Papa," Ilga persisted, "Angela is not a foreigner. Gatis and I are not foreigners either," she said calmly. "Only you and Mother are."

"Who asked you anything?" Kārlis shouted.

The thunder answered. Like Antigone, Ilga went to stand by her brother's side, but Kārlis grabbed her wrist and pulled her back. Ilga yanked herself free and said in a calm voice, "You are the miserably displaced persons, both of you, the DPs, not we, not my brother and I and not Angela either." She spoke while eloquent tears streaked her face. She turned that face toward the dark blue window, where raindrops crashed and broke into streams. "You are wrong," she said. "You are making us crazy." A lightning blade sliced the sky. "One, two, three," Ilga counted, and the thunder crashed down, it seemed, right in the middle of their living room.

Ilga turned and went up the stairs, but not to her room. She perched at the top of the stairs and watched. Holding their separate silences, they waited for the storm to pass. When it had blown over, Milda's voice, like thunder's distant rumbling, rose in a slow lament, "Oh, what have I done? Where have I failed? Didn't I do all that was possible to make my children love Latvia and us? Haven't we taken them to school every Saturday for twelve whole years? Haven't we sent them to so many summer camps so they would have wonderful, unforgettable times? Haven't we sacrificed? Haven't I read and sung to them?"

"Oh, shut your mouth" Kārlis yelled. But Milda could not, would not stop.

"Could you, my darling child, could you not have loved one of our girls? There are so many, and one is prettier than the next." She really hated to cry in front of her children, but the tears could not be stopped.

She knew they watched her, pitied her, but she could not help herself. The whole evening ran down her face as she sniveled and heaved. “Couldn’t you fall in love with Gunta, or Dzidra, or Skaidrite?”

“Love cannot be ordered,” Gatis said. “Love is free.”

Milda stopped crying. The words sounded familiar. She had said those words, when another girl of the Latvian circle had fallen in love with a black man and been thrown out of her parents’ house.

“Mamma, It’s all right, You should be pleased that I have found someone I love so much,” he said gently, comfortingly. And she was comforted.

“I forbid you to love this girl,” Kārlis said, but his words went flat.

“Good night,” Gatis said and bowed to his father, kissed the top of his mother’s head, and walked up the stairs. He almost tripped over Ilga, who now stood up. She opened her arms to him and embraced him. Her short disheveled hair against her brother’s light blue shirt lay like the crown of a sunflower against the sky. She cried and laughed at the same time. And then she straightened up and, holding her brother at arm’s length, sang the aria from *Carmen*:

Love is like a bird that will never be tamed
Love is like a Gypsy, lawless and free
Love is like an elusive bird
Just as you think you have caught it
The creature flies away . . .”

After this exhibition, Milda, rendered speechless, went up to her bedroom, even though she was not at all sleepy. Some half hour later, Gatis opened the door and asked her if she was all right. She told him she was not sleepy and asked him to bring her a glass of linden blossom tea to calm her nerves.

"Sure," he said, a bit too gladly, and hurried downstairs. Minutes later he brought the tea on a tray and sat down on the side of her bed. He watched her drink it all. Then he pulled her up and held her most tenderly. She breathed in his body odor that blended with Mennen cologne. "You have turned into a man too quickly for me." She ironed his wrinkled shirt with her fingers. "I love you so much," she whispered.

A while later, Kārlis called for his son to come down, and Gatis released himself from his mother's hand and, kissing her gently on the cheek, let her slide down onto the pillow. "I know," he said. "I love you too. Always."

His voice seemed very far away. She saw him go out the door. She heard her husband's voice, but no words, and then she heard words and no voice. Words rising and falling, going off into straight lines, words coming upstairs, taking on steps and running, banging doors, shutting her out. She tried to sit up, but her head was like a stuffed suitcase. She could not lift it. She felt a body lie down next to her, weigh down the mattress, tip her so she would roll downhill, down a green hill where daisies bloomed. She stretched out her arms and turned around, pushing herself over to her side of the bed. She forced her eyes to open wide. For a moment she stared at the sky, across which she had not bothered to draw the shades. She saw the night, washed clean by the storm, lying beside her, brilliant and cool. She longed for the stars to cover her.

In her twilight awareness, she became conscious of Kārlis, who tossed about as if he were pushing clouds or swimming in deep waters. His hands groped, scratching the sheets, tangling themselves in her nightgown, his sharp fingers groped at her dormant breasts, his alcohol breath fanning her, dragging her along, vaguely arousing her. He moved quickly, a night rider, riding on and on along island beaches with swaying palms, over meadows and across the Alps, on and on, she did not know where—a masked rider, galloping without stopping, without rest, until he collapsed. She heard him moan as in pain, Free, she tried to run away but got tangled up and fell exhausted. She felt him tossing and turning and moaning until he fell asleep, pressing down on her body, putting to sleep only her arms and legs.

She heard noises, like the distant rambling of thunder and saw the rays of a night-light through the crack at the bottom of the door. Vaguely she heard doors opening and closing and footsteps tiptoeing and vanishing. She knew she should rise and go to the window and look out, but her body hung limp and empty, like a nightgown blowing on a clothesline. At last, close to dawn she fell into a deep sleep. She did not hear the birds. She did not hear Kārlis rise and tiptoe out of their room.

The clock said nine-thirty, when she finally made herself rise out of the mangled, night-smelling sheets. She foolishly, deliciously, rolled in them, listening to the silence and marveling at her own sloth. She smiled, realizing that she had gotten by without making breakfast. She stretched luxuriously and swung her legs over the edge of the bed. She decided to go on with the self-indulgence. She would make an appointment for a shampoo and set and, perhaps, call a friend and go to lunch or maybe to the newly opened shopping center, where she would buy something soft and personal. End-of-season sales offered outdated luxuries "at low, low prices."

After slow showering that washed all traces of the night away, she dressed. Then she slid past Gatis's and Ilga's closed doors, glad that they, too, were sleeping off the commotions of the past day and night. "Yesterday was only a dream, ending in a nightmare, but now it is morning—a beautiful new morning!" she told herself. She heard the birds singing. "Thank God for that!" she said and went down the stairs.

In the kitchen, full of humid July sunshine, she saw a jar of instant coffee and the crumbs of dried bread. The knife lay at the side of the loaf she had baked a few days ago. So Kārlis had eaten very lightly and slunk out of the house and driven off catlike! She scowled at the mess he had left for her to wipe up as a matter of course and screwed the lid tightly on the jar of jam and went to percolate her coffee. The bread crumbs grated like gravel under her bare feet. She was disgusted by the way the dishrag felt and with a hard initial sweep almost plunged into deep cleaning, forgetting the plans she had made a while back.

Suddenly her hands stopped wringing the dishrag. She saw the corner of white paper under the pot of begonias above the sink and pulled out a wad of solidly filled pages. Her whole being choked up in fear, when she recognized Gatis's handwriting sloppily slanted in every direction. With shaking hands she unfolded and sorted out the pages, not written in Latvian but in English—and a careless, vulgar English at that. Flushed, she poured herself a cup of coffee and sat down. She read

Gatis's Letter.

Dear Mom [not *mīļā māmiņ*?]

I'm leaving home. Yeah, running away, as you never expected I would, so by the time you read this, I'll be far gone. Don't know where, but I'll send you some sign of life soon as we're settled. You might ask 'we?' Yes. Angy and me—we're eloping. She's gonna have a baby in 6 mos. so we gotta get married soon but I'm not marrying her 'cause I have to but because I want to—cause I love her and she loves me and we've been in love for over a year, going out when you and dad thought I was somewhere hitting the ball or being lectured at. Finally me & Angy had a fight and she said she'll go and meet you herself if I don't do things proper and treat her right and I still didn't have the guts and so I guess she quit taking the pill and got us in trouble. But like I said, I'm not marrying her cause I have to. I'm crazy about her. That black hair and those dark brown eyes like velvet, and when they smile I just go nuts. But I think we'll do OK. She'll help out and I'll find a job soon as we find a place we want to be at, with nobody around to run our lives.

Mom, Angy's just full of fun. She likes to laugh a lot and play practical jokes, but she's got a head on her shoulders. Guess she got it from her old man or grandma who made pizzas on her hill. She knows how to do things and how to speak up for herself. She told her mom right away that she was pregnant and proud of it, but her old man didn't like it. So she said tough and told him she doesn't need him. She thought she could stay with us but being the way things were last night she could tell right away that it wouldn't work and so we decided to make a clean break right then and there. We'd talked about all this stuff before, and that's when I took out the money so we wouldn't have to hang around. So that's what we'll be doing by the time you read this. We'll be going West just like in the movies.

Mamma, mamīt, don't cry! You did the best you could for an emmigrant, and I'll never forget you and tell everybody I had the best mother in the whole world! Sure, you were strict, but I could tell you love me. But Papa I never could figure out. Man, I could never touch him, and I don't think he ever touched me except those couple times when he whipped me with birch twigs. So I was scared of him. That's why I just did what he said and stayed out of trouble, and I think you thought I was just a good kid and we all got along so well and it was Ilga who always made trouble.

But yesterday Ilga stuck up for me and told you & dad that I'd turned into a MAN*. But I'm not sure how exactly she meant it. I expect she liked that I stood up to dad, but for me it's being in charge of my life that's important, specially now that I'll soon be a father. And that's why it's best for us to go away. Yes, I'm off (unless you wake up and stop me) to explore my country—the great US of A—where I was born. You—all with your schools and camps and all—kept me like in a ghetto. Except, our ghetto was pretty with trees and flowers and Latvian pots and pillows but it was always unreal —like our garden on our miserable street and how we lived wasn't like other people outside of our fence. We* *didn't even speak the same language or wear the same kinds of clothes or eat the same food. Every time I went with you people looked at us funny. I'd have these short pants and that prievite and I'd say stuff and people would stare. I hated to go to school too, but later I didn't care cause I was smarter than other kids in my class. Ilga used to tell me stuff so I wasn't afraid but tried to make a game of being different like she did.*

I remember one day we took off—this was just a couple of years ago—from Longlake and went to town to pick up some beer and chips. It was like we'd come in from outer space, man. The streets, stores, all looked unreal. Ilga even drove down a one-way street until the cop yelled, but she said 'let's beat it!' and stepped on it and we got away. She said 'let's get back to Latvia quickly.' Soon as we got inside camp all was OK. We were in our safety zone. I'm telling you all this & wondering if you knew at all how I felt because when I tried talking to you, you said we shouldn't feel that way. So what's the use? I'd have trouble saying it all in Latvian anyway.

The other thing I noticed that in school I hardly knew anything about what's going on in this country but I knew all that stuff about what happened in Latvia in the '30s or whenever. I started noticing how papa didn't talk about any news or anything except when there was something about commies. And then he was off somewhere marching where nobody gives a damn about him or anyone else who carries signs. But I guess he really thinks he's doing something, waking up the world or tearing down walls. And that Vanags always with him with his wooden arm and that black glove sticking out, giving me the creeps. . . When I was little I didn't know what was going on. I know you guys had some real rough times, but man, aren't they over? You, I'd bet, don't even remember what really happened but only what people told you. We used to sit there in that Sat school and listen when they talked about the future and how we're all gonna go there to live and clean up the mess, but I bet when it comes right down to it, nobody'd go and live like people 100 yrs. back.

We did feel a little dishonest, though, listening about how we were holding the future and how we could choose what our hearts belonged to, when all we really wanted was to have a good time, to be normal, like others. But you wouldn't see things our way and so that's why we listened to all the lectures and everything so we could do what we wanted afterwards. When the interstates opened, we'd really have a blast driving all over and you folks dishing out the money, writing checks for the future. Now Jimmy Carter wants to open things up, but the hawks don't trust him and yell he's soft on communism.

Man, how're you supposed to change things, if you can't open doors? I think the whole world's going nuts. That's another reason we're going away. Just couldn't take it anymore. Gotta figure things out for myself.

Keep thinking on what I missed out on. Baseball! I was about the only kid in school whose Pa never took him to a real live ball game. Man, I didn't even know how to keep score! That killed me. There was no way I could explain to anyone that my old man never watched a ball game, except soccer, and that we didn't play baseball at all those summer camps, only volleyball.

Mom, I was actually scared to tell Papa that I wanted to play baseball. I wanted a bat and ball for my 15th birthday so bad, but I was scared to speak up. I thought he'd whack me with the bat and I'd be flying way out into right field. (Get that, right field! Ha-ha!) But seriously, I had these dreams of swinging a bat and making a home run! I couldn't tell you about all this either. You'd have gotten me what I wanted—you always did because you were scared too—and then we would've had real problems. For the longest time I was afraid to play baseball even in PE cause I knew I'd get laughed at.

One time they did laugh—some of the guys, and there were these girls laughing and watching me miss three swings in a row. That was in 10th grade. Then I hear a girl say shut up! And walk up to me and say it's OK. And then she says why don't you buy me a Coke after school. I couldn't talk. She was so pretty—like Brooke Shields and she smiled over me like an angel in a painting. And I said sure, OK. she says,

"I'm Angela." I just stared. I said I'm Volly. You know me, don't you and she says I've been watching you and there's that sweet smile again. (Oh, I forgot to tell you that the kids called my Volly because I played volleyball.) And that's how we met, but it wasn't until the next year when we got serious. I kept looking at her for a whole year because I was scared you'd find out but then I couldn't keep away from her anymore and she really went for me and we were as much in love as we could stand.

Talking about my name. How could you name me something that looks like a misspelled gate? Where did you think I'd live? Who did you think would be saying my name all my life? So I was glad they came up with Volly. Later I told Angela my real name and she didn't laugh. Then I knew she really loved me. But when we settle down I'll change my name.

But you can keep calling me Gatiņsh. I wouldn't want you to call me anything else. I know Papa won't ever call.

Milda scanned the pages, looking for kindness, but finding no telling words, read on:

I'll miss you. I'll miss Ilga.

I remember how I never could get it the way she never bitched about her name or being Latvian. She'd make a big deal of her name. She'd make the kids say it right or she wouldn't talk to them. She'd make a show even of that. Once I saw her at the Dairy Q. holding out a cigarette and telling some bunch of kids from school what her name meant. Longing, she says. Oh, I'm so full of longing, so full of dreams and pains, she says with her eyes closed so as to only move her red painted lips over the banana split. She had guys all over her. You're full of shit, says one and pushes his finger right into her chest and she drops her cigarette and punches him so he lands off the bench backwards and then puts her foot on his chest. When she sees me coming, she asks, "My precious brother, would you want a chocolate or a vanilla ice cream cone?" Unreal!

When we fought, it was like she was hitting at phantoms. Everyone thought she was weird but they looked up to her. She was lots of fun, but it got to me. So I'd stay out of her way.

Mama, don't get so upset when Ilga fights. She's not really fighting you. She fights with these visions or soap bubbles that she loves to blow up. She'll never do what I'm doing. She'll never run away like me. Can't you see that she cannot run away? She'll probably live with you forever. She'll never find a guy that doesn't bore her. The only guys she likes are black. But mostly she needs Latvians. She needs all that for the theater she's always playing. She needs you and Papa to do the mother and father parts and you do all that so good! She gloats when she can twist and direct you so you get the act straight. Did you see how she worked last night? We were all playing the parts she gave us, and she loved it. I know she'll miss me because who'll take my part? She'll have to write a new soap.

Tell her I've gone like Columbus to discover America—she'll love it. Tell her I've gone to find my own way and life. (I'm starting to choke up.)

But tell Papa that I left in the night so we wouldn't have a fight. His voice and the way he thinks scare me. And I didn't want his ugly words ringing in my ears all the way into the sunset. It'd be bad for Angy and the baby. But I don't want to talk to him about me and Angy, specially after last night. Did you see how worked up he was? Did you catch the way he was making moves on Angy, leaning all over her when he had the chance? I know she asked for it. I talked to her about it, trying to be pretty strict the way papa is with you and us and she said she didn't mean it and then she was quiet and after a while she said your dad is neat, real handsome, and maybe he just wasn't in love and happy the way we were, and I said—so? And she said, o men! And then we talked about taking off and she was all excited.

I know I could never live without her and I could never stand Papa looking at her or fighting with me and telling me what to do and all that and I said be ready by 5 and she said I'll be waiting. Boy, I'm really glad Papa gave me the car for graduation! I guess I won't be driving it where he wants me to, but what's mine is mine. Tell him I really appreciate it. I mean it

Boy, it's getting light and I must close. Don't cry, mammīt! And Ilga. Keep laughing. We all should have laughed more and not taken all that Latvian stuff so serious that no one could say anything before Pa said we were disrespectful. Everyone is so hung up on respect! No wonder you got taken and lost the war. (I don't mean it, Mom, just kiddin'.) Still, we might have gone to see fireworks once in a while on 4th of July instead of always taking up the whole weekend with some Latvian consciousness building stuff. And we might have gone on a real vacation. Camping and fishing, stuff like that instead of always sitting in summer schools being fake Latvians, always repeating the same song and dance about communists and Hitler and all. About the only real fun we had was writing on the walls, sneaking in the beer and sucking joints. But I didn't get hooked on any of that stuff. I hate smoking, like you. I'll miss you mammiņ! I'll let you know where we are and you can come and visit. I hope you don't wake up now. I hope no one wakes up, but suddenly I'm so tired.

"You'll sleep long because I put Sominex in your tea last night and Papa was pretty zonked out after our talk. As long as he snores, I'm OK. Forgive me, but I didn't want you to stop me, I mean us.

So farewell, Mother, farewell Father and Sister! Farewell, my Latvian fantasy! I'm going West . . ..

With hugs, kisses and handshakes,
no longer yours only
Gatiņš

Hearts Broken

Milda folds the pages and stares out the window into a numbing sunshine, where chirping, anxious birds hop about guarding their nests. The shadows, transparent and evasive, play on the grass. Some clouds cross the blueness above. She hangs, motionless, in some void, disconnected and done in, but eventually her body rises and pours itself a cup of coffee and returns to the chair. Her lips sip the black, tasteless brew, and her eyes blink at objects around her—inside and out. She is the axis of her whole universe, suddenly twisted out of shape and broken. She has no idea how to mend herself. She wishes that the past twenty-four hours had been only a nightmare, but Gatis's letter lies on the table like pages torn from some banned, dirty book. She cannot, for all her probing, imagine her own darling boy leaning over those pages and pushing the pen across them with such cruel rapidity. Her body seems pricked as though he had drawn the ink straight from her major arteries and left her bleeding to death, her soul flowing out of her, trying to reach any one of the scattered cloud fluffs caught in the tree tops.

As if seeing a rerun of some movie, Milda's mind recalls coldly the scenes of the night just passed. She sees, on a white screen, mounted high and in a close-up, Angela's breasts barely covered with the T-shirt of hearts and flowers, heaving against her husband of twenty-seven years. She sees how the girl lured and upset him, toppled him over so much that in the night he had reached for her, substituting whatever his hands could find for the impossible he longed for.

Milda rests her head in her hands, pushing the images away, but another scene presents itself. She does not see it; she had only heard: Father and son talk; they shout; they are silent, while she sweats and kicks the sheets. She is certain of the inevitable victory: youth will win over age. The son will outrun the father. The son must defeat the father. She was merely a spectator high in the bleachers. She had not considered being attacked and defeated also. How could she suspect that her honey-sweetened linden blossom tea would be poisoned? How could she ever imagine that her son's eager offer to carry a tray to her room for an intimate nightcap turned into utmost hypocrisy? How could she know that men still risked murdering their mothers for the lust of women?

The screen goes blank, and Milda's fist hits the table. The coffee spills. The fine, lily-of-the-valley decorated cup rocks until it rolls off the table with a weak crash.

"Where is my brother?" A call from the top of the stairs cuts the air and causes Milda to tilt her head. "Where is my brother?" Ilga asks, hovering over her mother. "Where is he?"

Milda pushes the sheets of paper across the table and rises. "I must go and clean his room," she says. "I always pick up after everybody. I always pick myself up," she mumbles as she climbs the stairs clutching her stomach. The labor pains are intense. She cannot count the seconds of relief between them. The umbilical cord is cut. It hurts.

*

When, in the evening, Mr. Arājs learned what had happened, he broke out into a sweat, grit his teeth, and forbade both Mother and sister to talk about *the boy*." But Mrs. Arājs charged. She screamed, "You did it! You, lecherous, incestuous beast! . . . Insensitive despot! . . . Dictator! . . . Heartless, cruel father!"

Her fists rose against the man standing before her and beat his chest, but he gripped her wrists, squeezing them, cutting off her blood, and pushed her across the room. He watched her fall onto the sofa, her legs sprawling upward and going down, her skirt collapsing like a parachute. He saw her head pressed against the old bomb-shelter blanket she had insisted on hanging on their newly papered wall and cluttering it with the bric-a-brac she had hoarded. She hung like another piece of her hideous collection. He watched her slide down, down into stupefying silence. "Stop blinking!" the man shouted. "It gets on my nerves. It always does—always has." He stood above her, big and overpowering. "One more word out of you and . . .," he stammered.

"And what?" she screamed, pouncing up and leaping at him, but he grabbed her around the neck and shook her. She spit in his face, her mouth foaming. She showered him with spittle until his hands released her to wipe his face.

"I despise you! Frigid, manipulative snake," he said, looking down. "I see it all now," he snarled. "How you trapped me—you and my mother. I see your whole conspiracy," he exploded, leaning over her. "I hate women," he spewed, and with that he stormed out of the house. She threw a Latvian pot after him, but it hit only the slamming door and shattered into shards of clay. Sobbing, she stooped to pick them up, piece by piece, sliver by sliver. "I always pick up the pieces," she mumbled, pressing them hard, cutting her hand, unaware that Ilga was there beside her, helping her pick things up.

"*Mammīt*," she said. "Go to bed. Sleep. Rest. I'll bring some food up later."

"Are you also going to poison me?" Milda shouted, pale and frightened. "Are you all going to kill me?"

"No, *Mammīt*, of course not." Ilga took her hand and emptied the broken clay on to a newspaper. She got water and soap and washed the limp hands. She dried and held them, blowing on the red cuts. "Relax, *Mammīt*, you're in shock. We're all in shock." She guided her up the stairs and tucked her in bed. "It will be all right," she promised.

But it was not all right. Not for a long time. "Spoken words cannot be unsaid," goes a proverb. "Spilled water cannot be swept up." The episode had split husband and wife. For a long time she slept upstairs and he downstairs. They ate in angry silence. He stayed out without warning or explanations and resumed intense smoking. She contemplated divorce but could never say the word. She was terrified by the apparitions beyond it: the FOR SALE sign outside their hedge; he or she putting their divided belongings in separate U-Hauls and going into the unknown; their children losing their home base and being dispossessed, like she was—and he—displaced persons, DPs. Exile within exile. No. That alternative was out of the question at this point in her life, and so she resolved to endure; this was the "worse" part of their marriage; there had been better ones. Such is life, she understood. She learned to cope by watching talk shows, listening to TV marriage counselors, psychiatrists, and women with much more outrageous and horrid problems. She got hooked on *Days of Our Lives*. She escaped from her days into the lives of others, much worse and more complicated. *But they are scripted, rehearsed and acted out, while mine . . .*

"Bullshit, Mamma!" said Ilga and slapped the TV off. "Your problems are not like that. You are from another world that TV has not yet discovered. Why, if you would send your story in, you'd get rejected—like I was—*not pertaining to general interest*, et cetera and so on." Ilga made her get out of the house. They took rides; they walked miles. "Our joys are not of general interest either," said Ilga as she made a daisy wreath, waist deep in a strange meadow that looked like a spot of Kurzeme. Together they picked herbs that would heal the nerves. They laughed. Once Ilga took her mother to a secluded beach on Lake Michigan. They climbed up and down a huge, steep dune that looked like a tilted desert against the bright blue water and sky. Ilga, a blue sailor cap on her head, stripped as she went down to the sea. "Follow the leader," she called, as free as the breeze. At the water's edge she pulled off the cap and plunged into the water. Like a beautiful mermaid, she floated in and out of the waves, laughing, the sun slanting around her. And laughing, Milda followed the leader, swimming far out on a reflected, golden sunbeam. She turned over and swam on her back. It was marvelous, delicious, cold and hot. Ilga surfaced and sidekicked next to her. They swam out of the present world and into some other, nonexistent, pure and innocent. They were mere elements in an eternal universe until—the scream. They stood up, but quickly covered their nakedness with an oncoming wave. They saw a woman with a boy by either hand run away and disappear beyond a storm-twisted tree. "I guess we shocked them," Ilga said and they laughed. They waded out of the water and lay in the sand. Ilga buried her mother, leaving her head out. "This is wonderful, lovely, clean . . . This day is a gift of heaven," Milda said and kicked off the sand. Lying on their stomachs, they talked, hummed, giggled, and, when the sun fell into the lake, turning it a golden red, they, too, went back into the water and swam until Venus, the evening star, appeared and shone down upon them.

So Milda put divorce out of her mind. She would not say the word, would never propose the concept. *Let him. Let him ask or tell me, if he wants to. He still rules the house; he makes all major decision, while I just go along. Submit*. She was, after all, a traditional Latvian wife and, underneath the pain, still proud. Still beautiful, the mirror said.

Meanwhile, she—and sometimes Ilga—cleaned Gatis's room. They would start out in silence, but soon the words and phrases would break it. They recalled Gatis at various stages in his life. They talked and talked, as seldom before, weeping and laughing, drawing close, almost becoming one body again. They ended up wishing him good fortune. "He will be all right," comforted Ilga. "You'll hear from him when he's ready. Allow him time and space. He needs to work out his anger."

"Yes, I see."

"He's right about me," Ilga admitted. "He's so right. I won't leave you. I can't ever leave this world—the Latvian world, as he described it. But, *Mammīt*, please understand—I need to be free. I also need space. I need to do my own thing, be myself." Milda stroked her head. She understood. Only what to do with Papa? How to crawl out of the limbo of married misery?

"Put him on hold. First get yourself together," Ilga counseled. "And where will *he* go?" She asked knowingly. "Who will take care of him? Don't you see that he needs you? He has defined himself by you—us—and the Latvian flag. He is nothing without all that, an empty coat sliding off a hanger." *How wise is my daughter!* "Besides, our community would be outraged if you divorced, because everyone likes you. You both look so perfect together . . . So give him space and time. He hurts too. And don't blow up Angela's boobs bigger than they are. After all, they're not her fault, and she is pregnant. So Papa took a little fantasy trip, so what? Haven't you done the same?" *Yes. Right.* A slight, caught-in-the-act smile tilted the corners of her mouth.

"I like Angela," Ilga affirmed. "They'll be all right, you'll see." *Yes . . . We shall see, maybe.*

After this session, Ilga seemed exhausted. She vanished for days. When she returned, she watched her parents. She watched her mother slowly coming out of her grief, and when she heard again the first kind words between her parents, she glowed with joyous hope. She left them alone.

It was not long before Mr. Arājs came home at his regular hour and soon fell back into his routine. Still, he slept downstairs and never entered his son's room. "A man's pride—or shame—is the basis of tragedy," Ilga commented, "and Papa is drowning in both."

To pull her thoughts out of the husband-wife impasse, Milda decided to do something with Gatis's room. She arranged all the photographs she found in boxes in chronological order and pasted them in albums. She cleaned the frames that displayed ribbons, prizes, and certificates. She wanted all the evidence of her efforts out in the open, her case clear and ready for the inevitable trial of her years of maternal responsibilities. Men and women—even God—must find her *not guilty.* She dusted and vacuumed the room regularly. She kept fresh flowers in a green vase with precise Latgalian designs Gatis had made—in case anyone should drop by to investigate. On special days she kept long vigils in his room, looking through the accumulated remains of his childhood. In the evenings she would light candles and, sitting at his window full of night, would study the stars. They calmed her, and she would wish upon many stars that time would turn back and she could correct all the wrongs of which her darling accused her and of which she accused herself. She wanted to call back time. She wanted to tell him, "I understand you better. I have looked out of your window."

"Time, my dear friends," the old Baptist preacher had said in a choked voice, "cannot be turned back. Therefore, my brethren, redeem your time! Treasure every living moment so that later you will not lament." He had said it at his seventy-fifth birthday celebration—three years after his wife was laid in her grave. Now he, too, was dead and lay next to her. "Time can never be called back," he had belabored the point. "You only have the moment you live, and you live it in the place where you are, not somewhere else. Other times and places belong to others, not you."

•

As Ilga had predicted, in time news arrived. Before a month had passed, a postcard came from Garry Arrid. "So he changed his name, but not the initials!" exclaimed Ilga. "That says something."

Gatis/Garry and Angela had traveled West, as they stated. They were married in Reno. They would settle, at least for now, in Phoenix. "Everything is fine. Don't worry."

"You see!" shouted Ilga triumphant, happy, as she saw tension flow out of Milda's face, and Kārlis take his pack of cigarettes and go outside.

Just before Christmas, a white envelope with the Phoenix address carried the announcement of Mara's birth. "Mara!" Ilga rejoiced. Milda, too, was very pleased: a true Latvian name. The name of the earth goddess. "He chose that," said Ilga, "I'm sure, to make you happy. What more could you want?" At that moment, Milda—incredibly a grandmother—wished for nothing more, except, of course, to see the child, but that was impossible. Kārlis's face was still cold and distant. *Later, maybe later . . .* Meanwhile, she had to be content. Her son had confirmed his national loyalty more than she ever expected by naming his daughter Mara.

The next day Milda bought a hundred dollar bond in that beautiful name and enclosed a check for an equal amount to "the happy parents." Ilga sent a package of baby clothes. Eagerly they waited for thank you notes, but none came. They were hurt, angry. "She's so uncultured," Milda complained. "How can he stand it?"

Ages later came a belated Christmas card, followed by a frosty New Year's telephone call and then a long winter silence. Gatis's old window bloomed with ice flowers. His room was very cold.

There was no Easter Card, even though Milda *said it with flowers.* She wired a lily. At last Garry called. He made stammering excuses. Angela, too, spoke into the telephone, telling Milly that the lily was pretty and white. She let Mara jabber and promised to send a picture. Yet another eternal silence followed. "They're busy," Ilga said, and Kārlis restated the no-call rule at least "until he apologizes." Milda dared not risk any more rebellions. It was her husband's habit to scrutinize all monthly bills, especially the telephone. "I will not simply overlook his disobedience and insults. I will not aid and abet my own humiliation," he pronounced, standing firm. Yes, of course! Mr. Arājs lived by his principles, everyone knew that.

The promised photo of a beautiful blue-eye, dark haired baby came in time for Mother's Day. There was a note of run-on sentences, written in two entangled handwritings and a child's scribble, clearly guided by an adult hand. Milda was overjoyed; she could not hold out, and on Mother's Day, in the evening, she telephoned. "This is my day," she said tremulously to Kārlis, feeling a surge of hysteria pulling her down. But she did not fall. She merely stood tall and looked down on her husband with pity: she saw him tied up by his own knots, looking at his lap.

The telephone conversation was hopeful, cordial. Her words traveled freely across the valleys, mountains, and deserts. "It'll be your turn to call me," she said lightly and hung up with love and kisses. When she went to report on the conversation, she saw Kārlis slouched deeply in his chair. His face was tear-streaked and furrowed. He was feeling around for a handkerchief and Milda gave him hers. She took his hand and said, "Let's go to bed." And he followed her. That night she took him in her arms, and they shared a pillow. It was good. They were at home. They talked about planting new roses in their garden.

The days went on, blandly, predictably. Ilga was frequently absent, supposedly allowing them *space,* allowing her parents to close the space between them. Garry also gave them space. He didn't call. Except for the usual Latvian functions, nothing seemed to happen. They were alone in a long, space-filled summer silence.

At the edge of that silence Kārlis died far away from home, far away from his wife and children. He collapsed while carrying the Latvian flag down Pennsylvania Avenue in Washington.

Milda called Gatis, begging him to fly home. Ilga also called. But he said, "*Es nevaru.* I cannot. Impossible." Angela was pregnant and had morning sickness. It was very hot in Phoenix, and his place was there, with the living, with *his* family. "Besides, Father never . . . you know, he never apologized."

"Yes . . . No. Time was pulled out from under him," she said softly.

"I know you will be brave and strong," came her son's words. "Like always." When she hung up, she felt extremely weak. Alone, all alone. "The loss of your spouse is impossible to describe," the preacher had said. "The heart is cleaved. It is worse than losing your country."

Amen, she whispered with conviction, feeling the true weight of the preacher's every word and was glad that she had taken the time to drive to Cleveland for Reverend Gramzda's seventy-fifth birthday and patiently listened to his old stories about the escape, Esslingen, and his wife—her dear old namesake, who had been like a mother to her. *Oh, how will I ever live without him*?

The Death of Kārlis Arājs

The summer of 1979 was turbulent, hot and stormy. Milda worked on the house, the garden, and herself, leaning on Ilga, leaning on her memories, tidying her son's empty room, but mostly drawing on her own strength that would not let her crumble. She remembered the words of Mrs. Gramzda, who was her touchstone of quiet grace and fortitude. She remembered all the mothers she knew who had lost their sons in bloody battles and car accidents. She saw her Aunt Matilde again signing the papers that would send her beloved sons off to war. She remembered the slurred lists of names on town news posts. Names of dead sons, brothers, cousins. She remembered staring at Juris's name on that black-edged list glued on a round cement post in the middle of a bombed out town, and how she made for him a tiny grave in the meadow outside of the village. It was not a grave for his body, only for his elusive spirit and the memories of their words, touches, laughter, and lost promises. The tiny mound was only a place where she cried out all her tears for him—before Gert had found her and, hand in hand, they walked back to the village.

A lifetime away, she decided to pin the darkest episode of her adult life in her journal and tuck it away like a time bomb, hoping that one day her offspring would find the outpouring of her heart and be surprised. Relieved, she reasoned: *You are actually quite lucky. Your son went away of his own free will. He chose his path. You know where he is. You can telephone him. You can write. You still have him. He has strong roots.*

"Everything will be all right," Ilga kept assuring her. She liked mothering her mother. "Papa will come around," she said. "Old men mellow."

"He is not old," Milda shot back. "We have a lot of life left."

"Sure."

*

Once Kārlis returned to their double bed, Milda forgave him everything and catered to his many needs carefully, tenderly. She hoped that somehow she would bring out of him again the passion he displayed on the Tobago beach. She hoped that, if only one more time, it would erupt for her as it had for Angela, she would have at least a definite memory around which she could redefine her marriage no matter what might happen in days and years to come. In her effort to penetrate that sincere wish and hope, she swore never to allow her thoughts to dwell on Pēteris Vanags or any other man besides her husband, and in time, she succeeded. To her relief, and like an affirmation of her sincere resolve, the next time Vanags telephoned and she answered, she could pass the receiver on to Kārlis with calm indifference. *Never! Never will I let your hand touch mine! Not as long as we both shall live.* She swore and meant it. She hummed an old Schubert melody and sat down at the piano, which she had not touched for a long time. Recalling other dormant melodies, she watched her fingers travel over the keyboard, at first uncertain but soon becoming braver as the hours ticked on. *Oh, where have I been? In what caves have my senses slept? Awake! My soul, awake!* She promised herself that she would practice every day for an hour, and she did.

As spring turned to summer she felt nature's healing power flow through her also. Stepping out of the shower, one fine morning, she felt truly born again. All adulterous thoughts and images had stopped their visits and left her at peace. It had happened to her as to other heroines in inspiring novels. In almost losing her husband, she—like those heroines—realized how much she loved him and how dependent she was on his life that had become also her life. When she opened her eyes to that, it was as though she had opened all the windows of a mildewed house so that joy and sunshine could come in. From that day on, she humored her husband with greater intensity. She found enchanting places where they could be alone, where they could walk hand in hand and stop suddenly, on impulse, for a light kiss, a smile, a wink of the eye.

Still her husband remained aloof. He seemed embarrassed and awkward when thus taken by surprise and responded in cold, though polite and coherent tones. He talked to her as to a friend, perhaps a cousin. Her touch sparked nothing; it suggested nothing. His eyes avoided her penetrating, questioning pleas. But she forgave him. She was understanding: *we all operate by different timing systems. I'm just a few feet in front of him and must slow down so he can catch up.* She closed her eyes to his slothfulness. She refused to see that instead of matching his steps to hers, he was turning inside himself. *He is afraid*, she murmured with pity. *He needs more time.* But when she suggested small trips or visits to art galleries and concerts, he reminded her that he had no time. *Yes, he is busy and I'm selfish.*

He was the elected coordinator for Free Latvians of the World, and to Milda's dismay, was again on the road and in the air. He traveled as guest speaker to various summer retreats; he flew from the East to the West Coast—planning, organizing, persuading. As the confrontation with the Soviet Union became an urgent political issue in Washington, the Captive Nations representatives, gaining self-confidence and hoping for support and justice, also became more outspoken in pleading the case for freedom for their countries and spelling out the wrongs and mistakes that had been inflicted upon the small nations by the large and powerful ones. Kārlis wrote articles for *Avize* and chaired the Committee for Demonstrations. He did not want to be disturbed. Immediately after the June 14 demonstration in Chicago, he worked toward the August 23 demonstration in Washington. "This will be crucial. *We must be heard!* We *must* get the liberals out and the Republicans in. We *must* take the hard line in order to preserve democracy. We *must never tire of working for freedom*."

"Yes," Milda said. She, of course, understood that he had to keep things straight. He had to tell America—right in front of the White House, where there would be TV cameras and reporters. She agreed that it was up to him to keep the pain of the Baltic States alive; she agreed that the dangerous softness on communism that their own children expressed was taking over the minds of college students. She heard the mad news showing general disrespect for order. Frightening things were indeed threatening the world, but her indispensable Kārlis (with some other men) would read and explain the subtle warning signs. They would tell people to beware of worldwide communism.

The day he left, he rehearsed the speech he would deliver in Washington. Milda had wrapped herself in a bathrobe and crept down the hall and leaning against the wall, watched him. As the mirror cleared, she saw him lean forward as if to hypnotize his own image. He paused, smiled, cleared his throat and spoke:

"My fellow Americans," he said in a low voice, "my good brothers and friends, do not think that we are only telling you about what happened to us in our little country. No!" His volume rose. "We are warning you about what may happen here in this country, in this land of the free and home of the brave. It could happen also in this Capital of our free democratic and Christian world!" He turned up the volume:

"Communism is a power—a mighty force—that like a river in spring will flood the whole world, yes, even the whole globe!" He softened: "It might flood America in the night, while you are sleeping, or it might flood it in broad daylight even while your children are playing baseball and your men are at their jobs." Up again: "It will happen soon, unexpectedly, like a thief entering your house." Pleading and warning: "So watch out, my dear friends and fellow citizens, the Red Bear will stomp in your streets, farms, factories, and parks. It will walk from the East to the West, from the North to the South. Its big paw has already pressed down Cuba, as it pressed down Latvia, Lithuania, and Estonia, in fact, all of Eastern Europe. It will not be long before its tail sweeps across the whole of Central and South America. Its nostrils are blowing their noxious breath already on Florida. And right here, in Washington, secret agents and spies are at work, speaking clever words with the mouths of naive liberals, who try to persuade our congressmen that Washington should negotiate with Moscow. But I ask you, can there be any compromise on truth? Can a lamb negotiate with a hungry lion—or a ferocious bear?"

He shut the door. She tiptoed back to the bedroom and changed into a comfortable shift and then slipped down the stairs to make breakfast and wait. She had heard the same speech with only slight variations countless times throughout the years but she had never seen her husband so charged with emotion, as if the whole cause of freedom and liberty hung in his words, as if he had been chosen by the Almighty to save America. She hoped that the president would hear him.

Kārlis pushed the door open with a force that threatened the hinges. "Awake, America!" he called. "Be alert and strong! Don't spare your dollars for the best missiles and submarines!"

He paused. Then: "If not us—we—who? Whom?" He paused again and adjusted his voice to sound like Mr. Reagan's. "God bless you, my fellow Americans, and aid you in your great mission!"

He came into Milda's view and she, smiling approval, said, "Take me with you," her voice low and pleading.

"Please, this is no time for jokes." He, pushed past her.

"I'm not joking."

"Woman, can't you see I'm in a hurry? Where's the flag?"

She ran upstairs and came down with the new banner she had made especially for this occasion. Handing it over, she stepped aside. He brushed her cheek with a light kiss and saying a *see you soon* rushed out the door. A taxi was waiting. There was no time for breakfast. No time for her.

The next afternoon the telephone rang, and Milda swept up the receiver, "Hallo?"

"Hallo!" It was Pēteris Vanags. She stiffened. "Hallo!" he repeated.

"Yes, hallo."

"I regret to inform you, my dear, that your husband collapsed earlier today."

"What do you mean collapsed?" Milda asked in an icy voice, knowing very well what he meant.

"Your husband died, my dearest."

She forced out the dreaded word: "Dead?"

"Yes." Vanags's voice switched to oratory. "Yes, your brave husband and my dearest friend fell as he carried our banner down Pennsylvania Avenue. He died instantly . . . The banner fell over him. It covered him. He died a hero."

Milda had no tears. She hated the sound of Vanags's voice burrowing into her ear, uprooting the peace and happiness of recent months and days. She remembered the last moments with her husband—it seemed only hours ago. They had not kissed properly in parting, and now they would never kiss, never repair the damage they had inflicted on each other over the years *Nevermore* . . . She hung on to the receiver and the wall, closing her eyes. "Did he deliver his speech?" she asked blandly.

"No. I spoke instead."

"What did you say? How did you speak?"

"I spoke from my heart. I told the world about what had happened to our people on June 14, 1941, and on August 23, 1939. I said how America was falling under communism and that it was up to America to save the world, and that America must build up her military strength. I put in a strong word for Mr. Reagan. I said that a strong defense system was the only way. I said that Russians understand only force . . ."

"Then it was a fine speech," she cut him off.

"Yes. I think so, if I can say so myself." He paused and went on in a voice of, what seemed to her, mock humility: "But I could never speak as fluently and effectively as your beloved husband. We have lost the best speaker and the best voice for liberty and democracy. But, my dearest, we must carry on."

"Yes," Milda said, tasting the salt of her tears. She saw herself in the mirror, and she thought about Jackie Kennedy walking behind her slain husband's casket. She wished Kārlis had been a president. She wished they had all been spared the long exile and were in Latvia—at home. She was convinced that Kārlis would have become president had there been elections, had there been time to live in peace. At least he would have been some kind of minister, she was sure of that, or a diplomat.

She resented Vanags more than ever because he had walked beside Kārlis, carrying with his one arm the American flag. She could not endure his English. His accent grated on her nerves. She could not imagine him representing her nation on TV or anywhere else. *She* should have been next to her husband! *She* should have delivered his speech! *She* should have risen with him and flown away, not sunk down in her smug self-indulgence and fear, only to suddenly encounter the man who now breathed on the other end of the telephone line. *Why didn't I love and support my husband sooner instead of tampering with him as if he were my child? Why did I allow our children and stray men to come between us? Why, oh why?* But Kārlis had not invited her to put on her national costume and walk with him between the two flags, as they had walked together in Germany, even before they knew each other's names. *Oh, why was he in such a hurry to get away?*

"One more question, Mr. Vanags: were there many people, TV cameras?"

"Ah, yes. No. There was, of course, the Voice of America, and some others. I didn't turn around to look. People took pictures. A woman came up and said she liked the way our women were dressed. Another asked where we came from and still others wanted to know where we were going." Vanags paused long enough to emit his typical, cynically bitter laugh, like the neighing of a horse, that dissolved in a heavy sigh. He coughed. She heard his heavy breathing, then more words:

"Your Michigan congressman did stop to talk to us. He promised to help save our country, only he did not know where it was. He thought we were newcomers. But I set him straight. I told him how we came to these shining shores more than thirty years ago." He coughed again. "Oh, people still have no idea about what happened to us—only to them, the Jews, as though only they suffered!" Vanags's wounded voice rose to an uncomfortable volume, "My dearest Mrs. Arājs, can you tell me where these people have been? They still don't grasp what the Iron Curtain is all about. I doubt if anyone remembers Churchill's speech, do you, my dear?"

"I don't know," Milda said in a dead voice.

"I am sorry," Vanags apologized. "I don't mean to take away from your grief."

"You don't."

"Your husband died a hero." He paused. "We are fortunate."

"Oh please! Please leave me alone . . . I want to die with him . . . I wish you . . ."

"Had died? Oh no, you don't. We promised . . ."

"Stop it!" She cried out. "You *are* dead to me, have been for a long time or didn't you notice? I loved only him, can't you understand that and leave me alone?"

She waited, but he was silent. When he spoke again, his voice was even, businesslike: "I shall write an article about him in *Avize*. I would like some photos of home life. We want to show him as a caring family man, a loving husband. Most people knew him only as an ardent patriot. I'll put in that we all will try to follow his example and zeal but that none of us has his strength and his absolute and total conviction . . . I'll say that it was symbolic and proper that he died beneath the banner he loved so much . . . I shall give a perspective, a flashback of Esslingen, where he had emerged as a leader, where you both led many parades, and . . ."

"Oh, leave me alone! Write what you want!"

"I shall be at the funeral. Will you need my help?"

"No! Never!" She waited. She wanted a fight. She wanted to tell him that she had pushed him out of her life for good, but he was silent, thinking—she was sure—about what to say and how to politely remind her that he had outlasted his rival and now would come to collect the spoils. With a shaky hand she hung up the receiver and went outside.

She sat down on the swing and stared at the bright, unreal world, a world without Kārlis Arājs, and began staging his funeral. She began with the casket covered with the same flag she had made for him. She would place on it a white lily and two dark red roses, the darkest she could find. Ilga and Gatis would be on either side of her. She would, no doubt, look like her dead mother Katerina, all veiled in black, lost to life and saturated with grief. Her grief would protect her from Vanags, who will say his piece, as he must. *But how will it be later? . . . Oh God!*

She rose, ready to go out and buy yards of sheer black chiffon and heavy crepe. But where would she find all that? She wondered if there were funeral shops as there were bridal shops. She didn't like funeral parlors with their American ways. Kārlis must have a real Latvian funeral. She telephoned the minister, but there was no answer. She felt relieved. She was not ready to share her grief with anyone. She wanted to chop the evergreen branches herself and strew them on all the paths they had walked. Perhaps she should have her husband cremated so that someday she might carry his ashes to Latvia or, at least, to the edge of the Baltic Sea.

No! protested her alert voice of Reason. *To mix with Alma? To indulge in hysterical sentimentality? How inappropriate! How banal! A man—especially of his stature—needs a splendid funeral. A man needs a grave a woman can tend—a place for tears and flowers at least at the appropriate times. He deserves clear, engraved dates and an epitaph that summarizes the essence of his life.* And she must compose that carefully and reverently, for it would also reflect on her . . . *Strewing ashes in the sea! How melodramatic and selfish*! Milda could not do that. She could not imagine her husband so reduced, diluted, washed off the earth and forgotten. Moreover, she would be responsible for having no resting place herself, no place where their children could lay her down. She straightened up. The ceremony must be in the Cathedral. She will call the archbishop and the choir director—the maestro—and request their favorite cantata: *Dievs, Tava zeme deg*! (God, thy land is burning). She will request the complete work. Kārlis will lie in an open garlanded casket, with burning candles on either end. Yes, the funeral must be splendid—a state funeral as befits a leader, while she will take her place beside him, veiled in black and alone in the cold, dark night of her soul.

As the late sun pierced its long, hot beams through her open window, she looked backward and forward; their married life was like a closed book, mysterious, fully illustrated, precious, and she placed that book, placed his life, on a high shelf, which only she could reach. She arranged him along with all her precious dead, and like those others, he now belonged to her completely, and she could make of him whatever her heart and imagination allowed.

"All flesh is as grass," said the preacher. "A flower in the field, which is here today and gone tomorrow."

She saw an empty, flowerless field all around her. She was alone and lost in that field, a child crying for the setting sun, running after it, calling, but the sun did not wait for the orphan. The sun had no time.

Milda placed an oversized announcement of her husband's death in the major Latvian and local American newspapers:

Kārlis Arājs, born May 18, 1928.
Died August 23, 1979, Washington DC.
Latvijas tautai—neatkaībai un brīvībai.
For the Latvian people—for independence and freedom.
"To him who is faithful to the end,
belongs the crown of life."
Rest in peace, my husband and my love!
In deepest sorrow, your wife Milda
and our children Illga and Gatis.

*

A month after the memorable funeral, by the end of September, Milda was rushed to the hospital. She had been bleeding. Dark, clotted blood had hit the carpeted stairs as she tried to reach her bed but couldn't. An indefinite time later Ilga found her in the bathroom. The ambulance came quickly, its sirens and lights ripping the silence of the tree-lined autumn street, causing people to come out of their houses to look and listen and ask for whom the sirens cried.

Ilga sat in shock, holding Mother's hand as she was transferred from the stretcher onto the hospital bed quickly, impersonally. At the door, their hands were pulled apart, and Ilga was left alone waiting outside the operating room. The malignancy had not spread beyond the cervix. Milda's womb was scraped. "This is routine," the doctor said and told his patient to take it easy. He instructed Ilga, saying, "Take care of your mother. You can. You are unusually strong women." Then he picked up the telephone to answer another call.

At the end of the week Milda was released. She had been scraped and rearranged inside. She would be fine. Her reproductive, creative part had been aborted and thrown away. No fuss, no mess. Yet she wept silently, mournfully, her head turned to the wall. There, among the flowers and inside the sterile vault-like walls, she pondered the steps of the human life: how quickly and simply, she noted, life's ordained functions and purposes end! She was fine. Unbearably light and free, defying the specter of her aging and death.

That fall and winter she updated her dental work and accepted reading glasses. When spring came, she was surprised by new bursts of energy. New life budded and bloomed within and around her, and she forgot her age. She joined a spa and played the piano with renewed excitement. The doctor assured her that she was doing fine, just fine. She gloried in that truth. "Love your body," Mrs. Gramzda had said when she lay at the end of her life. "A healthy spirit lives in a healthy body. I don't believe in the separation of body and spirit. That's nonsense invented by sick men with undeveloped imaginations."

Milda planted a whole bed of red and white roses—enough for bouquets that would keep Kārlis's grave blooming. They would bloom dramatically against the shining black granite monument.

Miraculously, she injected her vitality into *those who had gone before* and wrote what she felt and remembered in her journal. Throughout the coming year, in all seasons and weather, early in the morning, people driving past the cemetery could see a lone woman, dressed in either black or white, her arms full of flowers, kneeling in the Latvian section, at the tallest monument (set by the people) and gliding on, pausing at other graves and giving each a flower and her sigh. Sometimes a young woman walked with her. Together they read the names of people and places, words a stranger to the Latvian culture could not pronounce: Kalniņš, Siliņš, Bērziņš (he was killed in Vietnam), Egle, Ozols—born in Riga, Liepāja, Jelgava, Alūksne, Saldus, Madona; died in Michigan.

All closed books, biographies buried in the earth.

"So many lands and seas lie between their births and death," one would say and the other respond, question, ponder. "Life is a rugged road," says one and glides on.

They would drive home and have breakfast, and then Milda would set to work on what Kārlis had left behind—unfinished and disorderly. Slowly and carefully she set things in order. She carted boxes to the Studies Center, where they were stored with many similar boxes. The director feels bad: there is not enough room for everything. People are bringing whole libraries—even donating the shelves, but there is no room, no room at all. And the funds are dwindling; the faithful supporters are giving out and dropping off. There is no money to hire a full time archivist. But—the director is pleasant—"later, perhaps later, you understand." She understands everything and leaves.

And so, slowly, box by box, bag by bag, Milda empties the house of her husband and wonders how she will continue going on alone, now that she felt the strangeness of exile pressing her down with a force she feared more than death.

And then uninvited, unsummoned, belatedly and slowly, as if crawling from the ground, the image of Mr. Vanags immerges. Where is he? What is he doing? She read the obituary he had written. She saw the formal photograph of Kārlis at a younger age. The writing was dry, factual, nothing what she had expected, nothing about past parades and symbolism. Only the facts, as if there were no space for elaboration, no space to celebrate a noble life. After she read and reread it, she wept. She nurtured her anger and affirmed her resolve to never let that man reenter her life. *So what's happening? Why is he suddenly here, on my mind?*

The Visit

"You *must* fly to him?" Ilga startled her mother, who, on her knees, with her back to the door, was cleaning Gatis's room.

"What?"

"*Mammīt*, fly down for a visit. You have the time. You also have the money."

"But Papa . . ."

"Is dead."

"No . . . Yes," she spoke waveringly, confusedly. "Dead, yes, of course, but more with me now than when he lived."

"That's exactly why you should go. Get away from here! This house's become a shrine—spotless, nothing out of place—a damned morgue. I can't take it anymore, Mamma!" Milda blinked bewildered, deeply wounded. "It's been over two years and you're still wearing black. That's pretty sick. Go! Do something, for God's sake! Get with it!"

Soon a long preparation for the visit began. Milda reserved a place on TWA for August at a supersaver price. She would have a whole month to get ready. She tried to imagine the babies. Mara would be exactly one year and eight months; Tony, seven months. That is how it would be in August 1981, but it would not stay that way. The children, her grandchildren, would grow, change, learn, develop, turn into people. Therefore, she bought gifts not for their toddler and baby stages but for the later, more aware years of their childhood. She would buy things for them that she hoped might help to shape their consciousness and establish a connection between her and them; between the long Aryan, Indo-European roots and the tender ones they were now pushing into the American Southwest. For the parents she would get token reminders, so they would not forget their origins. Gatis would not really need presents; she herself was all that he would want and all she could give him. The most precious gifts, she knew, were intangible, illusory, abstract. At this sensitive meeting, things money could buy, in fact, seemed banal.

As the time of departure drew near, Milda became irrepressibly excited. She saw her mirrored reflection becoming younger; her cheeks had a live blush, and her motions quickened. She bought a doll for Mara and dressed her in a *Nīca* costume: a bright red skirt with embroidery running down in streams, a gray vest with black embroidery down the front, and a white blouse decorated with black cross-stitches on the sleeves. When all was done, she braided the doll's long yellow hair and put on its head a beaded crown. This is the most colorful of all the Latvian costumes, signifying a rich district. It is the garb all little girls love. Ilga, too, had cried for such an outfit, but Kārlis forbade it. "Too much red," he said. "The Soviets have taken this one over and are using it for pseudo-national propaganda purposes. I cannot stand it!" And *Ilgiņa* had to accept the rather dull, striped Vidzeme costumes. But for little Mara, now asserting her right to do as she pleased, Milda, displayed the doll on the shelf below Kārlis's portrait, saying, "See!" Ilga saw her and loved the awakened spirit and the expressive artistry. "Why don't you make a series and sell them," she proposed, but Milda said, "Why don't you? I haven't had time to learn capitalism."

Next, she bought a book of beautifully illustrated Latvian folktales and another hardbound picture dictionary—*Kā to Sauc*? (*What is It Called*?) This would help Gatis teach his children Latvian words. It would be fun, she thought, as she remembered the word games she had played with her babies and, consequently, they could read and speak two languages before they started kindergarten.

For Tony she renovated Gatis's teddy bear, and, after some hesitation, folded up the old miniature Latvian flag Kārlis had saved and kept with him since the war. It had stood on his mother's bookshelf and was the only decorative item on his desk. It was his inspiration, Milda believed, therefore sacred. She hoped and trusted that Gatis would see it that way and also teach his children to cherish and respect the sad, courageous banner.

For Angela she had ordered a large silver brooch made in the ethnographic sun design. The large, clear amber eye gleamed in perfection. She placed the treasure in a dark blue velvet-lined jewelry box, knowing that she would have to explain its symbolic and real value. She would tell Angela that amber had been exported to ancient Rome, and that several amber routes stretched from the Baltic to the distant lands around the Mediterranean Sea. To be secure in her knowledge, Milda did some research and learned that Nero had ordered shiploads of amber and that the stretchers of gladiators were lined with it because of its healing properties. She also knew from reading Homer's Odyssey that one of Penelope's lovers had given her an amber necklace. From a more recent brochure, she had been reminded that amber in ancient times had been valued as precious as gold and that its other name was *electron* because it was charged with static electricity. All this, she hoped, would stimulate their conversations; she also hoped that for the growing and busy family time would always be set aside for learning and that learning would be fun. and new knowledge would increase the value of her gifts beyond any set price.

Thinking about all this, as she prepared for the trip, made her feel that Angela was not nearly as foreign as she had feared in the beginning, when she had so magnetized Kārlis. The nightmare came back, but she pushed it aside. It was past and gone, belonging to other dead ecstasies and events she had survived. Now she could look at it all from her vantage point and not begrudge Kārlis his lust for a young body any more than she would begrudge a traveler his visions of alluring but unreachable hemispheres.

Milda was pleased for being able to look back like that, creatively, rationally. It pleased her that she had always surpassed Kārlis with her imagination and that now she could indulge it without having to explain and justify why she saw things in a certain way and possessed her own peculiar sensitivities. Since his death, more and more bravely, she enjoyed skipping his full stops and using ellipses as she pleased. "You were the unreasonable one," she told his somber portrait on the wall. "Stop me, if you can!" She pressed the doll to her cheek and challengingly stared at the canvas.

The week of the trip Milda set to harder work. She baked Gatis's favorite bread, the Latvian sourdough. And when she was done with that—a three-day process—she baked *piragi.* She bagged dried linden blossoms in a fancy tea container. They had been picked from the tree that Kārlis had planted when Ilga was born.

From the birch, planted at the birth of Gatis, she took a bottle of sap, which, an old friend of the family was now drawing. The white-bearded man came at the precise time every March and tapped the tree, according to traditions, and bottled the sap. Latvians who nurtured old customs believed in the magic, health-giving properties of the graceful silver birch and had a celebration after the sap stopped flowing, just before the leaves came. Milda knew that Gatis would be pleased to learn that this ritual had not stopped. Everyone had enjoyed the parties when the whole community was young, happy, and not yet threatened with assimilation. "Our distilled spirit flows on forever," Ilga had once remarked and made Kārlis nod in approval . . . Recalling those times with a sad smile, Milda boxed two bottles, one from bygone springs and one of *birch nouveau.*

Finally, she spent a great deal of time in the garden, stopping at the flowerbeds, checking their moisture, and eliminating the smallest weed. She gazed at the goldfish in the water lily pond, staring into the water as if looking for Kārlis's reflection next to her as it had been for so many years—years when she took him for granted, immune to his mortality. She walked along the carefully sculptured paths, wide enough only for one person. Usually she had walked behind him. Now she was aware that she did not particularly miss him. She did not miss the shadow that so often fell over her.

She read the garden like a calendar, a diary, an outgrowth of their lives and imaginations and their thoughts and secret longings. The garden had grown and aged with them, and now, it seemed, it was not as green, nor as consistently bright. Something should be done about that—later . . . She walked under the linden tree, now spread out too much, and in need of trimming, but she felt helpless. How could she stop the tree or anything from growing beyond her strength and reach? She could hardly cut off the branches for her tea blossoms . . . Well, she'd call the old, wise pantheist as soon as she returned; he will be pleased and honored to lend his hands.

Walking on, she slid under the sacred birch branches and sat in the swing Kārlis had hung for Gatiņš. She kicked off her sandals and gave herself a hard push and then let the swing rock her of its own momentum. Lazily she leaned her head against the rope. She pulled the hairpins out of her bun. The braid untwisted itself. It hung, full of gray, down her side, but the wind did not care. The wind is colorblind. She gave the golden-haired little girl a push. She laughed, eyes closed and looking up at a bright sky as through a green sieve. Sadly she remembered that Gatis did not like the swing and that most of the time it hung unused, rocking in the breezes, swinging empty in the wind. Gatis was afraid of his tree. It all happened because he was caught stealing cookies.

Kārlis had come upon the little thief as he stood on the top of the kitchen counter reaching high above for the cookie jar. Milda was upstairs napping and was awakened by the crash, followed by a loud scream and some very clear words by Kārlis. "Go out and cut three branches off the tree. Take the smaller ones that hang low and bring them to me." Milda could not believe her ears. The boy was far too small! The pruning shears were too big for his little hands, but she dared not say anything. She heard the door close. She knew that both father and son had gone out. Kārlis, she trembled, was about to teach another of his unforgettable lessons . . . Milda heaved in fury. She rushed down the stairs and into the kitchen. Jar and cookies lay shattered all over the floor, but she headed for the window, flying into it like a mindless bird. She saw Kārlis's back just outside the door and little Gatiņš under the birch, holding on to the shears, cutting the branches. His little body was erect, his face set in hard man lines. He looked like a miniature of his father—a little elf—as he cut until his hands could hold no more. Still, with his face set in angry spite, he ran to his father and gave him the shears, hanging open, chillingly dangerous. Then he ran back, gathered the twigs and carried them like a bouquet of flowers. Milda heard the porch door close. They were inside. Kārlis said, "Now, my boy, receive what you deserve. You stole and you must be punished." Milda held onto the edge of the kitchen sink as she heard the switches fall on what she knew would be a bare bottom. She did not hear any screams, only suppressed gasps and, "Now thank me for this lesson." She did not hear the thanks, but she heard Kārlis say, "What? Say it louder!" And then the little man's voice came through clearly: "Thank you, Papa." Kārlis said, "That's good. Now let us shake hands. Man to man. I trust you will never steal again." She did not hear the answer, only the little steps as the boy ran past her, up the stairs to his room.

"Don't go to him!"

Hours later, after a tasteless supper, Milda went to her darling with a glass of milk and a slice of bread. She helped him undress. She saw the red stripes on his white bottom. She kissed and soothed it with vitamin oil and put on his pajamas. "Mammīt, I did not steal," he said, heaving, "I w-was hungry but you were asleep and I didn't want to wake you 'cause you were very tired and Papa is mean." She stroked his head, her lips whispering and kissing the pain away. She rocked him to sleep, softly singing, *Aijā, žūžu, lāču bērni . . .*

She did not speak to her husband for days. The children shunned him.

Some years later, the Easter Monday of Gatis's seventh year, Kārlis called him kindly, cheerfully asking his help. Milda saw her husband take the board, a rope, and, with the boy carrying the toolbox, go to the birch tree. So Milda knew that Kārlis was hanging the swing because the traditions demanded that. According to pagan customs, swings were hung the Monday after Easter Sunday. The young men had to swing the girls as high as they could to insure fertility and the propagation of their tribes. Kārlis was insuring his immortality, Milda thought. When the swing was safe, he pushed Ilga until she was giddy and then called Milda and pushed her a bit—symbolically. Finally it was Gatis's turn. But he was rigid. His hands went white as they held the rope, and his teeth clamped. Kārlis pushed hard, and the boy screamed until the swing stopped. He slid off and ran to Mamma. Kārlis only laughed, saying, "Sissy." And then cheerfully, "You are growing big just like your tree. Soon you'll swing the girls." Gatis said, "Yes, Papa." Papa tousled the boy's head and said, "He is now on a good path. He will be a fine man. Discipline and love make a man strong."

But Gatis hardly ever played under the tree. He avoided the swing, saying it made him sick to his stomach. Only when Papa was home, he thought it was his duty to swing and to twist himself inside the ropes, coming out in a dizzy spin. Left alone, Gatis usually played in a safe corner with his Matchbox cars. If he swung at all, it was in Ilga's hammock under the linden tree. Often he would fall asleep in her arms, rocking gently as though in a cradle—the way she (Milda) rocked now, waiting for the airplane to take her through the clouds to her darling boy.

*

She flew into Phoenix around seven o'clock in the evening. A much changed Gatis met her; he moved slowly and heavily, not like her little boy, nor the disciplined athlete. His hair fell in disarray, and he needed a shave. He approached her shyly and embraced her awkwardly. His long letter of confessions and accusations lay between them. Only the picking up of luggage, the moving out of the airport, and finding the parked car kept mother and son in some sort of balance.

As Milda stepped into the hot Arizona evening, she felt she had landed in a completely different world. The monsoon rains had left behind thick low clouds and puddles that steamed, creating circles of rainbows, mixing heaven with earth. She admired the tall, waving palms and the purple mountain silhouettes. Gatis watched her take it all in and then guided her to his car—also aged. "The wife drives the wagon," he remarked. Talking casually, they drove through the city that lay flat and spread out as far as she could see. It reminded her of nothing.

They pulled at last into a driveway. The small house sat in a huge sand box. Only one scraggly tree leaned against it, hot and drooping. Here and there different kinds of cacti squatted, somewhat bloated because of the rain. Their prickles and spears glistened. "Don't touch!"

The door opened, and a heavy black-haired woman holding an unruly baby stepped forward. In her smile Milda saw what she remembered of the sexy Angela. She was again dressed in red shorts, over which she wore a flowery maternity top. A little girl, calling "Daddy, daddy," rushed into Gatis's arms. He promptly introduced her to her grandmother. "Here is our Mara," he said, and Mara said, "*Labdien.*" Milda bent down and hugged her. They closed the door to keep the heat out and went inside.

A spaghetti supper was promptly served, but Milda reached for the salad. Hungry though she was, she could not possibly indulge in all the food Angela provided. She could not help seeing how much everyone ate. Gatis had seconds, and little Mara cleaned up her plate down to the last noodle. Milda imagined the colloids building up, the cells dividing and multiplying outward into unhealthy chubbiness. Distressed, she did not know what to do with all she had baked. Everything was still safely packed. She would divide her bread and *piragi* into seven days and suggest that Angela not work hard at cooking. Satisfied with her idea, she glanced around. Only one bookshelf with a few books, all unfamiliar, unliterary—*Reader's Digest* condensations, a set of smudged encyclopedias, and a line of paperback thrillers. No paintings on the walls. Only a lone crucifix and a large calendar with a picture of the Grand Canyon in August. She wished to see the canyon, but there would be no time. Not now.

Her attention was called again to the table. Cartons of different ice creams and a can of chocolate sauce offered choices of dessert. Milda took half a scoop of vanilla ice cream and a touch of the sauce. The others scooped and poured and argued about kinds and quantities. Milda accepted a cup of decaffeinated coffee.

Angela was not at all as Milda remembered. She had gained weight, not just the legitimate weight of pregnancy. Her bare arms were definitely fat and she had a double chin. Her hair was cut too short for her face, making her appear top heavy and sloppy. Milda could not understand how the beautiful sex kitten could do this to her son who had given up everything for her. She wished Kārlis could see Angela now!

She looked at Gatis, blinking, wanting to say something. Kid him about storing food around his middle like a camel and tease him by saying that just because he lived in a desert, he still was not a camel and did not need to make a hump in front of him. But he was not open to kidding and so she blamed, naturally, the woman who cooked. *The woman is responsible, after all, for a proper diet that will not go into extra fat but turn into energy and good looks.* She was proud that Kārlis had never been overweight. *I shall have to suggest, say something—but later. How?*

Luckily, Mara moved boldly toward her, saying, "Granny," as though trying the word out for size, startling Milda because she had never heard herself called that. Distraught, again unsure whether she was losing or finding her identity, she handed out the presents.

The evening was like a strange Christmas, set on the red planet Mars. The sunset sky burned in brilliant violets and reds while a lone blooming oleander filled the picture window like a lighted Christmas tree. Everyone was opening presents; everyone seemed happy. Milda explained each item and admonished the parents to guard these special treasures. But Mara wanted her doll NOW; she pushed the books aside. Milda would read to her later. Teach her a few words. There was plenty of time.

Angela said she just loved the pin and fastened it on to her light cotton maternity blouse. The brooch, tilted by the silver and weighted down, exposed the unpolished backside of the amber eye. Milda wanted to set it right, teach her daughter-in-law how and with what it should be worn, but she only blinked. She could not bring herself to touch Angela. Gatis caught it all and for a moment their eyes locked, as long ago. Only now it hurt—incurably. Slowly, hesitatingly, he took his gift and pulled at the ribbons. He *was* surprised. He stared at the rolled-up faded flag on its shining brass pole. It lay in the box like a knife, its point very sharp. Their eyes met at that point; she saw tears flooding his eyes—those unmistakably Latvian eyes that seemed to be either floating or sinking in this strange land. But she could not go to him, could not help him. She passed the still fresh *piragi* around—one for each, but everyone, except Gatis, said *no thanks*. He bit into the icon of old days and praised his mother. Eyes closed, he also inhaled the sourdough bread and put it aside to be savored later. He opened the canister of tea.

"Ah," he said, "I can smell Ilga. How is she?" Milda updated him. Animated, they exchanged small remembrances, and then he pulled the ribbon off the next present. His mood changed when he recognized what was in the bottles. "I'm surprised you're still tapping," he said. "How is my tree? How groweth my soul?" She heard the irony, the truth: his soul was left at home, with her, growing alone in their garden. He was split, cut, exiled! *Oh God* . . . He told Angela to keep the tea in the medicine cabinet, while he put the bottles of birch sap in his liquor cabinet.

"I'll keep them handy," he said, "for when I need special powers, when I need to jack up my anger." Blood rose to his face. "This is my father's bottled up rage," he said and told Mara about the trees in Grandma's garden. The child did not know what rage meant, and the father did not explain. Intensely, he looked into his mother's eyes. She stared back blandly, helplessly, and pitied poor dead Kārlis, who had never felt his son's love, only his trembling, submissive fears. She turned her eyes away. *Oh, why did I drag along all this baggage, when my son has tried so hard to escape? Why did I unload on him the outmoded traditions even I don't take that seriously? What am I trying to implant in this red desert heat?*

To steady herself, she reached for little Tony, who had been walking around the furniture but was now kicking against Angela's competing belly. He crawled to Grandma readily, jabbering, grabbing for the old teddy bear. Pleased, Milda picked him up and moved to a rocking chair. She pressed the teddy against his cheek, and they all rocked away, while Tony babbled in the universal language of babies that all mothers understand. *Blessed intimacy*! Milda felt her long-gone motherhood resurfacing and remembered. *This*, her soul whispered, *is happiness . . . a woman's golden age. This is what you had but don't have anymore. You brought them reminders—and they respond in kind. How do these things balance out? Whose gift hurts the most?*

She rocked on, pressing the child to her heart, closing her eyes and feeling her own babies. She is in her twenties, live, looking forward, building the Latvian Exile State with her own flesh, blood, and dreams . . . The baby goes limp in her arms; Angela stands before her ready to reclaim her child, but Milda rises and carries him down the hall to his room and puts him in his crib. Angela backs away. The baby whimpers, cries out, but Milda soothes him with words and kisses, softly singing, *Aijā žūžū lāču bērni* . . . And then she, too, finds her bed and goes to sleep.

By the third day, once the bread and *piragi* were gone, Milda was restless. They had been to the mountains and in the valleys where Westerns are still being filmed. They had explored the canyons, but hiking was hard for Angela, Mara complained, and Tony had a heat rash. Gatis was tense; his knuckles white as he held the steering wheel. His eyes avoided meeting his mother's hazy glances. Milda looked out. She was impressed and awed by the mountains, yet they did not draw her, not like the Alps. She was afraid of the cacti, feared stepping on snakes, spiders, and scorpions, while the F100+ dry heat made her want to bite the air. Her skin dried out and her hair hung limp. She felt lightheaded, her blood pounding against her temples, and like a thirsty mountain deer, she longed for an oasis, for streams of running water.

She also longed for grass, real green, growing grass that people mowed and walked on. How much she had taken its soft greenness for granted! How naturally she had kicked off her shoes and walked barefooted, soothing and cleansing her feet in morning dew and after soft summer rains! Here she had to keep her shoes on at all times. The cactus needles would even get into the house. You could not hang sheets outside because the needles would get stuck in them, Angela explained when Milda suggested a clothes line. The windows had to stay closed, the shades drawn. "We're trying to save on our electric bill," Angela said.

Milda felt clammy, covered with desert sands, and her feet, more than she herself, wanted to get up and start walking home—home where the grass was green and soft and where the nightingales and skylarks sang in the night and in the morning.

As they drove around the city, she thought she had come to the land of the aged. Old people were everywhere. Wrinkled ladies, sunburned and dried, hard like orange peels, walked around the shopping centers under the awnings, alone or holding onto shaking old husbands. Some carried their own oxygen as they shuffled into sunsets, hand in hand, feebly smiling. The Old drove carelessly, mindlessly, signaling right but turning left, demanding distance and patience. "Watch where you're going, you old fool!" someone shouted leaning out a window at an old man who stepped on to the highway and tried to cross it. Gatis said *fuck* and cursed the traffic jams.

Through her window Milda saw the dark people, the Mexicans, the Hispanics, the migrant workers, some wearing orange vests and working, while others stood at street corners, jobless and hot, waiting or dreaming the American Dream. She saw Indians baking tacos on their reservations, their canvas tents blowing in the wind, and felt sorry for these people, the humiliated, the cheated—deprived old kingdoms of Navajo, Apache, Pueblo—the bereft, the displaced, whose ancestors had been driven here on many trails of tears. "Like our people driven to Siberia," she said. "But the history books hide the truth in kinder, more dishonest words," she went on. "*Relocated*, they say of the poor Indians, as the communists say of our people. But they are worse off than Latvians."

"How's that?" Gatis asked yawning.

"Because they are victims and outcasts in their own land," Milda said. "They look out of their reservations, as from prisons. They see every day what the white man has done to them."

"Would you expect us to give America back to the Indians?" her second-generation American son asked. Milda did not respond, but Gatis braced himself for more arguments: "I suppose Latvians still think that Russia will give Latvia back to the natives. Hand it over because it is right so you all can go back and start over." He raced through a yellow light. "Get with it, Mother!"

Milda shut her lips tightly but could not keep silent. "I think all people should be allowed to live in their home countries. God put them there and nowhere else."

"Mother, you'll never change," Gatis said, but she heard Kārlis—hard, insensitive, putting her down and off track.

"No, I guess not."

The sun was setting beyond the purple mountains. She saw a coyote prowling at the edge of the city and showed it to Tony, who wanted to get into her lap but was tied in an infant seat. "Poor coyote, also dispossessed," she murmured.

"Nasty pests," Angela said.

They crossed a river full of rushing muddy water. "The rivers stay dry all year," Gatis explained. On the banks of the river Milda saw poor houses, shacks that could be flooded out by the next deluge. Certainly the people had no insurance, while in the foothills stood elegant houses like miniature castles, with locked, iron-fenced courtyards, green grass, and flowering trees. The beauty and opulence of the rich struck her as obscene, stark, showy, unnatural. She wanted to go home.

Yet she wished to hold time still. She needed this time to be with her son alone. Angela and the children always insulated them. Finally, almost pleadingly, she said to Gatis, "Could we be alone? Could we just please talk?"

On the fifth night, after the children were asleep, she sat down next to Gatis. Angela turned on the TV.

"Turn that thing down!" Gatis shouted.

"I've got a right to watch my show," Angela snapped back. Milda shrunk. They were really scolding *her.* She held on to a pillow.

"What did you want to talk about?" Gatis asked, composed, in the Latvian. *Ah, yes!* She knew him again. He was hers, her boy. She choked up and said nothing, but Garry Arrid was impatient, glancing from wife to Mother, as though whipped by both. At last Milda spoke softly, gently, and he turned to her. She told him about Ilga and his old friends and what *Avīze* had printed about his father and his importance. She showed him a photo of the elegant tombstone she had designed and the community had put up. She updated him on the relationship between the exiled and home communities, and then she talked about her daily life, the nearly empty house and his room. As *Gatiņš* responded, she could not help noticing how badly his Latvian had faded. The old language was polluted and eroding; he was throwing in American words, phrases, and clichés carelessly, mindlessly.

"Please," she said. "One language or the other. You're not mixing a salad."

"Lay off, Mom!" he said in English and told Angela to make popcorn.

Gatis made her move over to the corner of the couch. *Ah, I'm being punished and made to feel guilty—guilty about speaking Latvian to little Mara. Oh, I cannot win, cannot do things right!* She pouted, feeling Kārlis's disapproval for not enforcing the Latvian language enough with the whole family, but taking the easy way out and talking English in her accent. Catching disproving glances in her son's eyes, as blue as the dry sky, she saw her husband's disapproving scowls. Hurt, she wanted to cry, to bury herself in her son's shirt and have it all out, but she sat quiet and still, suspended in time. *How can I salvage so much in one week?*

"Time flies," she said softly. "Sometime down the road I shall have to sell the house and move."

"Where will you go?" Gatis sat up, glancing at Angela.

"I don't know," Milda said, and, having caught that glance, smiled. *They're afraid . . . We're having a communications gap . . . I'm stuck . . . Alma, dearest mother and aunt, help me! I know what you'd say.*

"It's only a stage, a phase," Milda said, straightening up, staring at her son, the stranger.

"Yea."

She talked about some alternatives. Ignoring Angela, she now spoke in the Latvian. She said the words clearly. Angela glared at her, but Milda's words pulled Gatis back into the world he was forgetting and from which he had escaped. Angela, left on the outside, quit talking. She armed herself with Tony and turned to her mother-in-law her full womb.

Little Mara, feeling the tensions rising, talked more as she scurried from one to the other, carrying or dragging the doll—the lovely Nīca doll—by one arm. Still, the child was charming, Milda had to admit. She had strange, large eyes: a dark violet, like Elizabeth Taylor's, that distracted her father. He took her in his arms and called her his *donna bella.* Mara smiled, showing a perfect row of baby teeth. Milda seeing their intimate connection, recalled that throughout the week, he had always called Mara to himself, whenever the conversation with her had become threatening, and in seconds she came to him dancing, shaking her hair and giggling as it tickled her bare shoulders. Milda saw that the little *donna* already moved her hips in unconscious provocation that clearly had not come from her side of the family. Even Alma had not moved like that. Ilga did not either.

As she watched the child, she was sure that Angela's hips had moved in just such a manner through the halls of East High when her son was still innocent and when, like a Venus fly catcher, that Italian *donna*, who since then seemed unendingly pregnant, had trapped him with her Sophia Loren gyrations. Such were the hot-blooded women of the South.

*

The room hung in suspended silence. Milda watched her granddaughter, projecting her into the future that would be only some short ten years away. She was concerned for all of them. *If they live here long enough Mara might marry one of the short stocky men with raven hair and a mustache*. She had seen many white girls walking with dark men—those migrants, legal and illegal aliens. Staring through the blooming oleander tree into the future as through a telescope, she saw her and Kārlis's thick Latvian blood, flowing into thin trickles, completely diluted, overpowered like thin streams of water that flowed in the mountains, afraid of the heat and the desert's ravaging dryness.

"I think you should make a conscious effort to speak Latvian to your children," Milda said directly. And: "I hope you look for a more appropriate place to live. This is ridiculous to be so far away from home." Gatis did not answer; still they argued. They argued without words, across the head of little Mara and behind Angela's full back, who threw in that she was teaching Mara Italian words. She said that they were planning to go to Florence next year while the babies could still travel for free. She said how she had always wanted to go back and see where she came from, now that roots were so important, and that Garry, too, was learning Italian. "Isn't that enough?" she demanded.

"*Bet*," Milda barely breathed. Garry understood. The full sentence would be: "But when Latvia is free, will your children not go there? . . . Shouldn't you teach them your mother's and father's language?"

But Garry did not answer that unvoiced question. Her *but* in the casual chatter of her Italian-Latvian-American granddaughter's innocent word games had been like a dull dart thrown at a freshly painted wall instead of a well-worn target. Her son had let the conjunction miss him; he had let it go past him where it would not imbed itself but would drop without so much as leaving a scratch. And then he stood up. He stood straight the way he had done that day when he had said NO to his father.

He knew that soon his mother would remind him that after Mara turned five, she should be enrolled in one of the summer programs of the Latvian consciousness-raising camps and that this would be possible only if she knew Latvian. The camps were generally fun, and the little kids liked them, but Garry also knew that unless the children were fluent in the language, they were shunned, embarrassed, taught separately at the end of the regular sessions so that they would not affect other children whose parents had not mixed their bodies with foreign "elements"—as the leaders pointed out.

Garry knew very well that Milda would be disgraced if her and her patriotic husband's grandchildren would only be accommodated during an allocated week at the end of the season. And Milda, on her side, sensed that her son's protective instincts were like her own and that he would never put his children, whom he so openly adored, in a humiliating, intimidating position. Tugging and pulling, Mother's and son's sharp eyes met over the heads of the children in a cold, wordless impasse.

Milda calculated how she would have to be responsible for any future Latvian education. She would have to pay for the trip and the camp. She would have to shower the children with presents and rewards if they learned well. It would be fun, she assured herself. *Or would it?* Gatis had not moved one step closer to meet her at least part of the way. Instead, he swept Mara into his arms and tossed her above his head, saying, *la bella donna.* He set her down deliberately, as if making a final point. He patted her head and then leaned forward and with the same hand patted his mother's aging cheek. Milda tried to grab that hand, but he moved away before she could catch it. Angela, observing the drama from her corner of the room, announced that it was bedtime and gathered up her children. Gatis escaped into the kitchen to pour himself a drink.

"Let's celebrate," he shouted, when Angela joined him. "Bottoms up!"

Milda heard the clanking of glasses as he refilled his and mixed margaritas for the ladies. Cautiously delivering the drinks, he went back for his and then plunked himself down between the two women, a full glass of amber liquid in his careless hand. While Milda licked the salted rim, she saw how quickly Angela drank and how that drink mellowed her.

"Milly, relax!" Angela said. "We just love it out here! We're doing good. It took a while, but now this is home." Milda recognized the look that had tripped Kārlis, and she swallowed a mouthful. She saw how her son pulled Angela down into the couch, kissing her, his giddy hands sliding down her back and up her leg. Milda sat on edge, as if watching an X-rated variety show, thinking how a mother-to-be should not drink alcohol, but *what can I say?* She was glad she was leaving the next day. And, she knew, so was everyone else.

*

On the airplane, Milda went over the days of the week past, which were already as nebulous as the clouds through which she darted. She recalled, as she looked down on the red sand of the desert and the dried-out rivers, that she had lovingly attempted to talk about Mara's and Tony's future but was cut off by her own son—the crucial link. She was desperately frustrated, hurt, angry, helpless. Her heart cried, *Pity me! I am, after all, your mother and I want to do what is best and what is right. I am alone in this world with no one to turn to except you and your sister, and she is lost too. And I am afraid, afraid that Pēteris Vanags will call me and make good on his promise. There are times when I hear him calling me and circling around me, ready to swoop down. How am I to resist? How am I to carry things through for us all?*

She looked into the sky and down to the earth. *How are we—you, she, and I and all who spring from our blood—to survive if we don't go on with at least some traditions? Sure, we have to make an effort, but what are we if we are not Latvians—all right—even part*

Latvians? What are we? Do you really want to be nothing but a chunk of vegetable in the American melting pot? Don't you see? And how long will Angela's kisses last? What will you do when they stop, when suddenly the sweetness becomes bitter, when she will have had enough of you and the children?

Milda was not just talking to herself in thin air. She had seen the tired marks on Angela's face, and she did not think that they were there only because of the visit. She wondered what Angela looked like and what she said, what was the sound of her voice, when no one was looking and listening. She noticed that Mara played her tricks on Gatis, not on Angela, and so it was obviously she—Angela—who controlled and disciplined. She had been and was controlling Gatis. Now, from the sky, Milda wanted to ask him what will happen when Angela grows tired of being the strong one. She wanted to warn her son. She wanted to tell him that women bloom twice and that the second blooming may be brighter than the first.

*

The pilot announces that they are flying at thirty-seven thousand feet. Still, Milda can see the desert clearly. She is intrigued by the clouds that are thick and creamy like beaten egg whites ready to be inverted for doneness. They would hold their peaks stiffly, even when turned upside down. Yet they would give nothing to the earth. The desert below is parched, the rivers dry and empty. Thirsty. But the clouds give nothing; only their shadows pass over, teasing the earth with their moisture, saying to it, *You can have water if you come up and get it; we shall never go down. We are reserved for other lands, the green ones, and the rivers and lakes that are already full. We will not touch you. We will not empty ourselves over you so you, too, might bloom like a garden. Therefore, be content with our shadows. There are as many shadows as there are clouds. Dark blue shadows from white clouds upon a red earth where no life seems to thrive, except such life as can survive next to death.*

Milda hears that they will be crossing the Rio Grande and Albuquerque; they will be flying over Las Vegas and Kansas on to St. Louis. There she will transfer. She will go on until she finds home. She hears a voice next to her saying, "Look, isn't that something!"

And Milda looks, her eyes blinking behind sunglasses. She sees the States and the clouds as if they were engaged in some dance. It's beautiful. She thinks about dancing, wishing she would dance again, longing for strong arms to hold her close. She consciously recalls Kārlis, but it is the image of Vanags that keeps emerging out of the blue. She brushes it aside, but it keeps reappearing as in a recurrent dream and in that dream her body longs for it while her mind rejects. She forces her mind away from the imposter and recalls her son. But his face is evasive and soon dims. When the shadows clear, to her mother's vision does not come a man's face but that of a little boy with golden curls, running to her in spring sunshine, splashing in puddles, playing under birch branches while the tree is little and before the father orders the boy to cut the cruel, useless twigs. And she holds the crying boy close to her heart, soothing and kissing him . . .

Flying high above the clouds, lost in the vastness of blue space, Milda hopes that she will have enough strength not to visit her son's home for a long time. He will have to come to her first. She can never again condone silently his cavalier, almost sadistically rude tossing in the wind all her values, her greatest value, that of keeping the threatened flame of the Latvian spirit alive until that land—which cannot boast of vast plains, rocky mountains, and burning deserts but is so little that, as one poet put it, it can be wrapped in a shawl—until that little land is free again. Next to that hope, she sees clearly, all other values, all actions, thoughts, everything fading away. Kārlis was right on this point. He understood. *Or?*

She looks deeper as the airplane dives into dazzling billows. Now the sun shines on them, through them. The clouds rise on either side like mountains; she expects angels to peek around the silver edges and walk up and down the slopes with harps and trumpets in their hands. She wishes she could see the throne of God on top of the highest cloud mountain the way men and women in past ages imagined God and his Kingdom before they found out that the world was round and the universe endless. She wishes that she, a mere particle in the vastness, might climb a stairway to heaven, like Christian in *Pilgrim's Progress*, with other absolved sinners and saints and ask for His justice, understanding, wisdom, and mercy. She wishes it could be like that—the way she pictured heaven when she was a child, when she walked with cousin Anna to Sunday school.

She remembers how she told Zelda that one day she would go and climb the mountains where clouds rested and she would choose one lovely pink cloud and fall into it and then float over Latvia, over Kurzeme. Her sister had called her stupid and told her it was not like that at all. Clouds are like fog, she explained; there's nothing to sit or stand on, and Milda had been ashamed of her visions and dreams next to her practical sister. Milda sees now that the sky is indeed a vapor. It is not a place. God is not there, neither are His angels. Kārlis is not there either, at least not in this American sky. She floats alone in the air—a permanent traveler, a stranger, widowed and childless, with all ties to the earth temporarily severed. She is tired, and she wishes that the jet would be high jacked and that it would, as if by some miracle, take her and parachute her down in Latvia, in Riga, Liepāja, or the castle ruins of Embūte, down on the only spot of earth where her feet would feel at home and where they could burrow in the grass and rest. She closes her eyes, waiting, waiting for her exile to end.

*

When she walked through the airport gate there, with a *Welcome Home* balloon stood Ilga. Milda embraced her with all the stored up warmth of the desert.

"Ah, my most precious child!"

"How did it go, Mother?"

"Fine! Just fine."

Into the Twilight

Milda tried to stay with the flow, driving slightly over the speed limit as she struggled through Chicago, then bore eastward, weaving around numerous MEN WORKING sites with narrowing lanes. She drove in the present, but her thoughts jumped back and forth through all the tenses, perfect and simple. At moments they triggered nerve sparks where her and Vanags's bodies had made contact, where her skin was fingerprinted. Dry and thirsty, her lips ached from his—or for his lips? She drank from her tepid water bottle, which did not cool her off. Longing mixed with desire, shame, pride, betrayal, while her foot on the gas pedal held the speedometer remarkably steady. "What must I do?" She called into the deaf traffic. "Where am I driving, really?"

Once past the quagmire of Gary, she turned on the radio and chuckled to herself as the news, the commercials, the music followed their scheduled bites. "Oh, why not?" She spoke out loud. "The world spins on as usual, while I'm veering off." She was getting sleepy, her eyes tired from the glare, the reflections of all the chrome around her. She bit into an apple and, holding it between her teeth, fumbled for the tape, saying, "Let's see what this is all about." Her hand nervously pushed the right buttons, while her head pondered the meaning and reason for what she was about to hear. *Is Pēteris bringing Kārlis back to life to torment and accuse me or to knock him down and away as men and bucks do?*

Suddenly a police car, with whirling lights and sirens appeared in her rearview mirror, and, alarmed, she pulled to the side, doing a dry run of her imminent excuses and pleas. But the car sped on, leaving the mirror empty—a dull, silent pewter rectangle, only reflecting two blue-gray eyes with a crease of anxiety between them. “Thank you, God,” she whispered and softly sang a hymn she had not heard in ages: “Lead me gently home, Father, lead me gently home. Lest I fall upon the wayside, lead me gently home . . .”

She drove on singing mindlessly, humming the forgotten words, until she pressed her foot on the brakes as her car became the tail end of a long line of backed up travelers. She inched on a bit, then stopped, crept on, and stopped again. She turned off the ignition and, irritated, eyed the equally frustrated drivers on both sides. No one moved for a long time. Some drivers got out, stretched and asked each other what was going on, but nobody knew. After about half an hour, a man with a portable telephone stepped out of his truck and announced that there had been a horrible accident: a semi truck had driven over a car, cutting the car driver in half. More police cars and an ambulance tried to get to the scene, whirling their signals, going as fast as possible, but it was too late: a man’s life was cut in half, in a moment, in the twinkling of an eye.

*

Another long hour passed before the traffic lines began to move, first slowly, then picking up speed and rolling on, and finally driving at full speed. Milda drove with the flow.

About a mile from where she had waited, she saw, as she passed, the residue of broken glass and crushed speed barriers. *On this spot a man was cut in half—swept out of life, having never reached his destination . . . Gone forever, without saying good-bye to anyone . . .*

And I can offer him nothing more than a glance of pity without tears . . . She picked up speed and drove on.

The sun was near setting when she crossed the Indiana-Michigan border. The traffic thinned out, and the landscape changed to various hues of green with tall trees and rolling fields. Squinting to avoid the blinding sunbeams, she pushed the cassette into place. The tape ran mutely on until, in a scolding, cold voice Vanags spoke: "I told you not to draw the curtain. I thought it was part of our gentlemen's agreement and I could trust you, but like a school boy you cheated and now you will suffer for it." He sounded like a principal or an interrogator or a police man. "Well then, look at her! There she stands, and here she is with me always." A silence followed and then, quite challenging, "*Mon ami*, how on earth will you go on living?"

"How indeed?" echoed Kārlis silently, and Milda imagined him clutching his heart. "But she is *my* wife," he gasped.

"Yes," Vanags articulated clearly, "your wife, but *my* love . . . Here she is *mine, my* goddess, *my* joy and torment."

"No!"

"Oh yes!" Vanags asserted calmly. "Do you, honestly not know? Cannot sense or feel the mutual pull, the invisible ties that hold us *all* together . . . forever—or until the Bony One with hollow eyes grabs us with her skeletal hands?"

The tape ran on in an elongated pause, as she held on to the steering wheel, now wide awake, listening. Vanags: "Don't give me that grin! Hey, keep your hands off me! What's come over you?"

Milda clutched on to the steering wheel like a life preserver, feeling her blood drain down to her feet, pressing the gas pedal. The speedometer needle hit ninety.

"I ought to slug you," Kārlis said, "challenge you to a duel, you son of a bitch!" Milda saw him rising, looming, fist ready, but then falling back. A static half cry downplayed the bravado exclamation. Pause. The other, mocked: "Go ahead."

Again silence reeled on, and then she heard Kārlis blowing his nose and sniveling, whimpering. Milda slowed down to 30 mph.

"I never could nor can satisfy her," he confessed. She turned up the volume. "No matter how hard I try . . . nothing I do is ever right or good enough."

"Is that so, my friend?" chuckled Vanags. She imagined him putting his strong hand on the weak, helpless arm. "It's true that man can control the world but not a woman's heart."

"Nor her manipulations," Kārlis amended, now loudly, bitterly. "She and my mother! Ha! Together they trapped me while I was still as green as a tadpole. They put me in a box called marriage. I always smell both. There's only one women smell, and I can never get out from under it, except . . ."

"Except?"

"Except when I am in the company of men, when I am with you. Like now. I don't smell them. Oh, don't look at me like that. Nothing unnatural, not like what's out in this so-called gay and free America. You see, with men, there's always a cause, a principle, a battle and then either victory or defeat, but with women . . . Sweaty sheets."

"Shut up!"

"No!"

Milda would not have recognized that tone and volume had she heard it out of context, and it also must have startled Vanags, for another droning silence followed. Then Kārlis: "You asked for it. You torture me as you torture her. If you love her that much, then why don't you take her, fight for her? You're the war hero, the brave knight! I'm only the duty-bound husband, the keeper of law and order. Well, I'm sick of it! I've been out in the world and there is work for us to do . . . I want to be free and go where I belong and can do some good, so why don't you help me and give me something definite, not this slow draining of nerves, and maybe I'll be free. Sure there'd be a scandal, but I won't be choked with garter belts, those raw rubber ones—remember? What do we have now anyway? The children are grown . . . Nothing's turned out the way it should've. It's all her fault. She spoiled the boy and never could handle the girl . . . I've got nothing to be proud of, nothing *I* could take back to Latvia after it's free of the Russian curse . . . Oh well." Kārlis laughed. "You've never lived with women, never felt the snap. So why don't you lay her? She'd probably like it, insatiable as she is."

Another long silence, then Vanags: "Are you sick, my friend?"

Not fair! You're taping the whole thing, You're making yourself noble, long suffering.

"I do not commit adultery. Only she alone will open the door for me . . . I must hold out until then . . ."

Ah . . . Someone behind her sounded his horn, and, jarred, she switched lanes.

"Let's drink to that," said Kārlis. "Give it to me straight. No rocks, no juices—straight up, for we are Latvian men."

"But old men with heart problems, no? Doctor's prohibitions, no?"

"To hell with them, to hell with it all, let's at least get drunk together, my best and dearest double-crossing friend," Kārlis carried on recklessly, and Milda, had she been present, would have pulled him away, as she often did, and take him home. He never could hold his liqueur.

Oh, stop it, don't!

"All right, as you wish . . . Cigarette?"

"Sure! . . . Doctor's orders." Puffy men laughs underlined the boyish joy of breaking rules.

Bastards!

"Love is an art, my friend," Vanags said, "or there is an art to love."

"Tell me about it," sneered Kārlis, "but only after you've lived with a woman."

"You've got a point there . . . We'll see. Here, drink up!"

She heard the liquid gurgle and hit the STOP button. *You both make me sick. Oh, dear God, help me!*

*

Gone cold and weak, she pulled into the next rest stop. She walked around and in the WOMEN's room threw cold water at her face, rinsing her eyes and rubbing her neck. Outside, back in the cooled down air, she jogged around a bit and then, refreshed, got back into the car. She yanked the tape out and pitched it in the DON'T LITTER bin and drove on toward the gathering darkness.

As the rolling, rain-soaked, exhausted clouds wove their thick night-veil all across the sky, streaking the moon and hiding the stars, Milda wondered—what veil, what forbidden curtain Kārlis had dared to draw so widely that all secrets gawked exposed, making hearts open and souls lie bare? What image of her stood or lay behind what curtain on what wall? And what had Vanags done with it, with her, all these years? The thoughts and the oncoming night, now framed with black, dune-rooted pine and fir trees, scared her. She drove faster, aware that she was heading straight north, where, had she been driving over Latvian clay roads, she would see a ring of amber light separating land from sky. It would give her hope and peace, as it did when she was a child and believed that heaven was there, at earth's edge. But now, in this weary exile, all was dark, and so many ghosts stalked the earth. She knew that she would again be suspended in waiting for yet another mystery to unveil itself in due time. She pinched her lips tightly, angrily and decided that she would not bring up what she had just heard about her husband to Vanags or anyone else. She would say nothing to her children. She would fiercely guard their father's, her husband's, image.

He lived his life the best he could, I am sure of that. It is I who am now forced to make yet other sharp turns.

The lines in the road blurred. Her tears jammed her eyes as she reviewed her married life and, in hindsight, saw the clues. But back then she had coped with her own guilt and accepted his accusations, criticisms, and withdrawals as deserving and just punishment.

She steered into the next rest area and parked in the farthest slot. She slumped her head on the steering wheel and sobbed until she felt as dry as an old leaf. She had not cried like that even at his funeral, when she cried for herself and her children. Now she cried for him, for what he had endured, what they had endured together, loving and hating, pretending and being most sincere. Her tear-drenched mind flew back with electronic speed to their separate, highly demanding, yet love-sheltered childhoods before the occupations that threw them overboard into such terror and tragedy no child should have to face. And then Germany, the ruins, the reconstruction, the DP camp of Esslingen, where forgetting and remembering were injected at every turn simultaneously, in equal doses, until they developed a kind of immunity that took the acute pain away and thrust them forward. Smiling and with hope, they carried their banners high and waving in the sun. They carried them above the heads of their own people, as strangers looked on curiously or indifferently. But they were too young to understand themselves and the world and the age in which they had been destined to live. And they had lived—he had—magnificently, faithfully, until death—his sad and glorious death . . . *Life, oh, life,* said the poet Aspazija. *It is worth dying thrice to live only once . . .*

*

Exhausted Milda continued on her journey. To herself she seemed split, very far away from herself; her head floating above like the new moon, now bright and unfettered by streaky vapors. The stars and the constellations, which she knew by name, seemed close, while her head spun among them—clear, cool, calm—sporting a vague smile, hardly visible from the earth below.

Men cut in half . . . my men . . . my life . . . In a moment, in the twinkling of an eye, at the last trumpet . . .

She searched blindly through her tape case and by the feel knew she had come upon Beethoven's Ninth Symphony. She slipped it into the slot and leaned back. Listening attentively, wishing to be distracted, to be back on earth, she drove on through the starry darkness.

Alle Menschen, alle Menschen . . .

An airplane flew through the sky, bright like a shooting star, and her thoughts fixed themselves on the other living man, the invalid, who had been up there, somewhere, looking down on cars like matchboxes, all exhausting their fumes, in lines of traffic, where someone was cut in half. She wondered if he was, at the same moment, thinking and remembering, wishing for her, hearing her heart's cry. Hearing the cries of millions as they crawled out of the ruins of Germany.

*

Milda rubs her eyes. She needs to watch for her exit. Grand Rapids with its lights is coming toward her at 80 mph. In minutes she will be home, back in her safe and empty house, and the festival with its songs and dances and rotating crowds speaking Latvian will seem like another dream—like so many other dreams and places where she had been for a while and then had to wake up to whatever reality lay before her. *So be it,* she said. "I'm dead tired."

Safely Home

When, close to midnight, Mr. Vanags telephoned, Milda hung up on him, but he called again and again. The telephone shrieked and cried, and, at last, she put the receiver to her ear.

"Please forgive me," he said.

"I don't know what you're talking about," she spoke into the mouthpiece, her voice sounding rubbery.

"Yes, you do, my precious . . . You know . . . The path is now clear between us. One life is finished and another must begin on a clean slate, don't you see?"

She said nothing, but listened to his breathing, waiting for him to say some final decisive words, but he only breathed deeper.

His palpitations exasperated her: "You bugged and taped the conversation only to trap him—a man who thought you were his best friend. Why? What was it for?" She tried to keep her voice impersonal.

"For you . . . For us. I tape all conversations with my guests. It's a kind of log or diary. My profession requires me to be precise and often I have to recall names and dates, so this was not as personal as it may seem to you, my darling."

"Isn't that illegal in *this* country, you goddamned *spy*?" she countered, ending on a cracked high pitch, but he heard only her mouth crying, not her heart. He knew she was his, but knew also that it would take time for her to succumb. So he would leave her alone until she called him, as he had said at the end of the tape, when he spoke to her, explaining and confessing. Besides, there were urgent matters for him to take care of . . . That cousin of his had finally caught up with him. *Well, maybe it's a good thing after all these years . . . Let him prove it, where there is no proof. We'll have our day in court, and until then, she must be left alone. This will play itself out,* so went his internal monologue. Milda waited for some words of explanation or denial, but he only panted and at last uttered in a tired man's voice, "Oh, my wonderful one, I've said it all in the tape. You heard it, and let's leave it at that. So you're finding out that I am at heart a coward who could not say those painful truths with your eyes cutting into my heart and conscience. How could I unveil the deep men secrets to you, when I don't understand them myself? Tell me, my treasure, does anything change the truth of our love and our anguish because we love, yes, granted, in spite of our reason, our hopelessness? You are as silent as that lovely painted form of yours on my wall. But you have been like that for many years. You only smile and reach your hands to me."

"I don't understand," Milda said quickly. "Explain. What are you looking at? What did my husband see that killed him?"

"Must I?"

"Yes, do! I cannot stand this."

"I'm afraid you'll laugh at me." He really did come across as a shy schoolboy.

"Please, I'm tired," she insisted.

A long pause, a clearing of the throat, then: "All right. I, years ago, before you were married and when we were all young, and I was sick for your love, I shared this apartment with an artist—a poor brother who couldn't make a living, so I had him paint a mural on my windowless wall of that ice-shattering scene in *The Golden Steed.* I gave him my treasured photographs of that play and you in it and let him choose. He reproduced in most exquisite colors the scene where you rise out of the glass casket and reach up—to your prince." She closed her eyes and tried to recall the lines:

> Antiņš: *Saulcerīte, Saulcerīte!*
> *She is saved from death at last.*
> *Now, my eyes, look upon her,*
> *Whom you only saw in dreams.*

"But he left off the prince. There is only you . . .

I can see her gentle face.
Her eyes shine through the fog.
They gave purpose to my thoughts,
On my way they guided me.

"He worked such artistry with your eyes so that they follow the onlooker. I never told that artist about my desire for you, let alone about my daily pain . . ."

Every day my eyes envision
Covers white of blazing sun,
Dazzling bows of crystal frost.
Slender, frail, transparent fingers,
Fragile like the melting ice
Gently hold a blue anemone
In her cold expecting hands . . .
Every night indeed I see her
Chilled and lifeless in my dreams . . .
Pale as death she glides beside me,
Head bowed low in deepest sorrow,
Silver dewdrops in her hair,
Long, dark lashes half concealing
Frozen tears in waiting eyes . . .

"But he must have known because he couldn't have caught my reflection in your face and gesture so accurately, so precisely."

"I see," she injected, shutting her eyes, shutting off the oncoming tears.

"I paid him a good wage, which made it possible for him to move out. Besides, I couldn't stand anyone else with us."

Only once I want to see her—
All my life I've lived for her!
Countless strangers will behold her.
Must she be denied to me?
All those thousands are indifferent,
But to me she is my life!

"I made that wall my shrine, my god and country. Everything, dear love. I placed my bed besides that wall, right below the casket. There we were, dreaming—sleeping out our separation, hoping for the day when we'll be together—hoping for a miracle . . .

Another miracle I see!
All her limbs are slowly moving,
Her pale lips begin to speak.
Saulcerīte! Saulcerīte!
Look upon the noonday sun!
Arise and live, my Saulcerīte!

"After a year, nightly paralyzed by your eyes and unable to endure my self-inflicted torment, I ordered a dark red drapery the shade of our flag. It covers the wall. I've disciplined myself to draw it only at night, when it soothes and lulls me . . . then I'm a child, and those dark days and nights . . . of war that have hung their shadows over my life . . . stop torturing me . . . I can sleep. My mind's eyes quit staring at those other dark and naked forms."

What is he saying? Milda wondered but did not ask. The tears stopped. Her mind cleared. She stood at attention, listening, pressing the phone tightly against her ear. "So . . . I need it, your portrait, I mean. I depend on it . . . I'm looking at it now."

"Oh, dear God," Milda sighed, surfacing from the play, from the poetry and the memories. "Oh dear," she tested her voice for coolness and then said, "I see. And poor Kārlis pulled the veil and saw the wall."

"Yes."

"He saw it but didn't understand, didn't see."

"Something like that. And it killed him."

"No!" Milda shouted. "No! That didn't. You didn't do it! His heart was bad, but he ignored every warning and thought that somehow he was immortal because he had this mission, this illusion that he would beat down communism . . . and with your and my help. We formed a union in his mind. He was driven and hated everything that got in his way—at the end even me," she said softly, aware of unveiling a secret mural of their marriage. He heard her sigh. "I'm tired," she said.

My eyes are full of melted snow.

"What was is no more and what was not is and must be," he said. "End of discussion . . . I know that this is very painful for both of us."

"Wait," she hesitated, then went on as if walking on stepping stones across raging waters. "I don't know how to say it . . . I really don't . . . want to deal with it, but there it is . . . as you put it. A clean slate, but now there is . . . this smudge on our slate which must be rubbed clean. Do you know?. . . Was my husband serious, I mean about me?. . . and us?"

"Ah, yes!"

He also sought for words and seemed embarrassed, his voice as on trial. "No, I don't know. As long as we have known each other, he talked about you with great admiration. I think, looking back, that when he clutched me, he was in pain. Perhaps had a small heart attack and panicked or something within him had snapped. Maybe he was more nervous about the demonstration the next day than I realized. But I don't know. Maybe he discovered something about himself he didn't know or could not admit that he had a problem. Perhaps the realization gave him the fatal shock.

"That night he slept on the couch, but not well. I heard him get up several times. Saw him leaning out the window, smoking. I heard him stumble about without turning on the light. The next day we hardly talked, but I did make us a good breakfast, and he ate well, and then we hurried to the demonstration site. But I tell you, I was worried, because he scared the hell out of me, because as long as we've known each other, he always seemed to me the proper scout, the flawless perfectionist . . . But now, since I've thought about him a lot deeper, I don't know."

"Yes . . . I don't really want to talk about him . . . So we'll never know and never understand . . . And it's too late . . . he's gone forever," Milda said softly, sadly, and fell into a prolonged silence. At last, exhausted, he finished, "The way I put things on the tape . . . what I said about you at the end, we'll go with that, all right?"

"Yes," she replied. She wished she hadn't thrown the tape away but didn't confess, didn't tell him that she could not, at the time and driving all alone, take any more devastating revelations, not then, and really, not now or ever. So she said, "All right." She listened to his breathing and imagined him looking at his wall with sad eyes:

Blue glass, green ice—
Twixt them white dress of snow;
Blue glass, green ice—
Twixt them lies a marble face.
Blue glass, green ice—
Twix them golden sunlight hair . . .

She wondered how he—how they—will cross the gulf that separated her image on his wall from herself, but she was also too exhausted to ask, let alone listen to more words. It was already past midnight.

"Good night," she said and hung up the telephone.

*

A ring! she mused, as she tucked herself in for the night. "In the morning I must go and find a ring. The script calls for it. *Blue glass, green ice* . . . *Blue glass* . . . It must be blue, of course. Blue sapphire."

Never wanting to burden her heart, she turned over on her right side and soon fell asleep.

The End

Printed in the United States
By Bookmasters